ALSO BY JULIA QUINN

THE BRIDGERTONS

The Bridgerton Series
The Bridgerton Prequels
The Smythe-Smith Quartet

ANTHOLOGIES

The Further Observations of Lady Whistledown
Lady Whistledown Strikes Back

OTHER SERIES

The Bevelstoke Series
The Two Dukes of Wyndham
Agents of the Crown
The Lyndon Sisters
The Splendid Trilogy

QUEEN
CHARLOTT

ALSO BY SHONDA RHIMES

BOOKS

Year of Yes
Inside Bridgerton (written with Betsy Beers)

TELEVISION

Grey's Anatomy
Private Practice
Scandal
Inventing Anna
Queen Charlotte: A Bridgerton Story

FILM

Introducing Dorothy Dandridge
Crossroads
The Princess Diaries 2: Royal Engagement

QUEEN CHARLOTTE

INSPIRED BY THE ORIGINAL SERIES
QUEEN CHARLOTTE: A BRIDGERTON STORY,
CREATED BY SHONDALAND FOR NETFLIX

JULIA QUINN

—AND—

SHONDA RHIMES

AVON
An Imprint of HarperCollinsPublishers

QUEEN CHARLOTTE. Copyright © 2023 by Julie Cotler Pottinger and Shonda Rhimes. All rights reserved. Printed in the United States of America. No part of this book may be used or reproduced in any manner whatsoever without written permission except in the case of brief quotations embodied in critical articles and reviews. For information, address HarperCollins Publishers, 195 Broadway, New York, NY 10007.

HarperCollins books may be purchased for educational, business, or sales promotional use. For information, please email the Special Markets Department at SPsales@harpercollins.com.

FIRST EDITION

Designed by Leah Carlson-Stanisic
All art from Shutterstock, Inc.

Library of Congress Cataloging-in-Publication Data has been applied for.

ISBN 978-0-06-330508-3

23 24 25 26 LSB 5 4 3 2 1

For Lyssa Keusch.
I'm not going to miss you because we'll always be friends.

And also for Paul. I'm saying it right here:
IT WAS ALL YOUR IDEA.

—J. Q

To my daughters. Each of you is a queen.

—S. R.

Dearest Gentle Reader,

This is the story of Queen Charlotte from *Bridgerton*.
It is not a history lesson.
It is fiction inspired by fact.
All liberties taken by the authors are quite intentional.
Enjoy.

Dearest Gentle Reader,

This coldest time of year has become that much colder with the sad news of the death of the Princess Royal. The granddaughter of our dear King George III and Queen Charlotte died in childbirth along with her baby.

And while our hearts grieve for the loss of the Princess Royal, our heads grieve more for the future of the monarchy itself. For the Crown now has a crisis on its hands. A crisis one can only imagine that Queen Charlotte must find galling after ruling over the matchmaking efforts of the *ton* and the marriage mart with such an iron fist.

This Author and all of England can only hope Queen Charlotte finally turns her matchmaking energies onto her own family. After all, Her Majesty has thirteen children, and now not a royal heir from any of them. At least not a legitimate one.

It causes one to wonder: Is the Queen's knowledge of how to make a good marriage nothing but talk?

Lady Whistledown's Society Papers, 10 November 1817

Fifty-Six Years Earlier . . .

CHARLOTTE

Like all members of the German aristocracy, Princess Sophia Charlotte of Mecklenburg-Strelitz was in possession of a great many names. Sophia for her maternal grandmother, Sophia Albertine of Erbach-Erbach, a countess by birth and a duchess by marriage. Charlotte for her father, Charles Louis Frederick of Mecklenburg-Strelitz, who was born a second son and had died before he could assume the position of head of the family. Then there were the many and sundry double-barreled lands and properties that made up her heritage. Mecklenburg-Strelitz and Erbach-Erbach, of course, but also Saxe-Hildburghausen, Schwarzburg-Sondershausen, and, if one wanted to go back far enough, Waldeck-Eisenberg.

She enjoyed all of her names, and she was proud of every last one, but the one she liked best was Lottie.

Lottie. It was the simplest of the bunch, but that wasn't why she liked it. Her tastes rarely ran to the simple, after all. She liked her wigs tall and her dresses grand and she was quite certain no one in her household appreciated the complexities of music or art as keenly as she did.

She was not a simple creature.

She was not.

But she liked being called Lottie. She liked it because hardly anyone ever used it. You had to *know* her to call her Lottie.

You had to know, for example, that in spring her favorite dessert was raspberry-apricot torte and in winter it was apple strudel, but the truth was she had a taste for fruit, and for sweets, and any sweet made of fruit was her absolute favorite.

People who called her Lottie also knew that when she was a young girl she'd loved to swim in the lake by her home (when it was warm enough, which it rarely was). They also knew that when her mother had banned the practice (stating that Charlotte was too old for such frivolity), Charlotte had not spoken to her for three weeks. Peace was reestablished only after Charlotte had written a surprisingly thorough legal document outlining the rights and responsibilities of all involved parties. Her mother was not immediately persuaded by Charlotte's arguments, but her older brother Adolphus had intervened. Charlotte had made a good case, he'd said. She'd shown logic and intelligence, and surely that should be rewarded.

Adolphus was the one who'd coined the pet name Lottie. And that was the true reason it was her favorite name. It had been bestowed upon her by her favorite brother.

Pardon, her *former* favorite brother.

"You give the appearance of a statue," Adolphus said, smiling as if she had not spent the last three weeks begging him not to marry her off to a stranger.

Charlotte wanted to ignore him. She'd have liked nothing better than to never utter a word in his direction for the remainder of both of their lives, but even she recognized the futility of such stubbornness. And besides, they were in a carriage in the southeast of England, and they had a long ride both ahead and behind them.

She was bored and furious, never a good combination.

"Statues are works of art," she said icily. "Art is beautiful."

This made her brother smile, damn his eyes. "Art can be beautiful to gaze upon," he said with some amusement. "You, on the other hand, are ridiculous to the eye."

"Is there a point?" Charlotte bit off.

He shrugged. "You have not moved an inch in six hours."

Oh. *Oh.* He should not have gone there. Charlotte leveled her dark eyes on his with a ferocity that ought to have terrified him. "I am wearing Lyonnaise silk. Encrusted with Indian sapphires. With an overlay of two-hundred-year-old lace."

"And you look beautiful," he said. He reached out to pat her knee, then hastily withdrew his hand when he caught her expression.

Murderous.

"Apparently too much movement could cause the sapphires to shred the lace." Charlotte growled. She literally growled. "Do you want me to shred the lace? *Do you?*"

She did not wait for him to answer. They both knew he was not meant to. "If that were not enough," she continued, "the gown sits atop a bespoke underpinning made of whalebone."

"Whalebone?"

"Yes. Whalebone, Brother. The bones of whales. *Whales died so I could look like this.*"

At that, Adolphus laughed outright. "Lottie—"

"Don't," Charlotte warned him. "Don't you dare call me Lottie as if you care."

"Come, *Liebchen*, you know I care."

"Do I? Because it does not feel as if you care. It feels as if I have been trussed up like a prized sow and placed upon an altar as sacrifice."

"Charlotte—"

She bared her teeth. "Shall you put an apple in my mouth?"

"Charlotte, *stop*. You were chosen by a king. This is a great honor."

"*That*," Charlotte spat. "That is why I am angry. The lies. You will not stop lying."

She could not stand it, these endless lies. This was no honor. She wasn't sure what it was, but certainly not an honor.

King George III of Great Britain and Ireland had appeared out of nowhere (or rather, his people had; *he* had not deigned to make an appearance) and inexplicably decided that she, Sophia Charlotte of Mecklenburg-Strelitz, should be his next queen.

Mecklenburg-Strelitz. They had traveled all the way to *Mecklenburg-Strelitz*. Charlotte loved her home, with its placid lakes and verdant lawns, but she was well aware that Mecklenburg-Strelitz was considered one of the least important states in all the Holy Roman Empire.

To say nothing of the distance. The King's advisors would have had to sail past dozens of duchies and principalities—with dozens of duchesses and princesses—before reaching Mecklenburg-Strelitz.

"I do not lie to you, Charlotte," Adolphus said. "It is a fact. You were chosen."

If Charlotte could have moved in her whalebone corset, she would have twisted to face him more squarely. But she could not, so she was forced to settle for a glacial stare. "And how difficult was it to be chosen?" she demanded. "What do they need? Nothing special. Someone who can make lots of babies. Someone who can read. Someone with all the social graces. Someone with a royal bloodline. That is all they required."

"That is not nothing, *Liebchen*."

"It is *not* a great honor. And you could have told them to choose someone else. Someone stupid enough to want it."

"They did not want someone stupid. They wanted you."

Good God, he could not possibly be so dense. "Adolphus, think," she implored. "Why me? He could have anyone. Anyone. And yet they came hunting all the way across the continent for me. There must be a reason for that."

"Because you are special."

"Special?" She gaped at his naiveté. No, not that. He was not naïve, he was merely trying to placate her, as if she were some calf-witted child, too blind or stupid to recognize the web of treachery that had been spun around her. "I am a stranger to them," she said. "They are strangers to us. You cannot think me this ignorant. There is a reason they wanted me, a stranger. And it cannot be a good reason. I know it cannot be a good reason because you have not looked me in the eye since you told me."

It took a moment for Adolphus to speak. When he did, his words were useless. "This is a good thing, Lottie. You shall be happy."

She stared at him, at this man she thought she knew better than anyone. He was her brother, the head of her house since the death of their father nine years earlier. He had sworn to protect her. He had told her she was good and worthy, and she had *believed* him.

She should have known better. He was a man, and like all men, he saw women as pawns to be shuffled around Europe without a thought to their happiness.

"You know nothing," she said in a low voice.

He said nothing.

"You proclaim that I will be happy as if you could possibly know that. As if your mere words will make it so. Did you ever once ask me what I want? No, you did not."

Adolphus expelled an irritated puff of air. She was trying his patience, this was easy to see. But Charlotte did not care, and her fury was making her reckless.

"Turn the carriage around," she announced. "I am not doing this."

Adolphus's face grew hard. "I signed the betrothal contract. You are doing this."

"No."

"Yes."

"Brother." She gave him an obnoxiously pleasant smile. "Turn this carriage around or I will bounce. Do you wish to know what will happen if I bounce?"

"You shall tell me, I'm sure."

"This corset of mine, made of the finest and most expensive whalebone, is rather delicate. And also, it is very, very sharp. And of course, I am in the height of fashion, so this corset is quite snug." Charlotte snapped a finger against her midsection to make a point, but the joke was on her. She'd lost all sensation in her rib cage, and she might as well have been tapping a wall.

"Shall we loosen it?" Adolphus suggested.

"No, we shall not loosen it," she hissed. "I must arrive on display, which means I must stay strapped into this monstrous thing. And thus if I give the appearance of a statue, ridiculous to your eye, it is because I cannot move. No, I *dare not* move. My gown is so stylish that if I move too much, I might be sliced and stabbed to death by my undergarments."

Adolphus blinked.

"How joyful it is to be a lady," she muttered.

"You are upset."

She wanted to kill him.

"Charlotte—"

"It is a viable option," she said. "Moving. I've considered it. Choosing to be killed by my undergarments. There must be an irony to it, although I confess I do not yet see it. Humor, yes. Irony . . . I'm not sure."

"Charlotte, I mean it, stop."

But she could not. Her mind was on fire. Her fury was righteous and she was scared, and with every mile she was hurtling toward a future she did not understand. She knew what was happening, but she did not know *why*, and it made her feel stupid and small.

"We have, what, an hour to go?" she railed on. "I believe if I am diligent with my movements I could most certainly bleed to death before we reach London."

Adolphus appeared to be suppressing a groan. "Like I said, you are upset. Emotional. I understand—"

"Do you understand? Truly? This, I would love to hear. Because I am not upset. Nor am I emotional. I am angry. And I cannot breathe. And both are thanks to you, Brother."

He crossed his arms.

"I shall do it," she warned. "I shall bounce, and I will impale myself on this ridiculous corset and bleed to death."

"Charlotte!"

At that, she finally shut her mouth. Adolphus rarely took that tone with her. In fact, she was not sure he ever had.

Before her eyes, her genial brother disappeared, replaced by the stern and powerful Duke of Mecklenburg-Strelitz. It was disconcerting. Infuriating. And it made the little girl who still resided deep in her heart want to cry.

"I know I should have taken a firmer hand with you when Mama and Papa died," he said. "I allowed you to read too much, and I indulged your every whim and frivolity. So I take full responsibility for the fact that you are now exceedingly headstrong and mistakenly think you can make decisions. You cannot. I am in charge. This is happening."

"I do not see why you could not just—"

"Because they are the British Empire and we are a tiny province in Germany!" he roared.

Charlotte shrank into herself. Just a little bit.

"We had no choice," he hissed. "*I* had no choice. You want a reason? Fine. I have none. There is no good reason. In fact, the reason might be terrible. I know that no one who looks like you or me has ever married one of these people. Ever. But I cannot question! Because I cannot make an enemy of the most powerful nation on earth. It is done." He leaned forward, vibrating with rage and impatience and maybe even resignation. "So shut up, do your duty to our country, and *be happy*!"

Charlotte flinched. Because finally, Adolphus wasn't lying. His skin was brown. Her skin was brown. Brown like chocolate, like warm, rich wood. She did not have to set eyes upon King George III of Great Britain and Ireland to know that his was not.

So why? *Why* was he doing this? She knew what the pale-skinned Europeans said about people like her. Why would he "pollute" his bloodline with a girl of Moorish ancestry? Her tree led to Africa, and it did not take many generations to get there.

Why did he want her?

What was he hiding?

"*Liebchen*," Adolphus said. He sighed and his eyes softened. Once again, he was just her older brother. "I am sorry. But there are worse fates than marrying the King of England."

Charlotte swallowed and looked out the window at the English countryside rolling by. It was green and bursting with life. Fields and forests, small villages with their quaint churches and high streets. She supposed it did not look so different from her homeland, although she had not spied a single lake.

Was it so much to wish for a lake?

"Will I ever return to Schloss Mirow?" she asked quietly.

Her brother's eyes grew wistful, maybe even a little sad. "Probably not," he admitted. "You will not wish to. In a year, we will be too rustic for your tastes."

Charlotte had the oddest sensation that if she were anywhere else, if she were anyone else, she might cry. Yesterday, her tears would have flowed. Hot and angry, with all the passion of her youth.

But now she was to be Queen. She did not cry. Whatever lay inside a person, creating tears, forming sobs—it had been switched off.

"Sit back," she said. She tugged her hands free from his and set them firmly in her lap. "You are endangering my gown. I need to look perfect when I arrive, do I not?"

Her palace awaited.

GEORGE

Most of the time, George didn't mind being King.

The perks were obvious. He had more money than one person could possibly spend, multiple palaces that he could call home, and a veritable flotilla of servants and advisors, all leaping over each other to satisfy his every whim.

Chocolate in the morning with precisely three spoonfuls of sugar and a dollop of milk? Right here, Your Majesty, on a silver-edged saucer.

A copy of *The History of Succulent Plants* by Richard Bradley? Never fear, it does not matter that it was published in 1739, we shall find it for you immediately!

A small elephant? That might require a few months to procure, but we shall get on it straightaway.

For the record, George had not requested an elephant. Of any size. But it rather cheered him to know that he could.

So yes, being King was frequently delightful. But not always, and one could not generally complain, because one sounded like an *ass* when one complained about being King.

But there were drawbacks. One enjoyed a disturbingly small degree of privacy, for example. Like right now. A normal man might enjoy a shave from his valet with nothing to fill his ears but birdsong drifting through the open window, but George's dressing room had been invaded by both his mother and one of his advisors.

Neither of whom were showing any inclination to shut up.

"She was being fitted for her gown when I left her," Princess Augusta said.

"Everything is as it should be," Lord Bute murmured.

"She wanted to wear some monstrosity from Paris. Paris!"

Bute nodded, a rather diplomatic motion that indicated neither agreement nor dissent. "I believe the French capital is known as a center of fashion."

George closed his eyes. It was odd, really, but people seemed to speak more freely in his presence when his eyes were closed, as if somehow he could not *hear* them.

It was not a trick George could employ often; it would not do, for example, to close one's eyes while sitting on a throne or receiving heads of state. But at times like this, reclining with a warm towel on his cheeks and throat as he awaited his valet's arrival with foam and a straight razor, it could be quite illuminating.

For his mother's discussion with Lord Bute centered on George's fiancée, which would not have been so remarkable, except that George had not yet met his fiancée, and the wedding was in six hours.

Such was the life of a king. One would think being anointed by God would grant one the right to clap eyes on one's bride ahead of one's wedding. But no, a king married for his country, not his heart or loins. It didn't really matter if he did not see Sophia Charlotte of Mecklenburg-Strelitz before they took their vows. In fact, it might be better, all things considered.

Still, he was curious.

"She is marrying an English king," his mother said. "She must wear an English gown. Did you see what she was wearing this morning when she was presented to me?"

"I am afraid I did not notice, ma'am."

"Fusses and frills. It was altogether too much for a morning call. Sapphires. In the middle of the day. And lace made by nuns. Nuns! Does she think we are Catholics?"

"I am sure she merely wished to make a good impression upon her future mother-in-law," Bute demurred.

Princess Augusta snorted. "These Continentals. They are entirely too full of themselves."

George allowed himself a smile. His mother had been born Augusta of Saxe-Gotha-Altenburg. One could not sit more squarely in the middle of the Continent than Gotha.

But Augusta had been a princess of Great Britain for twenty-five years. More than half her life. She was supposed to have been Queen, but that honor had been denied to her when George's father, then the Prince of Wales, was hit in the chest by a cricket ball and died shortly thereafter. The Crown would skip a generation, traveling from grandfather to grandson, and with no husband to be King, Augusta could not be Queen.

Still, she had devoted herself to this country. Princess Augusta had birthed nine princes and princesses, all of whom spoke English as their mother tongue. If his mother now saw herself as wholly British, George supposed that was understandable.

"She is attractive, though," Bute said. "Her face was most pleasing. And she held herself well. One could say that her posture was regal."

"Yes, of course," Augusta agreed. "But she is very brown."

George opened his eyes. That was unexpected. "The earth is brown," he said.

His mother turned to him. Blinked. "What on ea—" She stopped herself before she punned, which struck George as a mild tragedy. He quite liked puns, intended or otherwise. He loved the way words clicked together, and if sometimes this meant his sentences were four hundred and sixty-three words long, then that was a problem for someone else.

He was the King. Long sentences were his birthright.

"What," his mother said again, after a pause that didn't seem nearly lengthy enough to have contained the full stretch of George's thought process, "does that have to do with anything?"

"I love the earth," George said, thinking that explanation enough.

"Don't we all," Bute murmured.

George ignored him. He didn't *mind* Bute; he was mostly helpful, and the two of them shared a common love of natural philosophy and the sciences. But he was also occasionally annoying.

"The earth is brown," George said again. "That which springs all life, all hope. It is brown. It is lovely."

His mother stared at him. Bute stared at him. George just shrugged.

"Be that as it may," his mother persisted, "no one *told* us she was so brown."

"Is that a problem?" George asked. He closed his eyes again. Reynolds had arrived with the razor, and it was much more relaxing this way. Although logically speaking, one should never feel *too* relaxed with a razor near one's throat.

"Of course not," she said quickly. "*I* certainly don't care what color she is."

"You'd care if she were purple."

Silence. George smiled in his mind.

"You are going to give me a megrim," his mother finally said.

"There are a great many doctors in the palace," George said helpfully. It was true. There were far more doctors than any one person could possibly require.

Except a king, apparently. A king required a great many doctors. This king in particular.

"You know I'm not actually going to get a megrim," his mother said crossly. "But honestly, George, could you just allow me to finish?"

He motioned with his hand. It was a regal thing, that. He'd learned it at a young age, and it came in handy.

"We are not prepared for her to be so brown," his mother said.

"Indeed," Lord Bute said, adding absolutely nothing to the conversation.

"And it doesn't come off."

At that, George's eyes snapped open. "What?"

"It doesn't come off," his mother repeated. "I rubbed her cheek to be sure."

"Good God, Mother," George said, nearly rising from his chair. Reynolds jumped back, just fast enough to keep from slicing George's throat with the razor.

"Please tell me you did not try to rub the skin off my intended bride," George said.

She bristled. "I meant no insult."

"Nevertheless, you—" He stopped, pinching the bridge of his nose. *Don't yell don't yell don't yell*. It was important that he remain calm. He was at his best when he was calm. It was when he lost that calm that his mind started to race, and what he needed right now—what he needed always—was no mind-racing.

Calm. Calm.

He took a breath. "You are not an unintelligent woman, Mother. Surely you realize the rudeness of such a gesture."

Princess Augusta's posture, which had already been ramrod, grew even more impossibly stiff. "I am mother to the King. You are the only person above me. Thus, I am incapable of being rude to any but you."

"Your argument does not hold," George told her. "Have you forgotten that by nightfall she will be Queen? And thus most certainly above you."

"Pah. In rank, perhaps."

"Wasn't that precisely your point?"

But his mother had never been a friend of logic when it counteracted her arguments. "She is a child," she said.

"She is seventeen. Might I remind you that you wed my dear father at sixteen?"

"Which is why I know precisely what I am talking about. I hadn't a whit of maturity at my marriage."

That gave George pause. It was very unlike his mother to speak of herself in such a manner.

"She will need guidance," his mother continued. "Which I shall provide."

"She shall be most grateful for it," Lord Bute said.

Again, always so helpful. George ignored him, turning once again to his mother. "I am sure she will be delighted to receive your aid and succor now that you have treated her like some theatrical freak."

Augusta gave a little sniff. "You are always so quick to extol the virtue of science and inquiry. Surely you would not begrudge me my curiosity. I have never met someone of her color. I do not know how it works. For all

I know, a double tincture of applied arsenic would bring her right down to my complexion."

George closed his eyes. Dear God.

"I knew she was a *little* dark," Augusta said.

"Indeed," Lord Bute murmured.

Augusta turned to him. "Why did Harcourt not explain her color? He saw her when he signed the papers, did he not?"

"He mentioned some Moor blood," Bute allowed.

"*Some*," Augusta emphasized. "That could mean anything. I thought she'd be the color of milky coffee."

"Some might say she is."

"Not the way *I* take my coffee."

"Well, we all do pour our milk diff—"

"Cease!" George roared.

They did. Perk of being King.

"You will not speak of my bride like a bloody cup of coffee," George bit off.

His mother's eyes widened at his coarse language, but she held her tongue.

"Your Majesty," Bute said.

George silenced him with a flick of his hand. "Mother," he said, waiting until her eyes were fixed on his before finishing his question. "Do you or do you not approve of this marriage?"

Her lips pinched. "It does not matter if I approve of it."

"Cease your dissembling. Do you approve?"

"I do," his mother said. Quite firmly, in fact. "I believe she will be good for you. Or at the very least, not bad."

"Not bad?" George echoed.

"For you. Not bad for you." And then, as if they didn't all know what she meant, she added, "I don't believe she will exacerbate your . . . condition."

There it was. That *thing* they never talked about. Except when it was happening and they had no choice.

The last time had been particularly awful. George did not remember all the details; he never did, he just woke up later feeling exhausted and confused. But he recalled that they had been discussing *her*, his soon-to-be bride. She was on her way already, on a ship from Cuxhaven, but a voice in his head had warned him that this was not the right time for a journey. It was not a *safe* time for a journey.

She would lose the moon.

What the hell did that mean? Even he did not know, and the words had sprung from his lips.

He was not certain what had happened after that. As usual, giant chunks of his memory were gone. George always visualized the phenomenon like an atmospheric mist, seeping from his mouth as he slept, growing softer and thinner until it drifted away on the wind.

Memory as mist. It would have been poetic if it weren't *his* memory.

The next thing George remembered was waking up at the Royal College of Physicians. It was rather like he'd been shaken from a nap. His mother was there, along with a small handful of doctors.

One of them had actually been helpful.

Pleasant change, that.

"May I continue, Your Majesty?"

George looked at Reynolds, who had been standing quietly through the entire exchange, straight razor in hand. George held up a finger, signaling that he needed a moment more, and turned back to his mother. "You tell me that you support this marriage, and yet you appear apprehensive. I would have you explain."

Augusta took a moment before speaking. "We will need to make adjustments," she said. "Quickly."

"People will talk," Lord Bute said.

"People will talk," she agreed. "It is a problem. We do not want them to think we did not know."

"That her skin is brown?" George asked.

"Precisely. They must think we wanted it this way. Perhaps we are trying to make a statement. We wish to unite society."

"We have already made the trade deals," Lord Bute said. "But they *could* be canceled . . ."

"We cannot cancel the royal wedding on the day," Augusta said sharply.

"God no," George murmured. He could not even begin to imagine the nature of the rumors that would follow.

"The *ton* might not accept her," Bute said. "It's a problem."

Augusta was having none of that. "We are the Palace. A problem is only a problem if the Palace says it is a problem. That is a fact, is it not?"

Bute cleared his throat. "It is."

"And the King is the sovereign head of the Church of England and ruler of this great land. Therefore, nothing he does would ever be a problem for the Palace. Would it, Lord Bute?"

"It would not."

"So. This must be as the Palace wished it to be. Must it not, Lord Bute?"

"Yes. It must."

"Good." Augusta's voice was brisk, businesslike. "Then the King's choice has been most intentional. To make that clear, we shall expand the guest list for the wedding. And add to the new queen's court."

Bute's eyes widened. "Are you saying . . ."

"The King is saying." She placed her hand over her heart, the very image of feminine rectitude. "I am only his mother. I say nothing."

George let out a bark of laughter at that.

The only sign that Augusta heard him was a slight tightening around her mouth. She barely even paused before saying to Lord Bute, "*The King* wishes to expand the guest list for the wedding and add to the new queen's court."

George smiled. He finally understood. His mother was brilliant.

"Of course, Your Highness." Lord Bute looked at Augusta, then at George, then back at Augusta. "It is only . . . the King realizes that the wedding is in six hours?"

"He does," George said, grinning.

"The Danburys, I think," Augusta said. "Your grandfather spoke of them, did he not?"

"I could not say," George admitted.

"He did," Augusta said firmly. "Not of the current Danburys, of course. He would never have known them. But he knew the father. Stupendously wealthy. Diamonds, I think. From Africa." She looked at Bute. "Are you taking notes?"

"Yes," he said quickly, scrambling for paper. George wished him luck. He was not likely to find any in his dressing room.

"Who else?" Augusta asked. "The Bassets?"

"An excellent choice," Bute said, still looking for paper. And a pen. "Might I suggest the Kents?"

Augusta nodded her approval. "Yes, they will do. I'm sure there are more. I shall trust you and Lord Harcourt to determine who might be most appropriate."

"Of course, Your Royal Highness. I shall have the invitations issued at once." Bute cleared his throat. "It is very short notice. They may have other plans."

Augusta flicked her hand in the air. It was a regal thing, and George was fairly sure she found it just as handy as he did. "Other plans?" she echoed, disbelief painted across her face. "Who would not want to attend a royal wedding?"

AGATHA

If Agatha Danbury had known she'd be attending a royal wedding, she'd have worn a nicer dress.

Not that there was anything wrong with her current attire. To the contrary, her gown was the height of fashion, designed by Madame Duville, one of the top three modistes in London. The fabric was jacquard silk, the color a rich, lustrous gold that Agatha knew complemented the dark tones of her skin. Her stomacher, too, was a thing of beauty—adorned in the latest style with a single bow over the bosom, and then further dressed with silver embroidery and a magnificent Nigerian topaz.

So yes, objectively speaking, her dress was gorgeous.

The problem was that it had not been specifically designed to be worn at a royal wedding, and anyone with an ounce of reason knew that if one was to attend a royal wedding, one had to damn well pony up the funds to have a gown customized for the occasion.

But as it happened, when Agatha had opened her eyes that morning, she'd not been in possession of an invitation to the nuptials of King George III and his German bride. Nor had she any expectation of ever finding herself within spitting distance of royalty. *Her* side and *their* side did not mix.

Ever.

But one did not ignore a royal summons, and so now she and her husband were seated in a surprisingly well-located pew in the Chapel Royal, exchanging nervous glances with the other members of their set.

She was exchanging nervous glances. Her husband was asleep.

Leonora Smythe-Smith, who always used ten words when five would do, twisted around to face her. "Why are we here?" she whispered.

"I could not say," Agatha replied.

"Have you seen how they are looking at us?"

Agatha resisted the temptation to hiss, *Of course I see how they are looking at us.* Honestly, one would have to be a complete lackwit not to notice the glares coming from the nobility-filled pews.

Nobility that was, to a person, in possession of porcelain-pale skin.

And while the Danburys and the Smythe-Smiths—and the Bassets, and the Kents, and quite a few other prominent families—enjoyed a life of wealth and privilege, it was still a very separate sort of wealth and privilege from the traditional British aristocracy. Agatha's dark skin meant that she could never be considered a proper companion for their daughters, much less a possible bride for their sons.

It did not bother her. Well, only rarely. Truly, only at times like these, when she found herself in the same room with dukes and duchesses and the like. It was tempting to return their disdain with an announcement that she, too, was a descendent of kings and queens, that her birth name was Soma, and in her veins flowed the royal blood of the Gbo Mende royal tribe of Sierra Leone.

But what would be the point? Most could not find Sierra Leone on a map. Agatha would wager that half would think she was making up the entire country.

Idiots. The world was populated with idiots. She'd long since learned the truth of *that*, along with the depressing fact that there was very little she could do about it.

Such was the life of a woman, no matter what shade her skin.

Agatha stole a glance at her husband. He was still sleeping. She elbowed him.

"What?" he spluttered.

"You were asleep."

"I was not."

See? Idiots.

"I would never sleep in the Chapel Royal," he said, brushing a piece of lint from his velvet waistcoat.

Agatha shook her head. How had he managed to get lint on his coat between their home and St. James's Palace?

Her husband was . . . not her favorite person. She supposed that was as kind a way as any to describe him. He had been a part of her life since she was but three, when her parents had pledged her to him in marriage.

She'd wondered, as she was raised to be his perfect wife, what sort of man entered a betrothal contract with a three-year-old. Herman Danbury had been well past thirty when he had signed the papers. Surely if he was eager for heirs, he would have chosen someone who could provide them with a bit more haste.

She'd gotten her answers—such as they were—after her marriage. It was all about bloodlines. Danbury also came from royal blood, and he refused to mix his with any but the most elite of African-British society. Plus, as he'd cheerfully informed her, he'd secured himself fourteen more years as a bachelor. What man wouldn't be delighted with that?

Agatha suspected that there were more than a few Danbury bastards sprinkled across the southeast of England. She also suspected that her husband provided little to nothing as support for these children.

It ought to be a crime. It really ought.

At any rate, he'd stopped producing children out of wedlock after their marriage. Agatha knew this because he'd told her quite explicitly that she satisfied all his needs. And based upon the frequency with which she found herself satisfying those needs, she believed him.

She shifted slightly in her seat. She'd been satisfying his needs that morning when the royal invitation had arrived. As a result, she'd not had time to take her usual postcoital warm bath. She was sore. And possibly chafed.

Well, more sore and chafed than usual.

But she was willing to ignore her discomfort because one, she had no choice, and two, she was *at the royal wedding*.

Such astonishments did not happen often in a lifetime, and never before in hers.

"Shouldn't they have started by now?" Mrs. Smythe-Smith asked.

Agatha gave a little shrug. "I don't know," she whispered, mostly because it would be impolite to say nothing.

"The King will arrive when the King wishes to arrive," Danbury said. "He is the King."

This proclamation was delivered in a voice so pompous one might think Danbury actually had some experience with kings.

He did not. Of this, Agatha was quite certain.

But her husband was right about one thing, Agatha supposed. A king got to do what a king wished to do, including arriving late to his own wedding.

Or inviting all of London's dark-skinned elite to the ceremony.

Agatha hazarded another glance at the opposite side of the chapel. Not all of the nobility was glaring at her. A few looked merely curious.

Don't look at me, she wanted to tell them. *I am as clueless as you.*

At least there was much to look at while she was waiting. The Chapel Royal was as exquisite as she would have imagined. It was not in the current rococo style, which surprised her. She'd have thought the palace would be more *au courant*.

But this simpler style was lovely, and quite honestly more to her taste. The ceiling in particular was a wonder. Intricately coffered and painted by Hans Holbein himself. Or so Agatha had once read. She'd always had an interest in architecture and design. The recessed panels made her think of honeycomb, and each was—

"Stop gawking," Danbury hissed.

Agatha jerked her stare back down to eye level.

"You look like a peasant," he said. "Try to behave as if you have been here before."

Agatha rolled her eyes the moment he looked away. As if *anyone* thought either of them had ever set foot in the palace before this day.

But she knew what this meant to Herman. His had been a life of "almosts." *Almost* fitting in. *Almost* being accepted. He'd gone to Eton, but had he been allowed to play on the teams? He'd attended Oxford, but had he been invited into any of the special, secret clubs?

No, of course not. He had money, he had education, he even had royal African lineage. But his skin was dark as chocolate, and so he would never be accepted by the *ton*.

And therein lay the great contradiction of her life. Agatha didn't like her husband. She really didn't. But she felt for him. For all the indignities that pecked away at his heart. Sometimes she wondered if he might have become a different man had he been allowed to rise to his true potential. If he had not been stepped on or pushed away every time he approached his goals.

If society had viewed him as the man he truly was, maybe he could have seen her as the woman *she* truly was.

Or maybe not. Society was full of men who saw women as nothing but accessories and breeding stock.

Still, Agatha wondered.

"Oh!" Mrs. Smythe-Smith yelped, and Agatha followed her gaze to the back of the chapel. Someone important was arriving.

"Is it the King?" Danbury asked.

Agatha shook her head. "I cannot see. I don't think so."

"It's the Princess!" Mrs. Smythe-Smith said.

"Which one?" Agatha whispered. The bride? One of the King's sisters?

"Princess Augusta."

The King's mother. Agatha held her breath. Princess Augusta was without question the most powerful woman in the country. A queen in everything but name, she had long been rumored to be the true power behind the throne.

The congregation rose as one, and Agatha craned her neck for a better view. To hell with looking like a peasant, she wanted a glimpse of the Princess. And besides, Danbury had his back to her and was likely gawking himself.

Princess Augusta moved like a queen, or at least how Agatha thought a queen would move—with grace and purpose, her fan an elegant extension of her right hand. Her back was straight as an arrow. If she felt burdened by the obvious weight of her gown—the fabric alone must have weighed almost a stone—she gave no indication.

What would it be like to have so many eyes on oneself? Agatha could not imagine it. To be at the center of such attention, presumably every day. It must be exhausting.

But the power. The ability to do what one wished, to see whom one wished, and more importantly, to *not* see those one wished to avoid.

Sadly, Agatha could not imagine that, either.

She got a better view of Princess Augusta as she moved down the center aisle. She seemed to look at no one and everyone at the same time, as if to say, *I see all of you, but you are beneath my notice.* Her eyes passed over the crowd, fixing on no one until—

They fixed on *her.*

Agatha stopped breathing. This could not be right.

Princess Augusta continued her regal march, moving ever closer, and Agatha could not even begin to think what she and her husband could have done to insult the Princess, because why else would she be fixing them with such a single-minded stare?

She could not be imagining this, could she? Maybe the Princess was actually looking at the Smythe-Smiths. Except that was equally difficult to believe.

Five feet away, two feet . . .

She stopped. Directly in front of the Danburys.

Agatha curtsied. Deeply. When she rose, Princess Augusta was speaking to Danbury.

"Your father was friendly with his late Majesty, my son's grandfather, was he not?" the Princess inquired.

It was true. Danbury's father had known King George II. Agatha was not certain that their connection could have been termed a friendship, but His Majesty had very much liked the diamonds that had come from the family's mines in Kenema.

The Princess did not seem to be expecting an actual reply, because she did not pause before saying, "I am so pleased to have you here with us today on this family occasion, *Lord* Danbury."

Agatha felt herself lean forward. Had she heard that correctly?

"Lord?" Danbury stammered. "I . . . I do not know what to—"

Princess Augusta cut him off cleanly. "You shall be receiving the official proclamation from the King after his wedding. You are honored to be Lord and Lady Danbury now."

Lady Danbury? She, Agatha Danbury, was now Lady Danbury. And had been made so in front of dozens of witnesses, in the Chapel Royal in St. James's Palace.

This was not . . . It could not be happening.

And yet it was. Princess Augusta stood right in front of her, and she said, "All the members of the *ton* must be titled."

"The *ton*, Your Royal Highness?" Agatha echoed.

Princess Augusta acknowledged her with a tiny tip of her head. "It is time we were united as a society, is it not?"

Agatha's lips parted, but even if she'd had the presence of mind to speak, it mattered not, for Princess Augusta had moved on to the next pew and was greeting *Lord* and *Lady* Smythe-Smith.

What the *devil* had just happened?

Beside her, her husband puffed with pride. "Lord Danbury," he said in a reverential whisper. "Imagine."

"I am imagining," Agatha said softly. She watched as the new Lady Smythe-Smith sank into a deep curtsy, remaining there so long that Princess Augusta finally had to order her to rise.

"I am sorry, Your Royal Highness," Lady Smythe-Smith said. "That is to say, thank you, Your Royal Highness, I—"

"One last thing," Princess Augusta interrupted, except she returned her attention to the Danburys when she said it. "What is your name?" she asked Agatha.

"Me?" Agatha pointed to herself.

Princess Augusta gave a single sharp nod.

"Agatha Louisa Aminata Danbury."

"That is a good name."

"Thank you, Your Royal Highness."

The Princess regarded her with piercing eyes. "What does it mean, Aminata? I assume Louisa is in honor of our great princesses."

"Of course, Your Royal Highness." It was true. Agatha's parents had wanted their daughter to have a royal name, one befitting both of her cultures, and so for her second given name they'd chosen Louisa, a name popular in the British royal family. For her third . . .

"Aminata is—" Agatha cleared her throat. She was not used to speaking to someone of Princess Augusta's rank, and she was frankly terrified. But she remembered something her nanny had once told her.

Be terrifying.

Even if she wasn't terrifying, even if she was terri*fied* . . .

She could imagine that she was terrifying. She could imagine she had the strength and power to bring men and women to their knees. And maybe a hint of this dream would sift up to her skin.

She looked Princess Augusta in the eye. "Aminata is a family name. It means trustworthy, faithful, and honest."

"Are *you* trustworthy, faithful, and honest?"

"I am, Your Royal Highness."

Princess Augusta stared at her for several seconds longer than was comfortable. "Good," she finally said. "You will serve the Queen as a member of her court."

"I—" *What?* Agatha's mouth moved for several seconds before she managed to form words. "Yes. Yes, Your Royal Highness. It will be my greatest honor."

"Of course it will." Princess Augusta turned to Danbury, who was gaping at both women, and gave him a brisk nod. Then she was gone.

"What just happened?" Agatha whispered.

"Why you?" Danbury demanded.

"I don't know."

"It's your name," Lady Smythe-Smith said. "Animata."

"Aminata," Agatha corrected, "and it's not my name."

"You just said it was."

Agatha shook her head. Dear God, this woman was a fool. "It's not *why* she chose me."

"Then why did she?"

"I don't know. Why did she choose any of us? We are suddenly all nobles?"

"*We* are," Danbury said petulantly. "You are something more. You are a member of court."

"I am as astonished as you," she assured him.

"It was my family that had a relationship to the late King."

"I know."

"So why do they want *you*?"

"I do not know. I do not know these people."

"You will," Lady Smythe-Smith said, reminding them that she was still eavesdropping.

"Dearest," Agatha said, patting her husband on his arm, "I am sure it is only because of you and your reputation that they would choose me. After all, they cannot choose *you* for the Queen's court. You are a man. They could not have you, so they asked me in your stead."

"I suppose," Danbury grumbled.

"I am nothing without you, my dearest," she said. They were words she had uttered many times, and they had not lost their effectiveness. Danbury returned his attention to the front of the chapel, and Agatha continued her examination of the ceiling. She really liked the way the octagons and Swiss crosses formed a pattern, and the—

A movement caught her eye. Someone was up in the balcony. Agatha quickly glanced about. Had anyone else noticed?

No. No one else had been looking up.

It was a young woman. With skin the same color as Agatha's, maybe a shade different; it was impossible to tell in this light. But she was definitely not white, and she was definitely in a restricted area.

Agatha glanced again at the people around her. They were all looking at each other, some beginning to fan themselves as the room grew warm from the crowd.

She looked up again. The girl was gone.

Curious.

But not as curious as everything else that had happened that day.

Lady Danbury. Attendant to the Queen.

Gah.

BRIMSLEY

Bartholomew Brimsley was going to lose his job.

Or they would hang him.

Or both. Honestly, that seemed plausible. He would be dismissed from his position as royal attendant and then hanged, and then, because he happened to work for the Royal House of Hanover, and they owned half the world and could do anything they pleased, they'd probably hire a traveling troupe of Italian grape pickers to stomp on his corpse.

There would be nothing left of him but patches of hair and entrails, and it would be nothing less than he deserved.

"You had one task," he muttered to himself. "One. Task."

Unfortunately for Brimsley, that one task was shepherding Princess Sophia Charlotte of Mecklenburg-Strelitz to the Chapel Royal at St. James's Palace, where she was meant to marry His Majesty King George III of Great Britain and Ireland.

Right bloody now.

And he'd lost her.

To think he'd considered this a *promotion*. Sophronia Pratt, head maid to Princess Augusta, had pulled him aside only last week and said, "You have been given the honor of serving our new queen."

And while Brimsley was digesting that startling development, Pratt said, "She is known as Princess Charlotte, not Princess Sophia. That is the first thing you must know."

"Shall her regnal name be Charlotte, then?"

"We do not know. One can only assume, and when it comes to royals it is best to never assume."

"Yes, ma'am," Brimsley said. He wondered what sort of uniform he'd be given. Not the bright red of the footmen and drivers; surely he'd be issued something more distinctive, as befitting his higher station. The King's man wore naval blue, but Brimsley liked scarlet.

"She is to arrive next week," Pratt continued. "We do not yet know the exact day, but I have been informed that the wedding will take place immediately."

"Immediately, ma'am?" Brimsley echoed.

"Within hours. The very same day, to be sure."

"Is there a reason for the rush, ma'am?"

Pratt skewered him with a glare. "If there is, *you* shall not be privy to it."

"Of course not, ma'am," Brimsley said, but inside he was berating himself. Pratt could rescind his promotion just as easily as she'd extended it. So he bowed his head appropriately and said, "I shall be at the ready, ma'am."

"Good. Now then, you will walk five paces behind her. Always. You will be with her always. You will answer her questions—"

"Always?" Brimsley said.

"Sometimes." Pratt gave him a look that was equal parts stern and disdainful. "You will answer her questions *sometimes*."

Brimsley wasn't quite sure what to make of that.

"She will not know how we do things here," Pratt explained, disdain now *briskly* outpacing sternness. "It shall be one of your primary duties to help her learn."

"Would that not require that I answer her questions?"

Pratt's eyes floated heavenward, and Brimsley, while not a skilled lip-reader, was fairly certain she mouthed the words *Heaven help me*.

Heaven help them both. Honestly. He was getting thrown to the wolves, and they both knew it.

"The German princess must learn to live as we do," Pratt said.

Brimsley gave a solemn nod. "I understand, ma'am."

"In this court."

"Of course, ma'am."

"*Princess Augusta's* court."

Brimsley opened his mouth. Surely it would be the new queen's court, not Princess Augusta's.

Pratt lifted an astonishingly imperial eyebrow. "Yes?"

Brimsley wasn't stupid. Vain, perhaps, but not stupid. "I understand perfectly, ma'am," he said.

"I thought you might," Pratt replied. "It is why I recommended you for this position."

"Thank you, ma'am."

Pratt gave him a look that said his thanks were beneath her. "Do you want to know the other reason I recommended you?"

Brimsley was not sure that he did.

"It is your face," Pratt said. "It is a bit like a fish."

"Thank you?" He coughed. "Ma'am."

"That is another reason, I suppose. I just insulted you, and you thanked me. You will get a lot of that from the Queen."

Brimsley was not cheered by this. "Have you heard very much about her, then?"

"Not a word," Pratt said briskly, "but royals are all the same in that regard. At any rate, your fish face lends you an air of perpetual disdain. You appear rather pleased with yourself, when we both know you have no reason to be."

Brimsley was not sure he had ever been insulted so thoroughly, and if he were not the victim, he'd probably admire her for it. It was really rather deft.

"One last thing," Pratt said. "The questions the new queen asks might not be the ones most conducive to her learning how to adapt to our way of life. Do I make myself clear?"

"Yes, ma'am," Brimsley replied, because honestly, this woman was terrifying.

And he wanted the job. Which he assumed came with a raise.

So he had bowed and scraped before Princess Charlotte, who, it had to be said, was not *at all* what he'd expected, and he had begun what he assumed would be his life's work—that was to say, walking five paces behind her elegant royal form.

Except the Princess didn't seem to understand how any of this worked, because when they were walking down the long corridor to her rooms, she stopped.

So he stopped.

She stood still for a moment, possibly expecting him to join her, which of course he could not do, so he stood there in agony until she resumed walking, and then—

She stopped *again*.

He stopped again.

She didn't face him, but he could see by the tightness in her shoulders that she was irritated.

She took a step. Just one, not even fully shifting her weight. Then she whipped around, as if trying to catch him doing . . . what? He didn't know. Royals were strange, strange creatures.

"Why didn't you move?" she demanded.

"You did not move," he replied. "Your Highness."

"I moved."

"You did not move in space," he explained. "You only pretended to take a step."

She stared at him for a long moment, and it occurred to Brimsley that with time she would be even more terrifying than Princess Augusta or Mrs. Pratt.

"Your Highness?" he asked. Very carefully.

"Walk with me," she said. "I have questions."

He held himself still. "That is not how it is done, Your Highness."

"What do you mean?"

He did not point, because one never pointed in the presence of a future queen, but he did motion with his hand in the vicinity of her elegantly clad feet. "You walk there and I"—he motioned again, this time toward his decidedly less elegant footwear—"walk back here, Your Highness."

Her dark eyes narrowed. "You cannot walk with me?"

"I am always with you, Your Highness." He cleared his throat. "Five paces behind."

"Five paces behind."

"Five paces behind," he confirmed.

"Always."

"Always, Your Highness." *I am your shadow*, he thought with burgeoning hysteria. *Except that I am short and pasty and you are tall and glorious with skin the color of a majestic oak.*

She was different, he realized. Not because of the color of her skin or the texture of her hair. She was different on the inside. She had that magical, intangible quality that made people want to be near her. To hear her words and breathe the air around her. If Brimsley were a more fanciful man, he'd have said she sparkled.

But he was not fanciful. So instead he would describe her as clever. And poised. And he realized that they had both been thrown to the wolves that day.

"You are always there," she said.

Always, he vowed. But it would be unseemly to profess the fervent emotion that had very unexpectedly gripped his heart, so he merely said, "Whenever you need me, Your Highness."

"What is your name?" she asked.

"Brimsley, Your Highness."

"Just Brimsley?"

"Bartholomew Brimsley."

"Bartholomew. It suits you. I shall never use it, of course."

"Of course," he echoed. He was stunned she'd even asked.

"Brimsley," she said, with—in his opinion—just the right degree of sharpness for a future queen, "tell me about the King."

"The King, Your Highness?"

She regarded him as if he were a creature of considerably lesser intelligence. "The King," she said again. "He is to be my husband. I wish to know about him."

"The King," he said again, stalling desperately. He was fairly certain he'd entered a living nightmare. Surely this was one of those questions Mrs. Pratt had instructed him not to answer.

"Can you tell me *anything* about him?" Princess Charlotte persisted.

"Well . . ."

The Princess did not cross her arms, possibly because her gown was too gloriously trimmed to allow it, but the expression on her face was clearly of the crossed-arms variety.

"The King," Brimsley said.

"The King. You do know who he is."

"I do, Your Highness. He is the King."

"*Mein Gott*," the Princess muttered.

And so it was that Brimsley did *not* tell her about the King. In fact, he employed every conversational trick he could think of to avoid telling her about the King. But now he wondered if that had been a mistake. Maybe if he'd said the King was handsome, or that he was honorable—both of which were true—she'd not have run off mere minutes before her wedding.

Maybe if he'd said the King was interested in agriculture and astronomy—which was also true—he, Brimsley, wouldn't be slinking along the outer edge of the chapel, trying to render himself invisible as he made his way to the sacristy.

Fortunately for him, the wedding guests were far more interested in each other than they were in a lone servant, moving a bit like a terrified crab. He made it through one doorway, and then another, and then—

The King!

Brimsley tried not to piss himself. Mostly succeeded.

He scooted past the King, who noticed him not at all, bowed to the archbishop, who gave him some sort of priestly wave, and finally caught the attention of Reynolds, the King's personal man.

"There is a problem," Brimsley whispered.

Reynolds was taller than Brimsley, fitter than Brimsley, and more handsome than Brimsley. And they both knew it. But still, Brimsley did have a few advantages.

None right now, though.

"What have you done now?" Reynolds asked, condescending as always.

Brimsley gulped. "The bride is missing."

Reynolds grabbed his arm. "What did you say?"

"You heard me." Brimsley shot a panicked look at the rest of the room's occupants. The archbishop was clearly half-deaf, but the King was looking straight at him.

Brimsley shifted to the side. He could not turn his back on the

King—that was, if not a hanging offense, at the very least enough to have him thrown out of the palace. Although to be honest, his aforementioned misplacement of the bride was probably the bigger concern at the moment.

Regardless, he'd feel a lot better if he could position himself in such a way that he couldn't see that the King was staring at him.

"Brimsley," Reynolds hissed. "Where is she?"

"I don't know," Brimsley shot back. "Obviously."

Reynolds let out a sound akin to a growl. "You are useless."

"I don't see you keeping track of an unhappy female."

"It's not my job to keep track of an unhappy female. My job is the King."

He was right, damn him, but Brimsley would never admit it. Reynolds would lord it over him for days.

"Now is not the time to argue," Brimsley whispered, trying desperately not to look at the King. But how did one *not* look at a king? That was like not looking at the sun.

What an apt metaphor. If he looked too long at the King, he would surely burn. And yet, nothing existed without him. Not this palace, not this country, not—

"Brimsley!" Reynolds snapped.

"I do not know what to do," Brimsley said. It was the most painful admission of his life.

"Where did you last—"

But Reynolds's question was silenced by the sound of a chair scraping across the floor. The King had risen.

"Your Majesty," Reynolds said, and it was only his hand on Brimsley's arm that stopped Brimsley from prostrating himself at the King's feet.

"I'm apparently not needed," the King said. And he walked right out.

Brimsley stared. Reynolds stared. And then they looked at each other.

"What just happened?" Brimsley asked.

"I do not know," Reynolds replied, "but it cannot be good."

"Should we go after him?"

"*You* should not." Reynolds ran through the doorway after the King, leaving Brimsley alone with the archbishop.

"Your excellency," Brimsley said, smiling weakly.

"Are we ready, then?" the archbishop asked.

"Er, not quite." Brimsley hustled backward to the door—since one did not turn one's back on an archbishop, either—then he took off down the hallway in a fast-panicked walk.

They couldn't have gone far. That door led straight outside, and the other one went into the chapel, which meant—

Brimsley stopped short when he turned the corner. Reynolds was watching the King, who was speaking with a man Brimsley had never seen before. He wasn't close enough to hear what they were saying, but the King was listening intently, and then the King said something, and then the man said something, and then—

The man slapped the King across the face.

Brimsley nearly fainted.

Two guards rushed forward, presumably to clap him in irons, but the King stopped them, allowing the strange man to depart. And then he walked outside. On his wedding day. The King walked right out of the chapel.

Brimsley took a step forward, baffled by what he had just seen. And also wildly curious. Information was currency among the palace staff, and this was gold.

It was at that moment, however, that Reynolds saw him. "You should not be here," he whispered harshly.

"What just happened?"

"Not a word. To anyone."

"But—"

"Not. A. Word."

Brimsley clamped his mouth into a straight line. He had questions. Oh, he had questions. But Reynolds was the King's man, and he was not. In fact, he would be no one's man if he didn't locate Princess Charlotte.

"I have to go," he said suddenly.

Reynolds looked down his supercilious nose. "See that you do."

Brimsley retraced his steps through the corridor and back into the chapel. God, he hated Reynolds.

Sometimes.

Charlotte

Charlotte eyed the garden wall. She could do it. If she grabbed hold of the woody vine that crept up the brick, wedged her foot in that little nook behind the purple flowers, and hoisted herself up . . .

She'd be up and over in no time.

Not for nothing had she climbed all the trees at Schloss Mirow.

It would not be easy in her wedding dress. Princess Augusta's choice was plain, but the fabric was heavy, and her panniers were wide. Still, it was probably easier to move in than the one Charlotte had brought from Paris.

Thank you, Augusta. For this, at least.

Charlotte gritted her teeth, jammed her foot in the nook, grabbed hold of the vine as high as she could reach, and pulled.

She didn't make it.

"Bloody hell," she muttered.

She could try again. She was getting out of this damned palace if it killed her. No one would tell her about the King. She'd asked his mother, she'd asked that fool Brimsley, she'd asked the seamstress who had acted like this repellent wedding dress was actually fashionable, but no, not a one of them would tell her anything of substance.

Was he handsome?

Was he kind? Athletic? Did he like to read?

Maybe he was ugly. Maybe that was why no one would tell her anything about him. She'd been shown his miniature, but everyone knew that miniaturists were paid to make men look more handsome than they actually were.

She could get past it if he was ugly. Beauty was on the inside, was it not?

Very well, it was not. Beauty was very much on the outside, but she was a good person. She would overcome.

And what had these people—Brimsley and the seamstress, who theoretically worked for *her*—had to say to her questions?

Nichts. Nothing. Brimsley had replied first by saying the King was the king, second by saying he was ruler of Great Britain and Ireland, and third by reporting he'd been the monarch since October.

King, ruler, monarch. Three synonyms revealing absolutely nothing.

And the seamstress! When Charlotte had asked her if the King was cruel, she had said, "You are going to have wonderful children together, Your Highness."

What did that even *mean*?

She was leaving. She didn't care that the ocean crossing from Cuxhaven had been so miserable she'd thrown up on Adolphus six times. She was returning to Mecklenburg-Strelitz if it killed her. And besides, Adolphus had deserved every drop of her vomit. It was his fault she'd been thrust into this situation in the first place.

She backed up a few steps. Maybe if she took a running start . . .

"Hello, my lady."

Charlotte nearly jumped out of her skin. She'd had no idea she wasn't alone in the garden. A young man—older than she was, but still young—had come through a door she hadn't even noticed.

She gave him a quick examination and immediately dismissed the idea that he worked for the palace and had been sent to drag her back to the chapel. He was obviously one of the wedding guests; his silver-gray ensemble was far too well-tailored for him to be anything but. He did not wear a wig over his dark hair, a fashion choice of which Charlotte approved. His eyebrows were also quite dark and would have looked ridiculous with a fluffy white mop perched atop his head.

On some other day—any other day—Charlotte would have judged

his face to be quite pleasing. But not today. She had no time for such frivolity.

"Are you in need of assistance of some kind?" he asked.

She gave him a tight smile. "I am quite fine. Thank you."

It was an obvious dismissal, but he just stood there, watching her with a rather inscrutable expression. Not unfriendly, just not, well, scrutable.

She flicked her hand toward the chapel. "You can go back inside and wait with all the other gawkers."

"I will," he said. "But first, I am curious. What are you doing?"

"Nothing," she said quickly.

"You are clearly doing something," he said, rather affably, to tell the truth.

She put one hand on her hip and waved her other arm in an arc that motioned to absolutely nothing. "I am not."

He looked amused, and frankly, somewhat condescending. "You are."

"I am not," she ground out.

"You are."

Himmel, he was annoying. "If you must know, I am trying to ascertain the best way to climb the garden wall."

"Climb the . . ." He looked at the wall, then back at her. "Whatever for?"

Charlotte was so frustrated she wanted to cry. All she wanted to do was escape, and this complete stranger would not stop asking her questions. Worst of all, she had to conduct this conversation in English, which was a *dreadful* language. So unhelpful. In German, she could mash words together and make new ones, delightfully long and descriptive. Instead of saying, "I am jumping over the wall to escape my wedding," she could describe the whole situation as *preweddingwalljumping*.

A German would know exactly what she meant.

The English? Bah.

"Please leave me be," she said to the stranger. "I really must go."

"But why?" he persisted.

"Because I think he may be a beast," she burst out.

That got his attention. His brows—those lovely dark brows that would have looked so ridiculous under a wig—rose. "A beast."

"Or a troll."

He blinked a few times. "Who are we discussing exactly?"

"Well, that is impertinent. And it's none of your business." And then, because she was clearly losing her mind, she went and contradicted herself by telling him everything anyway. "The King," she said desperately. "I am talking about the King."

"I see." His face grew thoughtful. It was a handsome face, Charlotte thought with a tinge of hysteria. Unlike the King, who was being hidden from her.

"No one will speak of him," she said. "No one. He is clearly a beast. Or a troll."

"Understood."

Charlotte returned her attention to the garden wall. "You know, if I just grab there . . ."

"Right there?" He motioned to a spot.

"Yes." Charlotte looked at him with renewed interest. Truly, he was well-built, fit and athletic under his clothes. She had rather a lot of brothers, and she knew that tailors employed countless tricks to make men look stronger and more manly. She also knew how to recognize these tricks, and it was quite clear that this man's tailor had employed none of them.

He was definitely strong enough to be useful.

She smiled gamely. "Perhaps you could assist me by lifting me up?"

"Yes, of course," he said, all amiability and politeness. "I do have one question, though. You do not like beasts or trolls?"

She gave him a look. He was wasting time. Time she most certainly did not have. "No one likes beasts or trolls."

But the young man was not done with his questions. "What he looks like matters so much?"

"I do not *care* what he looks like," Charlotte practically cried. "What I do not like is not knowing. I have asked *everyone* about him. Not just what he looks like. What he *is* like. And no one will tell me a thing."

"That is a problem," he murmured.

"Here," she said, motioning him over. "Just take hold here. With a lift, I believe I can make it over the garden wall."

"You want me to lift you over the wall so you may escape."

Mein Gott, he was slow. "That is what I said, yes."

He glanced behind him, back toward the chapel. "People will notice you are missing, will they not?"

"I shall worry about that later. Now, if you please, I just need a little help." She motioned urgently. "Come, make haste."

But he just crossed his arms. "I have absolutely no intention of helping you."

Now she was irritated. He'd been so polite and chatty, giving every indication that he was a gentleman, when all he was really doing was wasting her time. "I am a lady in distress," she snapped. "You refuse to help a lady in distress?"

"I refuse when that lady in distress is trying to go over a wall so she does not have to marry me."

Charlotte went still. So still that she would have sworn her blood stopped flowing. She looked up. Into his eyes, which were very, very amused.

"Hello, Charlotte," he said. "I am George."

"I—I—"

His mouth curved into a devilish smile. "You . . . ?"

She sank into a curtsy. A very, very deep one. She would have scraped her forehead to the ground had it been anatomically possible. "I am so very, very sorry, Your Majesty."

He reached down and took her hand, tugging her back upright. "Not Your Majesty. George." His mouth made a funny line, and for a moment he looked almost flustered. "I mean, yes, Your Majesty. But to you, George."

Charlotte was quite certain that words did not exist to describe her current state of wretchedness. Not in English or German. But she tried, nevertheless. "Please accept my apology," she begged. "If I had known that you were you . . ."

"You would have what? Not told me you were trying to escape?"

He was teasing her. She could hear it in his voice. But this did little to ease her utter and complete mortification. And fear.

He *seemed* like a nice man. He hadn't flown off in a rage over her behavior. But they both knew he could make her life a misery with a snap of his fingers. And she had just insulted him in the worst possible way.

"Well . . ." she said, trying to find words that could possibly fit such a situation. "Yes. I mean, no. I mean, I do apologize, Your Majesty."

"George," he said. "Just George."

She couldn't take her eyes off him. He was so . . . kind. Not at all what she'd expected, even before she'd tried in vain to question everyone about him.

It wasn't that he was handsome, which he was.

He really was.

It was something else. Something she did not know how to describe, except that her arm had been tingling since he took her hand, and she would have sworn that her body was somehow lighter than it had been a moment earlier, as if she might suddenly find herself floating a few inches above the ground.

Everything felt different. *She* felt different.

He leaned in. "The King situation," he said, almost conspiratorially. "It towers over us. Accident of birth on my part. But I thought perhaps as my wife you could ignore that, and I could be Just George to you."

"Just . . . George?" she echoed.

He nodded. "That was of course before I found out that you do not want to be married to me."

"I did not say that," Charlotte said quickly.

"Oh, you did."

"I did not."

"You did."

"It is not . . ." Charlotte shook her head, utterly frustrated. "I do not know you."

He held his arms out to the sides. "I do not know you, either. Except that you are terrible at climbing a wall."

"You try climbing a wall in all of these garments," she retorted.

He chuckled.

She grinned.

"What?" she asked.

He shook his head, as if he could not quite believe his own thoughts. "You are incomparable. No one told me you would be this beautiful."

Suddenly, Charlotte did not know what to do with her hands. Or her legs. Her body felt strange, as if the air she breathed was some fizzy foreign substance, twinkling on the wind.

"You may be too beautiful to marry me," George continued. "People will talk." He tipped his head, quirking a devilish smile. "Given that I am a troll."

Charlotte wanted to die. "Your Majesty—"

"George."

"George," she forced herself to repeat. It was not easy. He was a king. No one called kings by their Christian names.

"What do you want to know?" he asked.

"What?"

"You do not know me. That is the problem, is it not? What do you want to know about me?"

"That is quite . . . I do not . . ."

He smiled expectantly, never taking his eyes from her face.

"Everything," she said.

He nodded slowly. "All right. Everything, eh? Well. I was born prematurely, and everyone thought I was going to die. But I did not. I am a fair fencer. An even better shot. My favorite food is mutton. I will not eat fish." He looked up sharply. "Do you like fish?"

"I—"

"No matter," he said, clearly uninterested in her answer. "We shall not eat it. I like books and art and good conversation. But most of all, I like science."

"Science?"

"Chemistry, physics, botany. And especially astronomy. The stars and the heavens. I am quite the farmer, probably would be a farmer if I were not already occupied."

Charlotte blinked, trying to keep up with him.

He pointed to his ribcage. "I have a scar here from falling off my horse. And one here"—he motioned to his hand, to the base of his thumb—"from just being incredibly clumsy with a paring knife. And I am very nervous about marrying a girl I am only just meeting minutes before our wedding, but I cannot show it and climb over a wall because I am the King of Great Britain and Ireland and it would cause a scandal.

But I promise you, I am neither a troll nor a beast." He paused, and Charlotte finally saw the hint of nerves in his warm, dark eyes.

He looked at her. Really looked at her. And he said, "I am just George."

Charlotte felt her face change. She was smiling. She couldn't remember the last time she had smiled so widely. She liked him. She *liked* him. It seemed a miracle, but she liked this man she had been commanded to marry. He talked a bit quickly when he got going, but he was . . . interesting. And funny.

And really quite handsome.

"George," she said, testing his name out on her tongue. "I—"

"*Liebchen!*"

She whirled around. Adolphus was hurrying toward her.

"We have been looking everywhere for you!" her brother said. "What are you—" He gasped. "Your Majesty."

Adolphus bowed. Deeply. Humbly.

"Ah," George said, in quite the friendliest manner imaginable. "You are the man responsible for my possible future happiness."

"*Ja,*" Adolphus said, looking highly ill at ease. "My apologies. Yes. No. I'm—"

"Well, you have arrived at a most opportune moment," George said. "Charlotte was just deciding whether or not she wanted to marry me."

An expression of great alarm came over Adolphus's face. "Charlotte is *overjoyed* to become your wife."

"No," George said sharply. "She is still deciding." He flicked his head toward the garden wall. "She might go over the wall instead."

Adolphus's mouth opened. Then started to close. Then opened again.

"The choice is entirely up to her," George said.

Charlotte decided then and there that she loved him. As much as one could decide such a thing. Also, she'd only known him for five minutes. She wasn't as fanciful as that.

George turned to her with a slightly sheepish smile. "I should go back because I suspect that by now there are some very anxious guards who think I am kidnapped. Charlotte?"

She looked up at him, utterly beyond words.

He took her hand and leaned down, brushing his lips across her knuckles. "I hope I see you in there."

She could only stare.

"And if so," George said, letting her fingers slip through his, "I shall be the one standing next to the Archbishop of Canterbury."

He strode off, resplendent in his richly embroidered coat.

"Do not tell me you are still hesitating?" Adolphus said.

Charlotte turned slowly to her brother. She'd quite forgotten he was there. "Well," she said slowly, looking down at the detestable gown Princess Augusta had forced on her, "first I need to change."

GEORGE

George was terrified.

Could a person be terrified and elated at the same time? It must be possible, because he was feeling both, along with dread.

Fear.

No, that was the same thing as dread.

Did that count? Both, together? If fear and dread were synonyms that meant they were the same thing and thus it was only one emotion he was feeling, not two.

He looked down at his hands. Were they twitching?

No, but were they *shaking*? Perhaps, but there was a chill in the air. That could be the reason.

Were shaking and twitching synonyms? Now that was an interesting question. He'd have to say no. Not really. There was an appreciable difference between shaking and twitching. Not like fear and dread. Fear was a lesser form of dread, but shaking was not at all the same movement as twitching. You couldn't compare the two.

The two *pairs* of words, that was. The whole point was that he was comparing *each* pair within itself.

He took a breath. *Stop*, he told himself. *Calm your mind.*

This happened sometimes.

Often.

More than he wished.

His brain seemed to run off without him, and he could not control his thoughts. That was the worst part of it, because shouldn't a man be able to control his own mind? He was the King. If he could not rule his own mind, how could he expect to rule anything else?

And now he was terrified. And elated.

As previously mentioned.

It was all because of her. Princess Sophia Charlotte of Mecklenburg-Strelitz. No, they were married now. She was Queen Charlotte of Great Britain and Ireland.

She was a queen now. His queen.

George had not been looking for her when they'd met in the chapel garden. It was just that they'd told him she'd run off, and he'd felt such overwhelming relief and embarrassment—again, with the contradictory combination of emotions.

He'd needed air.

He had been feeling so confident. They'd found him a new doctor, a Scot who practiced in London. It had only been a week, but George had been feeling quite himself again, like a man ready to get married. But then that little toad of a servant had come and told Reynolds that the bride had gone missing. George had looked down, and his hands had begun to twitch, and all he could think was—

Escape.

No bride, no wedding. He did not need to be there.

He'd always loved the chapel garden. It was not like being truly out of doors, where the fields rolled wide and the trees were majestic, but it was bucolic and relatively unpatterned for an ecclesiastical space. There were hedges, of course, but years ago someone had planted wildflowers in the open areas. George often escaped there when he needed a spot of privacy.

Plus, no one seemed to look for him there. It was a boon.

But Doctor Monro had been standing in the corridor, presumably put there by George's mother, who was taking no chances, and he had not accepted George's excuses or explanations. He had not bowed; he had not kissed George's ring. Instead, when George said that he was not ready, and he was not right, Doctor Monro had looked his king in the eye and said, "I have examined you thoroughly, and you are perfectly right."

"Do I look perfectly right to you?" George demanded, holding out his twitching hands.

He'd thought that would be the end of it, because any fool could see he was not well, but the doctor roared, "*You are perfectly right*," and then he'd slapped him across the face.

And that . . . had . . . done it.

The twitching stopped. His mind slowed and centered. George had blinked, put up a hand to stop the guards from hauling Doctor Monro off to whichever dungeon was nearest, and he'd thanked the doctor.

It had been revelatory.

A miracle.

There was something about Monro's voice. And maybe the slap, too, but mostly the voice. It was smooth and deep. Commanding. When Monro spoke, it brought George back to himself. His thoughts had stopped racing, and his hands had stopped twitching, and he'd felt ready.

He had stepped outside to breathe in the cool air, and there she was, attempting to climb a woody wisteria vine. Charlotte. His princess, soon to be his queen. He wasn't positive it was her before they spoke, but he'd had a good suspicion. Her skin was dark, like his mother had told him, and she was wearing a very simply cut ivory gown that had fit his mother's description. She was the right age, and she held herself like a royal.

He'd thought she was pretty.

That was all he'd thought, really, when he saw her standing by the wall. But then she spoke.

And he was lost forever.

When Charlotte spoke, the world came alive. She was fierce and stubborn and shockingly forthright. Her intelligence transformed her pretty face into something incandescent. Truly, he did not know a woman could be so beautiful.

She was a star. She was a comet. She was everything that sparkled in the night sky, brought down to earth by magic the church swore did not exist.

How did you explain that some people were special? That they were somehow *more* than everyone else? Were they born under the wing of an angel? Did their blood flow at a different speed?

All his life, people had told him that *he* was such a person, but he knew the truth. It was an accident of birth. He was born to be King, and thus he was coddled and praised. When he spoke, people listened.

But they were listening to their King. Not to George.

Charlotte was different. She could have been born in a sewer and people would have leapt over barricades to hear her words. Hers was a charisma that could not be faked.

Or taught.

She was, quite simply, magnificent. Far more so than he could ever hope to be.

It was not just her beauty. She was terrifyingly clever. That was the problem. If she were ugly, if she were dull, he might feel himself up to the task of being her husband.

George had known that he had to allow her to decide for herself if she wanted this marriage. He had somehow recognized that her spirit could not be commanded. Yes, he supposed he could order her to take her place in the chapel, and yes, he was quite certain that her brother *had* ordered her to take her place in the chapel, but George knew that a marriage under duress could never be a true union. Not with her.

She could not be tamed. It would be a crime to even try.

So he took a chance. He gave her the opportunity to abandon the marriage. And he gave himself thirty minutes of heinous anxiety.

He had been fairly certain she would decide to go through with the marriage. He certainly hoped she would. Their conversation had gone well. Maybe she had not been struck so cleanly by Cupid's bow as he, but she seemed to like him well enough, which was often the best one could hope for in a royal marriage.

But until he saw her enter the chapel, glittering in an ivory caped gown shot with silver and gold, he had not been positive that she would show up.

She walked up the aisle, and with each step his joy grew. He watched her, and he was so sure, so certain that this woman was perfect and this marriage was right.

This union would be the making of him.

Charlotte's brother took her hand and placed it in his, and George had smiled and said, "You changed your dress."

"I required something more befitting a queen," she replied.

His queen.

He would have sworn his heart sang.

But now, after the long, solemn ceremony and so many hours of making polite conversation with people whose names he would never recall, he felt something dark and ugly scraping at the edges of his happiness.

He was not worthy of this magnificent creature. And with time, she would know it.

Much of the time he was *fine*. Normal, or at least as normal as a king ever was. But then something would set him off. He could not explain it—something sparked in his mind, and he could not put out the strange, ungodly flame that burned and snapped inside of him.

He filled with words—that was the only way to describe it. His body filled with words, usually about the heavens and the stars but sometimes about the sea, and the gods, and ordinary men. The syllables twisted and jumbled inside him, burning his mouth, and pressing at his skin. Until finally it was all too much, and he had to *say* it.

And the worst—the absolute worst of it was that he *knew* when his mind was not working properly. At least at the beginning of an episode. He could tell that something was sick and rotten, and he did not know how to fix it.

But not right now.

He took a breath. He was perfectly well. He was perfectly right.

This was his wedding day, and he was perfectly well and right.

Charlotte was just a few yards away, speaking with her brother and the new Lady Danbury. She looked lovely and regal, her hair a perfect cloud topped with the most whimsical and fairylike tiara George had ever seen. It occurred to him that it was past time he led his bride in a dance.

He crossed the distance and bowed. "May I have this dance, Your Majesty?"

She smiled as if lit from within. "I would be delighted, Your Majesty."

George led her to the center of the floor. Other couples would join them soon, but it was understood that this dance would be for the King and Queen alone. And though they had shared words all evening, this was the first conversation since the ceremony that was theirs alone.

He waited for the music to begin, led her through the first steps, and then asked, "How does it feel to be Queen?"

She gave a little start of surprise. "I do not know," she said. "How does it feel to be King?"

"I hardly know anything else."

"That cannot be true. It has not been even a year since you ascended to the throne."

"True," he allowed, "but I have always known it was my destiny. I am the eldest son of the eldest son of a king. I was but twelve when my father died, and I became the Prince of Wales. I have never been treated as an ordinary human being."

Did she hear the note of wistfulness in his voice? He did not wish *not* to be King, but there were times when he'd gladly skip affairs of state to work in his garden.

Farmer George. That was what people called him behind his back. Little did they know he took it as a compliment. He had meant what he'd said to his mother that morning. The earth was beautiful. Soil was a miracle, and from it sprang all life and hope.

"You did not answer me," he said, taking her hand and raising it above their shoulders so that she might twirl. "How does it feel to be Queen?"

"It is an impossible question."

"Is it? I should have not thought it so. It would be an extraordinary change for any woman, even one who has grown up a princess."

"Perhaps." The dance drew them apart for a few seconds, and when they were once again face-to-face, she said, "It is far less special to be a princess in Europe. We are rather thick on the ground, to be honest."

He felt himself grin. "I cannot decide if the image is delightful or terrifying."

"A swath of princesses?"

"An army," he decided.

"That *would* be terrifying," she said. "You have not seen my sister shoot a gun."

George chuckled. "I do not know how many sisters you have," he admitted.

"Only one who is still living."

"I am sorry."

She gave a little shrug. "The rest were all gone before I was born. I did not have the opportunity to know them."

"As is so often the case." George's own parents had long been considered blessed that all of their children had survived infancy. His sister Elizabeth had passed two years earlier at the age of eighteen, and he had mourned her truly. But thus far, she was the only of his siblings to have died.

"You have a great many brothers and sisters," Charlotte said.

"I do. I hope that you will come to view them as your own. Caroline Matilda—my youngest sister—would be quite interested in your army of princesses, I'm sure."

"Is she a good shot?"

"God, I hope not. She's but ten."

Charlotte laughed. It was a rich sound, not particularly musical, but full of joy. "I must confess that I, too, am not handy with a weapon. Your sister and I shall learn together."

"A frightening prospect," George murmured. "And one I may have to take pains to prevent. But more importantly, what would we call this princess army?"

"This is where English fails us," Charlotte said with a disdainful wrinkle of her nose. "In German we would have a word for it. *Armeeprinzessinnen*. We would all know exactly what it means."

"I speak German as well," George reminded her. "And I don't believe a new word is required. Is there a reason we would not call it an *Armee der Prinzessinnen*?"

"Details," Charlotte scoffed. "I prefer long words."

"*Backpfeifengesicht*," George murmured.

Charlotte's face lit with a smile. "A face in need of a fist. Such a useful word. It is needed in English."

"I daresay it is needed in every language," George said. "But as it happens, you are the Queen. You can make up all the words you wish."

She grinned. "Fistneedingface."

"Faceneedingfist?" he countered.

"Yours is more accurate, but mine is more satisfying."

George let out a burst of laughter, loud enough that it drew curious stares.

"Careful," Charlotte said with a daring twinkle in her smile. "People will think we like each other."

"Don't we?" he murmured.

But she was saved from answering by the steps of the dance. They each made a stately circle before their hands once again touched, and she said, "I hope so."

"It is a gamble we take," he said, "these marriages of state."

She acknowledged this with a tiny nod, then said, "You must know that I had no choice."

"Untrue," he murmured. He took her hand as they walked down an imaginary center aisle. The rest of the guests had not yet joined them, so it was just they two, processing alone. "I distinctly recall telling your brother that the choice was entirely up to you."

"Surely you do not think I *truly* had a choice?"

George tried to ignore the little pricks of unease in his chest. "You gave every indication that you thought you did when you tried to go over the garden wall."

"This I cannot deny."

"And I did give you a choice. If you did not see it as such, that was entirely up to you."

She considered that for a moment before speaking. "I very much appreciated that you offered. I was surprised that you did."

"I am not such an ogre. Nor," he added with a tip of his head, "a troll or a beast."

The music swelled and then ebbed, indicating that the solo first dance had come to an end. George made a regal sweep with his arm, inviting his guests to join them. They did, swarming around the royal couple in a blur of perfumed satin and silk. And while he and Charlotte were still very much the center of attention, he felt not quite so much on display.

It was something of a relief, that.

"They told me almost nothing about you," Charlotte said.

"They did not tell me much about you, either."

"I am sure there is less to say."

"Impossible. There could not be enough words to describe you."

"Now I know you exaggerate." But she blushed a little. It was not as easy to see on her skin as it must be on his, but he found this thrilling. As if she were a greater challenge.

She would not be easy to understand. She was a diamond. Flawless. But no one knew how a diamond came to be without imperfections. They just turned up that way, magic of the earth.

"Come," he said, motioning to the side of the room. "Let us leave the dance floor to our guests."

They returned to the side of the ballroom. Charlotte looked out over the crowd, and he looked at her. "You are beautiful," he said. He had not meant to say it, not right at that moment, but it slipped from his lips like a poem.

She turned. "You are kind to say so."

He tried his best to appear nonchalant. "It is nothing but the truth, but surely you must know that."

"Is not beauty in the eye of the beholder?"

"If it is, then you are the most exquisite creature ever to be born, for I am the one beholding you."

She smiled at that, a real smile. But it looked as if she were holding back something more. A laugh?

"What?" he asked.

"What what?"

"You were about to laugh."

She drew back her chin. "I was not."

"Allow me to correct myself. You were holding back a laugh."

"Is that not the same thing?"

"Not at all. But you are avoiding my question."

"Very well, if you must know—"

"I must," he interrupted, and he grinned. He could not remember the last time he'd felt like this, like he needed to win and woo and most of all, he had to earn it.

"I was thinking," she said, "that such opulent language is not like you."

"You were, were you?"

She shifted her posture. A little wiggle of her shoulders. She looked rather pleased with herself. "I was."

"And how would you know that, given that we've only just met?"

"I could not say, except that I think I know you."

His heart leapt. Soared. And it would have been glorious except that the black hand of terror snaked out and squeezed in his chest. She did not know him. If she knew him, she'd not have married him.

George looked down at his hand. He could not see it twitching, but it felt like it was. Like it might.

Might. That was the problem. What might happen. He did not know. He never knew. All he knew was—he did not want to hurt her.

He could not hurt her. It was the most important thing. It had to be. He made a decision.

"I have a surprise for you," he said.

"For me?" Delight twinkled across her face. "What is it?"

"You will need to be patient. And you will need your cloak."

"Is it outside, then?"

"Not exactly. Well, yes, exactly. You will see." He took her hand and pulled her toward his mother, who was in conversation with members of the Mecklenburg-Strelitz delegation. "It is time we said our goodbyes."

Charlotte glanced at all the guests, still merry and dancing. "Already?"

"We are no longer needed. No one can depart until we do, so really, we're doing them all a favor."

"George," his mother said, once they'd reached her side. "You are looking well."

The unspoken message being—*sometimes you don't.*

George's lips pressed together before he spoke. "It is my wedding day, Mother. Of course I am looking well."

Augusta turned to Charlotte and curtsied. "Your Majesty."

For a moment Charlotte appeared not to know what to make of this. Just that morning she had been the one curtsying to Augusta. Finally she nodded and said, "Your Royal Highness."

"We depart anon," George said. "I am taking Charlotte to see her present."

"Her present?" Augusta frowned. "Oh, you mean—"

"Eh eh eh. Not a word. It is a surprise."

"I must bid farewell to my brother," Charlotte said. "I will return in a moment."

"She is good for you," Princess Augusta said once Charlotte was gone.

"Yes," George said.

"And of course you are good for her. You are the King. You would be good for anyone."

He did not really want to nod, but he did. He had to acknowledge her statement in some manner.

"You will bed her tonight?" Augusta asked. But it was really closer to a demand.

"Mother!"

"Every day you fail to produce an heir to the throne, our family's position weakens."

"Is that all a king is?" George countered. He was so bored of this conversation. It was one his mother introduced at least every other day. "A royal stud horse, trotted out for the chosen mare?"

Augusta just laughed. "Do not pretend you take umbrage. I've seen the way you look at her."

"I do not wish to have this discussion with my mother."

"I do not wish to have this discussion with my son, but apparently I must." The faint lines around her mouth tightened. "Do not forget your duty to this country."

"I assure you, Mother, it is never far from my mind."

"It is all so very modern now," Augusta said. "In my day, there were seven people in the bedchamber on my wedding night to witness the marital act. To confirm that your father and I did what was necessary to make you."

Dear God.

"Now," she went on, "it is the thing to give the couple privacy. Which would not be an issue ordinarily. But the thing about you, George . . ."

He closed his eyes. "Don't, Mother."

But she did. "It is just that you have your own mind."

The unspoken message being—*and a strange mind it is.*

George let out a breath. His hands felt funny. He needed to leave. And he was so bloody tired of all her unspoken messages. "Just say what you mean, Mother."

She brought her eyes to his. "Do what needs to be done."

"And damn the consequences?"

"I didn't say that."

"You didn't need to."

Augusta looked over at Charlotte, who was still saying goodbye to her brother. "She *is* lovely. Intelligent, too. That is a good thing, despite what most men say. She will make good babies."

He shook his head. "Good night, Mother."

She just tipped her head toward a spot past his shoulder. "She is coming back."

"Thank you for waiting," Charlotte said. "I am ready."

"I am so glad to hear that," Augusta said.

George shot her a look, one that fortunately Charlotte did not see. "Let us be away," he said, tugging on his new wife's hand.

"Is there no one else we need to bid farewell?"

"No one at all." He started walking quickly, eager to be out of the palace after his conversation with his mother. He loved her, he did, but lately she always seemed to set him on edge.

Their carriage was waiting in the drive, and less than ten minutes later, they were at their destination.

"Where are you taking me?" Charlotte asked. "Are we there yet?"

"Don't look. Keep your eyes closed."

Charlotte obeyed. Almost. He saw one eye peek through her lashes.

"I see you peeking," he said teasingly. "Do I need to send one of the footmen for a blindfold?"

"No, no, I swear," she said with a laugh. "I will not look."

He put his hand over her eyes. "I do not believe you."

"I cannot get out of the carriage with my eyes closed."

"You should have thought of that before you disobeyed me."

"George!"

He loved the sound of his name on her lips, especially like that, tinged with a laugh. She would appreciate this gift. He knew she would.

It was for her own good.

She would understand.

She had to.

CHARLOTTE

"Are you ready?" George asked.

Charlotte nodded, trying to rein in the silly smile that kept tugging along her lips. He'd put his fingers over her eyes, something she'd never liked as a child, and yet tonight she did not protest. His hand was large and warm, and its strength hinted at something wicked and wonderful.

How could she have been so lucky? She knew what it meant to be ripped from one's childhood home and sent off to marry. She may have been the first in her family to wed, but the other German nobles did not live so very far, and gossip traveled like the wind. Brides were bartered without a thought to their culture or language.

Or whether they cared for the groom. People were still talking about the dreadful match between Sophia Dorothea of Prussia and the "Mad" Margrave of Brandenburg-Schwedt, and that had occurred before Charlotte had even been born.

But George was perfect. Or maybe not perfect, because Charlotte was sensible, and she knew no one could be perfect. But he was everything she could have hoped for. And for the first time since Adolphus had informed her that she was leaving Mecklenburg-Strelitz, she was happy.

"Just a few more steps," George said, once they'd stepped down from the ornate Gold State Coach that had taken them through London. "I want you to have the best vantage."

"Of what?"

"Now, now, no need to be so impatient."

She let herself be led across crunchy gravel. A drive? It must be; they had arrived in a carriage.

"Almost there," George said. "One, two . . ."

And on three he lifted his hand to reveal a beautiful, stately home. Neoclassical in style, it was shaped like a U, with pillars and pilasters marching across its façade. A red carpet rolled down the stairs from the main entrance nearly all the way to the carriage.

"What do you think?" George asked eagerly.

"It is lovely." She turned to her new husband, watching the flames from the torches flicker in his dark eyes. "Who lives here?"

"I had it redesigned just for you."

Charlotte knew that could not be entirely true, not when their wedding had been agreed upon only a few months earlier. But still, she loved it. The stonework was much more to her taste than the brick of St. James's Palace.

Most importantly, she would be the head of her own household. Queen not just of her country, but of her home. That would not be easily attained at St. James's, where Princess Augusta was in residence.

Here, at—

She paused. "What is it called?"

"Buckingham House," he said. "But you may rename it if that is your desire."

"No, I like it. It has the sound of something that will endure."

"I pray that it will."

Charlotte could not stop smiling. She had not known she had it in her to feel such joy, that she could be made so happy by another human being. She could not stop thinking about how lucky she was. George was kind, and funny, and he seemed to be very intelligent. On the way over from St. James's Palace, he had told her of some of his scientific interests. He owned a telescope, apparently—a very large one—and something else called an orrery that predicted the positions of the planets and moons.

She had never been particularly interested in astronomy, but when George told her about it, it came alive. She wanted to know more. She wanted to *learn*.

Now he had bought her *this*? She looked back up at him. "This is truly our house? Oh, George . . ."

"It is your house," he said.

She blinked, certain she could not have heard him correctly. "My house. What do you mean?"

He motioned to the enormous building behind him. "This is where you shall live. I had all of your things moved here during the ceremony."

Charlotte kept staring at the building, as if she could somehow see through the stone to her trinkets and gowns, presumably tucked away in wardrobes and cabinets. "I am not sure I understand," she said. "If this is my house, is it not also *our* house?"

"I suppose officially St. James's is our house," he said, in a voice that indicated he had not considered the matter until that very moment. "But this is where you shall stay."

"Oh" was all she could say.

He patted her arm. "You shall be very comfortable here. It is very modern."

"Where will you stay?" she finally asked. Because he had not uttered one word about his own plans.

"I have an estate in Kew."

"Kew," she repeated. So many one-word sentences, and nothing but echoes of his pronouncements. She felt rather stupid, to be honest.

She despised feeling stupid. Truly, it was the one thing she could not tolerate.

"It's not far. Less than ten miles."

"So you shall live in Kew."

"Yes."

She looked back at Buckingham House, which had seemed so glorious when he'd lifted his hands from her eyes. Now it was just a house. Large, elegant, but just a house.

She forced a smile. Not much of one, though. "And I shall live here."

"Yes."

"George," she said cautiously. "It is our wedding night."

"And it is late," he said, his voice slightly brisk, as if he'd only been waiting for the correct sentence upon which to change the topic. "You have been traveling, and I should let you get inside. You will need to meet your staff, and you will want to get some sleep."

"No," she protested. "George. It is our wedding night. We are supposed to . . ."

He just stared at her, and she would swear something in his eyes . . . *changed.* What was the opposite of a flicker? Because that was what happened. Something went flat. Maybe even a little cold.

"We are married," she said. "Are we not supposed to do what married people do?"

His brows rose, and not with amusement. "Are you demanding I perform my marital duty to you?"

"I am not demanding. I am not even sure what marital duty is. I just know . . ." Charlotte felt herself flailing. She was uncertain, unmoored. She did not know what was happening, and worse, she was not sure what *should* be happening.

"Do we not spend this night together?" she finally asked. "My governess said that is what happens on a wedding night. The bride and groom sleep together in one bed."

"Fine," George said with a huff of annoyance. "I shall stay."

Charlotte watched as he stomped toward the house, utterly baffled by his abrupt change in behavior. "George?" she asked, her voice tentative.

He paused near the entrance, and even before he turned around, she could tell he was rolling his eyes at her. "I said I shall stay," he said. "Are you coming?"

"I— Yes." She gathered her skirts and hurried after him. What was happening? Where was the darling man who had teased her about princess armies and jumping the garden wall?

Answer: Stomping ahead of her, right past the row of servants who had lined up for their arrival.

"Ah, hello, hello," she said, pausing to nod and generally be polite, unlike her furious husband, who was already halfway down the hall.

"Thank you," she murmured to the woman she guessed was the housekeeper. "Brimsley, you're here. Of course you are."

He bowed. "Your servant, Your Majesty. May I present the staff?"

Charlotte threw a desperate glance at George, who was disappearing up a staircase. "Perhaps another time." She took off, moving as quickly as she could without actually breaking into a run. "George! George!"

But he was already up the stairs.

"George!" She picked up the pace, but there was only so much she could do in her wedding gown. "I cannot keep up. Please. Slow down."

He whirled around so suddenly she stumbled back. "I thought you wanted me in the bedroom," he said, flinging one of his arms out to motion down the hall. "Is that not where I should be?"

"No."

"No?"

"Not if you are going to behave this way. You are angry. What is wrong? What have I done? Whatever it is, I am sorry." She reached within for bravery, then she reached out to him. Took his hand. "Please," she said. "Forgive me. I do not know what is happening."

She felt his hand tremble in hers, heard his breath catch, and then slow down. "You have done nothing to be sorry for," he said. "I just . . . I just want to go to Kew."

"So let us go to Kew."

"No," he said, too loudly. "I . . ."

She understood. And it was awful. "You do not want *me* to go to Kew."

"This is your home," George said, but the words sounded mechanical, as if he'd practiced them in his head.

"And Kew is your home," Charlotte finished.

"Yes."

"I see," she said. But she did not. She did not see at all.

"You do?" George said brightly. He took back his hand. "Good. That is very good. You are all right, then. You will get settled, and you will be comfortable, and all will be well and right. I shall speak with you . . . later." He gave her a smile, one that she could not judge the sincerity of, and started walking back down the hall toward the stairs.

What?

No.

"I am not all right," Charlotte said forcefully.

He turned.

"Is this how it is to be?" she asked. "This is our marriage? You there and me here?"

He swallowed. "Yes."

"Why?"

"I thought it would be . . ." He swallowed again, and truly, he did not look quite right. "It is easier."

"For whom?"

"What?"

"Easier for whom?" she asked. "You or me?"

"I am not going to debate this with you."

"I merely want to understand. I had such a wonderful time with you this evening. *We* had a wonderful time. You cannot tell me otherwise. You need to at least tell me—"

"I do not need to do anything. I decide!" he thundered. "I have decided. I am your King."

"Oh." Charlotte lurched back, and somewhere, somehow, she located her pride. "My mistake," she said with crisp indifference. "I thought you were just George. Forgive me, Your Majesty."

She curtsied.

But then he said her name. He said it with regret, as if he cared.

As if she mattered, when she knew plainly that she did not.

When she spoke again, her voice was scrupulously polite. "May I withdraw, Your Majesty, or was there something more you wished to say to me?"

But if her voice was demure, her gaze was not. She kept her eyes on his throughout, refusing to be the one to break the connection.

"Charlotte," he said. "This is for the best."

"Of course, Your Majesty. Whatever you wish."

She stared at him. And then once he'd gone, she stared at the staircase. She took a breath. Tried not to cry.

Queens did not cry. Wasn't that what she had decided earlier that morning?

Good God, was it just this morning that she'd been in a carriage with Adolphus? That was a lifetime ago.

She looked down the long corridor. Which room was hers? George had motioned, but he had been so angry. She couldn't tell where he'd been pointing.

She squared her shoulders. She was not useless. She could find her own bedchamber. But when she started walking, she sensed a presence. She sighed. Brimsley. It had to be.

She said his name.

He materialized as if from smoke. "Yes, Your Majesty."

"You are here as well. In this hallway."

"I am wherever you are, Your Majesty." He held up a candle, illuminating her path.

"Right." She sighed, but the air tripped through her throat, and it sounded as if she might cry.

"Your—"

"I am *fine*, Brimsley." She had to cut him off. She could not bear it if he asked after her welfare.

"Yes, Your Majesty."

"My room," she said, trying very hard not to allow her spine to slump. "It is this way?"

"Yes, Your Majesty. The open door at the end of the hall. I am happy to show you."

"You need not follow me."

"But I shall, Your Majesty."

For the love of God. "Stop calling me Your Majesty."

Brimsley looked pained. Or maybe constipated. "You are the Queen of Great Britain and Ireland, Your Majesty. I cannot call you anything else."

She sighed. Deeply. "Well then, stop following me."

"I cannot do that, Your Majesty."

"Is it against the law for me to kill you?" she muttered under her breath.

"What was that, Your Majesty?

She straightened. "As your Queen, I order you to stop following me!"

Brimsley's expression did not change a whit. "It is my sworn duty to take care of you, Your Majesty. At all times."

"I do not want you here."

She wanted *George*. But not the man who had brought her to Buckingham House. She wanted the man from the garden.

Just George.

She thought he had been *her* George.

"I hope in time you will become used to me, Your Majesty," Brimsley said.

"Wonderful," Charlotte said, utterly exhausted. "We can spend the rest of our lives together."

She let him lead her to her room, and then she let her new maids prepare her for bed. And then, when she was finally alone, she lay in the middle of her giant bed and stared up at the exquisite stitching on her glorious canopy.

She closed her eyes. "I should have gone over the wall."

BRIMSLEY

Brimsley loved his new job.

He had been given a completely new uniform with a gold brocade vest, and the move to Buckingham House meant that he was at the top of the belowstairs hierarchy. Who could be more important than the chief servant to the Queen?

He might not sit at the head of the table in the servants' quarters—that was the butler—but he was at the butler's right hand.

He selected the choicest cuts of meat for his plate when they ate. He never had to worry about there being enough pudding for everyone because there was always enough pudding if you were the second person to be served.

Everyone looked at him differently, too. The maids no longer looked down their noses at him. Now he looked down his nose at *them*, even the ones who were taller, which, to be honest, was most of them.

Fish face, his ass. He was on top of the world.

The new queen had yet to appreciate his many virtues, but to be fair, not even a week had passed since the wedding. She was adjusting to her new life, just as Mrs. Pratt had said she would need to. But at least she wasn't stuck over at St. James's, where Princess Augusta was still firmly in charge. Brimsley was quite certain the Queen would be happier here at Buckingham.

Once she adjusted.

If she adjusted.

Which she would. He would make sure of it.

Her days were much as Brimsley had anticipated:

She rose.

She was dressed.

Her hair was styled.

She ate breakfast.

She looked out a window.

She ate lunch.

She read a book.

She was ushered back to her room where her clothes were changed and her hair was restyled for dinner, and then she went to the long, formal dining room, and ate dinner.

Some days she read the book before she looked out the window.

She seemed a little bored, to be honest, but Brimsley would have traded places with her in an instant. A life of leisure? Of gorgeous clothing and elaborate coiffures and only one's favorite foods?

He wouldn't have been able to fathom it except he watched her live it every day.

He spent a great deal of time trailing her as she explored Buckingham, and it was during one of these jaunts that she suddenly stopped and said his name.

He stepped forward. "Your Majesty."

"What is in my engagement diary for the week?"

He was not sure he heard correctly. "Engagement diary, Your Majesty?"

She turned to face him. "I assume there will be charity visits? The poor. Or orphans?"

"There are no orphans, Your Majesty."

Her regal brows rose. "No orphans, Brimsley? In all of London?"

He coughed. Somewhat painfully. "None in your engagement diary, Your Majesty."

"Can we put some there?"

Brimsley had a vision of himself, physically lifting small orphans and placing them next to the Queen.

He did not enjoy this vision.

"I would not think this is the best week for orphans, Your Majesty."

The Queen let out an impatient noise. "Very well, then. I know I must meet with my ladies-in-waiting. That is important. And there is much to take in here. The art. Seeing the galleries of London. I have always loved theater and music. Are there concerts in my engagement diary? Operas?"

"Your Majesty."

She stared at him expectantly.

"There is nothing in your engagement diary, Your Majesty."

"How can that be?" she demanded.

Brimsley felt his toes curling in his boots. He had a desperate urge to fidget, and he never fidgeted. It was one of the reasons he'd been promoted to this role. Or so Reynolds had told him, and Reynolds seemed to know everything.

"Is there nothing in my engagement diary?" the Queen demanded. "Nothing at all?"

"No, Your Majesty."

She took a step in his direction. He tried to take a step back, but she quelled him with a look. He was quite frozen in place.

"Brimsley," she said. "I am the Queen. I have duties. Official duties, do I not?"

"You do, Your Majesty. Many duties."

"Then how can there be nothing in the Queen's engagement diary?"

It had not occurred to him that she did not realize why her days were so empty. "You are currently enjoying the privacy of the first days of marriage, Your Majesty."

She stared at him. "This is my honeymoon," she finally said.

And for the first time since he'd laid eyes on her, he truly felt sorry for her. "Yes, Your Majesty."

The following week was an exercise in repetition.

The Queen rose.

She was dressed.

Her hair was styled.

She ate breakfast.

She looked out a window.

She ate lunch.

She read a book.

And so on. All of it, alone.

Except for Brimsley, always five paces away.

She was miserable, and he had not a clue what to do about it.

He considered consulting Reynolds. The Queen's misery was clearly caused by the King, and no one knew the King's situation better than Reynolds.

But that required admitting to Reynolds that he was failing in his new position with the Queen, and nothing could be worse.

Then he received a letter from Princess Augusta.

St. James's Palace

Princess Augusta's Sitting Room

...

Later that Day

"I assume you know why I have called you here this afternoon," Princess Augusta said.

Brimsley did not, in fact, know why she had called him there. Especially since Reynolds was also in attendance, along with Earl Harcourt and Lord Bute, two of the King's most long-standing advisors.

Reynolds, with his shiny blond hair, piercing blue eyes, and remarkably deep voice. Reynolds, six feet tall if he was an inch, with a mien and demeanor that would not have been misplaced on a duke. Brimsley would have hated the man if he ever bothered to think about him.

Which of course he did not do. Why would he think about him? Reynolds was with the King, and Brimsley was with the Queen, so the only reason he, Brimsley, would ever need to picture Reynolds's ridiculously symmetrical face was when the King and Queen had business together.

Or when he and Reynolds had business together, which they sometimes did. Of a sort.

Brimsley would not say that they were friends, but they had certain interests in common. And so sometimes they did find themselves in each other's company.

Sometimes.

Occasionally.

Really, only now and then.

They had certainly never been simultaneously summoned to a meeting by the King's mother. It was frankly terrifying. It did, however, give Brimsley a small measure of satisfaction that Reynolds did not seem to know what to make of the situation, either.

"A report, if you will," Princess Augusta demanded. "I wish to know of the King and Queen. How are they getting along?"

Oh.

Oh.

Oh dear.

Brimsley swallowed uncomfortably and then lied through his teeth. "They seem very content."

This did not seem to appease the Princess. "I would hope for more news than the appearance of satisfaction and contentment," she said.

"They are a wonder together," Reynolds said with uncharacteristic drama. "He is smitten with her beauty."

"Really?" Princess Augusta's brows came together, and her lips, which were always somewhat pinchy, tightened into a line. "King George is smitten? So quickly?"

Brimsley very nearly rolled his eyes. He knew Reynolds had been overselling it. "I would not dare to define the emotions of the King," he pronounced.

"Of course not," Reynolds quickly added. "I only meant that he seems happy."

"And what evidence do you have of this?" Princess Augusta demanded.

"A great deal of talking," Brimsley said.

"Talking?"

Brimsley nodded. "And walking."

The Queen walked. Brimsley assumed the King did, too.

"Laughter," Reynolds added. "There is laughter. It warms the heart to witness."

Princess Augusta somehow gave the appearance of leaning forward without actually moving a muscle. "And what of their relations?"

Brimsley just stared. Surely she did not mean . . .

"Their marital bonds," she clarified.

"Bonds," Reynolds echoed.

Brimsley stole a glance. Reynolds looked every bit as horrified as he, but he masked it quickly with a shrug and an expression that seemed to say, *I don't know what she's talking about. Do you know what she's talking about?*

Brimsley responded by similarly expressing, *I don't know what she's talking about, either. Perhaps it's something about flowers. Or cake.*

They turned back to the three dignitaries with equally blank faces.

Lord Bute slammed his hand down on the arm of his chair. "The Dowager Princess wishes to confirm that the marriage has been consummated."

Brimsley wondered how much longer he could feign stupidity.

"Sexually," Earl Harcourt practically barked. Then he adjusted his cravat. "She asks for the good of the country, of course."

"Of course," Brimsley said weakly.

"So?" Lord Bute demanded.

Brimsley looked at Reynolds. *He* was going to have to answer this one. It was the King's fault, after all. All of Buckingham House had seen what had transpired on their wedding night. The Queen had been completely prepared to do her duty and lie with the King. *He* had been the one to take off for no apparent reason.

Reynolds squirmed. "Certainly," he finally said, although he didn't sound too certain to Brimsley's ears. "I mean, from what I can tell, I would say yes."

"From what you can tell?" Princess Augusta said.

"I did not accompany them into their bedchamber, Your Royal Highness."

Brimsley choked on a laugh.

"Have you something to say?" Lord Bute asked.

"Yes, Brimsley," Reynolds said in a peevish tone. "Have you something to say?"

"I also did not accompany them into their bedchamber," Brimsley blurted out.

Reynolds groaned.

Princess Augusta gave them a look that said she was not accustomed to dealing with idiots, then asked, "So would you say it is a successful honeymoon?"

"Indeed," Reynolds said. "Do you agree, Brimsley?"

Brimsley forced himself to nod. "Most successful."

The Princess's eyes narrowed, and Brimsley's nightmare returned—the one with his corpse being stomped on by Italian grape pickers. Except this time, there was a goat.

But then Princess Augusta clapped her hands together and beamed. "This is good!" she exclaimed. She looked to her companions. "We feel it is good?"

"Very good," Lord Bute said.

"Excellent," Earl Harcourt chimed in. "Most excellent."

"Perhaps we shall have an heir on the way before the next fortnight," Princess Augusta said. "Wouldn't that be splendid?"

"Yes, Your Royal Highness," Brimsley said before he realized she wasn't speaking to him.

She motioned to the door. "You may go."

He took a step backward, and then another, Reynolds moving in tandem beside him. Together they backed up to the door, and then finally escaped into the corridor.

"What just happened?" Reynolds whispered.

To which Brimsley replied, "Can we be hanged for this?"

Reynolds stared at him. "Really? That's what you're wondering?"

"You're not?"

"You are so selfish," Reynolds said.

"And you are blind," Brimsley shot back. "We don't serve at the pleasure of the King and Queen, we *exist* at their pleasure. And by extension, of the King's mother. If she is displeased . . ." He made a slicing gesture across his throat.

"You belong on the stage," Reynolds said. He had a way about him, as if he were always talking down to Brimsley, and not only because he was nearly a foot taller.

"We just *lied* to Princess Augusta," Brimsley hissed. "She's going to realize something is wrong when there isn't, in fact, the promise of a baby in the next fortnight."

"Well, I don't know what *we* can do about it."

"There is no *we*," Brimsley said. "There is only you. *You* have to convince the King to summon her."

"I cannot."

Something flickered through Reynolds's eyes so quickly Brimsley almost missed it. Pain. Worry, maybe.

Brimsley's mind flashed with the memory of that man in the hall outside the Chapel Royal. The one who had slapped the King across the face.

He chose his words very carefully. "Is there something I should know about the King?"

"Just that he is your King."

"But the Queen . . ."

"The Queen has been elevated to the loftiest position in the country, if not the world. The Queen cannot possibly have a worry to her name."

Brimsley nearly groaned. "Reynolds—"

"I must depart," Reynolds said suddenly. "I do not like to leave the King unattended for long."

"What could happen to him?" Brimsley scoffed.

Reynolds's expression darkened. Then he strode away.

BUCKINGHAM HOUSE
THE DINING ROOM
···
12 SEPTEMBER 1761

Brimsley was still stewing over that conversation the following day as he watched the Queen take her evening meal. She was seated at the foot of the table, as she always was, resplendent in a round-necked gown of gold.

Table for twenty, place setting for one.

There wasn't much for him to do while she was eating. Six footmen were in attendance to tend to her meal. The minute she finished her soup (chicken consommé this evening), Footman Number One appeared on her right with a small urn if she desired another serving. Footman Number Two appeared on her left to whisk away her bowl if she did not.

"James," Brimsley whispered to Footman Number Three. They were all named James. It was easier that way.

He turned a quarter inch. Just enough to indicate that he'd heard.

"Does she seem quite right tonight?" Brimsley whispered.

"The Queen?"

Brimsley would have groaned if he were allowed to make a noise. Of course he meant the Queen. She was the only *she* in the room.

All he did was nod, though. It was dangerous to alienate a James. They tended to stick together. And they were all quite athletic.

The footman just shrugged. Useless. Brimsley leaned a little to the left, trying to get a better view of Queen Charlotte. She'd seemed unsettled on the way in, although he could not have explained why he thought so. Maybe it was just because *he* was unsettled.

He was still quite concerned about the conversation with Princess Augusta. If by "quite concerned" one actually meant terrified to the point that his digestive processes had not worked for a solid day.

Surely at some point the Princess would realize that the King and Queen were living in separate households. It was frankly a miracle that no one had informed her yet.

Or had they?

Acid crawled up his throat.

Maybe the Princess was just toying with them. Maybe she *did* know that the royal marriage was already stale. Maybe the only reason she had not had Brimsley sacked was that she was pondering something worse.

Did they still garotte people?

Or what if—God forbid—she had him demoted? She could send him out to the stables. Forget sitting at the head of the table. They wouldn't even let him in the kitchen with the stench of the stables on him.

And the *looks* he would get. Not even pity. Just contempt.

Maybe the garotte would be better. He could—

"Brimsley."

He jumped to attention. The Queen had set down her cutlery, but she was still on the soup course. She wasn't nearly done with her meal.

He moved quickly to her side. "Yes, Your Majesty?"

"Ready the carriage."

He blinked. This was most unusual. But if it was what she wanted . . .

"Of course, Your Majesty." He headed for the door, then paused to inquire, "May I say our destination?"

"We are going to see my husband."

Oh.

Oh.

Oh my.

KEW PALACE

LONDON

...

LATER THAT EVENING

"Where is he?"

Brimsley ran to keep up with Queen Charlotte. He'd never seen her move so fast. He'd barely got the carriage door open before she had her feet on the ground and was stalking across the drive, her deep purple cloak billowing behind her.

A small flotilla of servants came rushing out the palace door, including Reynolds, who, it had to be said, did not look his usual unflappable self. Brimsley tried to get his attention and unfortunately succeeded.

"What have you done now?" Reynolds demanded.

"Oh, this is my fault?" Brimsley shot back.

"You!" the Queen said imperiously, pointing at Reynolds.

He made a hasty bow. "Your Majesty, we were not expecting you."

"Where is he?" she demanded.

"The observatory, Your Majesty."

The Queen stared Reynolds down. Brimsley *loved* it.

Reynolds pointed. "It is that way, Your Majesty."

She marched in the correct direction, and Brimsley took his place five paces behind.

But then she held up a hand. "Wait here."

For once, Brimsley allowed her to move out of his sight. "Will he be cross with her?" he asked Reynolds.

"Absolutely," Reynolds answered, still staring in the direction of the Queen. "But she is standing up to him. Perhaps this is good."

"Perhaps," Brimsley echoed, not so sure. "Perhaps it is bad."

Reynolds cleared his throat. "Would you like to step indoors while we wait to find out?"

"Whether it is good or bad?" Brimsley asked.

They were standing side by side, both looking ahead. Brimsley glanced at Reynolds, but only with his eyes. It would not do to appear too eager.

Reynolds made a small murmur of assent. "You should come in and warm up. It is a cool night."

It wasn't. The air was quite pleasant.

Brimsley felt a frisson of excitement. It would be more pleasant inside with Reynolds. "I thank you, sir," he said, allowing a hint of flirtation to enter his voice. "That is very kind and generous of you to offer."

Reynolds walked inside, clearly expecting Brimsley to follow, which he did. They had done this before—not as often as either would have liked, but often enough that Brimsley knew the way.

Reynolds was too pompous by half, but the man kissed like a dream.

"I am always jealous that the King's Man has far better quarters than the Queen's Man," Brimsley said, once they'd reached Reynolds's room.

"To be expected," Reynolds replied. "I am more important than you."

Brimsley decided to ignore that, partly because he'd already backed Reynolds against the wall, and partly because it was true.

But there was still much to discuss. "We have a problem," Brimsley said, getting to work on Reynolds's breeches. Their moments were always stolen; they needed to be quick.

"To be sure."

"Are we going to talk about it?"

Reynolds whipped Brimsley's shirt over his head. "Did you get another letter from the Princess?"

Brimsley nodded, then arched his neck to give him better access. This time of night, Reynolds had just the right amount of stubble to make Brimsley's skin shiver with delight. "The palace is asking for a report." He yanked off Reynolds's breeches and pushed him down on the bed. "What are you going to tell them?"

"Me?" Reynolds started working on Brimsley's breeches. "Why should I be the one to tell them anything?"

Brimsley crawled on top and kissed him with urgency. "It was the King who refused to consummate the marriage."

It was divine until Reynolds pulled back and said, "She could have seduced him."

"She is a lady. Pure and well-bred."

"Fine," Reynolds said, wrapping his fingers around Brimsley's length. He smiled coyly and squeezed. "Still, she could have shown him a little ankle, or—"

Brimsley pressed down so they were skin to skin. He was hard, and Reynolds was hard, and it had been weeks since they'd had a chance to be alone. He ached for this man's touch, and now that he had it, he could not get close enough. Still, even in these few moments of stolen passion, he had to defend his Queen.

"She asked him to stay." Brimsley kissed him. "He demanded to return here to Kew." Another kiss. "Without her. As you are aware."

Reynolds rolled so he was on top. "You say that with a note of accusation."

Brimsley rolled right back. "You might have done something."

"I do not control him."

"You serve him. You know him. Is there a problem? A deformity?" Brimsley could barely voice the question. "Is something wrong with his . . . bits?"

Reynolds sat back. "That is beyond the pale."

"I am just asking. We have a problem."

Reynolds let out a groan, as if he could not believe he had been reduced to such reports. "I believe his bits to be fine. Large. From what I have seen, he has large, healthy bits. No deformity."

"Well. She is a beauty. A jewel beyond compare." Brimsley paused, aware that he needed to speak very carefully. "But perhaps she is not pretty to him. Not his type?"

Reynolds regarded him with confusion. "I do not know that I can define his type."

Brimsley glanced pointedly at their penises, both slightly deflated now. Understandable, given the conversation.

"Female," Reynolds said. "His type is most definitely female. After that, I have never paid attention."

"Well." Brimsley pondered this. "Perhaps what they need is to simply spend time together. As they are right now."

Reynolds nodded slowly, and then he trailed his knuckles down Brimsley's chest. Lower, then lower, until he finally took him in hand. "Do you suppose they might spend fifteen minutes together now?"

Brimsley touched a finger to Reynolds's lips. "Let us hope for twenty."

GEORGE

KEW PALACE
THE OBSERVATORY
...
TEN MINUTES EARLIER

She had come to Kew.

He had not expected this.

George had done the right thing, the honorable thing. He had done his duty to his country and his crown, and he had married the German princess. Then he had left her alone.

No one seemed to recognize what a sacrifice that was. He was entranced by his new bride. Maybe this would turn out to be nothing but a grand infatuation, but Charlotte was all he could think about. Her beauty, her wit, the way she seemed to sparkle in his memory. In the days since his wedding, he'd kept his eye glued to his telescope because sometimes, when he was staring up at the heavens, trying to calculate orbits and distances, he was actually able to forget that he had a wife.

He was afraid. He did not understand his mind, could not puzzle why sometimes it raced and sometimes it did not. He had seen the look of terror in his mother's eyes when he began to twitch, when words spewed from his mouth, strings of nouns and verbs that made sense in his head but nowhere else.

He'd once asked Reynolds to write it down, to keep a record of his ramblings so that he could try to decipher them when he was in a more sensible state of mind. It was horrifying. He could not allow Charlotte to see him when he was like that.

He needed to protect her from it.

He needed to protect himself from her disgust.

But the heavens were safe. The sun and the stars and the planets. Meteors and moons. He could not hurt them. And they would never look down upon him with shame.

So George had sequestered himself in his observatory at Kew Palace, where he whiled away his hours with his giant Gregorian telescope. It was a masterpiece, designed by James Short himself, rivaled only by the one the French king had recently commissioned from Benedictine monks in Paris.

He'd been told that Charlotte was settling in at Buckingham House. He'd asked a few trusted servants to keep an eye on her, and they reported that her days were peaceful. She seemed to like reading and looking out windows.

That seemed normal.

So why had she suddenly come to Kew?

He listened. He could hear footsteps approaching. Just one set. She was alone, then.

He brushed the crumbs of his dinner off his shirt. Was he presentable? He did not look very kingly. He'd been in the observatory for days, even choosing to sleep on a cot in the corner. The dishes from his evening meal had not yet been cleared away from the table. There hadn't been time. Reynolds had come racing up the stairs mere minutes earlier to tell him that the Queen's carriage had been spotted at the bridge.

He moved back to the telescope and pressed his eye to the eyepiece. He did not want to look like he was waiting for her.

He paused. The footsteps drew closer.

Finally, her voice. "What is this place?" she asked.

George drew back, trying to pretend that he had not been listening for her. "Charlotte. Oh. Hello. Here you are."

Her lips moved, but not quite into a smile. "Here I am."

"This is my observatory," he said, motioning with his arm. "It is where I look at the stars." Would she be interested? He rather thought she would. "This is a perfectly clear night," he said, beckoning her to the telescope. "You can see the constellations. And I think I am getting a glimpse of a planet. Come. Look."

She took a slow step in his direction, her face marred by a light frown as she took in her surroundings.

"Don't mind the mess," he said, shuffling a few piles of paper into one. "I didn't know you were coming."

"Else you would have tidied?"

"Probably not," he admitted.

He watched as she took in the room. It was strange to have her here, and it set him on edge. He did not like having other people in his observatory; it was one of the few places he could be truly alone. He did not even allow the servants to enter. Except Reynolds, of course. *Some*one had to bring the dishes in and out. And Reynolds knew when not to speak. More importantly, Reynolds knew when to listen. Because sometimes George just needed someone to listen.

Charlotte wandered over to the far wall, where he had pinned up several drawings. One was of a design for a new type of telescope. Another was a chart of constellations in the southern sky.

"Is this what you have been doing?" she asked suddenly.

George blinked. "Excuse me?"

"Since the wedding." She motioned to the chart on the wall, and then to the telescope. "Is this how you have been spending your time since the wedding?"

He brightened. This was a question he could answer. "Well, yes. It is most exciting. There is an alignment—"

"In this room," she said, and her voice seemed to develop an edge. "This whole time you have been in this room."

"Observatory," he corrected. "But yes. Would you like to look through the telescope? It's a remarkably clear night, as I said, and I'm almost positive I have found Venus. I mean, I *am* positive I have found Venus, but I *should* verify against my charts. It is the way of science, you know. One must record, one must verify."

She did not speak, and he felt compelled to fill the silence, so he motioned to the chart she'd been looking at. "Not that one. That one is for the southern hemisphere. Did you know the austral skies don't look the same as ours? One sees entirely different constellations. I should like to go sometime, but I doubt I will have the opportunity. Too much to do here at home."

He looked at her expectantly. He had not anticipated that she might be interested in astronomy.

But she was just shaking her head. "What have I done wrong?" she asked.

"I beg your pardon?"

"What mistake did I make?"

"You have made no mistake." It had not occurred to him that she might think their separation was her fault. But he did not know how to correct her misapprehension without revealing his own deficiencies.

"Did I say something to offend you?" she asked.

"No." Of course she hadn't. She was perfect. That was the problem.

"Did I *do* something to offend you?"

"No. Of course not."

"Then what is it?" she cried. "What is so wrong with me?"

"There is nothing wrong with you," he said simply.

She was his comet, his shooting star. She sparkled like the heavens, and when she smiled it felt like mathematical equations sliding into place. The world in balance, each side properly weighted.

She was everything that was beauty, and everything that was brilliant, and he was—

He was not well.

He was not well and he was not right, but worse, he could not predict *when* he would be not well and not right. If he had one of his spells in front of her, if she saw him at his worst . . .

He did not know how he could bear it.

But how did one explain such a thing? One could not, of course. So he repeated his words and hoped they would be enough. "There is nothing wrong with you, Charlotte."

Her voice rose in volume. "There must be, or you would not have so easily cast me aside."

He did not know how to speak to her. Would her heightened emotions trigger his own? He needed to remain calm. That was the most important thing he had learned from Doctor Monro. What was it he liked to say? George needed to learn to govern himself. How could he govern others if he could not govern himself?

He took a breath. Charlotte was unpredictable. Capricious. She had abandoned her honeymoon chambers at Buckingham House in violation of all custom and decorum, not to mention his direct order. She had burst in here, his observatory, his private sanctum, unannounced.

Who did that? What measure of woman was she?

"Why do you hate me?" she asked.

"I don't hate—" He muttered a curse. He was losing control of the conversation. This was not acceptable. "Do not become unreasonable."

"George, I thought you were visiting a brothel!"

He drew back, flabbergasted. "Do you even know what that word means?"

"I know what a brothel is," she said testily. "Almost. I have brothers. But that does not signify. I am saying that I would almost *rather* you were visiting a brothel."

"I don't think you do," he said.

"I could understand it more," she said with a frustrated roll of her eyes. "But this— Do you truly prefer stars to my company?"

"I did not say that I prefer—"

"You have been in this room—"

"Observatory," he said again. "The only one of its kind in all of England." He smiled gamely. "I can show it to you, if you like. The telescope in particular is a masterpiece."

She stared at him, and for the love of all that was holy, he could not begin to guess what she was thinking. "Let me make sure I understand," she said. "You have been in this one-of-a-kind observatory room sleeping and eating and staring up at the sky and feeling most excited by the constellations since the night of our wedding while I have been stuck in that stuffy house being changed like a doll three times a day with nowhere to go, no one to talk to, and nothing to do."

"You are the Queen," he said plainly. "You can do whatever you like."

"Except spend time with my husband."

"Come now, Charlotte—"

"Stop patronizing me!"

"I do not understand what you complain about."

"I am seven and ten years old, and suddenly I am Queen."

He found himself backing up as she spoke. He didn't mean to. He didn't want to. It was just that he could feel his mind getting riled.

Words shot through his brain like dice, and it took everything he had not to keep jerking his head to the side.

"I am in a strange country," Charlotte said. "With strange food. And strange customs."

"We can ask the chefs to prepare familiar dishes," he suggested. "Schnitzel? Strudel? I am sure they can learn."

"It is not about the food," she burst out, even though she had, just a moment ago, said it was about the food. "You do not understand because this is who you were born to be. You say I can do whatever I like, but I cannot. The Queen is not allowed to go to the modiste or the galleries or the ice shops. I cannot make friends. I must hold myself apart. I do not know a single soul here. Except for you, and you will not be with me."

He *could not* be with her. It was different.

"I am completely alone," she said, her voice growing small. "And you prefer the sky to me."

He did not speak. He just stared at her. He wanted her to be happy. He wanted her to feel at home. Could she not see that he was trying?

"Say something!" she begged.

He shook his head. "I do not want to fight with you."

"I *want* to fight with you!" she cried. "Anything would be better than this—this neglect. This disregard. I cannot bear it."

He held himself still. He was a statue. It was the only way.

"Fight with me," she begged. "Please."

He did not move. If he could just hold still, he might make it through this night without an episode. Or at the very least, he could stave it off until she departed.

Venus, Transit of Venus . . .

Not now. He could not lose control right now.

Venus, Venus, Mars, Jupiter . . .

"Fight *for* me, George," she whispered.

He did not want to hurt her.

He didn't even shake his head. He just turned back to his telescope and said, "Go home, Charlotte."

He placed his eye to the eyepiece and brought his fingers to the focusing knob, even though it was already exactly where he wanted it to be.

He needed to pretend that he was busy. She would leave. She would not see the expression on his face.

But she did not leave, not as quickly as he thought she would. He was forced to stand there, eye to the telescope, pretending that he was not painfully aware of her presence.

Was she watching him? Judging him?

He looked at the stars. Located Venus.

Prayed she would leave.

Finally, she did.

KEW PALACE
THE OBSERVATORY
...
THE FOLLOWING MORNING

"Your Majesty," Reynolds said, "Doctor Monro has arrived."

"Show him in." George shuffled his papers as he stood. He did not like to receive people in the observatory. The doctor would be his second guest in as many days, but desperate times and all that.

"Thank you for coming so quickly," George said as Reynolds led the doctor in.

"Of course, Your Majesty." Doctor Monro cast several admiring glances at the observatory's equipment. "A most impressive scientific collection. I do not know that there is another to match it in England."

George offered him a self-deprecating smile. "There are a few advantages to being a monarch. One of them is you get the best stuff." But for once, George did not want to talk about his philosophical table or his microscope. He took a breath. He did not like asking for assistance. But he knew he must. "Monro, I, ah—I need your help."

"Of course. I am near at hand for whenever Your Majesty feels a fit coming on."

"The thing is, that is not enough." George raked a hand through his hair. His mother was always telling him this was not a regal habit, but right now he couldn't be bothered to care. "Look, I have learned a thing or two about science, and one thing I have learned is this: Scientists keep the best of it to themselves. Am I right, Monro?"

"I am not sure I understand, Your Majesty."

"It can be years before the public learns of the newest discoveries. And I do understand—there is good reason for this caution. Say a doctor is brought in to treat a king."

"We speak in hypotheticals?" Monro murmured.

George was willing to play this game. For now. "Of course," he allowed. "It is merely an example. This doctor—who is treating a king—he could not risk failure, or God forbid, harming his sovereign. So he would employ only his safest, most proven treatments. He would keep the cutting edge of his methods to himself until they are proven beyond a doubt."

George fiddled with the lodestone on his philosophical table before bringing his eyes to the doctor's. "Do you understand me now, Monro?"

The doctor slowly nodded. "I may begin to."

"It is not enough to cure the fits once they start. If the Queen were ever to see me like . . . *that*, I could not—" He could not imagine it. He could not allow himself to do so.

"May I assume the Queen does not know of your condition?" the doctor asked.

"She does not." George fought the urge to pick up an instrument. It was hard to keep still, but he needed the doctor to see how deadly serious he was. "If God forbid I were ever to hurt her . . . Surely there must be something you can do? Something to end the fits before they begin."

And then he said the one word he'd never allowed himself to dream. "Forever?"

Monro took a moment to consider his request. "I have been experimenting with something more . . . proactive."

"Please. I want to be well."

"I would require rooms in the Palace. Full access to Your Majesty. At any time. And license to pursue rather more"—he cleared his throat—"extreme measures."

"Anything," George said eagerly. "Whatever you have to do. We have the time and privacy of my honeymoon."

Monro glanced about the room. "This is your honeymoon?"

"You see my problem. I do not dare spend it with my bride. I cannot risk her seeing me when I am not myself."

Even as he spoke the words, though, George wondered if he was a fraud. What if *that* was what he was? What if the man who lapsed into nonsense, who lost hours of his time to fits and twitches he did not remember the next day . . . What if that was the real man?

Maybe *this* was the mirage. Farmer George, Scientist George. The man who wanted to love his wife. What if *he* was the false king?

"I am ready, Doctor Monro," he said. It was time to learn the truth.

"We can start today," Monro suggested.

"Excellent. What do you need?"

"Ehrm . . . nothing to start. We will simply speak. But I will need to establish a laboratory on-site. Can you provide men to move my equipment to Kew?"

"At once," George said.

"And an ice bath for later this afternoon."

"You wish to take an ice bath?" George couldn't imagine much that was less pleasant, but if the doctor liked his waters cold . . .

"*You* shall do so." Monro regarded him with a sharp expression. "If I am to treat you, you are not my king. You will do whatever I say, whenever I say. Do you understand?"

"Yes," George whispered. Because he wanted to be well. And for the first time in months, he felt a whisper of optimism. It felt good to have made a decision, to have finally taken the reins of his own care, even if he was then placing those reins into the hands of another.

"Can we begin right now?" George asked.

Monro blinked in surprise. "Yes," he said, a look of satisfaction—or maybe delight—flitting across his face. "Yes, we can. Take a seat." He pointed to a straight-backed wooden chair. "Right there will do."

George followed his direction and sat.

"Do not move while I speak to you," Monro said.

George gave the tiniest of nods.

"The problem in your case is clear. You are a king."

George wanted to nod again, but he didn't. He was determined to follow the doctor's orders.

"As such, you are used to the obedience of others."

George watched as the doctor began to slowly pace in front of him. Three steps one way, three steps the other.

"You yourself have not learned to obey."

George wondered if this was true. It quite possibly was.

"Above all, you have never learned to submit. Your mind ranges, undisciplined. Unbound, it tests the limits of reason. That is the origin of your fits. Do you understand?"

George did not speak. He did not know if he was supposed to.

Monro stopped short and then brought his face close to George's. "*Do you understand?*" he roared.

George startled. "Yes," he said. "Yes. I understand."

"Your Majesty!" Reynolds came skidding into the room. "What is happening? Are you all right?"

"We require solitude," Monro said. He flicked barely a glance at Reynolds. "You are dismissed."

Reynolds looked to George. Clearly, he would not leave without his King's say-so. George swallowed and nodded. He had to do this. It was his only chance.

Reynolds did not look happy, but he moved to the door.

"Wait!" Monro barked.

Reynolds turned. "Sir?"

"My patient requires a change of diet."

"You mean the King?" Reynolds's voice was edged with insolence. George couldn't help but be gratified by it.

"I mean my patient. That is what he is for the foreseeable future. Please direct the kitchens to change his morning meal to porridge."

"Porridge, sir?" Reynolds said.

"Thin porridge."

"We do not even feed that to the scullery maids here at Kew," Reynolds said.

Monro did not see fit to reply.

"You want to feed the King gruel," Reynolds stated, his face printed with disbelief.

George pressed his lips to hold back a smile. Reynolds was loyal. A friend, even. It warmed the heart.

But he needed Monro's help, so he turned to Reynolds and said,

"Please do as the doctor orders. It is a new treatment, one with great promise."

"Your Majesty." Reynolds was clearly unconvinced.

"I am certain, Reynolds," George said. "Go."

KEW PALACE
THE OBSERVATORY
...
14 SEPTEMBER 1761

The following day, George was less certain. But he was still determined to see this through. Doctor Monro had set up a laboratory in the basement of Kew, and he had moved George's treatments to this dank level.

George should have felt some kinship there—it was a place of science, after all, with anatomical charts on the walls, and shelves full of books and jars. But all George could summon was terror. Unlike his celestial observatory, this place was dark and subterranean. The flickering torches cast sinister shadows, but worst of all, Monro had brought in cages filled with animals. Rats, mostly. A rabbit or two. Even some dogs.

They did not look well.

"This is the cure," the doctor said, directing George to a straight-backed chair that had been bolted to the floor. "Submission. It is as I told you before. If you cannot govern yourself, you are not fit to govern others."

George eyed the chair with horror. It was simply made, of iron and wood, but there were ominous knobs and levers, and what were those straps dangling from the headrest? Surely they were not meant to wrap across his face?

"Strap him in," Monro said to his assistants.

George tried to control his breathing as leather restraints were secured around his wrists and ankles.

This is necessary, he told himself. This is right.

Govern yourself. Control yourself.

But his heart was racing, and his breath was moving through him with faster and heavier gulps. He was scared. This was necessary, and it was right, but he was scared. Surely that was normal. It had to be.

"Until you are fit to govern yourself," Monro said, "I shall govern you. Do you understand me?" George nodded, and he started to say yes, but one of Monro's assistants shoved a gag in his mouth.

"*Do you understand me, boy?*" Monro roared.

George nodded frantically.

"I do not give a damn who your father was, how many titles you have, or whether you are God's own representative on Earth. In here you are just another animal in a cage. And just like an animal, *I will break you.*"

George closed his eyes just as Monro's assistants pulled another leather strap tight across his forehead. He was ready to be broken.

Agatha

And now she was having tea with the Queen. Agatha truly did not understand how she'd come to this moment.

Of course she *understood*. The Queen had dark skin and the Palace wanted to make sure she felt welcome and at home. Thus, they had decided that others with dark skin might be finally considered appropriate company. But Agatha did not understand how it had come about that the former Princess Sophia Charlotte of Mecklenburg-Strelitz had been selected to be Queen in the first place.

Whispers were that the "old" *ton*, as the light-skinned nobility were calling themselves, were still wondering if the marriage might be annulled and a new queen found amongst their ranks. Many, if not most, still refused to accept the newly elevated peers. Several of the new lords, including Lord Danbury, had attempted to take up membership at White's.

They had all been rebuffed at the door.

Agatha could not help but think that the Palace had not anticipated Charlotte's skin color. If so, wouldn't they have issued wedding invitations to London's dark-skinned elite with a *bit* more advance notice? Agatha was not complaining; who complained about an invitation to a royal wedding? But it was a known fact that the old *ton* had received their invitations weeks ahead of the event.

So now England had nobility with a full range of complexions. Parliament was calling it "The Great Experiment." And it was, Agatha supposed. Both great and an experiment. She eyed the new queen over the elaborate afternoon tea that had been laid out on the table between them. Did Charlotte have any idea the change she was fomenting? Just by her very existence? Agatha suspected that she did not, sequestered as she was in Buckingham House.

"It was kind of you to invite me to tea," Agatha said.

Queen Charlotte smiled and nodded. It was all very polite.

Agatha motioned to the food on her plate, realized she had not yet tried it, and then took a hasty bite. "The scones are delicious."

"Yes. I had not tried them before coming to London. We have different foods in Mecklenburg-Strelitz."

"Do you? Of course you must. Are you enjoying the food here in England?"

"It is delicious. Everything is delicious." As if to make her point, the Queen picked up an apricot biscuit and took a bite. But the motion was very sudden, and there was something about it that struck Agatha as inherently nervous.

Which was the oddest thing. Why would the Queen of Great Britain and Ireland be nervous to meet *her*?

"How wonderful," Agatha murmured. She took a sip of her tea, desperate to do something with her mouth other than make conversation. Honestly, this was the most awkward tableau. How did one talk with a queen? Forgetting the matter of rank (as if that were possible), there were at least six servants in the room.

And a harpist. Who played just ever so slightly louder than was conducive to conversation.

"I am glad you could come," the Queen said.

As if Agatha could have declined. She smiled politely and asked, "Are you meeting each of your ladies-in-waiting individually?"

"No."

"Oh."

The Queen waved carelessly at her servant. "Brimsley said to invite you. He said you would be the most discreet."

This gave Agatha pause. "We require discretion?"

"Because I am on my honeymoon."

"Your honeymoon?" Agatha echoed. Dear heavens, why had she been summoned to the palace during the Queen's honeymoon? She cast a furtive glance at Brimsley. He looked alarmed.

Agatha gave him the tiniest of nods, one it was possible he would not even see. But she wanted *some*one to be aware that she understood the delicacy of the situation. It should not get about that the Queen had felt the need for companionship during her honeymoon.

Other than that of the King, of course.

But the King was nowhere in sight, and before Agatha had been directed to this glorious sitting room decorated in shades of teal, gold, and cream, she'd heard whispers that the King was not in residence.

"It is going *wonderfully*," Queen Charlotte said. "It is a splendid honeymoon. My husband is the best of husbands. He is most intelligent. And very handsome."

"The King has always been regarded as pleasing to the eye," Agatha said carefully.

"Yes."

Agatha took another sip of her tea.

"More?" the Queen asked.

Agatha nodded gratefully.

The Queen raised a hand, and three servants hurried forward. One refilled Agatha's tea, another splashed a bit of milk in the cup, and the third dropped in a cube of sugar.

"The Dance of the Tea Maids," Agatha said under her breath.

"What did you say?"

Blast. She had not meant that to be audible. "I was admiring the precision of your servants," Agatha said. "They moved as if in a beautifully choreographed dance."

The Queen considered this, and then nodded. Smiled even. "It was, wasn't it? But that was not what you said."

"I called it 'The Dance of the Tea Maids,'" Agatha admitted.

The Queen's smile grew. Not much. Not even enough to show her teeth. But Agatha got the sense that she might actually be starting to feel at ease.

The poor woman. Poor girl, really. She was only, what, seventeen?

Agatha had been of a similar age when she had been married to Danbury, but at least she hadn't had to move to another country.

Those early days of marriage had been awful. It was still awful most of the time, but at least she understood what she was doing. She was in her own culture and, until she had been unexpectedly elevated to this position of lady-in-waiting, she had known how to navigate her society.

Queen Charlotte was adrift.

Agatha took a sip of tea. It would have been a crime not to, after the servants had prepared it with such flair. But she and the Queen had fallen into another awkward silence.

"Do you like music?" the Queen asked abruptly.

"I do. I would not say I am knowledgeable on the subject, but I enjoy listening."

"I am a great afficionado."

"How fortunate for us. Will you be hosting concerts?"

The Queen glanced at Brimsley, who gave a tiny nod. "Soon," she said. "Once my honeymoon is over."

"Ah." And that was the end of that conversation. Agatha was saved from trying to come up with another appropriate topic by the entrance of a footman. He shared a few quiet words with Brimsley, who Agatha was coming to realize was the Queen's most trusted advisor.

As much as anyone could be trusted on less than two weeks' acquaintance.

Brimsley stepped forward. "The King has sent you a gift, Your Majesty. It is waiting in the foyer. And there is a note, ma'am." He handed it to the Queen.

"A note?" The Queen's face positively lit with excitement. It was almost painful to watch. Agatha waited patiently as she ripped open the seal.

"Oh, this is lovely," the Queen said. "Is this not lovely?" She held the note forward, and it took Agatha a moment to realize she was meant to take it.

The private correspondence between King and Queen, and she, Agatha Danbury, was meant to read it?

If she had been Catholic, she would have crossed herself. Honestly.

"Read it aloud," Queen Charlotte commanded.

"*I never want you to feel alone,*" Agatha read. She cleared her throat. "*George R.*"

"His signature."

"Yes, of course." Agatha looked down at the elegant handwriting one more time before setting the card on the table. "I don't believe I have ever seen a monarch's signature."

Queen Charlotte considered this for a moment. "I suppose neither have I. No, wait, we signed the register in the chapel, did we not?"

Agatha nodded. "It is customary, ma'am."

The Queen turned to Brimsley. "Show me the gift."

Brimsley made a sound of mild discomfort. "Ehrm, this might not be the best time."

"Nonsense. I will see it now."

Agatha tried to hide her apprehension. She suspected Brimsley had a far better understanding than the Queen of how the palace worked, and if he did not think this was the correct moment for the King's gift, he likely had a very good reason.

But one did not disobey a direct order from royalty, so a moment later, a wicker basket was brought forth.

"What is that?" Queen Charlotte asked.

Agatha leaned forward. All she could see was a giant puff ball of caramel-colored fur.

"That is the gift from the King, Your Majesty," Brimsley said.

"But what is it?"

"I think it is a dog, Your Majesty."

The Queen looked at the puff ball, then at Agatha, and then at Brimsley. "No," she said firmly. "Dogs are big and majestic. A pinscher, a shepherd, a schnauzer. That is a deformed bunny."

Agatha snorted a laugh.

"Then you agree," the Queen said, turning sharply to face her.

"Er, well . . . I have never been fond of dogs," Agatha admitted. "Of any sort."

"Are you fond of deformed bunnies?"

"Certainly not."

The Queen regarded the dog for a moment. "Does it have a name?"

"Pom Pom, Your Majesty," Brimsley said.

"*Pom Pom*?" She muttered something under her breath in German.

"The King's man told me the King named it himself," Brimsley said.

"The King's man? The one I met at Kew?"

"Reynolds," Brimsley confirmed.

"He knows the King well, this Reynolds?"

"Quite."

The Queen considered this. "And Reynolds said the King wanted me to have it?"

"Very much, ma'am. He said the King is most concerned with your happiness."

The Queen's eyes narrowed. "You seem to know this Reynolds quite well."

Brimsley coughed and blushed. Agatha's brows rose. Now *this* was interesting.

"Reynolds and I have both worked for the royal family for a number of years," Brimsley finally answered.

But the Queen was no longer paying him any attention. "I suppose it is a thoughtful gift," she said, poking one finger into the fur. She looked back at Agatha, a determinedly happy expression on her face. "My husband is the best of husbands."

Agatha did *not* say, "Yes, you'd mentioned." She did, however, nod.

"It is our honeymoon," the Queen said. She swallowed, and the movement looked almost painful on her delicate, jewel-laden throat.

Agatha could stand it no longer. Carefully, she set down her tea. When she spoke, it was in a lower voice. "May I speak freely, Your Majesty?"

The Queen turned to Brimsley, who managed to clear the room with a curt nod. He took the basket with Pom Pom and walked to the door. "I shall be no more than five paces away," he assured the Queen.

The Queen waited until he was gone and then turned to Agatha with something akin to relief in her eyes. Or maybe it was desperation. "Please speak freely," she said. "No one else does."

Agatha took a metaphorical breath for courage and then dove in. "First, you are a terrible liar. I did not believe a word you said about your honeymoon. Do not try that in front of society. It will cause scandal."

The Queen's eyes went wide. "Oh. I did not realize I—"

"My honeymoon was a disaster," Agatha said frankly. "On my wedding night, I did not know what to expect, and my husband was old and impatient. He still is old and impatient."

"I am sorry."

Agatha shrugged. She had long since accepted her lot in life. Luxury and wealth, with not a whit of true comfort. "The whole event was painful and quite terrifying. I am here to tell you that it is normal if your wedding night was not perfect or splendid."

The Queen said nothing.

Agatha waited.

Nothing.

Dear God.

"Your Majesty," Agatha said, very, *very* carefully, "you did *have* a wedding night?"

It was as if a dam exploded. "He was mean," the Queen cried out. "And rude. And selfish. He just wanted to leave. He felt bad, I suppose, and he did not seem to understand why I did not want him to live at Kew while I am stuck here with no one to talk to and then he gives me that beast as if that is to make everything better but that does not make up for—"

"*Your Majesty,*" Agatha interrupted.

Queen Charlotte stopped talking and gave a little nod. Dear God, she looked young.

"I am still allowed to speak freely?" Agatha said.

The Queen nodded again.

"I am talking about consummating the marriage. You and the King did consummate the marriage, did you not?"

But the Queen just sat there with an utterly blank expression on her face.

"Your Majesty," Agatha said with rising alarm. "*Charlotte.* If you did not consummate the marriage, you are not actually married to the King. Your whole position is in danger. The Great Experiment is in danger. My God, you *did* consummate?"

The Queen did not speak.

"You do know what I mean when I say consummate?" Agatha asked, dreading the answer.

The Queen's face took on a vaguely helpful expression. "Does it have something to do with this great experiment?"

Oh, Lord. Heaven help them both.

Agatha squared her shoulders. She was about to cement her place in history, not that anyone would ever know it. "Let us send for Brimsley," she said with grim determination. "We will require supplies."

The Queen gave her one nod, then turned toward the door. "Brimsley!" He came rushing in.

The Queen motioned to Agatha. "Whatever she needs."

"Drawing paper," Agatha said. "And charcoals. Or pencils. Either will do."

If he was puzzled by the request, his face did not betray it. He had the supplies in hand in under ten minutes.

"I'm not a very proficient artist," Agatha said, starting to sketch.

"Nonsense. I am sure you are excellent. Although . . ." Charlotte leaned forward. "What *is* that?"

Agatha wondered, and not for the first time, if she were in a waking nightmare. "That," she said, "is a man's member."

"His what?"

"His—"

"*Ma'am*," Brimsley choked out.

Agatha snapped around to face him. "Would you have her continue in ignorance?"

"Yes, Brimsley," Charlotte prodded, "would you have me continue in ignorance?"

Brimsley swallowed visibly. "Of course not, Your Majesty."

"Is that really the shape of it?" Charlotte asked, tracing the drawing. She looked at her fingers, gray with charcoal dust, and then rubbed them together to clean off the worst of it. "It does not seem practical."

"Well, it does change," Agatha said.

"Truly?" The Queen turned to Brimsley. "You have one of these, do you not?"

Brimsley's cheeks burned pink. "Yes, Your Majesty."

"And does it change when—" She looked to Agatha.

"When the man desires his wife," Agatha confirmed.

"Then," the Queen said to Brimsley. "Does it change then?"

Brimsley shot a desperate look at Agatha. "This is really not the type of conversation—"

"I'm well aware," Agatha bit off.

"Brimsley doesn't have a wife," the Queen pointed out.

"Well, yes," Agatha said. "It doesn't have to be a wife, strictly speaking. Any female could do, I suppose."

Brimsley swallowed.

The Queen looked back down at the drawing. "What does he do with it?"

Agatha looked over at Brimsley. He was visibly sweating, and his eyes were fixed firmly on the ceiling.

"He puts it inside you," Agatha said.

The Queen drew back, her chin practically disappearing into her neck. "You're joking."

"I'm afraid not."

The Queen turned to Brimsley for confirmation. "Brimsley . . ."

"Please, Your Majesty," he pleaded. "I beg of you."

She turned back to Agatha. "We are making him uncomfortable."

"Quite," Brimsley choked.

"He puts it inside you," Agatha said again. "Between your legs. I don't—" She looked down at the paper and let out a tiny groan. "I don't think I can draw it."

The Queen looked at Brimsley. "Can you—"

"No!" His face was now a tomato.

The Queen turned back to Agatha. "And how many times does he insert it?"

"As many times as necessary, Your Majesty."

"How long does it take?"

Agatha could not lie. "Sometimes it feels like it takes forever."

The Queen nodded slowly, absorbing this information. "Will I enjoy it?"

"I never have. But I do not believe I have ever thought of it as something to enjoy. More of a chore, really. Perhaps it is different if one does it with someone one likes." Agatha gave a shrug. "I do not know."

And she likely never would.

"Well, I do not like George," the Queen said plainly. "So I do not see why we should need to bother ourselves to do this at all."

"No!" Agatha burst out before she could temper her reaction. "You must. Your Majesty, this is Britain. It was not that long ago that Queens were beheaded for not bearing children."

"And this is the only way to fall pregnant? You are sure?"

"Quite sure."

The Queen frowned. "Surely there is no rush."

Agatha grasped the Queen's hand, well aware that this was strictly against protocol. "Your Majesty," she said with considerable urgency, "the marital act *must* be performed or you are not Queen."

"But we are married."

"Not fully."

The Queen muttered something—Agatha thought it was *We have seeds in German*, but sure that couldn't be right. "Ma'am?" she asked hesitantly.

"I said I need my German," the Queen said in a most frustrated tone. "I need my long words. This halfway marriage. It is ludicrous. We would have a word for it in German, and then I would *know* about it."

"Of course," Agatha murmured, not entirely certain what she was talking about.

The Queen's eyes flashed. "I am not stupid. I am not."

"No," Agatha agreed, startled by the sudden change of subject. But she was not merely paying lip service. Charlotte was not stupid. On the contrary, Agatha suspected she was one of the most intelligent people she would ever meet. But she had been thrust into an impossible situation.

Except it wasn't impossible, was it? Because this was Charlotte's life.

She was lonely. The Queen was desperately lonely, and Agatha had no idea what to do about it.

"I am not stupid," Charlotte said again. "But every day they make me feel so. They dress me up and tell me where to go and who to see and who *not* to see, and what I might—" She looked up quite suddenly. "I cannot even eat fish!"

"I beg your pardon?"

"The King hates fish, so I may not eat it even though we do not live in the same house. I love fish. Did you know that?"

"I did not."

"Herring. I grew up near the Baltic Sea, and we eat herring. It is a Danish thing."

"Danish," Agatha repeated weakly.

"We are very near to Denmark. But does anyone know that? No, they do not, because they do not care about me."

"I am certain that is not true."

"Are you?" Charlotte turned to her sharply. "I do not see how you could be. This is only the second time we have met."

"Well . . ." Agatha flailed for words. "You are the Queen. By definition, everyone cares about you."

Charlotte arched a brow. "You clearly know very little about being a queen."

"As I am growing increasingly aware."

Charlotte's mouth clamped into a firm line. "This," she said, motioning to the drawings on the table. "It truly must be done?"

"It must." Agatha managed a small smile. "I'm sure you have a word for it in German."

Charlotte stared for a beat, then let out an unexpected laugh. "You are funny." She pressed her lips together, then sighed. "Well. I have been left ignorant in both languages, clearly."

"I am sorry," Agatha said.

"It is not your fault."

"No, but I am sorry for your situation. It is the lot of women, I am afraid. It is not fair, and it is not right."

"No, it is not, is it? This—" Charlotte waved her hand above the table, indicating the lurid drawings. "This is not my failing. The King clearly does not want me. And I cannot somehow force him to want to do this with me. And maybe that is a good thing. If I am not Queen, if we are not married, then maybe we can forget all about this, and I can go home."

"No!" Agatha exclaimed.

Charlotte looked at her with some surprise. It *had* been a sudden outburst.

"I hope you will stay," Agatha said, forcing her voice into a calmer register. If Charlotte departed, so too did the Great Experiment.

"He does not want me," Charlotte said.

Agatha did not know how to respond. Finally, she said, "It is a Pomeranian. Your deformed bunny."

"Pom Pom?"

"It is a dog. A very rare, purebred Pomeranian. If it were a jewel, it would be a diamond."

Charlotte touched the jewels at her neck.

"Diamonds," Agatha said.

"My favorite," Charlotte whispered. She turned and looked at Brimsley.

He nodded. "I will fetch the dog."

ST. JAMES'S PALACE
PRINCESS AUGUSTA'S SITTING ROOM
...
AN HOUR LATER

Agatha had not even departed Buckingham when a servant intercepted her with a summons. She was not to go home. Rather, she would proceed directly to St. James's Palace. Princess Augusta required her presence.

"God help me," she sighed to herself in her carriage. This was a lot of royalty in one day. Her husband might be jealous of the attention, but honestly, it was exhausting.

"Lady Danbury," she reminded herself. "*Lady* Danbury."

Apparently she had to earn her title.

The Princess did not make her wait, and she was escorted immediately to the sitting room.

"You know Earl Harcourt, of course," Princess Augusta said.

Agatha did not know Earl Harcourt. Earl Harcourt would never have deigned to acknowledge her existence before the royal wedding. But she curtsied and said, "Of course."

Princess Augusta motioned for her to sit, then turned to her with icy blue eyes. "Please elaborate on your meeting with the Queen."

Agatha schooled her features to contain her surprise. News traveled fast. The Princess must have quite the network of spies. "I am not sure I understand."

"You met with Her Majesty," Princess Augusta said.

"I did."

"I am asking you to elaborate."

Agatha feigned ignorance. "We had tea."

The Princess looked at her.

She looked at the Princess.

Finally, Augusta said, "You had tea."

"Yes," Agatha said.

"And?"

"I met her puppy."

"Her puppy."

"Yes." Agatha smiled blandly. "She has a Pomeranian."

The Princess looked at her.

She looked at the Princess.

The Princess made a very impatient noise and then looked at Earl Harcourt.

He cleared his throat. "What did you speak to Her Majesty about?"

There was no way in hell Agatha was going to reveal the contents of *that* conversation. "I am sure I do not remember," she said.

Earl Harcourt's brows came together in an irate furrow. "I am sure you do."

"Does it signify what two ladies discuss at tea? Tea is often about gowns and flower arranging and embroidery and the social season gossip, and if we are bold, the latest musical compositions—"

"I do not think the girl knows," Earl Harcourt interrupted, directing this statement to Princess Augusta.

"She knows," the Princess said sharply. She turned to Agatha. "We know what tea is generally about. What was *this* tea about, girl?"

"This tea?" Agatha asked, all innocence.

"You are being purposely obstructive, Agatha, and I will not have it."

"Lady Danbury," Agatha said quietly.

"Excuse me?"

"Lady Danbury. That is my title, Your Royal Highness. The one you were kind enough to bestow upon me. Lady. Agatha. Danbury. And I do remember one thing about this tea. It was when I understood that our Queen does not yet realize that our titles are shiny and new. Is that not an interesting topic for an *upcoming* tea?"

The Princess stared at her.

She stared at the Princess.

"Harcourt," Princess Augusta said without looking at him, "perhaps the two of us should speak in a womanly way."

"Let me handle her for you," Harcourt blustered. "If Lord Bute—"

But Princess Augusta's interruption was sharp. "I believe I can manage."

The two women waited in silence as he departed. Then Princess Augusta looked at Agatha assessingly and said, "You surprise me. I always thought you were a quiet one."

"I am not quiet. It is simply that my husband is loud."

Princess Augusta took this in. Agatha thought she saw grudging respect in her face.

But it was impossible to be sure.

"Lady Danbury," the Princess said. "I need to know what is going on at Buckingham House. I need a trusted ear. Do you understand?"

"I do."

"Well then . . ."

Agatha chose her words very carefully. "Traditionally, when a title is bestowed, it comes with income and land. An estate. Without those things, a title is simply . . . a title." She folded her hands in her lap. "We all have needs, ma'am."

Augusta's lips tightened. "You want money."

No, she didn't want money. She wanted respect. She did not know why she suddenly felt so protective of her husband—she did not even like the man—but she could not bear the expression on his face every time he came home after a new slight or insult. He had been made a lord. He had been proclaimed by the King to be one of the most important men in the land, and no one was treating him as such. No one was treating any of the new lords with their due deference.

Agatha forced herself to look the Princess directly in the eyes. *Be fierce*, she told herself. *Be fearsome.* And she said, "You forget that the reason your father-in-law the King knew my family is that my father-in-law is also a king. And Sierra Leone is very rich. We already have money. We have more money than most of the *ton*. What I need is for my husband not to be denied entry to White's. I need him to be invited on the hunts. I need to be able to cross the street to the best modiste, to take the finest seats at the opera."

"That is grasping," Augusta said. "Asking for rather a lot. You should be grateful for what we have given you."

Agatha regarded the Princess with a cool stare. "You say you need to know what is going on over at Buckingham House. I assume the reason you need that is so that Lord Bute believes you have the situation in hand. Because if you do not, the House of Lords will be at your door. Is that not a fact?"

"Careful, Lady Danbury," Princess Augusta warned.

"I am merely pointing out that we both have needs. You need to know what is going on over at Buckingham House. We need to be equal members of the *ton*." She brought her tea to her lips. "We can be grateful to one another."

"You are more than you let on," Princess Augusta said after a long pause.

"As are you."

The Princess gave her a shrewd look. "I believe we have an understanding."

"Do we?"

"But of course an understanding is just that. An understanding. It is nothing without currency."

"The currency of information," Agatha said.

"Exactly." Augusta's head tilted very slightly to the side. "So I ask you, Lady Danbury, what do you know? What is happening at Buckingham House?"

"It is not so much what is happening," Agatha said, "as what is *not* happening."

Princess Augusta stared at her for a *very* long moment. "I see," she finally said.

"I think perhaps you do."

"You are certain of this?" Augusta asked.

"Absolutely."

Princess Augusta had the sort of face that did not betray emotion, but Agatha had spent her entire life being dragged to events where she was supposed to be silent. She knew how to read people.

Augusta was angry.

And scared.

And frustrated, and calculating, and already plotting her next move.

"Go home, Lady Danbury," she said. "I will be in touch."

Agatha rose and curtsied. "I await your direction, Your Royal Highness."

The following day, a letter arrived addressed to Lord Danbury. It bore the royal seal. Agatha stood with quiet rectitude while her husband opened it.

"We have been given land!" he exclaimed.

Agatha placed a hand on her heart. "No!"

"Right here in London. And the boys have been guaranteed spots at Eton."

"Their futures are assured," Agatha murmured.

"I never thought I would see this day," Danbury said. His lip quivered. "After everything that I . . . After all I endured . . ." He turned to Agatha. "Do you know how this happened?"

She could have told him. She could have said she'd struck a deal with the King's mother, that she'd betrayed her own Queen. She could have told him that it was *her* intelligence, and *her* cunning, but when she looked at his face, so awestruck, so delighted at finally having been granted the dignity and respect he'd been so long denied, she decided it wasn't worth it.

He deserved this moment.

Agatha smiled and touched his hand. "I have no idea."

"I will tell you," Herman announced, raising his arm like some sort of victory cheer. "The King sees me. For who I am. My value. My worth. He understands that the old ways are over, and this is a new world. That men are men, regardless from whence they come."

"And women are women," Agatha said quietly.

"What?"

"Nothing, darling." She patted him gently on the shoulder. "Tell me more about our new home."

"It is a most fashionable address. We shall be the envy of all. Basset will never believe . . ."

But Agatha had stopped listening. This was her victory. She had done this. She would never get the credit, but she saw herself. For who she was. Her value. Her worth.

The old ways were over. It was a new world.

GEORGE

KEW PALACE

THE KING'S PRIVATE QUARTERS

...

15 SEPTEMBER 1761

"Is Your Majesty quite all right?"

George paused in his efforts to dress himself for the day. Reynolds was standing in the doorway, holding his breakfast tray.

"Of course," George said, although in truth he was having a devil of a time with one of his buttons. "Why wouldn't I be?"

"You are shivering, Your Majesty."

"Am I?" George looked down at his arms. They were indeed shivering. "Is it cold?"

"It is not," Reynolds said, "but a prodigious quantity of ice is delivered each day."

"Yes. The baths are . . ."

Hideous.

The stuff of nightmares.

Very bad for one's ballocks.

George cleared his throat. "Well, I am sure they are helping."

At least he hoped they were. Much of his time in the bath consisted of Monro's burly assistants plunging his head underwater. It was dreadful, but George was getting used to it. And he had to trust in Monro's conviction that this would eventually put a stop to his fits.

What other choice did he have?

Reynolds's mouth pursed into a displeased frown. "As for this food," he said, setting the tray on the table, "I do not know that I would see it fed to our lowest stable hand. I would not even see it fed to the horses."

"Are you questioning the doctor's methods, Reynolds?"

Reynolds, ever circumspect, did not speak.

"I have my own doubts," George admitted. "But I must try. It is the only chance I have of being with her."

"With respect, Your Majesty is . . . His Majesty. His Majesty can do as he pleases. His Majesty could be with her right now."

It was so tempting. It was all he thought about. But he knew he was not ready.

"I cannot take the risk," George told him. "Especially with a woman so unpredictable. So capricious. Could you believe her the other night? Arriving at Kew unannounced?" He smiled at the memory. She was more than her beauty, more than her brains.

She was magnificent.

"Why, she's almost as mad as I am," George murmured.

"Your Majesty," Reynolds reproached.

George gave him a nod of acknowledgment. He knew that Reynolds did not like it when he referred to himself as mad. They had been together since childhood, since before it became obvious that George would be King, and Reynolds would be, well, Reynolds. They had a bond of friendship and shared secrets.

"Very well," George said. "I shall rephrase. A woman like that is too dangerous for a man like me."

"Or maybe a perfect match."

"Do you think?" This pleased George more than he could have said.

"I think we cannot know until His Majesty spends more time with her."

George dipped his spoon into the gruel. It truly was abysmal. But it was all he had. "I cannot be with her," he said with a sigh. "But perhaps you have heard word? That servant fellow of hers. The small one. Has he told you anything?"

"Brimsley," Reynolds said. "We have spoken."

"And?"

Reynolds took a moment to choose his words. "I believe she is lonely, Your Majesty."

"Lonely. Imagine that. I have spent my whole life longing for time to myself."

"It is what you have here at Kew," Reynolds pointed. "By your own design."

"I am hardly alone, Reynolds. The good doctor and his lackeys shadow me everywhere."

"Again, sir, that is by your choice. One you could easily reverse."

George shook his head. Everyone seemed to think it was easy being King, that the ability to order everyone about somehow made life a frolic. But directing the kitchen to make one's favorite pudding—and getting it, every time—was a far cry from ceasing one's medical treatment just because one found it unpleasant.

"I must see this through," George said. "This separation . . . I am doing it for *her*."

Reynolds held his tongue, but only for a moment. "She is just married, Your Majesty. It is her honeymoon. She may miss her husband."

George allowed himself a wistful smile. "I think I miss her, too."

Reynolds looked as if he'd like to say more, but George quelled that with a shake of his head. Reynolds was repeating himself now; they'd had this conversation more than once. And besides, Doctor Monro had arrived.

He came through the door without knocking, as was his habit.

"Doctor," George said.

Reynolds bowed, but it was very shallow.

Monro seemed preoccupied. "Is Your Majesty quite confident in his security?"

"My security, Doctor?"

"Your Majesty's guards, footmen, retainers." His hand moved angrily through the air, jabbing to all corners as if he could cast aspersions on every last man at Kew. "In these sad days there are so many enemies of the Crown, one would hate to think a spy had penetrated Your Majesty's circle. To say nothing of rogues, charlatans, petty thieves—"

"Doctor," George cut in, because honestly, he was impossible to follow. "What are you saying?"

"My dog is missing."

Oh.

"How dreadful," George said carefully. "Which one?"

"The Pomeranian. I only just purchased it two weeks ago. I have not even had a chance to perform any experiments on it."

"Pity," George murmured. He did not look at Reynolds, and he was quite sure Reynolds did not look at him.

"Indeed." Monro let out a grunt of displeasure. "I arrived at my laboratory this morning to find the cage unlatched and the stupid beast nowhere to be found."

George sighed and shook his ahead, almost giving the appearance of sympathy. "It may be that the beast was not so stupid. Lapdog or wolf, soon enough an animal tires of its cage. Do you agree, Doctor?"

Monro looked at him sharply. George immediately reschooled his features into boredom. Or blankness. Both seemed appropriate.

"Your Majesty has been spending too much time in the observatory," Monro decided. "I do not like the pallor of Your Majesty's skin, the color around your eyes. I worry another fit may be imminent."

Reynolds cleared his throat. "His Majesty's . . . ah . . . episodes, have never been presaged by a change in his complexion."

Monro turned to face him.

"Sir," Reynolds added.

"I do not take medical advice from a valet," Monro bit off, and he turned back to George. "We have forgotten our objectives. Grown too lax in our routine. But no matter, we can right ourselves. I will have an ice bath prepared immediately, and then it is straight to the chair."

George took a steadying breath. He hated the chair. Almost as much as the ice baths. But they were necessary. He was prepared to do whatever was necessary to be well.

But as Monro headed for the door, a footman arrived with a piece of paper on a platter, folded and sealed. Monro reached for it.

"It is for Reynolds, Doctor," the footman said, moving the platter to the side.

"Can he even read?" Monro spat.

"Doctor," George said sharply, "such insults are unnecessary."

"Forgive me, Your Majesty."

George acknowledged this with a flick of his hand, then turned his attention to Reynolds. It was not common that he received correspondence, or if he did, it was not common that he received it in front of the King.

"News from Buckingham House," Reynolds said, looking up once he'd finished reading.

George brightened. "Really?"

"Yes. The Queen has received your, ah"—he eyed Monro—"your gesture."

"Oh?" So they were speaking in code. George was highly entertained. "And what did she think of it?"

Reynolds hesitated.

"Go on," George said.

"Er, she called it a deformed bunny."

A deformed—

What?

And then George laughed. He laughed as he had not laughed in days. He pictured his wife. He pictured that ridiculous puff ball of a dog. And he laughed, and laughed, and laughed.

It was as if the light of the sun had finally reached his face.

"You know what?" he said, coming to his feet. "No ice bath. No chair today."

"Your Majesty," Monro said sternly. "That will not be permitted. We have much work to do, you and I."

"Sorry, Doctor. Today I would rather work on my farm. Fresh air and exercise will be just the thing."

"*Boy*," Monro boomed. He moved in front of George, attempting to block his way. "I command you to stay."

But for once, Monro's voice did not compel George to obey. Instead, he gave the doctor a grin and moved across the room to fetch his coat. "The carriage, Reynolds!"

"With delight, Your Majesty."

George strode down the corridor, moving with speed and purpose that had almost become unfamiliar.

"Shall you be in the fields all day, Your Majesty?" Reynolds inquired.

"As long as it does not rain."

"Very good. And dinner?"

George took a few steps down the stairs and then paused. "That is a good question."

"There are options."

"Indeed." George tapped his hand against his leg. He was filled with a nervous energy, but it was not . . . *bad*. He felt aware. Expectant.

Hopeful.

"Sir?"

He made up his mind. "I think I will dine with my wife."

"Excellent, Your Majesty. I shall alert Buckingham House."

"Right. Although perhaps *don't* inform the Queen. Just in case I . . ."

George didn't want to say it.

"Change your mind?" Reynolds suggested.

George let out a little breath of relief. "Exactly."

Reynolds smiled. "You won't, Your Majesty."

BUCKINGHAM HOUSE

THE DINING ROOM

...

LATER THAT EVENING

This was a mistake.

It should have been easy. He was a king, and this was his castle.

Metaphorically.

Buckingham House was just that—a house. But he had bought it for Charlotte. It was hers. He'd heard the household was already calling it the Queen's House.

He was the interloper.

This was the first time George had even stepped foot in the new dining room here. Servants lined the wall, most of them new to royal service, and in the middle of it all was Charlotte's empty chair.

She would arrive soon. Of that he was certain, if only because she did not know that he was there. The servants had been instructed to keep the news from her. He supposed they all thought it a romantic surprise on his part, when the truth was, he was scared she would take a tray in her room if she knew he was waiting for her.

This could go badly.

The Transit of Venus was coming soon.

Transit of Venus, Venus, Venus, Mars, Jupiter . . .

He gripped the edge of the table. That was not what he wanted to think about right now. It didn't matter. Well, it did matter. Of course it mattered. It was vitally important, actually, but it didn't matter right *now*, which was why he should not be thinking about it. He should be thinking about Charlotte. His wife. His bride. She was beautiful. Too beautiful. Too beautiful for him.

He was a troll, not a troll, maybe a troll, she was so beautiful—

"Your Majesty."

It was Reynolds. He put a calming hand on George's shoulder. Kept it there until George's breathing settled and he was able to take a sip of wine.

"Good color on this wine, Reynolds," George said.

"I shall let the kitchen know, Your Majesty."

George nodded slowly. He could do this. He *wanted* to do this. He could—

She was here. But she did not see him yet. She was not looking at the table; instead, her gaze seemed to be set on something off in the air, maybe nothing at all.

She did not look quite like herself. She looked . . . unmoored.

He felt his heart cracking. This was not the sharp-eyed, sharp-tongued woman he had married.

He stood. "Hello, Charlotte."

She stopped in her tracks. Even in the candlelight he could see her eyes flick this way and that, as if she were plotting her escape.

"Hello," she said, perhaps a little cautiously. She did not move toward the table. Her little servant stood behind her, taking in the scene.

George motioned to the feast laid out before them. "Is it all right if I join you for a meal this evening?"

"A meal?" she echoed.

He started to reply, but she was not done.

"A meal?! Are you—*A meal*?!"

She was angry, then. But at least she seemed once again to be herself.

"You truly think I would just sit across the table from you and share a meal after—" She threw up her arms. "You are mad."

George winced. Reynolds stepped forward.

"That can be the only explanation." She was talking to herself, but each word pierced George to his soul. His throat felt tight. It was hard to breathe.

"Your Majesty," came Reynolds's voice, low and reassuring.

George forced a nod. Then realized she was leaving. "Charlotte, please. Don't go."

She did not listen.

George hurried after her, pausing only to jab one finger in Brimsley's direction. "Stay."

Brimsley looked as if he might disobey, but Reynolds put a hand on his arm.

"Charlotte!" George called again. She was moving fast, faster than anyone in a gown like that ought to be able to. "Where are you going?"

"I do not know! Just . . . away from you!" She turned around for just long enough to spit out, "Wherever you are not!"

"Charlotte," George pleaded. "Charlotte, please. If you will give me a chance to—"

There was nothing for it. He had to be the King. "*Charlotte,*" he commanded. "*Stop walking this instant.*"

She did. But she didn't turn around.

"I realize you have no reason to like me," George said to her back. "You have no reason to trust me."

"None," he thought he heard.

He cracked his neck to the side, the motion somehow helping him to rein in his emotions. "You are justified in those emotions. I marry you and then I disappear into my observatory, and then I come here to dine as if . . ."

As if what? Even he didn't know.

He exhaled. "But if you will just give me one evening of your time. Allow me to show you where my mind has been. It will not make you forgive me, but it may make you hate me a little bit less."

She sighed. He did not hear it, but he saw it in the gentle rise and drop of her shoulders.

"Please," he said.

She turned around.

He held out his hand, and miracle of miracles, she took it.

CHARLOTTE

"Look. Do you see it?"

Charlotte adjusted her position in front of the eyepiece. George had brought her back to his observatory and was trying to show her something through his enormous telescope. But she had no idea what she was looking at. It was all just pricks of light with the occasional sparkle.

"Not like that," he said. He put his hands on her shoulders and readjusted her. "Now. What do you see?"

"I do not see anything."

"Well, concentrate."

She rolled her eyes. Or rather, she rolled one of them. The other was still fixed on the eyepiece. She squirmed her shoulders, trying to get him to give her space. "I cannot concentrate with you hovering and breathing and telling me to concentrate."

He let out a tiny puff of air. This annoyed her.

"All right." He reached in front of her. "Just let me turn the focus a tiny bit."

"Would you just step away and let me—"

She gasped.

"Oh my word," she exclaimed. "What is that?"

"That is Venus," George said with palpable pride.

"Venus. *Venus*." Charlotte pulled her head back for just a moment.

George looked utterly delighted, and perhaps a bit proud. Charlotte could not even begin to imagine the breadth of emotions traveling across her own face. Wonder, perhaps? Awe?

She moved back to the eyepiece. "The planet Venus. I am staring at *Venus*?"

"You are. I have—"

"The planet," she clarified, looking back up at him.

"Yes, the planet." He gave her an amused smile; he was clearly charmed by her delight.

"The planet," she said again. "I am staring at a *planet*. Surely I—" She had to pause just to consider the ramifications. "The wonder of it. Someone invented this"—she motioned to the telescope—"and it is capable of allowing us to see thousands of miles—"

"Millions," George said.

"Millions?"

He grinned.

She just stood there for a moment, blinking. "I don't even know how to *conceive* of such a distance. From here to Mecklenburg-Strelitz is, what, five hundred miles?"

"About. A little more, perhaps."

"It's—I—"

He grinned. That same unaffected grin he'd given her back in the chapel garden. When he was Just George. "What?"

"I am trying to do the arithmetic. A million miles is . . . I think . . . Well, two million times more than five hundred miles. Correct?"

He nodded. "And Venus is far more than a million miles away."

"*Mein Gott.*"

"My thoughts exactly."

"It is remarkable. It is *wunderbar*." She shook her head in amazement. "I do not know a word in English that is up to the task."

"Perhaps you shall have to make one up," he said. "If you recall, that is your right as Queen."

She laughed. She couldn't believe it. She'd been so angry at this man. She still was; he would not be let off the hook so easily. But still, he had managed to make her laugh.

"I cannot imagine what scientists might invent next," she said.

"It is something I think about every day," he said earnestly. "What if we could go to the moon?"

"Don't be absurd," Charlotte scoffed.

"What if we could see inside our bodies without cutting them open?"

"That's just disgusting."

"But what if we could?"

Charlotte shivered with distaste. "I prefer to ponder Venus."

"Excellent choice." George's face shone with excitement. In truth, his whole body did. He seemed almost electrified, lit from within. This was what passion did to a person, Charlotte realized. It was rare to find someone who cared so deeply about something. She'd thought she felt that way about music, but seeing George . . .

She was clearly a dilettante.

"I have been studying it," he told her. He sifted through a stack of charts and pulled one out, excitedly pointing at a dotted line. "A rare occurrence is coming. It is several years away, but it will take scientists time to prepare. Venus will travel in a specific arc and give us a single moment to take very precise measurements. And from that we shall know the distance from the Earth to the sun."

"That is amazing," she said.

He beamed. "The Transit of Venus, it is called. It will be quite the spectacle."

"And from this"—Charlotte held up a finger, as if anyone might be able to tell she was referring to Venus—"you can work out distances between two entirely different celestial bodies?"

"That is the idea."

"Could you teach me?"

"Well, I—" George stumbled over his words. Clearly, she'd surprised him. "I do not see why not. You have studied mathematics?"

"Not of the sort I suspect is required for this type of calculation," Charlotte said with some annoyance. "There is a gap between what is thought to be suitable schooling for a girl and a boy."

He shrugged. "If you wish to learn something, then you must."

Charlotte tried not to smile. It was moments like these that made it very difficult not to fall in love with him.

She moved back to the telescope, taking a moment to relocate Venus.

It was bright and brilliant in the night sky, outshining every star. "It is beautiful, George," she murmured.

"It is."

And he sounded content.

She pulled back to look at him. "This is what you have been doing? This entire time?"

He nodded. "There is something about the heavens. In this world we live in where I am given so much power and attention, it is good to remember that I am but a bit of dust on a small dot in the universe." He smiled boyishly. "Keeps one humble."

Her hand itched to reach out. But she could not. Not yet. She did not quite trust him.

"Being King is a hazard," he continued. "My world has been made to revolve around me. It has made me selfish." He looked away, briefly, then dragged his eyes back to hers. "I cannot imagine how painful and cruel it must have been to have me ruin your wedding night."

"It was your wedding night, too," she reminded him.

"I am so sorry."

"Yes, well." She swallowed. "I do not forgive you. Yet."

"Yet." There was a smile in his voice. "Yet is good. Yet is hope."

"Perhaps," Charlotte allowed.

"You know," George said, taking a small step in her direction, "it almost does not quite count as a wedding night."

"No?"

He shook his head. "We did not actually have the night part."

Charlotte recalled her conversation with Lady Danbury. Agatha's warnings had made her somewhat less eager for her marital duties. But at the same time, she understood that it had to be done. Consummation. Without it, she was not a true queen.

"We could start over," George suggested. "Try again?"

"That seems a reasonable idea," Charlotte said. She brushed imaginary dust from her skirt, eager to appear unconcerned. "We have been married over a week now."

"Yes," George said softly. "And I have kissed you but once."

"At our wedding."

"I have been longing to do it again."

Her eyes met his. "You have?"

"Every minute"—he stepped closer—"of every day."

"Why?"

"Why?" he echoed.

She gave a little nod.

"Because you exist," he said, as if it were the most obvious thing in the world. "I saw you, and I met you, and I spoke with you. I am enchanted. I can barely breathe for wanting to kiss you again."

Charlotte had the oddest sensation that she was somehow suspended in space. That the air around her had turned a little bit solid, and it was holding her up, keeping her steady as her breath tickled through her body.

"Will you let me?" George whispered.

She nodded. She did not know what to expect, just that she thought she might die if she did not touch him.

But it was still awkward. And funny, almost. He smiled, and she realized he was as nervous as she.

So she smiled. Because she couldn't help it.

And then his hand touched her cheek.

"Charlotte," he whispered.

"George."

His lips met hers. "Always."

His hand found its way to her back, and he pulled her close. Charlotte had never stood so near to a man before. The heat of him, the strength held in check—it stole her very breath.

She touched his hair, soft and crisp, and he let out a small sound of delight.

"You like that?" she asked shyly.

"Very much. I daresay there is nothing you could do that I would not like."

She laid her hand on his chest.

"I like that," he said.

Emboldened—and amused—she reached up and tweaked his earlobe.

"That, too."

"I'm out of ideas," she admitted.

His arms tightened around her. "I have many."

"Do you?"

"Mmm-hmm." His lips came once again to hers, and this time his mouth was more demanding. "This, for example."

After that, there were no more words. George kissed her with the same passion she'd heard in his voice when he spoke about the stars. He kissed her as if she were the rarest of jewels, precious and yet indestructible.

She felt worshipped.

Adored.

He was, once again, Just George.

But he had been Just George in the chapel garden. And he had changed. Warily, she stepped back. Her hand trailed down his arm until only their fingers touched. She needed to know what this kiss meant.

"Does this mean you are coming home?" she asked. "To Buckingham House?"

"Yes," he said. "I am coming home to Buckingham House."

"Tonight?"

He nodded. "Go back to your carriage and return. I shall follow posthaste."

"We may not travel together? We did right after the wedding."

He gave her one of his sheepish shrugs. "Rules to protect succession, I am afraid. Right after the wedding, there was no possibility that you might be carrying the next king."

"There is no possibility now."

"They do not know that." George kissed her again, his lips a tender promise. "And after tonight, there will be."

BUCKINGHAM HOUSE
THE KING'S BEDCHAMBER
...
LATER THAT NIGHT

In the time since the wedding, Charlotte had not allowed herself to peek into George's bedchamber.

This had not been easy. His room was next to hers, and in fact, the two were connected through a series of small sitting rooms. She was curious. And perhaps a little vengeful. Many a night, Charlotte had wanted to rip her covers off, tramp over to his suite, and break something. Sometimes she wanted to break something that looked like it mattered to him. Sometimes she wanted to break something small, something no one would notice right away. It could fester.

Just like she was festering.

But she had resisted.

It was a strange existence, her new life. She was Queen of the most powerful nation on earth. If she wanted to break something, the mess would be cleaned up straightaway, and then the servants would probably think they ought to applaud her for it.

Oh very good, Your Majesty. Your skills of demolition are beyond compare.

She could imagine that. Easily. A small army of maids and footmen, praising her for making their lives a little more miserable.

So no, she wasn't going to go into George's bedchamber and break something. All she had left was her dignity. Or at least, that was what she had control of. She might be headstrong. She might even be capricious. But she refused to be a monster.

But now everything was different. She was not sure what had prompted George to reconsider his decision to live separately, but she had decided not to question it. There was nothing to be gained in the poking of wounds. Not when they had the chance to start fresh.

And she liked him.

She liked him *so much*.

So here she was, at the threshold of his bedchamber. It was the same size as hers, but every decoration, every piece of furniture, proclaimed the presence of a king. The paintings of kings and princes past. The sumptuous, plush carpets. The headboard of his bed, regally red, crowned with gold.

She was nervous, but she was also excited. And she was ready.

Tonight, she would become a wife.

A queen.

He was standing by the fireplace in his black dressing gown, a glass of something in his hand. He set it down when he heard her enter.

"Charlotte."

She smiled shyly. "George."

He walked toward her. She didn't move. She wasn't scared, precisely, but the butterflies in her stomach were dancing a *Schuhplattler*. These things she was meant to do with him—they were new to her. She'd never liked being anything less than competent. She *hated* feeling stupid or unlearned.

He stopped just before her, then reached out and took her hand. "You are breathtaking."

Charlotte motioned to her nightgown. "It is pretty, but it has a thousand tiny buttons. I am suddenly concerned that my maids made the wrong choice."

George's smile was full of wicked promise. "I am very good with buttons."

His fingers made good on his words, nimbly slipping each button free of its satin loop. The entire time he stood close, his forehead nearly touching hers, the warmth of his breath wafting across her lips.

She was aching for him.

"I have dreamed of this," he whispered.

"I think . . . maybe . . . I have, too."

His eyes flared, and one of his large hands settled on her hip. "You have no idea how much that pleases me."

"I liked it when you kissed me," she said shyly.

He grinned, a boyish half-smile that made her insides flip. "I'm glad."

And then the space between them was gone, and he was kissing her again. His mouth was hot and hungry, and when she moaned against him, his tongue slid inside, sweeping against hers.

It was glorious, and she wanted more, but he drew back. "Charlotte," he asked, "do you know what happens on a wedding night?"

"Oh, yes," she said, relieved to be talking about something she knew about. "I know everything. I have seen drawings and had a detailed explanation of what is to occur."

"Well." He seemed surprised. Rather. "That is good to know."

"I—" She bit her lip. Was it appropriate to make requests? Was she allowed to?

"What is it?" he asked.

She decided she had nothing to lose by making her wishes known. "I do not like the part where my head hits the wall over and over again. Is there a way to avoid that?"

His eyes went wide. "*Who* instructed you?"

"It does not matter," Charlotte said. Agatha had shared her experiences in confidence, and it seemed disloyal to reveal her identity. "It's only that—"

"*Yes*," George interrupted. "There is a way to avoid that."

"Are you certain? Because if it must be done that way . . ."

"It doesn't." He bit his lip. "I promise."

Her eyes narrowed. "Are you trying not to laugh?"

"No!" he said, with a bit more energy than she thought was necessary.

"You are."

"I am not."

"You are lying."

"Only a little bit," he admitted.

"I knew it." She punched him lightly on his shoulder. "Why is this so funny?"

"I . . ." He seemed not to know how to answer.

"Tell me," she insisted.

"I just do not know how I might . . . Well—" He frowned, but only with one side of his mouth. It was somewhat adorable. "I suppose I could figure out how to make your head hit the wall over and over again," he went on, "but I cannot imagine why I would want to."

"That is a great relief."

"Charlotte," he said, taking her hand, "I do not know what you have been told, but this—our wedding night—it does not have to be painful. At least, not after the very beginning. It might be awkward, and in fact it probably will be awkward, but I hope it will bring you pleasure."

Charlotte blinked. This contradicted everything Agatha had told her.

George brought her hand to his lips. "Will you allow me to try?"

"To try . . ."

His fingers returned to the thousand tiny buttons. "To bring you pleasure."

His words let loose a torrent of shivers across her skin. "I think I would like that."

He undid a few more buttons, then brushed his lips against the patch of skin he'd just revealed. "Come," he murmured, and he took her hand and led her to his bed.

The covers had already been pushed back, and Charlotte lay against the silken sheets. George allowed his dressing gown to fall from his shoulders. She looked away. She hadn't meant to, but she hadn't been expecting him to disrobe just then.

"Do not be afraid," he said, climbing in beside her.

"I'm not."

He propped himself up on his side. "Good," he said, brushing a spiral of her hair from her face. For a moment, he just stared at her.

"What?" she asked, embarrassed by his scrutiny.

"You're just so beautiful," he said. "I can't believe you're mine."

She felt herself flush with pleasure. She was not unused to compliments, but from him, it felt different. It was not mere flattery. It was something so much more.

Eventually looking was not enough. George reached out and pulled her closer. One of his hands slipped underneath her nightgown, trailing along the length of her leg. Higher and higher, until it curved gently around her hip.

Her breath caught. When he touched her, she felt it on the inside. It made no sense, but she was slowly moving beyond sense. Gently, he removed the gown entirely and she was naked beside him.

"There is one thing I forgot to tell you," he said.

She looked up, her question in her eyes. His hand reached around her and then he rolled them both until he was poised above her, his dark eyes meeting hers.

"It goes both ways," he said. "I am yours."

He kissed her with unchecked passion, with a hunger that made her feel like the most priceless treasure.

This was *not* as Agatha had said. This was glorious.

He settled between her legs, and she felt him against her opening. "I hope this will not hurt," he said, "but if it does, it should not be for very long."

She nodded. "I trust you."

He pushed forward. Slowly. Then pulled back a bit before moving again. "Is this all right?" he asked.

She nodded. "It's very strange, but . . . yes."

He moved again, and it was the oddest thing, but *he* looked as if he might be in pain.

"Are *you* all right?" she asked with some concern.

"Quite," he said, but he was gritting his teeth.

"You look—"

"Shhh . . ." he begged. "I'm trying so hard."

"To do what?"

He smiled. He actually smiled. But it was the sort one made when one could not quite believe what was happening.

"George!"

"I'm trying, Charlotte," he ground out.

"To do what?"

"To go slowly. I don't want to cause you pain."

Oh. She thought about this. "Do you want to move faster?"

"*God*, yes."

Charlotte couldn't help but feel delighted by the desperation in his voice. It made her daring. "Maybe you should," she said.

He shook his head. "Not yet. But soon."

His hand moved between their bodies. "You will like this," he said. "I hope."

She gasped. His fingers were gently rubbing circles along her flesh. It made her feel hot, and she felt it all across her body. She could not think about anything else, just his wicked fingers, and then, before she knew it, he was fully seated within her.

"Charlotte," he said.

"George." She didn't know it was possible to smile a word, but that's what she did.

"Here I am."

"Here you are."

And as he began to move within her, as their motions grew more frenzied and uncontrolled, that was her only thought.

There they were.

Together.

THE NEXT MORNING

When Charlotte awakened, she was alone in George's bed. This did not bother her; perhaps he was an early riser.

They still had much to learn about each other.

She slipped on her nightgown and made her way through the connecting rooms to her own bedchamber. A basin had already been laid out for her morning ablutions, and after she splashed water on her face, she rang for the coterie of maids who dressed her each day. But for once, it did not feel like a chore. She had nothing but happiness. Nothing but delight and anticipation for the day ahead.

When she stepped into the corridor, Brimsley was waiting, as usual. His arms were full of squirming fluff.

"Pom Pom!" Charlotte exclaimed.

If Brimsley was curious about the marked increase in her excitement upon seeing her dog, he did not say so. "Your Majesty," he said, depositing the Pomeranian in her arms.

"Is it not a lovely morning?" Charlotte said.

They passed a window that revealed the skies to be gray and dripping with drizzle.

"It is a picture of bucolic splendor," Brimsley said.

She rewarded that lie with a radiant smile.

"Have you seen the King?" she asked. "If he has gone out for a ride or a walk we shall hold breakfast for him. I would like us to eat together."

"I do not think he has gone out, Your Majesty. I believe he has a visitor."

"A visitor?"

"His mother," Brimsley confirmed.

"Ah." Charlotte didn't really feel like talking with Augusta, but she was eager to see her husband again, eager enough that she was willing to interrupt their conversation to extract him. She turned to Brimsley. "They are in the sitting room?"

"Yes, Your Majesty."

Charlotte headed in that direction (Brimsley five paces behind, *natürlich*), but before she made her presence known, she stopped. Augusta's voice was very sharp. Even more so than usual.

"Do not make me ask the question," Augusta said.

Charlotte shushed Brimsley with a wave of her hand and then stepped back. She did not want to be seen.

"I am not making you ask," George said. "This is none of your business. It is my marriage."

Whatever qualms Charlotte had about eavesdropping evaporated instantly. They were talking about *her*. Surely she had a right to listen.

"Your marriage is Palace business," Augusta said in that terribly precise accent of hers. "Your marriage is Parliament business. Your marriage is the business of this country."

"Mother—"

"This cannot go wrong," she interrupted. "I need to know if you have properly bedded her."

Charlotte's hand flew to her mouth.

"I should not need to remind you that the fate of the Crown rests upon your shoulders," Augusta said.

"My head, I should think," George muttered.

Charlotte smiled, pleased with his quip.

"Don't be a fool," Augusta snapped. "Tell me now. Have you done what is necessary?"

"You told me I had to wed for the Crown," George said, his voice laced with impatience. "I did. You told me to charm her to make it easier for the Crown. I have done my best. You told me I could not let her *know* me because I must protect the secrets of the Crown. I have not."

Charlotte froze. He had not let her know him? *What did that mean?* She looked back at Brimsley, still five paces away. Was he hearing this?

But George was not done. His voice rose as he continued his speech. "You told me to bed her. I have done so. I understand. It has been abundantly clear since my first breath that I am born for the happiness or misery of a great nation, and consequently must often act contrary to my passions."

Charlotte did not want to hear anything more, but she could not move. Something began to die inside of her.

No, it wasn't death. It was rot. This awful feeling—it wasn't going away anytime soon. It was just going to get worse, slowly, inch by putrid inch.

"I am the picture of duty," George said, and now his voice was sour with sarcasm. "The Crown resides within me, embedded like a knife. You do not need to explain it to me, Mother. *It is me.*"

Charlotte took a step back. Then another. Then turned entirely away. Brimsley was watching her with a careful expression. She stepped past him and walked back toward the dining room.

"I shall have my breakfast now," she said, once she was certain she could not be heard by George and his mother. "There is no need to wait for the King."

George

Marriage. Marriage was Palace business. Parliament business. Parliament, House of Lords, Lord, Lord, Lord Bute, not Lord Bute, new lords, there were so many new lords . . .

George squeezed his eyes shut. His mind was racing again. This wasn't supposed to happen. Not today, not the best morning of his life.

Morning, morning. Morning sun, warmth of the sun, sun was a star. Not proven, not proven.

Charlotte. Think of Charlotte. Her face, her smile.

He took a breath.

Govern yourself.

Why had his mother come to call that morning? He had been so happy. So himself.

His mother had been so demanding, so determined to turn something beautiful into cold duty. Her voice had been piercing, and he had just wanted to be rid of her.

He would have said anything to get her to depart.

All he wanted was this one day. Just one day to feel like a man. Just a man.

Just George.

A throat cleared behind him. Reynolds.

"She is gone?" George asked.

Just George Just George.

He was just George. He had to remember that.

Govern yourself.

"Your mother has departed, Your Majesty. I saw to it myself."

George nodded, even though his back was still to Reynolds. He held himself straight. He needed to keep control. "And Charlotte?"

"The Queen is at breakfast in the dining room. If you would like to join her . . ."

Reynolds's voice trailed off. George looked down at his hands. They were trembling. Not much.

But just enough.

Just George. Just George.

Charlotte was in the dining room. She would not see him. If he fell, if he lost control . . .

His knees buckled, and he grabbed the arm of the nearest chair before he tumbled to the floor. Reynolds rushed to his side, easing him down onto the cushioned seat.

"Your Majesty," Reynolds said. He took George's wrist, felt for the pulse. "Your heart is racing."

"I know."

"Shall I send for the doctor?" Reynolds asked.

"*No.*" He could not face Monro. Not this morning. Not when he had been so happy. "I am fine. I do not need him."

But he was shaking. His entire body was shaking now. And if Charlotte saw him . . .

"Yes. *Yes.* Get him here." He needed to be better. He could not be like this. Not anymore.

He looked up at Reynolds with pleading eyes. "Charlotte . . ."

Reynolds gave him a single, sure nod. "She will never know of it."

BUCKINGHAM HOUSE

THE CELLAR

...

FIFTEEN MINUTES LATER

It had been decided that Doctor Monro would relocate his laboratory to the lower levels of Buckingham. But only in part. He could not move the full menagerie, nor the grotesque iron chair. Some things were simply too strange to be put on display in a well-occupied house. Even in the farthest corner of the cellar.

Only a few people were aware of the makeshift laboratory, and among the Buckingham House staff, only Reynolds knew the doctor's true identity and reason for taking up residence. It could not get out that the King was being treated for a nervous disorder.

Parliament would erupt in chaos. Britons would lose faith in the Crown.

And then there was Charlotte. George could not bear it if she witnessed one of his fits. He wanted just one thing in his life to be pure. Untainted by his position, by his duties.

By his madness.

If all went to plan, Doctor Monro would cure him. George would become whole again—the sort of person he wanted to be. The husband a woman like Charlotte deserved.

"I am eager to begin immediately," George told Reynolds as they made their way down to the cellar.

"Eager, sir?" Reynolds was clearly dubious.

George allowed himself a wry smile. "Eager for the results," he clarified. He was not eager for the treatment. But thus far, Monro was the only doctor who had achieved any measure of success. The day of the wedding he had managed to snap George back to reality. It had required a slap across the face, but George had calmed down. His racing thoughts had been tamed, and when he came across Charlotte in the chapel garden, he had felt enough like himself that he'd been able to converse with her. Flirt with her, even.

Their first conversation had been magical, and it would not have been possible without Doctor Monro.

So he was willing to give the doctor the benefit of all of his doubts.

An hour or so after George descended to the cellar, the doctor arrived, his two burly assistants in tow. George nearly flinched at the sight of them. Reynolds was openly hostile.

"I predicted this," Monro said by way of greeting.

"I did not have a fit," George stated.

Monro gave him a look that said clearly, *Then why am I here?*

"I felt one coming on," George said. Then he amended: "I felt the possibility of one coming on."

"Explain."

George told him about his conversation with his mother, about how she kept pushing and pushing, and it felt like she was turning something beautiful into a chore.

"You do not deserve beauty," Monro said.

George did not know what to say to that.

"You are just a man. You are not special."

"I am not special," George repeated.

"You must understand that you are no better than anyone else."

"I understand."

"I do not believe you," Monro spat.

"Doctor!" Reynolds interjected. "You may not doubt his word. He is the King."

"*He is nothing!*" Monro slammed his hands on the table. "He is only a man, no greater than you or I. In fact"—he began to pace, stalking the room like a predator—"he is *less* than you or I."

Reynolds ground his teeth together.

"He is far less," Monro continued, "and he must be brought down to nothing before he can be rebuilt." He looked directly at George. "When you are in my laboratory, you will be referred to as *boy.*"

Reynolds turned to George, aghast. "Your Majesty," he implored. "You cannot—"

"Do not interrupt me!" Monro yelled, spittle flying from his mouth. "I have been granted full rein over him. Every moment you waste threatens his recovery."

"We must allow him to try," George said to Reynolds.

"Sir, I do not think—"

"He helped me once," George said. "Before the wedding. I must believe he can help me again."

Reynolds stood down, but he was clearly unhappy about it. Monro, on the other hand, smiled as he said, "I understand we are to operate in secrecy."

George nodded his affirmation.

Monro motioned to his assistants. "Then they cannot run my errands. Not if they do not officially exist."

He looked at Reynolds.

"*No*," Reynolds said. But it was not so much a refusal as a statement of disbelief.

"Please," George said. "I need to try."

Reynolds acknowledged this with a shudder and a nod.

Monro looked at him with triumph, then flicked his head at George. "The boy requires an ice bath."

Reynolds turned to George, who nodded. Only then did he depart.

Monro directed his assistants to wait behind him, then gave his full attention to his patient. "You are used to splendor," he said, steepling his fingers as he paced the room. "Luxury. Comfort. You have never known the salubrious powers of Spartan habits."

George considered this. "If opulence leads to a disordered mind, why are not all kings mad?"

"Who is to say they are not?"

"I am fairly certain my father was sane. My grandfather, as well. Cruel," George added, almost as an afterthought, because his grandfather had never spared the rod, "but certainly sane."

"I could not say. I never examined them." Monro moved in, bringing his face uncomfortably close to George's. "To most of the world, you give the impression of sanity. It is only a select few who know your true nature."

"I would like to keep it that way."

Monro nodded. "Simple ways are needed. First, we must return you to your diet of porridge and turnips."

"I'm afraid that will be impossible," George said. He motioned upward, toward the rest of the house. "How would I explain it?"

"I told you it was a bad idea to leave Kew. We will not be able to achieve optimum results here."

"Then we must do our best."

Monro's mouth pursed into an angry bud. "My methods are meant to be all-encompassing. They will not work if you pick and choose."

"Then I pick and choose everything that can be done at Buckingham House," George said. "Surely that is better than nothing."

Monro let out a huff of annoyance. "Gag him," he said to one of his assistants.

George did not struggle. He had the first time. It had been pure instinct. Now he knew better.

He would submit. This would make him whole.

By the end of the day, George was exhausted. And he was freezing. Monro had utilized the ice bath twice, claiming that doubling up was necessary to make up for the loss of the iron chair. October was arriving with a chill, and despite the relatively new construction of Buckingham House, it was drafty. Reynolds had brought him a blanket, but George refused to be seen walking through the house wrapped like a baby.

Monro wanted to break him. George understood that. But surely he was allowed some pride.

He was eager to see Charlotte. She, along with his science, was what brought him joy. She was the reason he was subjecting himself to this.

He did not know how she had occupied herself that day. If his reports from before were accurate, she had most likely read a book and looked out the window.

Perhaps played with Pom Pom. He'd heard that she had finally taken to the dog.

Either way, she had certainly had a more pleasant day than he.

He'd hoped to see her after he'd eaten and had a warm bath, but they happened upon each other in the corridor outside their bedchambers. She had already dressed for dinner, wearing an elaborate gown of sumptuous burgundy. Her hair had been styled in a manner that George suspected was deceptively simple.

It looked simple to him, that was. She'd probably had to sit for an hour to achieve such pastoral perfection.

Women were mysterious creatures.

"Charlotte," he said. He smiled. He was happy to see her, even if he was not at his best.

"George."

He frowned. She did not sound pleased. In fact, she sounded quite *dis*pleased.

He noted the book in her hand. "Have you been reading?"

"Yes." She held the book to her side. Brimsley immediately materialized and took it.

"Anything interesting?"

"Poetry."

"And did you enjoy it?"

She shrugged.

The tenor of this conversation was not what he had expected. She was almost sullen. Still, he persevered. He glanced over at Brimsley, who was staring at him with thinly veiled hostility.

What the devil?

George looked at Reynolds, who was still holding the blanket. He was also looking at Brimsley. If George didn't know better, he'd have thought the two of them were silently trying to communicate.

Did they even know each other?

He let out a sigh. He was exhausted, and he did not have the patience for palace intrigue. He returned his attention to Charlotte, trying his best to remain cheerful despite his abysmal mood. "May I inquire the author?"

"Shakespeare," she said.

"Ah. Sonnets, then."

"Yes."

My God, it was like pulling teeth. He had never known her to be so uncommunicative. Not that he had known her for long. But still, this was clearly unlike her.

"Do you have a favorite?" he asked.

She stared at him. Not with anger. Just . . . without emotion.

"*Shall I compare thee to a summer's day?*" he suggested.

No?

He tried again. "*My mistress' eyes are nothing like the sun?*"

She arched a brow and recited from memory: "*When my love swears that he is made of truth, I do believe him, though I know he lies.*"

That was unexpected.

George took a moment to clear his throat. "I believe you altered the pronouns. Is not Shakespeare writing of a woman in this poem?"

"I have put my own interpretation on it."

"Charlotte," he said, and he finally grabbed the blanket from Reynolds. Heaven only knew how long he would be in this hall bickering with her, and damn it, he was cold. "Is aught amiss?"

She smiled, all teeth and insincerity. "I am perfectly marvelous."

That was patently untrue, but he did not have the energy to fight her. They stared at each other for a moment, and then she motioned that she would like to step around him.

"I have much to do," she said.

"I have not seen you yet today."

Her stance grew tense. "And whose choice was that?"

"Charlotte, you must know that I have duties as King." Technically, it wasn't a lie. He did have royal duties. They just weren't the reason he had been absent.

"Yes, I know all about your duties." She gave him another false smile. "I am one of them, am I not?"

Where was this hostility coming from? He shook his head. "You are far from a duty."

She scoffed.

He tilted his head rigidly to the side as he held his temper in check. He'd spent the day being violently screamed at. He'd been brutally submerged in an ice bath—twice—all for *her*.

She could not even speak to him politely.

"I plan to take my dinner in my bedchamber this evening," George said. The thought of donning full evening dress was exhausting. And maybe her mood would soften when they were alone. "Will you join me?"

"I have plans."

"Plans," he repeated dully.

"I have already dressed," she said, motioning to her exquisite attire. "I will dine formally."

"I would rather you dined with me."

"Brimsley," she said sharply. "Am I expected in the dining room?"

"Er . . ." He looked frantically between King and Queen.

"Brimsley," she said again.

"Yes, Your Majesty, I believe that you—"

"Ah, but she is Queen," George interrupted. "She sets her own schedule, does she not?"

Brimsley swallowed reflexively. "Yes, Your Majesty. She is—"

"Brimsley," Charlotte all but barked. "Do you or do you not work for me?"

Brimsley was now visibly sweating. "I do, Your Majesty. I serve you in all—"

"Brim*ley*," George said, his voice rising in volume on the second syllable. "Who hired you?"

Brimsley's head jerked to and fro, until he finally turned to Reynolds in desperation.

Reynolds looked at his feet.

"I was hired by the household, Your Majesty," Brimsley finally said to George.

"Which is headed by . . . ?"

"You, Your Majesty."

"Traitor," Charlotte hissed.

"*Your Majesty*," Brimsley pleaded.

"Never mind," George said, his patience gone. "Do what you will, Charlotte. My time is too valuable to stand here and argue with you."

He stepped to the left, trying to get around her, but there were four people in the hall, and her bloody skirts blocked the way.

He cursed under his breath.

She gasped. "What was that?"

"Your skirts are too damned wide," he ground out.

She drew back. Really. *That* was what offended her?

"I will have you know I am the height of fashion," she snipped.

"I am sure you are."

"I *set* the fashion."

"How lovely for you. Now if you will excuse me . . ." He pushed past her skirt, and maybe he was as malevolent a person as Doctor Monro kept insisting because he did take a bit of glee in the fact that she stumbled.

"Perhaps you are a duty to me!" she burst out.

He turned slowly to look at her. "Is that so?"

Her chin jutted out.

"Fine," he said.

"Fine."

But just then, Reynolds stepped forward. "Your Majesty," he said. His back was to the Queen, so she could not see when he looked pointedly at George's hands.

They had started to shake.

"Good night, Charlotte," George said. "Enjoy your meal."

"I will. I—"

But George had already allowed Reynolds to usher him away.

CHARLOTTE

BUCKINGHAM HOUSE
THE QUEEN'S BEDCHAMBER
...
LATER THAT NIGHT

Charlotte was tucked in bed, scrubbed clean and wearing her oldest, softest nightgown when a knock sounded at the door.

Odd, that. The maids never knocked. They just slipped in and out like ghosts. Charlotte wasn't supposed to notice them, and most of the time, she didn't.

It was probably Brimsley. He would not enter unannounced after she had gone to bed. He was too easily embarrassed, that one.

Well. He was going to have to see her with her sleep bonnet and her undereye creams and all those other secret feminine tricks men weren't supposed to know about.

"Enter!" she called out, fully expecting his small frame to appear in the doorway.

But it was a much taller man who entered her bedchamber. A much broader man.

George.

She felt her lips part with surprise as she hurriedly rubbed at the cream on her face. Why was he here? She was naught but a duty to him. He had said it quite clearly, and she remembered each word with surgical clarity:

You told me to bed her. I have done so. I understand. It has been abundantly clear since my first breath that I am born for the happiness or misery of a great nation, and consequently must often act contrary to my passions.

She was a duty. A chore. And he had not even truly wanted her.

She could have borne it better if he had not lied. He had made her feel wanted. Adored, even. He had told her she was special, she was incomparable. A rare jewel.

He had made her feel that theirs would be an uncommon union, more than just a diplomatic treaty.

Worst of all, he had made her hope.

He had led her to think that with her he might be Just George. And maybe she could be Just Charlotte.

It would have been better if he had stayed awful. She would not feel so betrayed.

"Good evening," she said. All things considered, she was rather proud of her civility. She'd wanted to say, *Why the hell are you here?*

And maybe throw something.

"Good evening," he said in return. He wore his dressing gown, the same one he'd had on the night before. Surely he did not think they were going to do . . . *that* . . . again? After what he'd said about her?

Except he did not know that she'd heard.

This was a predicament. She did not wish to admit that she'd eavesdropped. Such behavior was beneath her, and besides that, there was something awful in admitting that she knew the truth. How could she possibly be expected to look at him and say, "I know I am just another one of your royal duties."

It was easier to pretend that *she* did not care for *him*.

"I did not see you at dinner tonight," he said.

"I told you, I wished to dine formally."

"Did you enjoy your meal?"

She stared at him. Was he truly going to come into her bedchamber and make polite conversation? To what purpose?

"I was not hungry," she finally said.

"I was," he replied. He crossed the room and propped himself against the edge of her bed. "Quite."

And then he just stood there. Looking at her.

"I'm going to read," she declared. She grabbed one of the books she'd left on her bedside table and picked it up. He was not unintelligent. He would get the hint.

He didn't say anything, so she opened the volume with more of a snap than was strictly necessary and flipped to the title page. It was in German. Good. She could use something familiar this evening.

"Very well." George pushed himself off the side of the bed and walked around to the other side.

"What are you doing?" she half-shrieked.

"I'm getting into bed. I should have thought that was obvious."

She squirmed over to the far edge of the mattress. "You can't sleep here."

"I was under the impression ours was to be a true marriage."

"Perhaps," Charlotte said. "But not tonight."

He paused in his movements and regarded her with a coolly assessing stare. "May I inquire why not?"

"Do I need a reason?"

His brows rose. "If you want me to judge you as something other than a fickle female, then yes, you do."

"Fine," she said, closing the book on her finger as if she needed to mark her place. He might as well think she'd actually been reading it. "I did not see you today."

"*That's* your reason?" His face betrayed his surprise, and he looked as if he might well laugh at her. "You did not see me today."

Even Charlotte had to admit that it was a weak argument. "Well . . ." she stalled.

"*To*day. This day. This one day."

She stiffened. "Please don't mock me."

"I do not mock. I am only trying to understand."

"I feel mocked."

He tilted his head to the side as if he were taking the time to catalogue his thoughts. "Very well. Yes, I'm mocking you. But only because you are being ridiculous."

"If I do not have bodily autonomy, what do I have?"

Now he *did* laugh. Harshly. "Neither of us has bodily autonomy. We are both required to make a baby."

"Yes, I know," she muttered. "You live for the happiness and misery of a great nation."

"Ah. So you have heard me say that."

She froze. She was going to have to admit she'd been eavesdropping.

But then he added, "I have made that speech countless times. So much so that I fear it may supplant 'God and my right' as the official motto of the sovereign. But you should know something. I have meant it, every time I have said it. I am not my own man, Charlotte. The Crown rests heavy on my head."

It would soon rest on hers, too. Literally. Coronation was not far away.

"As sovereign, I have duties. You know this."

"Duties," she scoffed. She was coming to detest that word.

He took a breath. A rather long and awkward one, to be honest. "I have had a trying day," he finally said. He paused, and he seemed to be doing something odd with his hands. Eventually they formed stiff fists, and he placed his arms at his sides. "I do not wish to argue with my wife."

"You do not need to argue with your wife. You need only to go back to your own bedchamber."

"I want to sleep here," he said, and it sounded as if each word was ground out of his very soul. "I was hoping for comfort."

"Comfort," she echoed.

"Yes, comfort. From my wife, for whom I have been—" He swore under his breath. And then the oddest thing happened. His mouth did not move, but she would have sworn he was speaking to himself.

"You are my wife," he finally said out loud.

She shook her head. "You cannot ignore me the entire day and then expect me to lie here and—and—"

"And?"

"And—service you in the evenings."

His mouth fell open. "Service me? Is that what you're calling it?"

"It was my first time. I hardly know what to call it."

He yanked back the covers with enough force to send one of her pink cushions flying. "I was under the impression that you enjoyed yourself."

"It was . . ." Charlotte tried very hard to appear nonchalant. "Pleasant, I suppose."

"Pleasant." He crawled up on the bed.

She tried not to look at him, but he was looming over her, and it made her feel things. "Pleasant," she repeated.

"Which part was pleasant?"

"I beg your pardon?"

"Which part"—he crawled closer—"was pleasant."

"I . . . Well . . ."

His face took on a wolfish expression. "Was it when I kissed you?"

"Well, yes, but—" Damn it. She did not want to admit any of this to him.

"Was it when I touched you . . . here?"

She slapped his hand away before he could stroke the side of her neck. "I don't want you," she said.

"Liar."

"Fine. I don't *want* to want you." She tried to twist away, but he had inadvertently pinned the damask bed covering around her when he'd moved closer. She yanked at it, with little success. "And I certainly don't want you tonight."

This seemed to amuse him. "You don't want me tonight, or you don't *want* to want me tonight?"

She shook her head. "You're mad."

He let out a grim laugh.

Charlotte finally managed to loosen some of the bedclothes and scooted a few inches away. "You can't just promenade into my bedchamber and expect me to do my duty."

"If I recall, you enjoyed your duty. And also—*promenade?*"

"Don't be pedantic."

"I don't promenade." He sat back on his haunches with an expression of disbelief. Maybe disgust. "I don't have time to promenade."

"And how could I know that since I *never see you?*"

He rolled his eyes. "There are things I have to do."

"What things?"

"Private things."

She rolled *her* eyes.

"There are things in my life that have nothing to do with you." His voice began to rise in volume, and he started doing that funny thing he did with his hands when he was nervous.

Oddly, it was one of the things she liked best about him—that he, too, sometimes felt nervous when they were together. It made her feel less alone.

"You may be my wife," George said, "but that does not grant you access to every corner of my existence."

"Then you don't get access to every corner of *my* existence, either." She didn't care that she sounded childish; she had to make her point.

"Charlotte, this must be done." He motioned to the bed. They both knew what he meant.

"I don't want to," she said in a very small voice. Because she was lying. She knew she was lying. She did want him. She wanted her husband. She'd been evicted from her homeland and sent overseas. Alone.

She wanted to feel close to another human being.

But she wanted that human being to be the George she'd thought he was. Just George.

Just George was kind and funny and when he kissed her, she lost all reason.

This George—the one who called her a duty and reminded her that "this must be done"—could probably also make her lose all reason with a single kiss.

But her heart would remain untouched.

And yet still, she could not stop thinking about him—the way his head tilted when he smiled, or the exact sound of his laugh. She could not stop thinking about their kiss in his observatory at Kew, and how he'd told her he'd been aching to touch her. But most of all, she couldn't stop thinking about their one, perfect night. When he'd licked his way down her body, and—

"Arrrrrrrrrgh."

"Did you just growl?" he asked.

"No." Dear God, this was mortifying.

"Well, move over, it's time to do this."

"And I told you. I do not want to."

He practically bounced along the mattress until he was barely a foot away. He grinned. "I do not believe you."

"So you would force me?"

He smiled. Like a rogue. "It would not come to that."

"Well, I won't have you."

"Kiss me," he said abruptly.

"I beg your pardon."

"Kiss me. Once. If you still do not want me, then I will go."

She scoffed at that. "Don't be absurd."

"Are you afraid?"

"Afraid? Of course not. I'm not afraid of you."

"Good," he said. "I never thought you were. You're afraid of yourself."

"I am not."

"You are."

"I am *not*."

"You sound like a child."

She did, and she blamed him. He was the only person who brought out such truculence. With everyone else, she was a *sparkling* conversationalist.

"What day is it today?" she asked suddenly.

He blinked and shook his head, befuddled by her lightning change of topic. "Tuesday, I believe."

"The date," she said sharply. "I meant the date."

"September the sixteenth."

"Even days, then," she said, waving her arm expansively toward the rest of the bed. "We shall do this on even days."

"Even days," he repeated.

"That's what I said." And if she sounded proud, so be it. She'd retaken control of the situation. He might get what he wanted, but it would be on her terms.

But he was still regarding her as if she were somewhat addled. "We will have a schedule for copulation."

She shrugged. "If you wish to speak about it so clinically."

"Given the lack of feeling between us, clinically is the only way to speak about it."

"Obviously."

"Well, then." He nodded at her book, still in her left hand.

"What?"

"Get rid of it. We have work to do."

She felt her head shaking in confusion. What was he talking about?

"It's an even day," he said. He took the book from her and tossed it aside.

"Oh."

Oh.

George

It was a Pyrrhic victory, but George decided he just didn't care.

"Not love sonnets this time?" he quipped.

"It wasn't love sonnets last time."

He pulled the covers aside and moved over her, still on his hands and knees. "It won't be love sonnets right now," he warned. It was cruel, but her rejection of him had also been cruel. He'd thought their wedding night had *meant* something.

It had meant something to him.

He looked down, searching her eyes for hints of fear—he did not think he could live with himself if she feared him. But all he saw was excited defiance. Her eyes glittered with energy, and her breath grew fast and shallow.

Just like his.

"It's too bad you hate my touch so much," he taunted, trailing his fingers down the side of her throat.

She reached right between his legs and squeezed. "It's too bad you hate *my* touch so much."

Oh, she was going to play it that way, was she? He rolled them so she was on top, grabbed the hem of her loose-fitting nightgown, and whipped it right over her head.

"No buttons," he said approvingly.

She gasped at the swiftness of his actions, but if she felt embarrassed by her nudity, she did not show it. Instead, she squeezed harder.

A little too hard, to be honest.

But she was new to this. She did not know the border between a man's pleasure and pain.

At least he hoped not. Otherwise, she was trying to do him serious damage.

"A little less vigor," he said, wedging his hand between hers and his member. His dressing gown had fallen open, and for all intents and purposes, he was now as naked as she.

"Like that," he instructed, showing her how he liked to be held and stroked. And because fair play was in order, he returned the favor.

"Do you like this?" he whispered, touching her gently between her legs.

She nodded. "Yes, that. No, *that*."

He smiled wolfishly. He'd moved his fingers ever so slightly and had apparently found the spot that most gave her pleasure.

He rubbed, very softly.

"Oh, yes."

And then in circles. "Like this?"

She nodded frantically.

"I can do even better."

She didn't look like she believed him.

"Just you wait," he murmured, and then, before she could possibly figure out what he was up to, he flipped her over, scooted down her body, and planted his face right between her legs.

She shrieked with surprise.

He licked.

"George! What are you doing? You can't—"

"Oh, I can," he said, taking just a moment to look up at her. "You'll like it, too."

"Are you sure?"

He paused again. "If you don't, tell me."

She nodded. At least she trusted him in this.

He'd done this before, but not often. The courtesan his uncle had sent him to at the age of sixteen had assured him women loved it.

"They'll be yours forever," she'd said, right after giving him a condescending boop on the nose. "Provided you do it well."

He was fairly certain he had learned to do it reasonably well, but in truth, it had always felt like a bit of a chore to him.

He was not unselfish; he did care that a woman felt pleasure in their joining. But for him, it was frankly a little boring.

No longer.

Kissing Charlotte so intimately was a revelation. The taste of her, the heat . . . the sounds she made with every tiny lick and nibble . . . Her pleasure sparked his in a way he had not known was possible. Each time she moaned and squirmed, he felt himself growing impossibly harder. He didn't know how much longer he could possibly maintain such excitement, and yet something within him would not let him stop.

He was going to make her explode. It had become his life's ambition.

He slid a finger into her.

"Oh!" She let out a breathy squeal. It made him smile against her.

"You like that, do you?" he murmured. He turned the one finger into two.

Her hips bucked, and she cried out his name. "Wait!" she gasped. "I can't!"

He smiled again. She could and she would.

And he would bring her there.

"No more," she moaned. "No more."

He looked at her, wondering if she could see the way she glistened on his skin. "Do you really want me to stop?"

"No!" she practically howled, jamming her fingers into his hair and pushing him back down.

He laughed with delight and redoubled his efforts. She could say she didn't want him, but they both knew the truth. He would bring her to climax, and she would never be able to say she did not desire him.

She might someday decide she did not like him, but he would always know that she wanted him.

"George," she panted again. "George George George."

He moved his fingers as he licked her, mimicking the movements of lovemaking but adding a little twist and then—

The next time his name left her lips, it was a scream.

He slid up her body until his face was a breath away from hers. "Enjoyed that, did you?"

She could not speak.

"I'll take that as a yes." He positioned himself, nudging her already slack legs wider. "Are you ready?"

She gave a dazed nod, and he thrust forward.

She was gloriously wet, but this was only her second time, and he knew he had to give her time to accommodate him. "You will tell me if I hurt you," he said.

She nodded furiously.

He went still. "I'm hurting you?"

"No, I just mean I'll tell you."

Thank God. He would have pulled out. He would have. But it might well have killed him.

He moved slowly, or at least as slowly as he could, until he was finally fully within her. "Charlotte," he moaned, because truly, in that moment she was his entire world. He pulled back, the friction sending shivers of pleasure down his spine.

Her fingers gripped his shoulders, and her hips arched up, and he plunged forward. And then again, and again, until his movements lost all rhythm, and all that was left was need.

The bed shook and creaked, and he kept slamming into her, but she was meeting him thrust for thrust, and then he felt her climax again, squeezing him so tightly it sent him right over the edge.

"Charlotte!" he cried, and he poured himself into her, spending of himself like he'd never dreamed possible.

He collapsed, rolling to the side so he would not crush her.

"My God," he said.

She just breathed. Heavily.

"That was—that was—" He had no words. Truly. She had robbed him of sense. It was probably ironic.

"Did we make a baby?" she asked.

George turned his head, startled by the question. "We won't know for a bit."

"Really?"

He felt himself frown. "I thought you said someone explained it."

"They did. They said we might have to do it many times, but I assumed we'd know right away if it worked."

"It's when you miss your courses. That's how you know."

"I know *that*," she said, sounding a little impatient. "I mean, I know what it means to miss one's courses. I just assumed that one already knew by then. That . . . somehow . . ."

"You could tell when it happened?"

She nodded.

"No," he said, returning his gaze to the ceiling.

She made an irritated noise. She did not like being ignorant—he had already learned this about her.

Frankly, he could not blame her.

"Well," she said. "I suppose you should go now."

"Go?"

"You're in my bedroom."

Yes. And he thought he'd stay there. She'd spent the night in *his* bedroom when they'd done this the night before. But that was before she'd turned so cold and distant.

She sat up, holding the bedcovers to her body. For warmth? For modesty? That seemed absurd, given what he'd just done to her. Women made no sense to him, and she the least sense of all.

He'd thought she liked him. She'd given every indication that she thought him a worthwhile human being. He'd left his bed this morning, brimming with joy. But by the time he saw her again, late that afternoon, she was cold. Somehow she had realized the truth about him. Or if not the truth, an approximation of it. He was not worthy of her. Quite possibly, he never would be.

"Well?" she said, tipping her head pointedly to the door.

"You're truly asking me to leave?" he asked. "After"—he tipped his head toward the bed—"*that*?"

"That changes nothing."

He whipped back the covers, unmindful of their nudity. "Apparently not."

"It is our duty to make a baby," Charlotte said. "Nothing more."

George attempted to retrieve his dressing gown from the foot of the bed. Their exertions had been so acrobatic that it had tangled itself around the post. "Nothing at all," he grunted, yanking the damned thing free.

"I'll see you in two days," she said primly.

He tied his belt into a savage knot. "And not a minute before," he growled.

"It shall be my greatest delight not to see you."

"Indeed," he returned in kind. "The sooner you are with child, the sooner we can cease this"—he motioned toward the bed with his best royal disdain—"performance."

She shrugged. "Our duty will be done. You can go back to your stars and sky at Kew, and I will no longer have to view your face."

He swooped into a mocking bow. "Your Majesty."

She gave him a regal nod. *Him!* And then she pointed to the door. "Get out."

"With pleasure." He slammed open the door and left.

BUCKINGHAM HOUSE
MONRO'S LABORATORY
...
18 SEPTEMBER 1761

The next few days were no better. George still had no idea why Charlotte was so upset with him, but in all honesty, he was so angry that he wasn't sure he cared any longer.

More to the point, he didn't have time to worry about her. Monro had stepped up his treatment, and George was now spending the better part of each day in the Buckingham House cellar.

The doctor lamented the loss of his iron chair and was convinced that George's progress was hampered because of it.

"Your diet, too," Doctor Monro said. "It is a problem."

"If I could eat the gruel at dinner, I would," George said wearily. "But it would cause too much talk."

"It is a problem."

George resisted the urge to say, "Yes, you'd mentioned." It did not do to display insolence with the doctor. It earned him extra time in the ice bath, and Monro's assistants had taken to holding his head underwater for increasingly longer periods of time.

"We will have to make up for these deficiencies in other ways," Monro decided. "The gag!"

One of his assistants rushed forward and did his bidding. George's wrists and ankles had already been bound to the hard wooden chair, so now he was well and truly diminished.

"You cannot speak," Monro said, "so you must think the thoughts as I give them to you. Do you understand me, boy?"

George nodded.

"You must learn to submit. You must realize that you are no one. You are no better than anyone else." Monro walked to the wall, where several of his instruments had been hung on hooks. He took some time selecting the right one, eventually settling on a thin rod.

"With every strike, you must think to yourself, 'I am no one.' Do you understand?"

George nodded again, eyeing the rod with trepidation. Up to this point, Doctor Monro had not struck him with anything other than his hand.

Monro handed the rod to his assistant. "We shall begin." He nodded, and the assistant brought the rod down across George's thighs. It stung, but it wasn't as painful as George had anticipated.

"Did you think it?" Monro demanded.

George had forgotten. He shook his head. He needed to be honest if he wanted his treatment to progress.

"Harder," Monro instructed his assistant.

The rod came down with a slap.

I am no one, George thought.

"Did you think it?"

This time George nodded.

"Did you believe it?"

George gave a little shrug. Maybe? Honestly, he was not sure.

Monro regarded him for a moment, then must have decided it was still progress because he nodded and moved to the other side of the room, where he sat and picked up his notebook. Barely looking up from his notes, he said, "Again."

Slap!

I am no one.

"Again."

Slap!

Monro frowned. "He does not seem to be reacting."

George's eyes widened and he grunted from behind his gag.

"Move to his hands."

George strained against his restraints. Unlike his thighs, his hands were bare. This was going to—

Whack!

George screamed.

"Much better," Monro grunted.

Whack!

"Are you following my directions?"

George nodded.

Whack!

I am no one.

Whack!

I am no one.

Whack!

"Careful not to let him bleed," Monro said. He frowned as he leaned to the side to get a better look at George's hands. "It will cause questions."

The assistant nodded, and the next blow landed on George's forearms, which had heretofore been spared.

"Although I suppose we could just put him in gloves," Monro said.

I am no one. I am no one.

Whack! Back on the hands.

I am no one.

"Are you following my directions?" Monro asked.

George nodded vigorously. Tears had escaped his eyes and had soaked into his gag. He was mortified.

"Good. Then it is working." Monro looked back at his assistant. "Let's keep at it."

Whack!

I am no one.

Whack!

I am no one.

I am no one . . .

TWO DAYS LATER

He was the King.

He kept saying that he was no one and thinking he was no one, but when he awakened in the morning, he knew he was King.

It was all he had been born to be.

But George wanted to be well, and every time he saw Charlotte in the hall, her distaste for him written on her face, it renewed his determination to see this treatment through to the end.

Did she somehow see through his façade? Had she detected the madness behind his eyes?

Even at night, on those even days when they yelled and screamed and, yes, fucked, there was no tenderness on her part, nothing to indicate that she saw him as anything other than a source of physical pleasure.

And a baby. Mustn't forget that.

It made him want to redouble his efforts. Once they got her pregnant they wouldn't have to see each other again, and wouldn't that be marvelous? No more insults hurled at him from every corner. No more glares from that annoying diminutive servant of hers. What was his name again? Burdock? Bramwell?

Brimsley. That was it. Brimsley. He kept glaring at George as if he were to blame for the current palace mood, which ranged between explosive and already on fire.

It was Charlotte. It was *her* fault. He was being reasonable—well, as reasonable as one could expect from a madman—and furthermore, he'd been submitting to bloody torture trying to cure himself.

True, she wasn't precisely aware that he was doing this, or that he was occasionally touched in the head, but somewhere someone was keeping score, and he was definitely doing his part.

"God *damn* it," he tried to say.

Tried, because per usual, he'd been gagged.

"What was that?" Monro asked, looking up from his infernal little notebook. "Ungag him."

One of the assistants, the one George had decided to call Helmut, untied the gag.

George spat as it was removed. "We have been at this for days. How much longer?"

"As long as it takes to achieve our goal," Monro said with all calmness. "That was our agreement."

"Our goal was to restore me to myself. Much more of this and I will not have a self to return to. Is a broken king really better than a mad one?"

Monro set down the notebook and moved his hand through the air, much like a teacher might visually punctuate a lecture. "I do not call it the 'terrific method' for nothing. Terror is its very basis. But from that terror, what result."

George was not reassured by the way the doctor shivered with delight when he said, "what result."

"The wolves of the German Black Forest were famous," Monro continued, rising to his feet. "The fiercest in the world. Not content to steal chickens and cattle, they would run off with children. The old. But where are those wolves now?"

George really hoped this was a rhetorical question.

"They are gone!" Monro barked. "They exist only in legends, fairy tales. Through science and force of will, the Germans transformed their wolves into pathetic creatures like that Pomeranian I used to have. See, boy, animal nature is clay. With enough strength, you can mold it. I will do to you what the Germans did to their wolves. Mold you. Until you are as harmless and obedient as that bloody Pomeranian."

"The Pomeranian escaped," George whispered.

Monro whirled to face him. "I have seen the Queen's new pet, *Your Majesty*."

George fought to keep the defiance from his face. He was not supposed to defy the doctor. He did not want to.

"You disobeyed me," Monro said. "You will pay."

"I am King," George said.

"*You are no one!*" Monro screamed. "You are who I tell you to be. Do you understand me?"

"I am King," George said again.

Monro slapped him. "Say it again," he dared.

"I am King." But George's voice was weaker this time.

Another slap. "Again."

"I am . . . King."

Another. "Again."

"I am . . . I am . . ."

He was King. But was this worth it? Was there any reason to say so? It would just earn him another slap, and Doctor Monro was trying to help him, was he not?

"Who are you?" Monro asked. His voice was low. Commanding.

"I am no one," George said. He didn't quite believe it, but he was willing to say it. If it made this stop.

So he said it again. And again. But he was thinking something else altogether . . .

It was an even day.

And somehow, he smiled.

BRIMSLEY

Brimsley was nervous.

He would, of course, be the first person to admit that this was not an uncommon state for him.

Well, he'd admit that to anyone but Reynolds.

The thing was, usually when Brimsley felt nervous it was because he'd done something wrong. Or was about to do something wrong. Or possibly someone else had done something wrong and he was likely to be blamed for it.

Regardless, it had a lot to do with things going wrong.

Right now, however, everything was going right. In theory. The King and the Queen were living in the same household, and he no longer had to fear the fiery wrath of Princess Augusta because they were *definitely* having relations.

Very loud relations.

Brimsley spent a lot of time shooing other servants away from the corridor outside the royal bedchambers.

But still, he was uneasy. Reynolds was hiding something from him, which meant that the King was hiding something from the Queen, which meant that Brimsley was not doing his job of protecting her.

This was his sworn duty.

Furthermore, the King and Queen, for all their loud relations, seemed to detest one another. This did not bode well for the future. Anyone's future.

And now it was Coronation Day. Which meant that King George and Queen Charlotte of Great Britain and Ireland had to give the appearance of tolerating each other's company. Brimsley was confident the Queen would manage it. She knew what was required of her. It was the King who concerned him. His moods were much less evenhanded than hers, and more to the point—

Where the devil was he?

It was the royal wedding all over again, except now the King was the one who'd gone missing.

Brimsley put his hands to his face, using them to literally unclench his jaw. The King and Queen were going to be the death of him. He was going to grind his teeth to powder. And then he wouldn't be able to eat. He'd slowly starve, and wouldn't this make it all so much easier for the Italian grape pickers and their goat?

This had to end. For the sake of sanity *and* his teeth. He needed to find Reynolds. It was time he knew what was really going on.

Brimsley suspected Reynolds was down in the warren of rooms and hallways that made up the subterranean level of Buckingham House. He'd caught him on his way there before, slinking down one of the back staircases when he thought no one was looking. And he had definitely been slinking. Reynolds usually had the air of a man who expected the rest of the world to step out of his way, but when Brimsley had spied him, he'd been acting in an extremely furtive manner, looking this way and that, making sure that no one saw him leaving his post on the main floor.

There was no reason, none at all, why Reynolds—*the King's own man*—would have business so far belowstairs. This was where the laundry was done, where food was stored and pots were washed. It was a world apart from the glittering palace above, and hardly anyone crossed the border.

Today—Coronation Day—the halls were teeming with servants, all dressed in their finest. There would be a parade later that afternoon, and most everyone had been given a half-day off to celebrate. But Reynolds was six feet tall, and his hair was such a lovely, shiny blond it was difficult for him not to stand out.

It took Brimsley all of two minutes to spot him. He sidled up. "I need to speak with you," he said under his breath.

"Why are you down here?" Reynolds demanded. "You do not come belowstairs."

"Why are *you* down here?" Brimsley countered.

"I need be. I am on an errand."

"Then I need to be, too. I am here because you are. You hold the King. And she is looking for him."

"I thought they were not speaking."

"It is Coronation Day," Brimsley whispered urgently. "It does not matter if they speak. They must be united. So where is he?"

Reynolds yanked him into an alcove where they were less likely to be overheard. "You shouldn't come down here."

"You gave me no choice."

"Don't be ridiculous. Your duty is to the Queen."

"And the Queen needs the King." Brimsley fought the urge to roll his eyes. Or punch Reynolds. They were talking in circles. All they ever did was talk in circles.

Reynolds looked down the hall before answering. "The King shall be with her soon enough. He is studying his sciences up in the library."

Brimsley frowned. He'd been by the library just an hour or so earlier. There had been no sign of the King.

"Move along," Reynolds said in that annoyingly superior way of his. "Attend to your Queen."

But he seemed nervous. Almost shifty. And he kept glancing over his shoulder. As if . . . maybe . . .

Was he consorting with someone else? They had never said explicitly that they would not see other men . . .

"What's going on?" Brimsley asked suspiciously.

"Nothing's going on." Reynolds gave him an exasperated look. "You have an overactive imagination."

Brimsley lifted his chin. This could not be tolerated. "Listen to me well, Reynolds," he said. "If you allow yourself another rider, do not think I care. But"—his mouth formed an angry pucker as he regarded their unimpressive surroundings—"mind he is of the right station."

Reynolds drew back indignantly. "I am not . . . that is not what . . ."

Brimsley crossed his arms. Reynolds might be his superior in the household, but the bedroom was a different matter entirely.

"There are no other *riders*," Reynolds finally sputtered. "I am simply belowstairs."

"And yet you never are," Brimsley muttered.

"How would you know? *You* never are."

"I was looking for you."

Reynolds let out a big huff. It sounded one part annoyed and one part . . . well, honestly, Brimsley wasn't sure how to interpret it. Finally, Reynolds said, "I am simply belowstairs. That is all. Go attend to your Queen. Coronation Day is a great day for her and the country."

Brimsley frowned, strangely unready to move. "I'm not jealous," he said.

"Of course you're not."

"I have no reason to be. We made no promises."

"None," Reynolds said.

Brimsley swallowed. Did he want a promise? It had never occurred to him that he might be in a position to ask for fidelity. Because what would that even mean? A promise between two men? They could not take it to a church. They could not show it to a magistrate.

And yet, when he looked at Reynolds . . . when they caught each other's eyes in the hall . . .

It meant something to him.

"Brimsley," Reynolds said. And then: "*Bartholomew.*"

Brimsley looked up. Reynolds was raking his hand through his hair. His unflappable demeanor was . . .

Flapped.

"There is no one else," Reynolds said quietly. "You may be assured of that."

Brimsley gave an uncomfortable nod. "Nor for I."

"You should go back," Reynolds said. "There is much to do today. Too much."

"Yes." Brimsley sighed and turned to leave, but then a door opened at the end of the hall. Someone emerged holding medical equipment, and—

Was that the King inside?

Reynolds practically jumped in front of him to block his view.

"Is that a physician?" Brimsley asked. "Why is the King being examined by a strange doctor in the cellar?"

"Brimsley."

"Why is he not being examined by the Royal Physician?"

"*Brimsley.*"

There was something in Reynolds's voice. Brimsley stopped speaking instantly.

"You have seen nothing," Reynolds said.

Brimsley wanted to say more. He really did. But Reynolds's eyes were begging him not to, and Reynolds never begged.

Brimsley nodded. "I must attend my Queen," he said. He turned on his heel and left.

BUCKINGHAM HOUSE
NEAR THE ROYAL BEDCHAMBERS
...
3 OCTOBER 1761

The coronation was splendid. Everyone said so. The King and Queen looked glorious, both. They'd played their roles well. In fact, the only time Brimsley had seen them crack was right when they returned to Buckingham House. The weight of their crowns was quite literal, and they were both exhausted.

So exhausted, in fact, that they'd gone back to their respective rooms and stayed there for the rest of the evening.

On an even day, even.

"How do you think this pact came about?" Brimsley asked Reynolds as they walked down the hall together, each with a silver tray for his employer. It was early evening; the sun was on its way down, and the air at Buckingham House was gold with dusk.

"Even days, you mean?" Reynolds asked.

"Yes."

"I shudder to think."

"It is most peculiar."

"It is not for me to question the ways of the royals," Reynolds said.

"But . . . ?" Because there was clearly an implied *but*.

"I shall not finish my statement."

Brimsley glanced up through his lashes. "You are no fun."

"I am exactly as fun as I need be," Reynolds said.

"Precisely my point. Only someone wholly lacking in humor would make such a statement."

Reynolds gave him a look of exasperation, but Brimsley rather thought there was a bit of affection mixed in with it.

"Don't smile," Reynolds said.

Brimsley grinned. "What have you for the King?" he asked, motioning toward the silver tray Reynolds carried.

"Correspondence. And you?"

Brimsley looked down at the papers on his tray. "She is planning a concert. With a child pianist. It seems very strange to me, but she insists she has heard him, and he is remarkable."

"He is coming over from the Continent?"

"Vienna," Brimsley confirmed.

"How does one travel from Vienna?" Reynolds pondered. "Overland? Or by sea?"

They were at the King's and Queen's bedchamber doors by now, and had been for at least a minute. Just chatting.

"I'm not sure," Brimsley replied. "The Queen came by sea. Crossed from Cuxhaven. She said it was ghastly. Puked all over her brother."

"Sisters," Reynolds said with a knowing chuckle.

"Have you any?" Brimsley asked. He suddenly realized he didn't know. And he wanted to.

"Sisters?" Reynolds repeated. "Two. Both older. You?"

Brimsley shook his head. "It was only me. My parents had me late in life." And then, even though Reynolds hadn't asked, he said, "They're gone now."

"I'm sorry."

"So am I," Brimsley said softly. He'd been alone for so long. Maybe it was why he loved palace life so much. It had given him a place to belong.

But he did not want to grow maudlin. He nodded toward the bedchamber doors. "Do you think they will want to see each other?"

"It's an odd day," Reynolds reminded him.

"So perhaps . . . a quiet one?"

"The King has already—" Reynolds suddenly clamped his mouth shut.

"The King has already . . ."

"Taken care of his kingly duties."

Brimsley was positive that was *not* what Reynolds had been about to say. He also knew that Reynolds would not say more, no matter how tenaciously Brimsley pressed him.

He was a vault, that one.

"Will the King be coming down for dinner?" Brimsley asked.

"I don't know," Reynolds replied. His face took on an uncharacteristically pensive expression. "He's tired. He might wish to remain in his room."

"If he makes a decision, please do inform me so that I may relay it to the Queen. She may wish to alter her plans accordingly."

Reynolds turned his head slightly as he quirked a brow. "So what you are saying is: If he stays in his room, she is *more* likely to eat in the dining room?"

"I honestly do not know. They're most unpredictable."

"Royals?"

"Yes." There was a world of exhaustion in that word.

Reynolds chuckled. Then, after another few moments of companionable silence, he sighed and straightened his shoulders. "We had best return to our duties."

"Once more into the breach?"

Reynolds gave him another smile—the kind that made his heart flip. "Something like that."

Reynolds turned toward the King's chamber and Brimsley turned toward the Queen's, and they said goodbye without saying a word.

For one brief moment, the world hung in perfect balance.

BUCKINGHAM HOUSE
THE DINING ROOM
...
22 OCTOBER 1761

An even day.

One had to be especially on one's guard on even days.

The King and Queen had not chosen to dine together the night before, and while Brimsley held every hope that the two would reconcile (which did require that they spend time in each other's company) even he had to admit that it was nice to have an evening away from the unrelenting tension.

If fury were a solid thing, the entire palace would be swimming in custard.

Except custard tasted good. And it did not throw vases.

But today was a day that ended with a two. So Brimsley and Reynolds were stationed in the dining room along with six Jameses and a host of maids, and they were all watching the King and Queen with lip-biting trepidation.

"Would you please not breathe so very loudly?" the Queen sniped.

Really? Brimsley winced. Even he thought she was being unreasonable. And he always took her side.

The King stabbed a piece of meat and glared at her. "Would you please not talk?"

"I will talk if I wish to talk."

"Well, then, I will breathe if I wish to breathe."

She let out a long-suffering sigh. "It is just that you do it in such an unpleasant manner."

"Breathe?" he drawled, his eyes gogging with as much sarcasm as disbelief.

She did a little royal flick with her hand as if to say, *I said what I said*.

"That is the thing about life," the King droned, much as if he were delivering a lecture. "Human life, to be more precise. One needs to breathe. One might even say *you* need to breathe, although right now I'm not entirely convinced you are human."

"You would know."

"What does that mean?"

She shrugged and looked up at one of the Jameses. "Have we any herring?"

"No fish near the King," Reynolds reminded the room.

"Yet another reason why I prefer to dine without him," the Queen announced.

The King slammed his fists on the table. "What exactly is the problem? You have been behaving like a child since my first morning here and I have been—"

But the Queen had jumped to her feet. Brimsley took a step forward. Then he caught sight of her face and took a step back.

"You have been breathing my air!" she yelled.

Dear God. They had gone over the edge. The both of them.

Brimsley shot a look at Reynolds. Should they go?

Reynolds did one of those tiny head shakes one does when one wants only one other person to see it.

Not that the King and Queen would have noticed a volcano erupting beside them by that point. The King growled and strode around the table. When he finally stopped, he was mere inches from the Queen.

Brimsley gulped. This was not going to end well.

"Shall I leave?" the King said, his voice low and provoking.

"Yes." The Queen's chin jutted out in defiance. "Leave. Now."

And then—

Oh dear God.

The Queen had grabbed the King by the back of the neck and they were kissing.

"It is an even day," he practically spat.

"It is," she definitely snarled.

Brimsley jumped back just in time to miss an entire plate of roast chicken flying through the air. The King had swept the table clean of the dishes and food and—

"Out!" Reynolds yelled, and together the two of them practically pushed the rest of the staff from the room.

Don't look at the King's bottom. Don't look at the King's bottom.

He looked at the King's bottom.

But to be fair, it was a marv—

"Brimsley!" Reynolds barked.

"Go, go!" Brimsley shooed the Jameses down the hall, along with three maids who had been eavesdropping. He made it back to the dining room doors just as Reynolds got them both closed. They leaned against them, wincing at the sound of glass breaking.

Reynolds sighed. "The crystal."

There was a loud thump. Then a moan. Then a *tremendous* noise, the provenance of which Brimsley could not even begin to imagine, and then the King began to grunt.

"Even. Day."

Brimsley closed his eyes in mortification.

"Even. Day."

He'd seen the King's bottom. It was fairly easy to imagine what he looked like against the table, with the Queen—

He felt his face go *very* hot.

"Are you unwell?" Reynolds asked.

Brimsley adjusted his cravat, keeping his eyes forward. "The day has been . . . heated."

The Queen shrieked.

Reynolds cleared his throat. "My thoughts exactly."

Another sound came from the dining room, loud and lewd. They both flinched.

"I do not suppose you would allow me to . . . ah . . . cool down in your chambers later?" Reynolds asked.

Brimsley straightened. It had been some time since Reynolds had done the asking. It felt rather nice, to tell the truth. "I might allow it," he said. "You can tell me about the doctor."

"There is no doctor."

Brimsley turned and faced him. He was sick of being lied to. "You—"

"Yes! Yes! Yes!"

He snapped back to attention. Forget Reynolds for now. He had a door to guard.

BUCKINGHAM HOUSE
THE ORANGERY
...
2 NOVEMBER 1761

It turned out that it was difficult to maintain a five-pace distance when one had actual business to conduct, so Brimsley permitted himself to walk alongside the Queen while they reviewed her engagement diary.

"Now that the honeymoon has ended," he said, "we have galleries, operas, and plays for you to see. Your Majesty can also do charity works of your choice."

"Wonderful." She beamed. Her mood was beyond cheerful these days, despite her constant arguing with the King. Brimsley suspected it had everything to do with their even day activities, but of course, it was not his place to speculate.

"I should like to do something for poor mothers in the hospital," she decided.

"Very good, Your Majesty. I shall see to—"

The Queen reached up to pluck an orange from a low-hanging limb.

"Orange!" Brimsley barked.

Two attendants came rushing forward. The quicker of the two picked the orange and set it gently into the Queen's hand.

"As I was saying," Brimsley continued, "I shall see to those arrangements posthaste. Also, you will meet the rest of your ladies-in-waiting tomorrow."

"This is absurd." The Queen frowned at the orange in her hand, then frowned at him. "I will get my own oranges from now on."

Brimsley pondered the delicacy of the situation. It was indeed absurd that she could not pick her own oranges. On the other hand, there likely wasn't enough work in the orangery to justify the employment of two attendants. Right now, half of their job consisted of standing around and picking oranges for whichever royal personage happened by.

"Your Majesty—" Brimsley began.

"It is ridiculous to make someone else pick my orange. I shall pick my own oranges. There will be no discussion."

"I—" But he decided not to argue. How could he? She was the Queen. Instead he gave his most gracious nod and said, "Yes, Your Majesty."

"And what about formal engagements?" Charlotte inquired, blissfully unaware that she had probably just cost a man his job. "Balls? Dinners? How often am I to host palace events?"

"The King does not allow social events at the palace. Of any kind."

The Queen paused in her promenade. "How very odd. Well, we can go out to socialize, I suppose. I merely thought—"

"He does not socialize," Brimsley said. He would have thought she knew this by now.

"Surely with the titled class . . ."

"He does not attend any gatherings of the *ton*, Your Majesty."

She turned and regarded him with a piercing expression. "Why not?"

"I . . ." Brimsley blinked. "You know, I truly do not know, Your Majesty. It is simply his way."

"Has it always been his way?"

Brimsley thought back over the past few years. "For a time. Yes."

"But why? He does not seem shy with people. He has no stutter. His social graces are intact. He has a nice smile. He is tall and strong and handsome and smells like . . . a man."

Brimsley smiled. She could have been describing Reynolds.

"It may have something to do with the doctor," Brimsley thought aloud.

"Doctor? What doctor?"

Bloody. Hell. He had not meant to say that.

"I could be incorrect," Brimsley said quickly. "In fact, I'm sure I misspoke."

Charlotte leaned in, imperious and terrifying. Then she backed up and snapped at the rest of the servants. "Leave us!"

Brimsley took a step back, but she quelled him with a stare. "Not. You. Now tell me," she said, "*what doctor?*"

Agatha

Agatha hated these teas.

The tea was exquisite. The biscuits divine. The company?

Far too royal.

One could not say no when the King's mother extended an invitation. One stopped everything one was doing, pulled out one's finest day dress, and headed out to the carriage posthaste.

The urgency of the whole thing provided one small favor, though. Lord Danbury had been about to pounce when the summons had arrived. So Agatha had managed to get out of doing *that*.

Even Danbury understood that the King's mother took precedence.

"You are good to come," Princess Augusta said once Agatha had settled into her chair.

"You are kind as always to invite me."

Augusta got right to the point. "I am told you have visited with the Queen several times."

Agatha accepted a teacup from a maid. She did not have to tell her how she took it. They knew this by now.

"We enjoy walking in the garden," Agatha said.

Princess Augusta leaned forward. "So she is confiding in you."

"She is."

"Well?"

Agatha decided to lie. "She and the King are now very happy to-gether."

"Really."

It was not a question, more of a statement of doubt.

"Indeed," Agatha said, taking a delicate sip of her tea. "After a few strained first days, they enjoyed a wonderful honeymoon. And the coronation has only drawn them closer."

"They did look lovely in the abbey," Princess Augusta murmured.

"Oh, indeed. The very picture of bliss." This, at least, was not a lie. Whatever faults the King and Queen had, no one could say they were not splendid actors. They had smiled and waved, held hands and kissed . . . If Agatha had not been forced to listen to all of Charlotte's complaints, even she would have thought the royal couple madly in love.

"I hate him," Charlotte had said just the day before. "He is infuriating. He makes everyone think he is so very polite, but it is a lie. He is a lying liar who . . ."

Dear God, save me, Agatha had thought.

". . . lies," Charlotte finally finished.

But Agatha knew what it was like to be in a loveless marriage, so she tried to be as supportive as she could. "You shall survive this," she told Charlotte. "As long as you remain steadfast on—"

"Becoming with child," Charlotte interrupted testily. "Please. I know."

Agatha opened her mouth to say more, but Charlotte was not done.

"I *am* steadfast," Charlotte said. "I am the very definition of steadfast. I am *standhaft*. I am *inébranlable*. I will be steadfast in a fourth language if you but find me an interpreter. It is all I do. All we do. Try to fill my womb with a baby."

"I am so sorry," Agatha said, for truly, it sounded dreadful.

"It is a nightmare."

"It is difficult. I know. The act . . . ." Agatha thought of Lord Danbury, pounding into her, over and over. It was awkward, it was uncomfortable, and God in heaven, it was mind-numbingly boring. She'd taken to composing her shopping lists and correspondence while he did his business.

Charlotte had to endure all that under the watchful gaze of an entire nation. Not *literally*, of course, but still. The Queen had power but no privacy. Her every move was remarked upon, dissected, turned inside out.

Agatha would never have traded places with her, and that was saying a lot. She was married to Herman Danbury, after all.

"I hate everything about him," Charlotte said. "I hate his ridiculous face. I hate his voice. I hate the way he *breathes*."

Breathes? Agatha arched her brows. Surely that was a bit much? "Your Majesty," she said, "you can't possibly—"

"It's intolerable!" Charlotte burst out. "I can't— He—" *Huff huff puff huff puff puff.*

Agatha stared in horror. The Queen was jerking around like she'd been possessed by marionette strings. "Your Majesty," she asked carefully. "Are you unwell?"

"That is how he *breathes*!" Charlotte practically yelled.

That was definitely not how the King breathed, but Agatha was far too wise to make a point of this.

Just as she was too wise to share any of this with Princess Augusta.

"Is she showing any signs of being with child?" the Princess asked. "Do we think there will be a baby soon?"

Agatha forbore to point out that the King and Queen had been married for barely two months. Even if Charlotte *had* managed to get herself with child so quickly, there wouldn't be any signs yet. Instead she said, "I have not noticed anything."

"Keep your attention on it," Princess Augusta commanded. "There is pressure."

Now this was interesting. Agatha kept her face purposefully bland as she asked, "From Lord Bute?"

"It is none of your concern where the pressure comes from."

Agatha waited. One, two . . .

"Yes, Lord Bute," Princess Augusta said testily. "We need a baby. A royal baby is a cause for celebration for the commoners. For the entire nation. It is a sign of love to all and ensures the succession of the bloodline."

"Of course," Agatha said.

Princess Augusta leaned forward, but just an inch. "A baby seals the Great Experiment. We cannot fail."

Agatha saw her opening. "Perhaps," she suggested, "a ball would help with the Great Experiment?"

"A ball?"

"Yes. Lord Danbury and I would like to throw the first ball of the Season."

This was not strictly true. Lord Danbury very much wanted to throw the first ball of the Season. Agatha thought it was a terrible idea. Danbury was sure everyone would attend and make merry now that he'd gained membership at White's, but she knew better. Most of the *ton*—the old *ton*, that was—would decline an invitation from the Danburys. They would coo and fake their smiles and say things like, "We are so sorry to miss it," and then they would gather somewhere else at the same time and laugh.

Agatha had warned him that Princess Augusta was unlikely to approve. His response had been so despondent that it had almost broken Agatha's heart. He had looked so sad and small when he said, "They dangle joy in front of me and never let me grasp it."

Agatha, despite all the ways she disliked her husband, had said to him, "You are every bit as good as they are."

Because it was true. The things that made Herman a terrible husband were true of all men, at least as far as Agatha could make out. And she could not abide him being made to feel less than a man simply because of the color of his skin.

And so Agatha had promised she'd try. Maybe she'd even succeed. She had talked the King's mother into giving them property, after all. How hard could a party be?

"Your Royal Highness," she said with all due deference, "as one of the Queen's ladies, it makes sense that I would host the first ball of the Season. It would be such an uplifting display of unity for the *ton*, would it not?"

The Princess was shaking her head before Agatha even finished. "The first ball of the Season? With you? No. That will not be accepted."

Agatha had led a far more sheltered life than her husband. She had not experienced the day-to-day cuts and insults that wore a body down, that slowly added up until the wounds gaped and festered.

Or maybe it was just that she had not tried. Unlike her husband, she had not tried to enter establishments she knew would not accept her. She had not attended schools where she would never be treated as an equal, she had not entered banks only to have them take her money but not offer her tea.

Now Princess Augusta was cutting her off before she could even make her case. She was telling her point-blank that she was not good enough, that the Danburys were not good enough, that the entire new *ton* wasn't good enough.

This was not acceptable.

Agatha set down her cup. It was time to be a bit more direct. "Your Highness, I know you would like our teas to continue. It would be so difficult for you to hear about the Queen being with child long after the fact, would it not?"

The Princess sighed.

Agatha picked up her tea again. She needed the porcelain to hide her smile.

"I shall take it up with Lord Bute," Princess Augusta said.

Damn. Agatha knew what that meant. No permission would be forthcoming.

She had a decision to make.

It took her three seconds.

The Danburys would indeed host the first ball of the Season. She just needed to make sure the invitations were delivered before Princess Augusta had a chance to take the matter up with Lord Bute.

Purple, she thought as she made her way home. She'd always liked purple. It would be a marvelous color for the decorations. Purple with silver and white. She could picture it all in her mind.

Which was where it would likely stay. Lord Danbury would want to do the house up in gold. His favorite color.

No matter. It was a small battle. Meaningless in the long run. Herman might think he was in control, and she was mostly content to allow him this fantasy.

She knew the truth. She might not have thought of the Great Experiment, but she was now in charge of it. And she would not allow it to fail.

A week later, Agatha was not feeling so sure of herself. The replies to the Danbury Ball invitations had begun to arrive, and thus far, not a single member of the old *ton* had accepted.

Princess Augusta had formally asked her to cancel.

Well, *ask* might be overstating it. What Augusta had actually said was, "Your ball will be the ruin of the Great Experiment. You will cancel it."

The worst part was, Augusta was not wrong. It would be a disaster if the Danburys hosted the first ball of the Season and only half the *ton* attended. It would prove all the naysayers right: Society could not be united, and it was useless to try.

Through all this, Queen Charlotte was oblivious. She made no effort to understand British society beyond the pretty stone walls of her palace. Agatha tried not to be angry; the poor girl was barely more than a child. She had been ripped from her home, married to a stranger, and tasked with changing an entire culture.

Except no one had told her this. It would have been funny if it were not so dire. Great Britain stood on the precipice of something truly great and uplifting, and all because a young girl with brown skin had been chosen as Queen.

But she didn't know. Charlotte did not realize that she was the symbol of hope and change for thousands. No, not the symbol. She *was* the hope and change.

Agatha tried to be patient. Charlotte deserved time to acclimate to her new life. She was only seventeen.

But Agatha—and the rest of the new *ton*—didn't have time. The Great Experiment was *now*.

Princess Augusta liked to talk about how important this all was, that the Palace must remain steady in its quest to unite society, but Agatha knew that Augusta did not truly care about the fates of the Danburys and the Bassets and the Smythe-Smiths. She simply did not want to look like a failure. Augusta wanted the Great Experiment to succeed because *she* had orchestrated it. Nothing mattered more to the King's mother than the reputation of the royal family.

But for Agatha—and Lord Danbury and the Bassets and the Smythe-Smiths and so many others—it was more than reputation. It was their lives.

Agatha had to fight for this. She had to.

So for the first time, she traveled to Buckingham House without a summons. No one anticipated her arrival when she walked through the grand portico and informed the head butler that she was there to see the Queen.

It was hard to believe that this was her life, that she could walk into a royal palace with every expectation of being received. She liked to think that such disbelief had nothing to do with the color of her skin. Surely anyone would be astonished to find oneself on such close terms with royalty.

And yet here she was.

"Lady Danbury."

She looked up. It was Brimsley, the Queen's favorite servant.

"The Queen is in the library, my lady," he said. "I shall bring you to her."

"Is she reading?" Agatha asked, making conversation as they made their way down one of Buckingham House's long, elegant halls. "She mentioned she wished to read more in English. She said she still thinks in German much of the time."

"I could not speculate on her thoughts," Brimsley said, "but no, she is not reading."

"Oh. What is she doing, then?"

He cleared his throat. "She enjoys the view."

"From the library?"

"It looks out on the vegetable garden, my lady."

"The vegetable garden," Agatha repeated, because surely she had not heard correctly.

"Yes," Brimsley said with a nod.

"How scintillating."

"She finds it such."

Royals, Agatha thought. She would never understand them.

Indeed, when they entered the library, the Queen was standing by a window, practically pressed up to the glass.

"Lady Agatha Danbury, Your Majesty," Brimsley announced.

"We were not meant to gather today," Charlotte said without turning around.

"I hoped to speak with you without the other ladies-in-waiting," Agatha said.

"All right," Charlotte said, her attention still fully on the scene outside. She motioned with her hand for Agatha to come near.

"It is about the ball I am hosting," Agatha said, once she'd joined her.

"You are hosting a ball. How lovely."

Spoken with complete disinterest. Still, Agatha pressed on.

"I know that you will not attend," she said, "as the King does not accept social engagements."

"Is that not odd?" Charlotte finally turned to face her. "Do you know why?"

"I do not. I . . ."

But Charlotte was back to the window. What on earth was she look-ing for? Agatha stepped beside and peered out. There was nothing there. Just gardens and . . . more gardens. The Queen was literally watching cabbage grow.

Agatha took a breath. "The ball," she said succinctly. "I wanted to ask if you would encourage the other ladies-in-waiting to attend."

"Did you not invite them?"

"I did."

"Then what is the issue?"

Agatha reminded herself that Charlotte was young. In a strange place. A strange country. Surely she had to be forgiven for being so un-fathomably dense. "Your Majesty," Agatha said, very patiently, "they will not come if—"

"There he is!" Charlotte exclaimed.

Agatha almost groaned.

Charlotte's entire face scrunched as she scooted to the left for a bet-ter view of—

Agatha peered across her.

—the King, apparently.

Now Charlotte was shaking her head. "Is he actually . . . ? I believe he is actually gardening."

"Your Majesty?" Agatha said.

"It's George," Charlotte said in utter bewilderment. "He is gardening. With his own hands. Why would he do that? There are people." She turned to Agatha. "We have people."

"Your Majesty," Agatha practically ground out, "about the ball . . ."

"I thought perhaps it was a ruse, but every day he marches into that garden. It is so curious."

For the love of—

Agatha snapped.

"Your Majesty," she said sharply, positioning herself squarely between Charlotte and the window. "Please."

"What are you doing?"

"Princess Augusta has asked me to cancel my ball."

Charlotte gave her an impatient look. "I do not understand how this relates to me. If Princess Augusta has already asked—"

"You are the Queen," Agatha cut in. "And I understand that this feels beneath you. But if you were not the Queen—"

"But I am," Charlotte said quite simply.

Agatha fought the urge to strangle her. "But if you were *not*, your life here would be very different. Do you not understand? You are the first of your kind. You have opened doors. And made us the first of *our* kind."

Charlotte grew still.

"You have changed things for us," Agatha said quite explicitly. "We are new. Do you not see us? What you are meant to do for us? I tell you to consummate your marriage. I tell you to become with child. I tell you to endure. *For a reason.*"

Agatha dared a quick glance at Brimsley to see if he would interrupt. She was treading on very thin ice. But the Queen's man did nothing, and Agatha grew ever bolder.

"You are so preoccupied with whether a man likes you. You are not some simpering girl. You are our Queen. Your focus should be your country. Your people. *Our side.* Why do you not understand that you hold our fates in your hands? Please, you must look beyond this room." She motioned out the window at the King, who was hoeing, of all things. "You must look beyond this garden."

Charlotte said nothing.

Agatha did the only thing there was left to do. She curtsied. "Your palace walls are too high, Your Majesty."

CHARLOTTE

Charlotte was not accustomed to being scolded. As a child, yes, she supposed her mother had criticized when she was not behaving in a ladylike manner, but that had never really bothered her. When Princess Elisabeth Albertine scolded her youngest daughter, her youngest daughter generally made a game of it.

How many ways was *Mutti* wrong? How could Charlotte outwit her? The document insisting upon her right to swim in the lake had been only the beginning. Charlotte was smarter than her mother. She was smarter than everyone in her family except maybe Adolphus, and even he could only hope to call it a tie.

But Agatha Danbury was also intelligent. Very. When she'd taken Charlotte to task in the library, it had stung. Because Agatha was right. Charlotte had been selfish. She hadn't been paying attention to the people around her.

She had every excuse. She'd been in London, what—two months? No one could expect her to change the world in two months.

Except she was Queen.

Like it or not, she was not the same as other people. And apparently, people *did* expect her to change the world in a month.

She sighed and made her way to the edge of the orangery. It was rain-

ing, and the water hit the glass walls with satisfying pats. The sound
was even and regular, like a well-trained percussor in an orchestra.

She missed music. She'd had young Mozart out to perform, but other
than that—

Charlotte looked at her hand. She'd picked an orange without realizing it. She turned and looked at Brimsley, five paces away as always.

"I have picked my own orange," she said.

His face remained impassive. "You have, Your Majesty."

Charlotte looked around. "Where are the men who serve the orangery?"

"They are not needed, Your Majesty."

"You dismissed them?"

"You pick your own oranges now, Your Majesty," Brimsley explained.

"You did not tell me they would be dismissed."

"You would not have a discussion, Your Majesty."

No one had told her . . .

If she'd known . . .

Brimsley should have tried harder to tell her.

Or maybe she should have listened.

She stared at the orange in her hand. "You have it," she said to Brimsley. She'd lost her appetite.

Charlotte was still feeling contemplative and unsettled later that night.
It was an even day, and she was in George's room, in bed. She was still
thinking about that orange, and the two men who had lost their positions because she had not bothered to ask questions.

She remembered another conversation she'd had with Brimsley, when
he'd mentioned the doctor in the cellar.

It was time she started asking questions.

She sat up, tugging the sheets to cover her nudity, and looked at
George. "Are you not well?"

He blinked, clearly startled by her question. "Was that not up to
your standards? Because I felt that was quite—"

"No," she said, cutting him off. "You saw a doctor the other day. In
the cellar."

She watched him closely, but his face betrayed nothing.

"I'm not sure what you mean," he said. But his tone was too careful.

"It was Coronation Day," she said.

"And you were in the cellar?"

"Brimsley was. He saw you."

"Ah."

She waited for him to say more. When he did not, she suppressed an exasperated sigh and said, "That is all you're going to say? Ah?"

He picked at the sheets with his fingers. "I do not like being spied upon by your servant."

"He wasn't spying on you. He was down there for— Well, I don't know why he was down there. He just was. And he saw you. With a doctor. But not the Royal Physician. He said it was someone else."

George frowned. Charlotte could not tell if he was trying to remember the occasion or decide what to say.

"You say it was Coronation Day?" he finally replied. "That was why. The Crown must be examined on Coronation Day."

"In the cellar?"

He shrugged.

"You would think they would want to examine the Queen as well," she said. "It is all anyone cares about. Me making a baby. You would think there would be doctors all over me."

"You would not like that," he said.

"I did not say that I would. In fact, I'm quite certain I would hate it."

His nose crinkled, and he glanced over at the window. But Charlotte did not get the impression he was looking at something so much as he was *not* looking at her.

Especially since it was night, and the curtains were drawn.

"And yet," she said, almost thinking aloud, "there were no doctors for me. Even though I'm the one who has to carry the baby."

"I'm not sure—"

She cut him off. "Instead there are doctors for you. In the cellar, of all places."

"It seems important to you that we were in the cellar."

"Because the cellar feels like a secret."

"The cellar is where his examination room is."

"His examination room is in the cellar," she repeated.

"That is what I just said."

She shook her head. "It seems very strange. Why would a doctor be in the cellar?"

"I do not know who assigns such spaces," he said with a shrug.

"No, of course not," she murmured. He was far too busy to take responsibility for such mundane tasks. And then, just when she would have normally donned her dressing gown and headed back to her own room, she asked, "Why will you not let me know you?"

"What?" He looked startled.

Wary.

"What are you about?" she asked. "You refuse to hold court. You will not go out."

"I have duties to attend."

"Your duties are not like any king I have known. How do you spend your days?"

He gave a little shrug. "Farming."

"Truly?" It seemed impossible to believe, despite what she'd seen with her own eyes. What sort of king chose to spend his days in the dirt? Perhaps as a hobby, an hour here or there . . .

He nodded.

"And you find that satisfying? To spend the entire day in the garden?"

"I rarely get to spend the entire day there. I wouldn't mind it, though. I told you that I enjoy science. Part of that science is agriculture. I enjoy farming."

"So King George is Farmer George."

"Yes," he said, almost as if he were daring her to mock him. "Farmer George. I am Farmer George. These are the hands of a king and farmer. A farmer king."

He held them out. His nails were square and neatly manicured, but one had a dark line of dirt underneath. She smiled. He must have somehow missed that one when he'd bathed.

He truly did love to work with his hands, she thought with some wonder. Not everyone did.

She traced that little line of dirt with her thumb.

"Sorry," he said quickly. "I—"

"No," she said, covering her hand with his. "I like it. It's honest."

It felt like *him*.

Just George.

What would his life have been if he had not been born to be King? Would he have been happier?

The clock chimed.

Midnight.

"It is no longer an even day," George pointed out.

"It is not. It is decidedly odd."

"What is going on, Charlotte?" he asked. "Why are you asking so many questions? You usually leave after . . ." He tipped his head toward the bed.

"You live for the happiness and the misery of a great nation," she said softly.

"Charlotte—"

"No." She laid a gentle hand on his arm. "I am saying I understand. You live for the happiness and the misery of a great nation. That must be exhausting. And lonely. You must feel caged. No wonder you spend so much time in the garden."

"In the garden I am a regular man."

"Farmer George."

"Do not feel sorry for me. I do not know anything else. I have always been this. An exhibit instead of a person."

It sounded awful. It *was* awful. She knew this because it was what her life had become. She, too, had become an exhibit. She was never alone. Even when there was no one to talk to, when she sat at a dining room table with a dozen empty chairs, she was not alone. There was always a small horde of servants standing at attention, watching her every move.

When she was a child, though, she'd run free. She'd run wild, even. He had never been given such autonomy.

The irony. A king with no freedom. What a life he led.

She took his face in her hands. "You are a person to me. You can be a person with me."

His eyes met hers, and for the first time in weeks, she forced herself to truly look into those depths. She saw caution, and wariness, but she also saw hope.

He touched her cheek.

"Will you kiss me?" she asked softly.

He nodded, and his lips brushed against hers. It was gentle, and it was real.

"No more even and odd days," Charlotte said.

He smiled and rested his forehead on hers. "We shall just have days."

"Days," she murmured. Days sounded lovely. Just Charlotte and Just George.

He took her hand, rubbing his thumb lightly over the backs of her fingers. "Can I ask, what brought this on?"

"I picked my own orange."

"You picked your own—"

"Do not ask. I could not possibly explain."

He nodded. "Very well."

"George," she said. "I know you do not owe me anything after how I have behaved. And I know you do not like social events. But I need us to do something."

"What do you need?"

She thought about Agatha Danbury. And all the new nobles whose lives and positions hung in a balance for which she held the scales. It was not difficult, what she had to do. In fact, it was almost laughably easy.

She turned to her husband and said, "Our palace walls are too high."

DANBURY HOUSE

THE BALLROOM

...

6 DECEMBER 1761

"Are you ready, Your Majesty?"

Charlotte turned to her husband and beamed. "I am, Your Majesty."

They had dressed in their royal finest, George in silvery white brocade and Charlotte in an intricately draped gown of the palest of pink. The fabric had been studded with hundreds of crystals, and she sparkled like the night sky.

George nodded to the Danbury House butler, who boomed, "His Majesty King George III and Queen Charlotte!"

The ballroom, which had been a hive of activity, went silent in an instant. Charlotte swallowed her nerves; she was going to need to get used to this sort of thing. She stepped forward, her arm linked with George's.

She looked to the left side of the room. The old *ton*.

She looked to the right. The new *ton*.

Utterly separate.

"This will not do," George said quietly.

"No," Charlotte said. "It will not."

Together they made their way to their hosts.

"Lord and Lady Danbury," George said, his voice perhaps a little louder than it needed to be. "Thank you for having me."

Lord Danbury swept into a bow. "Your Majesties."

Charlotte met Agatha's eyes. Silently, she said, *I am here. We will not fail*.

Aloud, she said, "Your home is exquisite, Lady Danbury. We are so grateful for your invitation."

"Indeed." George kissed Agatha's hand, then turned and smiled at Charlotte. "I think every Season should begin with a Danbury Ball, don't you, my love?"

"I do," Charlotte agreed. She returned her attention to Lord and Lady Danbury but said loud enough for everyone to hear, "We command it."

Lord Danbury appeared incapable of speech. Luckily for him, Lady Danbury possessed her usual dignity and composure and said, "We are honored, Your Majesties. It will be our very great privilege to host the first ball of each Season."

"We shall of course attend," Charlotte announced. "We would never miss the first ball of the Season."

George gave their hosts one more nod, indicating his intention to move on, and held out his hand to Charlotte. "Shall we?"

The orchestra had gone silent upon the King and Queen's arrival, but when they stepped to the middle of the dance floor, the music began anew. The song was slow and richly romantic.

"Just George," Charlotte whispered as they joined their hands.

"Just Charlotte," he replied with a smile.

Out of the corner of her eye, Charlotte saw Agatha being led out to the dance floor by a member of the old *ton*. Charlotte was not sure of his name, but she thought he might be the husband of Vivian Ledger, one of her ladies-in-waiting.

Old *ton* and new *ton*. United.

Another united couple joined them on the floor, and then another. Then came the Smythe-Smiths, and after that an old *ton* couple, and before long the dance floor was full. Some couples were a blend of old and new, some were not, but they were all dancing the same minuet.

"Thank you," Charlotte said to her husband.

"You never have to thank me," he replied. He tapped one finger to her nose, a quick, affectionate gesture that was absolutely not a part of the dance. "We are a team," he said. "Are we not?"

"We are. We shall do great things."

"Together."

"Together," she agreed. "But I do need you to do one thing without me first."

"And what is that?"

"You must dance with Lady Danbury. The moment our dance is done."

"I would rather dance with you."

"And I would love to have all your dances, but this is more important."

He mock-sighed. "Let us hope all of my kingly duties are as easy as asking Lady Danbury to dance."

"Indeed."

"I do not know if you understand what you have done," George said quietly as they left the dance floor. "With one evening, one party, we have created more change, stepped forward more, than Britain has in the last century. More than I would have dreamed."

Charlotte squeezed his hand. "You can do anything, George."

And maybe she could, too. She was not just Charlotte, not just Lottie.

She was a queen.

She was more than a person, she was a symbol. She had known that, of course, but had not truly understood the import of this before this evening, when she saw it with her own two eyes.

She had power. An accident of birth, as George had once called it. Or maybe it was an accident of marriage. Either way, she had power, and it was time she used it.

It was time she earned it.

"Go dance with Lady Danbury," she said. "I will stand with your mother and appear delighted to converse. It will have much the same effect."

"Mine is the smaller sacrifice," George said.

"Go," Charlotte said, giving him an affectionate nudge. "The sooner you dance, the sooner we can go home and be alone."

"I do like the way your mind works."

She beamed up at him.

"But first, I think there is one more thing we can do."

"Oh? What is that?"

He smiled. "Kiss me."

"Or you could kiss me."

He pretended to consider that. "No, I think you should kiss me."

"Oh, very well." She rose to her tiptoes and gave him a peck on the cheek.

Someone gasped.

"Only a true wife would do that before an audience," George said quietly.

"Am I a true wife?"

"Forever," he vowed. He cradled her cheek with one of his large hands, then leaned down and brushed his lips to hers. It was a soft kiss, a gentle kiss, but it was also a promise. Of love, of respect, and of determination.

Together they would change the world.

Tonight was only the start.

Agatha

Danbury House

...

Later that night

"Thank you, thank you so much."

"It was a delight."

". . . clearly a favorite of the Queen . . ."

"The lemonade was exquisite."

". . . such a beautiful home."

The *ton*—old and new—were making their way from the ballroom to the front door. Agatha and her husband stood on the portico, bidding them farewell.

The ball had been a triumph.

Agatha had danced with the King.

The King!

The King had danced with the Queen, and then he had danced with *her*. And no one else. Not even his mother. He could not have made his approval any clearer.

The Danburys were officially royal favorites.

Society was to be united.

It was a new day in Britain.

There were two victories that night. The first was loud, and everyone understood the implications. The way of the old *ton* was over. Society would mix, and the color of one's skin would no longer determine one's rank.

But the second victory . . . That one was quiet. And it was hers. Agatha would never be able to share it with anyone, but she knew. *She* had done this.

She had spoken truth to power. She had made Charlotte understand that she had responsibilities, that she could use her position as a young queen to change the world.

Just as Agatha could use her position as a young queen's confidante.

Agatha knew of no society or culture where women were afforded explicit power. They had to work behind the scenes, manipulate their men into thinking they came up with all the good ideas.

Being a woman meant never getting the credit for one's accomplishments.

But not for a Queen. A Queen could *act*. She could *do*. She could make things happen.

Or could she? Agatha frowned. She'd asked the Queen to unite society by attending the Danbury Ball, but what Charlotte had really done was get the *King* to attend the Danbury Ball.

Agatha decided not to split hairs. She deserved to feel proud of her accomplishments. And she was certain that as Charlotte grew more comfortable in her new role, she would learn to exert her own power for good.

"Thank you again," the final guests said as they descended the front steps.

"Good night!" Agatha called. She and her husband moved back inside, where the entire staff waited in the front hall.

The butler shut the door. Lord Danbury held up a hand, and everyone watched, breath held. He peered out the window, waiting for the last carriage to depart. And then, when it was clear no one would ever hear, he let out a whoop of joy.

They all did. Danbury, Agatha, all the staff—they roared with happiness, united in their triumph.

"We are a success," Agatha said to her husband. She could not remember ever seeing such a look of joy and pride on his face. She almost hugged him.

He deserved this. For all his faults, and they were many, he deserved this moment of triumph. After a lifetime of slights and insults, he had been named a favorite of the King. He was finally the man he'd always felt himself to be.

It was a beautiful thing.

"The King!" Herman crowed. "He personally wrote to the *ton* to inform them he planned to attend. His favor could not have been more explicit."

"Indeed it could not," Agatha said.

"Lord Ledger invited me on one of his hunts," Herman went on. "And the Duke of Ashbourne mentioned a house party."

"It is marvelous," Agatha said.

"All these things I have been waiting for. They needed only to see me."

"It is true."

"I am a success!" Herman cheered. "Let us go and celebrate!"

He grabbed Agatha's hand and pulled her toward the stairs. He was laughing with happiness, and Agatha wanted to laugh, too, except that—*ugh*—he clearly wanted her to lie with him, and that was the last thing she wanted to do just then.

But it was her job. Just as Coral drew the baths, and Mrs. Buckle baked the bread, Agatha had to lie with her husband and grow the occasional baby. It wasn't as bad as it used to be; for the most part she'd grown accustomed to it. She sometimes even used the time to plot out her weekly tasks and correspondence.

But it wasn't the way she wanted to celebrate the evening.

She sighed as they entered her room. Danbury was very excited. Maybe he would not last long.

"Up you get!" he said, patting her on her bottom.

"Of course, dearest," she said. "Let me just change into my nightgown first."

"No need. We shall do it in your royal gown," he crowed.

And thus she found herself on her hands and knees on her bed, golden silk rucked up on her back. Danbury was having a fine time, thrusting back and forth. Agatha's mind was elsewhere, counting her dance partners. Let's see, first there had been Lord Ledger, then the King, and then she'd danced with Danbury because no one but a husband was brave enough to follow the King.

Then Lord Bute—Agatha suspected that Princess Augusta made that happen—then Danbury's friend Frederick Basset. Then Lord Smythe-Smith, then Sir Peter Kenworthy, then—

That was odd.

Her husband had stopped.

"My lord?"

She turned her head. She hadn't thought he was done, but she hadn't really been paying attention.

"My lord, have you finished?"

He was silent, and heavy on her back. She twisted, struggling under the weight of him, and then he fell over, landing on the floor with a loud thud.

"My lord?" she said again, but this time it was barely a whisper. She crawled to the edge of the bed and looked down. "Herman?"

But there was no reason to say his name. He was flat on his back, eyes wide open.

Dead.

Agatha swallowed. This was . . . She was . . .

Carefully, she edged around her husband's body and gathered her dressing gown. She wasn't quite certain what she was meant to be feeling just then.

She moved back to Lord Danbury and nudged him gently with her toe. Just in case.

He was still dead.

Well.

This changed everything.

She looked ludicrous, her purple dressing gown pulled over her ballgown, but nonetheless, she opened the door and poked her head out into the hall. Her maid, Coral, was waiting in a chair a few feet away.

"My lady," Coral said, rising to her feet. "I have had the upstairs footman bring up water for a bath."

Agatha nodded. This was their standard procedure. Coral had been with her since before her marriage. She knew that Lord Danbury's vigor often meant that Agatha needed a warm bath to soothe her skin.

"Thank you, Coral," Agatha said. She cleared her throat. "Erhm, you need not draw baths as often."

"Nonsense, my lady. It is quite simple now that we have a full staff. Today I have even had the new housemaid press lavender oils. It smells divine, and I'm told it makes the skin less ashy—"

"*Coral*," Agatha said.

Coral blinked.

Agatha spoke slowly and clearly. "You need not draw baths as often."

Coral's eyes went wide. She inched forward. "My lady," she whispered. "We are done?"

Agatha stepped aside and allowed Coral to peer into the room. "We are done."

Coral sucked in a breath, then held up a finger for silence. With a careful click, she closed the door.

Agatha could hold it in no longer. She let out a tiny shriek of joy and threw her arms around the other woman. Together they did a little dance, jumping up and down, then scooting to the side because good heavens, Lord Danbury was still on the floor, and yes, this was undignified and probably amoral, but *she was free*!

Agatha Danbury was finally free.

Coral pulled back, her eyes shining. "Do you want to change first?"

"No, I think— Well, I suppose I should not have the dressing gown." Agatha allowed Coral to pull it off her shoulders and set it back in its place on a chair.

"Are you ready?" Coral asked.

"I am," Agatha said. She was. She really was.

"Good luck. I shall be back in my chair."

Agatha nodded and shut the door. She counted to three, giving Coral enough time to return to her post, and then she screamed.

Good heavens, she had not known she could make such a sound.

"Help! Help! Oh no! Help!"

The door flew open. Coral appeared to be in full panic. "Oh, my lady!" she yelled. "What has happened?"

"It is Lord Danbury!" Agatha cried. "I think he is—"

"No!" Coral exclaimed. "Oh no!"

"My love!" Agatha sobbed. "Oh, my love!"

The hall quickly filled with footmen and maids, most still in their evening uniforms.

"Something has happened to Lord Danbury," Coral said. "Henry, you fetch the doctor. Charlie, wake his valet. Do it now!"

"He is gone!" Agatha wailed. "My love is gone!"

Coral turned back to the rest of the staff, still gathered in the hall. "Wait here. I must make sure everything is dignified for my lady, and then you can come and help."

She poked her head into the room and gave Agatha a look.

Agatha sobbed anew.

"We must remove you from the room," Coral said. "You cannot remain here with his lordship's body."

"Noooo! Noooo! I must stay with him. I must!"

"Come with me, my lady." Coral took her arm and led her out, past all the servants, gazing upon her with compassion. Agatha felt a twinge of guilt at deceiving them all this way, but certain façades had to be upheld.

"I shall take you to the guest room," Coral said.

"What will become of me?" Agatha whimpered. "What will become of us? My children . . . my children . . ."

"Come, my lady, come. The others will see to the doctor when he arrives."

Agatha nodded tearfully, and she let Coral take her to a guest room.

"I will fetch you something else to wear," Coral said, once Agatha was settled.

"Yes." Agatha was still in her golden gown. Herman had called it her royal gown. It was beautiful. Exquisite, really, and it looked gorgeous on her.

But she wasn't sure if she was ever going to wear quite that shade of gold again. She wanted to choose her own colors. She wanted to choose her own gowns.

She wanted to choose her everything.

DANBURY HOUSE
LORD DANBURY'S STUDY

...

SEVERAL HOURS LATER

Agatha had been wandering the house for nearly an hour. She wasn't sure why, except that she wasn't tired, and she felt so odd, and it somehow seemed like she ought to look at her late husband's things.

His relics.

He had been a relic.

But the house was new. Its walls held no memories. That was a good thing. It would be *hers*. Not his.

Never his.

She touched the spines of his books. Had he ever read them? She could not remember seeing him read.

The newspaper. He'd read the newspaper.

The butler ironed the newspaper then gave it to Lord Danbury. Agatha read it when he was through. After that, it went into the fire.

Was there metaphor in that? There must be, but Agatha couldn't find it. Not right then, at least.

"Lady Danbury?"

Agatha looked to the doorway. Coral was there.

"My lady, what are you doing here?"

"Nothing," Agatha said.

Everything.

"Can I do anything for you?" Coral asked.

"No," Agatha said. Then, "Wait."

"Yes?"

"Nanny said the children went right to sleep."

"Dominic had a few questions, but that is to be expected. He is the oldest." Coral regarded Agatha with a kind expression. "Are you cold? Or hungry?"

Agatha shook her head. "They did not seem to feel much upset at the death of their father. Which I suppose is not a surprise. Lord Danbury was a stranger to them. They saw him only a few times a month."

Coral seemed not to know what to say to this. "I can wake Charlie and have him light a fire. Or Cook can prepare a cold plate. Or early breakfast."

"Breakfast?"

"It is almost four o'clock in the morning, my lady."

Agatha's lips parted with surprise. "I did not realize. I am sorry. Coral, please go back to bed."

"I shall not leave you. It is not surprising that you should mourn him. He was your husband, even if—"

Agatha's brows rose.

"Perhaps some tea," Coral said. "Instead of . . . what are you drinking?"

Agatha looked down at the glass in her hand. "Port wine. It is awful. But it is Lord Danbury's favorite. *Was.* Was his favorite."

She set it down. She did not want to drink it.

Her hand was shaking. Why was her hand shaking? She was not upset. She would not miss him. Why was her hand shaking?

"My lady?" Coral sounded concerned.

Agatha slid the glass a little farther away from her. "I was three when my parents promised me to him. Did you know that?"

Coral nodded.

"Three years old. I do not think I fully understood how very small that is until last year, when Dominic turned three. Promised to a man at that age. What were they thinking?"

Coral remained silent.

"I was raised to be his wife," Agatha said, staring at the wall. "I was taught that my favorite color was gold because his favorite color was gold. I was told my favorite foods were his favorite foods. I read only the books he liked. I learned his favorite songs on the pianoforte. I am drinking this port wine because it is his favorite and therefore it must be mine."

She looked at Coral. "I do not like port wine."

"No, my lady."

"As many times as I dreamed and imagined and hoped and planned, I never thought what it would actually feel like to have him be gone. Wiped from this earth. I was raised for him. And now I am . . . new."

Agatha looked at the wine.

"I am brand-new," she said. "And I do not even know how to breathe air he does not exhale."

She turned, faced the door. "I think I will go to bed now."

"Of course, my lady." Coral stepped aside to allow her to pass, but Agatha wasn't quite ready to move.

"This world keeps changing," she said.

"That it does, my lady."

Agatha nodded and finally left. It was time to find her place in this new world.

But first, sleep.

George

George would never be sure why he awakened in the middle of the night. A sound from outside the house, perhaps? The wind? A bird? Or maybe no reason at all.

Who knew why a man's eyelids fluttered open while the moon still shone? All he knew was once he was awake, he was *awake*.

He was, he realized, too happy to sleep.

He was also hungry. He wanted . . . What did he want? Anything but gruel. He would never eat that miserable slop again. Tomorrow—or was it today already?—he would inform Doctor Monro that they were through. He'd thought the doctor's unconventional treatments had been working, but now he could see that it had been Charlotte all along.

She was the key to his health. She fed his happiness.

She would be the making of him.

Just look at what they had accomplished that evening at the Danbury Ball. Society was transformed. And it had been so easy. George had spent so much time bemoaning what it meant to be King that he'd forgotten what it meant to everyone else.

It was an accident of birth. He'd said as much to Charlotte, and he'd meant it. But he could do *good* with that accident. With his new wife at his side, to guide him, to help him . . .

There was nothing he could not do.

But first he needed a snack.

Careful not to wake Charlotte, he slipped from the bed, donned his dressing gown, and exited the room. He wasn't sure of the time. Two? Three in the morning? Buckingham was asleep, and he saw no reason to wake anyone in his quest for a bite to eat.

How difficult could it be to find a piece of bread and cheese?

He knew where the kitchens were; he passed them each day on his way to Doctor Monro's laboratory. Would he have known where to go at St. James's? Now there was an interesting question. He didn't think he'd ever been to the kitchens there.

No matter. Buckingham was his home now. With Charlotte. This was what mattered.

It was colder in the cellar, and he was regretting not having donned his slippers as he neared the kitchen. Why *did* feet get colder than the rest of one's body? It must be the distance from the heart. One's blood wasn't as warm when it reached the toes.

He paused for a moment to rub one foot against the other, then stepped through the doorway, and—

He was not alone.

"Monro," he said, stopping short just a step into the room. "What are you doing here?"

Monro looked up from a pot he was stirring on the stove. "Can't sleep, Your Majesty?"

"No, just—"

"Your insomnia does not surprise me," Monro cut in. "This is not the correct environment for you. We were making much more progress at Kew."

"I am not returning to Kew."

Monro's mouth puckered with irritation. "I worry about the effects of this whole place. Since you moved to Buckingham, you have not been to the chair once. If we do not resume treatment soon, we risk losing everything we have accomplished."

"We?" George almost laughed. "You and I, doctor, have accomplished nothing. Anything accomplished for me has been the work of my bride. Her methods have done more for me than you and your chair ever could."

"*Methods*," Monro scoffed. "Bah. She has no education. No learning. If Your Majesty thinks she helps you—"

"I know she does," George interrupted. But there was no way Monro would ever understand the redemptive power of joy. That evening—at the Danbury Ball—it had done more for George's soul than any ice bath or birch rod ever could.

"Your Majesty forgets himself," Monro said testily. "You grow reckless. You give free rein to your most capricious urges."

George crossed his arms. "So does she."

"My point exactly," Monro muttered.

George walked slowly across the kitchen, trailing his fingers along a wooden counter. "When I was an infant," he mused, "my colic was never just colic. My colic was a disaster, an ill omen, the potential ruin of England. When I was a boy, a refusal to eat my peas was the potential ruin of England. An incorrect sum at mathematics, the potential ruin of England. I have lived my entire life in terror of acting incorrectly, because every incorrect action threatened the ruin of England. That terror nearly broke me. I found places to hide. My farms. My observatory."

He turned back to Monro, his eyes hard. "My madness."

Monro said nothing. George located a loaf of bread and tore off a piece. "I thought that terror was the price of being royal. But now . . ."

He popped a chunk in his mouth and chewed. Swallowed.

"Now I have met a woman who is never terrified. Who does as she pleases. Breaks rules. Courts scandal. Commits unthinkable impertinences. And she is the most royal person I have ever known."

Monro shrugged.

"*She* will heal me." George's voice grew sharp. He did not understand the doctor's lack of reaction. It unsettled him.

"It is late, Your Majesty," Monro said. He took the spoon out of the pot, gave it a sniff, and then resumed his stirring. "You'll have to go back to bed. I am not free for treatment just now."

Good God, did the man never listen?

"Perhaps I failed to speak clearly before," George said. "You are no longer my doctor."

"No? A pity." Monro kept stirring, seemingly unbothered. "Nevertheless, I remain the Queen's."

George froze. "What did you just say?"

Monro motioned to the bubbling concoction in the pot. "I am preparing this poultice for her right now."

George's arms began to tingle. A rushing, roaring sound echoed in his ears. His voice, when he found it, felt ripped from his throat.

"Stay away from her."

Monro smiled. "But, Your Majesty, she came to me."

"She wouldn't," George said.

But Monro was already talking over him. "She heard that the King's doctor was here and apparently, she figured she should not settle for anything less than the doctor to the King." He looked up from his work. "Intelligent woman."

George ignored this little quip. "Why would she need a doctor?"

"Well, obviously, because she is with child."

George's mouth began to shake, lips quivering as if he had something to say. But there was only terror.

"She was not sure," Monro said. His mouth smiled. His eyes did not. "But I am."

"No," George said. "No."

"But why should you be so surprised? It is what you have been working toward, is it not?"

Yes. No. Not yet. He was not ready.

Monro sniffed at the spoon again. "Perfect." He tapped the stem against the side of the pot, letting the errant drips fall back into the swirling mixture. "We shall apply this directly to her— Well, you don't really want all the details, do you?"

George took a step back. It was still black as pitch outside; the only light came from the lanterns he and Monro had brought into the kitchen. The flickers cast sinister shadows onto the doctor's face. George could only wonder what they did to his own.

Did he look scared?

Grotesque?

Insane?

He felt all that and more.

He felt . . .

He felt . . .

He felt too much. He felt much too much. He did not know what to do with it all.

"A royal baby," Doctor Monro said. "Congratulations, Your Majesty. A joyous day for England."

Slowly, George backed out of the kitchen. He did not know what to say. He did not know how to think. This was good news. A baby. It must be good news.

Charlotte. Charlotte with a baby. Charlotte with a baby with a doctor. Doctor Monro.

Doctor Monro liked his chair. And his ice baths. His birch rod and his straps.

Charlotte with a baby.

Charlotte with a baby with the doctor with the chair.

No. Charlotte would not see Doctor Monro. He would not allow it. There must be someone else. Someone who did not know—

Charlotte. Charlotte was a star. A comet. She sparkled. She sparkled with the baby with the doctor with the chair.

He blinked. He was back in his room. How was he here? Had he walked? He did not remember walking.

He looked at his bed. The headboard was red. Red like love. Red like blood.

He looked at Charlotte. She was sleeping. She looked so peaceful.

Did she know?

Did she know she was pregnant?

Did she know he was mad?

Which was stronger? Love or blood?

Charlotte with the baby with the doctor with the—

What was happening? This wasn't the same. Similar, but not the same. Where were the heavens? Where were the stars?

Venus, Transit of Venus.

He ran to the window, wrenched it open.

Why were there clouds? He could not see. He was King. He commanded them to be gone.

Venus. Where was Venus?

He could calculate it. If he could find one star, he could find another, and then he could calculate Venus.

Venus, Transit of Venus.

Charlotte was a star. She sparkled.

A pen. He needed a pen. Where was his pen?

He ran to his desk. No pen, but he had charcoal. Why was there charcoal? He did not care. It didn't matter. He could use charcoal.

He found an empty spot on the wall and began to write. Calculations. Calculus. Equations in balance.

"Transit of Venus," he said to himself. He wrote it, too. *Transit of Venus. 1769. One plus seven plus six plus nine.*

He wrote. He calculated. He wrote more.

George the Farmer, Farmer George, Farmer King, Finding Venus, need to get it right.

Pictures. He needed pictures, too. Geometry. Angles. Isosceles obtuse. Isosceles acute. *Acute acute acute acute.*

"George?" It was her voice, but she was a star. She should not be able to talk.

Transit of Venus, Farmer King, George the farmer, that is not right.

"George, what is going on?"

"Be quiet, you are a star."

He scribbled. He wrote. He calculated.

One plus seven plus six plus nine.

"George, you're scaring me."

"Stop. No. I need to try." He added the numbers. They did not make sense. "Farmer King," he reminded himself. "Astronomer King. Recalculate to find it. Transit of Venus. Venus, Venus, Venus."

He looked at her. Who was she? She was a star. Why was she here? "I have to go," he told her. "I need to see."

Out into the hall. This way to the outside. He could see the sky there. He needed the sky.

Someone stepped in front of him. "Your Majesties. Can I help?"

"George is working," the star said. "Go back to your post. We will be fine."

He was not fine. He needed the sky. Which way to the sky?

The sky the sky. The heavens. Venus. Transit of Venus. One plus seven plus six plus nine. One plus seven plus six plus nine.

This way. Then that way. So many twists and turns to go outside. It was not right. He should be free. He was a farmer. Farmer George. He belonged outside.

"George, it is cold," the star said. "You have nothing on your feet."

His feet did not matter. *One plus seven plus six plus nine.* He was almost there. *One plus seven plus six plus nine.*

He threw open the door and sprinted into the night.

"I SEE YOU!" he yelled. He ran across the grass. Faster. Faster.

But the star kept chasing him. She sparkled like the sky, and she was quick.

"I'm right here," she said. "Don't worry."

"You are not a star," he said. He stared with wonder. He knew who she was. How had he missed it? "You are Venus."

"I am Venus," she said. "Yes, I am Venus."

"I see you! Venus! My angel! I am here!"

He reached for her, but she stepped away. Why? Why did Venus not want him?

"Talk to me," he pleaded. "Do not go! Talk to me! I knew you would come. I knew it. Venus, do not go. Do not go. Do not be afraid. It is me. Do you not know me?"

He tore off his robe. Bared his skin to the night. "Do you not see me?"

"Your Majesty!" someone yelled.

George turned. It was a golden-top. It looked hot. The top was on fire. He should not touch it.

Hot like the sun. Burning like a star.

"Your Majesty," the golden-top said. "I thought perhaps you would like to warm up. Do you remember? When we were small? Hot tea. Or warm milk. With sugar to make it sweet like dessert. We could go inside . . ."

George shook his head. He was not cold. "It is Venus!" he said, pointing to her. "Do you see her?"

"I do, Your Majesty," the golden-top said.

"Say hello!"

"Hello, Venus," the golden-top said. "Your Majesty—"

"Farmer George!" George cried happily. He threw his arms out, stretched them toward the sky. "Astronomer George!"

"Astronomer George, let us cover you up with this . . ."

George eyed him warily. What was the golden-top holding? What was he trying to do? "No, I want Venus," he said. He feinted to the side. The golden-top would not get him. He was too fast. "Only Venus." He looked at Venus and smiled brightly. "Hello, Venus!"

"George," Venus said.

He stepped to the right. The golden-top was still after him.

"George," Venus said again, louder this time. "FARMER GEORGE!"

He stopped. Looked at her.

"I am Venus," she said.

"I know. Hello, Venus. You are Venus."

"Yes. And Venus is going inside. You need to come with me."

"All right." He liked Venus. Venus sparkled. Venus was kind. But wasn't it strange that she was here in the garden? He looked at her curiously. "I thought you were in the sky?"

"I was in the sky," she said, laying a soft hand on his arm. "But now I am going into Buckingham House. Won't you come with me?"

He looked at her, at the house, then at the golden-top.

"Here," she said, and she put something over his shoulders. "This will keep you warm."

"It is cold," he said.

"Come with me," she urged, and together they walked into the building.

"Venus is indoors," he remarked. "A planet. Inside the house. So very odd."

"It is very odd," Venus said. "So very odd."

He turned around. The golden-top was following them, but Venus did not seem to mind. He looked at her, then jerked his head behind them, just in case she had not noticed.

"He is a friend," she said.

"You are sure?"

"I am sure. Come. We are inside now. Venus is indoors. With you. She is with you."

Venus.

He was with Venus.

He smiled. "Thank you, Venus."

She nodded, and for a moment he thought she might be crying, but no, that was not possible. Planets did not cry.

It was just a sparkle. Because Venus sparkled.

Venus was inside.

So very odd.

But she was inside.

With him.

CHARLOTTE

"This way," Charlotte said, gently guiding George through the quiet halls of the palace.

"Venus," he said with a tired smile.

He looked like he might fall asleep on his feet.

"He is heavy," she said to Reynolds, who was hovering two steps behind. Reynolds immediately came forward and supported the King from the other side.

"He is a golden-top," George said.

Charlotte and Reynolds exchanged a look.

"Golden-tops are good," Charlotte said to George. She didn't know what else to say. "They are kind."

"I shouldn't touch it," George said. He giggled. "But I will." He reached out and patted Reynolds's hair.

His shiny *golden* hair. Charlotte finally understood.

"It wasn't hot," George said. "I thought it would be hot."

The blanket slipped from his shoulders, and Charlotte paused to push it back up. He was naked under the blanket, and they were in a very public hall in Buckingham House. It was the middle of the night, and no one seemed to be around, but still.

"Brimsley has secured the area," Reynolds said.

Charlotte just looked at him. She had no idea what those words meant.

"He is making sure no one comes to this part of the house. I told him to lock the servants in their quarters if necessary."

"Oh. Thank you. I suppose." Her words sounded a little bit dead. Certainly blunted.

It was strange. She should have been in a heightened state. She should have been filled with rage, or worry, or something hot and volatile, but instead she felt as if she were sleepwalking. As if her mind and body had cleaved into two.

Somehow her body knew what it had to do—take the King back to his bedchamber, wash the dirt from his body, put him to bed. Her mind, though . . . It was somewhere else. It had questions.

"How long?" she asked Reynolds.

"Your Majesty?"

"How long has he been like this?"

"I . . . could not say exactly, Your Majesty."

Charlotte would have hit him if she'd had the energy. And if she weren't holding up the King. "Could you say inexactly?"

"Some years," he admitted.

"Is this typical? Tonight?"

"This was worse than usual," Reynolds admitted.

They had reached the King's bedchamber. George yawned. "I'm very tired," he said.

"We shall get you into bed soon enough," Reynolds assured him.

"We need to wash him," Charlotte said, her voice still heavy and dull.

"Yes," Reynolds agreed. "Can you stay with him while I fetch some soap and water?"

Charlotte nodded. Whatever devil had possessed George, making him run and yell like a maniac, it was gone now, leaving a very tired man. He yawned again, and she and Reynolds supported him as he sank gently to the floor. They leaned him against the wall—the one now covered with his charcoal scribblings—and he closed his eyes.

"Is he sleeping?" Charlotte asked. It looked as if he was sleeping, but what did she know? She'd never seen a man act as her husband had that night. For all she knew, sleep was no longer sleep.

"I believe so," Reynolds said. "It is common for him to be very tired after . . ."

She looked at him, daring him to say it. To call it what it was.

"I will get soap and water," he said.

"Do."

Reynolds departed, leaving Charlotte alone with George, who was still leaning against the wall with his eyes closed. He was mumbling, though. Nothing she could understand. She could not even make out the odd word here or there. It was as if he had been powered by fire, and the massive flame that had propelled him outside was now down to a flickery little ember.

Exhausted, she sat by his side on the floor. He was twitching, so she took one of his hands in hers, hoping to steady him.

"What is this, George?" she said aloud.

He sighed.

"Was this why you left me and went to Kew? You didn't want me to see you like this."

He mumbled. More nonsense.

Charlotte closed her eyes, then shut them tight, squeezing a tear down her cheek. She was married to this man. And she liked him. She even loved him.

Or did she? The George she loved . . . Did he even exist? Was he just a piece of an unknowable whole, and if so, what size was that shard?

What if Just George—*her* George—was only a sliver?

He talked of mathematics. Very well, she could do sums and products and percentages, too. What percent was *her* George? Would she get him half the time? Three-quarters?

Less?

"What am I to do with you?" she said softly.

He didn't answer. She hadn't thought he would.

There was a soft knock at the door, and Reynolds opened it without waiting for her response. He brought in a basin of water. Behind him, Brimsley carried towels.

Charlotte stared at him. Had Brimsley known? Had he served her all these weeks, five paces away, and never told her that her husband was a madman?

Brimsley swallowed uncomfortably. "If Your Majesty prefers to retire, Mr. Reynolds and I are perfectly capable—"

"Am I not permitted to wash the King?" Charlotte demanded.

Brimsley looked pained. "It is just not . . . usual."

"I confess I still have much to learn about palace procedure," Charlotte snapped. "For instance, I just pulled the King out of a hole in the vegetable garden. Where he was busy discoursing with the sky. *Is that usual?*"

Brimsley did not reply, which was fortunate. Whatever he wanted to say, she did not want to hear it. Not tonight.

"We will do it," Reynolds said to Brimsley. "Just . . . keep watch in the hall."

"Of course," Brimsley said. He stepped out, shutting the door behind him.

"Concentric circles," Charlotte said.

Reynolds looked at her. "I beg your pardon."

"We are concentric circles around the King. You and I, the closest. We wash his body. Then Brimsley. He guards the door. Then— Well, I do not know who then. His mother, I suppose. Lord Bute? Earl Harcourt? I assume they all know."

"They do, Your Majesty."

Charlotte dipped a towel in the basin. The water was warm, but not too hot. Gently, she got to work on George's hands. Reynolds did his feet.

"They all knew," Charlotte said. "How they must have laughed at me."

"No, Your Majesty. They did not."

"And how would you know? I can see that you are close to the King. His most trusted confidant most likely. But you do not attend government meetings. You do not have Parliament's ear."

"Servants hear more than you would think, Your Majesty."

Charlotte let out a grim laugh. "So it was *you* who laughed. The staff."

"No!" Reynolds said. He turned to Charlotte with a fervent expression. "We—I—never laughed at you. On the contrary, you are my greatest hope."

She looked at him. She could feel tears welling in her eyes, but she would not cry. She was the Queen. She would not cry in front of this man.

"You have done more for him than I could have ever dreamed," Reynolds said. "You are good for him."

But is he good for me?

It was a question she could never speak aloud.

St. James's Palace

...

The following morning

Charlotte had not slept.

Once she and Reynolds maneuvered the King onto his bed, she'd returned to her own bedchamber. She'd crawled under her quilts, her body wrapped in the softest of bedsheets, and she lay on her back, staring up at her canopy.

At some point, her numbness had bled into despair. And at some point after that, the despair had given way to rage.

Which was where she was right now.

Enraged.

On fire.

And on her way to see Princess Augusta.

"Your Majesty—"

Charlotte strode down the hall, her boots making angry clacks with each step. "Stop following me, Brimsley."

"I beg you, this will not end well."

Charlotte whirled around, her expression so fierce Brimsley stumbled back a step. "This will not end well, you tell me? This will not end well, you tell me *now*? Where have you been all these weeks up to now? You say you are here to serve me. You say you have pledged your life for my welfare. And yet you keep this secret?"

"I did not know, Your Majesty."

"You did not know," Charlotte practically spat. She had seen him last night. "I do not believe you."

"I did not know," Brimsley cried, and he reached out, almost as if he might grab her arm. But of course he did not. "I suspected," he admitted. "Not this. I could never have suspected this. But I knew that something was being hidden. I tried to find out what. I swear to you I did."

"I can understand this of *her*," Charlotte said, throwing her arm out in a violent motion toward Princess Augusta's sitting room. "She is self-ish. She cares only for the Crown. But you were supposed to be on my side."

"I *am*, Your Majesty."

Charlotte did not respond. She had already reached the sitting room. She barged in without a care for decorum or protocol. Princess Augusta was taking her breakfast with a friend.

"Charlotte?" Augusta smiled with both surprise and affection. "I did not expect you. The Danbury Ball was a triumph. Well done, my girl."

Charlotte could not listen to this. "Has Your Highness ever tried cutting English mutton with a dull knife?"

Princess Augusta went quite still. "I beg your pardon?"

"The knives at Buckingham House used to be sharp enough. Then one day, they were all quite dull."

"I'm sure I do not know what you mean."

"It was the day the King joined me there."

Charlotte fixed a placid expression on her face, waiting for Augusta to respond.

Augusta turned to her companion. "I believe we may have to break our fast another morning, Lady Howe."

Lady Howe departed with all possible haste. Still, Augusta held a hand up until several seconds after the door had been closed behind her.

"You were saying?" Augusta said.

"The knives," Charlotte reminded her. "Suddenly dull. Odd, I thought, but surely a coincidence. Surely a coincidence, too, that the very same day the windows were sealed shut on the upper floors. I found that a little bothersome. I do like fresh air while I sleep."

"I—"

"But suddenly there were locks everywhere. Locks on the armory, in the kitchen, the shed where the gardeners keep their shears. A coincidence, surely." Charlotte stepped forward, her eyes narrowing as they cut into Augusta's. "What I could not quite convince myself was a coincidence, though, was when the library's set of Shakespeare was suddenly missing *King Lear*."

"Forgive me," Princess Augusta said, stone-faced. "I am not a Shakespeare enthusiast."

"Are you not? Then let me educate you. King Lear is the one about the mad king."

"*Charlotte.*"

That was what set her over the edge. Augusta's patronizing, placating tone, as if Charlotte were imagining everything. As if Charlotte were stupid, as if *she* were the one who was losing her mind.

"Do you know what I have realized, *Augusta*?"

Augusta bristled visibly at Charlotte's use of her given name.

"I am living in a madhouse." She paced a few steps to the left, trying to control her emotions. She failed. Whirling around, she practically screamed, "*The King is mad, and I live in a madhouse.*"

"You forget yourself," Augusta warned.

"All this time I thought I was the damaged one, that somehow *I* was deficient. When he is—"

"The King is not mad," Augusta hissed. In front of her, her hands froze into tight claws, as if she needed that moment, that tension to steady herself. "The King is merely exhausted from holding the greatest nation in the world on his shoulders," she said, each word a precise clip of syllables and lies.

"Don't—"

"No, *you* don't," Augusta snapped, shoving her chair aside as she came to her feet. "You come here as if you know everything. You do not. You are a child."

"I am a pawn."

"And perhaps you are. What of it? Are you going to complain? You have been made Queen of Great Britain and Ireland. How *dare* you complain about that?"

"No one told me—"

"Who cares?" Augusta spat. "I certainly don't. What could you have known about it? What could you have understood? The weight of a nation on a boy's shoulders? The weight on his mother as she watches her son start to crack? If, God grant, you ever do bear an heir, then you may start to learn, and your first lesson will be this: You would do anything to stop the cracking. You would engage hideous doctors and their thousand disgusting treatments."

She looked Charlotte straight in the eye and said, "You would scour Europe for a queen grateful enough to aid him."

Charlotte flinched. She wished she had not. She wanted to be strong and proud and unfeeling. More than *anything* she wanted to be unfeeling. Anything to not feel *this*.

"You think the color of my skin makes me grateful?" she said.

"I think you have changed the world."

"I did not ask to change the world."

"I did not ask for a son with rough edges. But that is what I have, and I will protect him with everything I am."

"Rough edges?" Charlotte echoed in disbelief. "He was talking to the *sky*."

"And what of it? You were nothing. You came from nowhere. Now you sit at the helm of the world. What matter is it if your husband has his peculiarities?"

"Peculiarities? You call this a peculiarity? Your Highness, you did not see him last night."

"I have seen him before," Augusta said in a low voice.

"He thinks I am Venus."

"Then be Venus."

Charlotte shook her head, barely able to comprehend what she was hearing. "I did not ask to sit at the helm of the world. I did not ask for a husband. But if I must have one, if I must leave my home, my family, my language, my life . . ."

"What, Charlotte?" Augusta asked. Her voice was oddly flat. "What?"

"It cannot be for a man I do not know. A man I am not *allowed* to know."

"You know him now."

"You fed me a lie!"

"And you ate it willingly."

Charlotte almost laughed. What did it matter now if she had been willing or not? She was married to a king. There was no dissolving it. And she didn't know if she wanted to dissolve it. She just wanted—

What?

What did she want?

Honesty?

Truth?

Trust?

She wasn't going to get any of those things from Princess Augusta.

"Tell me," Augusta said. "Are you with child?"

"I don't know," Charlotte lied. She was fairly certain she was. Doctor Monro had certainly thought so.

"You will tell me the moment you are sure," Augusta ordered.

"I will tell you when I wish to tell you."

"You will find that there is nothing to be gained by being obstinate for the sake of being obstinate."

"Oh, I don't know about that," Charlotte muttered. The pinched expression on Augusta's face was the only bright spot of her morning.

The only bright spot in her whole damned life.

Neither woman saw the man standing in the hall just outside the sitting room. Neither heard his footsteps as he exited the palace and climbed back into the carriage that had brought him there from Buckingham House. And neither knew that he then traveled to Kew, where he found Doctor Monro in his laboratory.

"Your Majesty?" the doctor said. He had been packing his things. He had not expected to see the King.

George walked across the room and sat down in the ghoulish chair.

"Strap me back in."

AGATHA

DANBURY HOUSE
AGATHA'S PRIVATE READING ROOM
...
12 JANUARY 1762

"Lord and Lady Smythe-Smith are here to see you, my lady."

Agatha sighed heavily. She did not want to receive guests, but it had been a month since her husband's death. Good manners dictated that she be left alone for the first few weeks of her mourning, but now it was time for society to pay their respects.

She stood, smoothing her black skirts. "I shall receive them in the drawing room."

"Very good, my lady," her butler said. "I have already put them there."

"Of course."

"Along with the Duke of Hastings."

"What?" Agatha groaned. She had not liked the man when he was Frederick Basset, and she did not like him now that he was the Duke of Hastings.

"And Lord and Lady Kent."

"Is the Tsar of Russia here as well?"

"No, my lady."

The Danbury butler had never had a sense of humor. Herman had hired him, of course.

"But Lord and Lady Hallewell are here."

Agatha regarded the butler with something approaching horror. "And they're all in our drawing room?"

"I sent for tea, my lady."

"But no biscuits," Agatha said. "I don't want them to stay long."

"Of course not, my lady." He opened the door to her reading room so that she could exit, and then followed her out.

"It is so kind of you all to call," she said once she'd entered the drawing room. It was packed to the gills. It seemed like half the new *ton* were there.

She greeted each of them separately, then took a seat on her new sofa. Gold damask, of course. It had been ordered before Lord Danbury's death.

"Agatha, darling," Lady Smythe-Smith said. "We are devastated for you. For your loss. We grieve."

Do you? Agatha wanted to say. No one had liked Herman Danbury, except maybe the new Duke of Hastings.

"He was a great man," the duke said.

"He was a champion," Lord Smythe-Smith said.

Rounded out by Lady Smythe-Smith once again chiming in. "We do grieve."

Agatha waited for a moment. She looked to the Kents and the Hallewells, standing behind the Smythe-Smiths. Their faces were painted with their most compassionate expressions, but they seemed inclined to let the others do the talking.

"However," Agatha finally said. The air positively strained under the weight of unspoken words. "There is a *however* here, is there not?"

Because surely they would not have all come at once to pay their respects. Condolence calls were normally made one by one.

Lord Smythe-Smith cleared his throat. "There is indeed a *however*. And we do apologize for descending en masse. But we need to know. What happens now?"

"What happens now?" Agatha echoed.

"What have you heard?" he asked.

"What do you become?" his wife wondered.

"What do *we* become?" the Duke of Hastings said with greater force.

"Forgive me," Agatha said, looking from one face to the next. "I have not the faintest notion of what you speak."

"You are a trusted member of the court," Lord Smythe-Smith said.

"You are a favorite of the Queen," his wife said.

The Duke of Hastings leaned forward. "Surely the Palace has given you some word. On procedure. On what will happen next."

Agatha blinked. Next?

"Lord Danbury was the first of us to pass away," Lord Smythe-Smith burst out. He mopped his brow with a handkerchief. "The first titled gentleman on our side. And you have a son."

Oh.

Oh.

Agatha finally understood. "You are asking me if my four-year-old son is now Lord Danbury."

"We need to know whether the laws of succession on *their* side will apply to *our* side. Does he inherit the title?"

"I never thought . . ." Dear God. Danbury had been dead for a month, and it had never occurred to her to wonder if they would keep his title. She had just assumed her son's position was guaranteed.

She looked up. At the dozen or so faces fixed upon hers. "We could lose it all in a generation."

"Yes," Lady Smythe-Smith said. "What you lose, we lose. You set the precedent. You *are* the precedent."

The Duke of Hastings regarded her with a surly frown. "Will you remain Lady Danbury or are you just *Mrs.* Danbury?"

"I . . . will find out," Agatha said. What choice did she have?

"As soon as possible, if you please," the duke said.

Lady Smythe-Smith laid her hand on Agatha's. "We are depending on you. All of us."

Agatha smiled weakly. Once again, the fate of the Great Experiment lay heavily on her shoulders.

DANBURY HOUSE
LORD DANBURY'S STUDY

...

LATER THAT DAY

Agatha opened yet another drawer, rifling through papers. She should have done this sooner, if not to settle the matter of inheritance, then because she was now a woman alone, and she ought to understand her finances.

Frankly, she ought to have understood her finances when Lord Danbury was alive, but he would never have allowed access.

"Damn it, Herman," she muttered. His files were ordered with no rhyme or reason. He was not a stupid man. He should have done better.

Coral slipped into the room and shut the door behind her. "His valet did not have any information," she said. "Neither did the butler. Maybe Lord Danbury did not have a solicitor."

"My husband had a solicitor," Agatha said. "He met with him numerous times about . . . things." What sorts of things, Agatha did not know. She had not paid attention. Clearly, she should have done. "I only need find his name."

Coral stood by the door for a few moments, idly picking at the fabric of her apron. "I do try to look on the bright side, my lady."

Agatha looked up with either astonishment or disbelief. She honestly wasn't sure which. "The bright side?" she echoed. She was having difficulty locating that lately.

"You are free," Coral said. "Is that not what you wanted?"

Agatha let out a humorless sigh. "Do you think me free? I thought I would be. I thought Lord Danbury's death would leave me unencumbered, but all I find is that I am saddled with the burden of what it means to be a woman not tied to a man."

"Is that not good?"

Agatha shrugged. "Who knows? I am on my own, but life is out of reach. I have no new freedoms. All I can be certain of is mourning, embroidery, and quiet teas with other widows. Forever."

Coral said nothing. What was there to say?

Agatha slammed one drawer shut and yanked open another. "And now I cannot find the name of the solicitor! I am tasked with preserving the titles of dozens of good people, and I can't even find the name of the man who can help me."

"Would it be so bad, my lady?" Coral asked. "Losing the title."

Agatha looked up. "Yes, Coral. It would be bad. They showed up here—all of them—looking for answers. Depending on *me*."

"Surely it's not your responsibility."

"I made it my responsibility when I insisted on hosting that ball. When I asked the King and Queen to attend. We have given the new *ton* hope. A taste of rare air. Equality. They will not be able to let it go so easily." She flipped through another stack of papers. "And why should they?"

"But—"

"I found it!" Agatha held up a letter, triumphant.

"The solicitor?"

"Yes." She looked at the name. "A Mr. Margate. He will handle this. He will know what to do. I will write to him, and he will come."

Agatha took her seat behind Lord Danbury's desk and began to compose a letter. But then Coral asked, "Do you really think a solicitor will come to see a woman?"

Damn.

Sometimes she hated men. Truly.

"I shall simply sign the letter 'Danbury.' Let us hope he assumes I am a man with poor etiquette."

"But won't he know that his lordship has died?"

"He shall think I am a brother or cousin or anyone but me. That is how men are."

"I do hope you are right, my lady."

"I have to be," Agatha said with a sigh. "I cannot be wrong. Not in this."

DANBURY HOUSE

AGATHA'S BEDCHAMBER

...

THREE DAYS LATER

"A gentleman is here to see you."

"A gentleman?" Agatha looked up from her book.

"He says he is the solicitor," Coral said. "Looking for the lady who does not sign her full name."

"Oh my goodness." Agatha shot off the bed. "Am I presentable? Does this dress look serious enough?"

"It is black, my lady. Black is always serious."

"Yes, I suppose you're right. Mourning is a serious business."

"He is waiting in Lord Danbury's study."

Agatha nodded, shoving her feet into shoes. "Wish me luck."

"You shall not need it."

Agatha gave her a grateful smile and then hurried down the stairs.

"Mr. Margate," she said when she reached her late husband's study. "Thank you for coming."

He was old, and bewigged, and looked as she supposed a solicitor ought.

She moved to Lord Danbury's side of the desk and motioned to the other chair. "Please, sit."

"I am afraid I do not have good news."

Agatha clenched her teeth, but somehow she managed to sound calm when she said, "Please elaborate."

"There is simply no precedent for a case such as this. Not for nothing did they call it an experiment."

"And my husband was the first to die."

Mr. Margate grimaced. Agatha had little experience with solicitors— none, really—but even she could tell that his expression was a special one they employed when they were about to deliver bad tidings.

"The trouble is," he said, "the title and estate were very specifically bestowed on the late Lord Danbury, God rest his soul. Not on you."

"Of course not," Agatha said impatiently. "Titles are almost never bestowed on women."

"Normally it would all pass to the next Lord Danbury."

"I do have a son, you know."

Mr. Margate acknowledged this with the briefest of nods. "But no- where was it clarified whether these new peerages pass to a new genera- tion. It's quite possible they revert to the Crown."

"Leaving me Lady Nothing. With nothing but my husband's old house and money."

Mr. Margate made that expression again.

"Oh no," Agatha said. "Now what?"

"It is only . . ." He sighed heavily. "When your husband accepted the new estate, he used a sizable amount of his holdings to support your new life. Tailors, club payments, horses, extra staff . . ."

Agatha shook her head. There was no way she believed what she was hearing. "My husband had one of the greatest fortunes in all the Continent. Have you heard of Sierra Leone, Mr. Margate? Do you know the riches there? The diamond mines?"

"I am afraid your husband may have exaggerated his wealth to you. He also spent quite a bit to maintain a life worthy of a lord."

"He had not possessed the title for long."

"But even before. His clothing. *Your* clothing . . ." He eyed her black bombazine as if that were somehow responsible for her current downfall.

Agatha wanted to scream. She wanted to leap across the desk and wring this man's throat. But she didn't. She held on to her dignity, because apparently that was all she had to hang on to.

"You say he spent more freely once he was made a lord," she said.

Mr. Margate nodded.

"So, due to this peerage, which we may not even be able to keep, I am to be left . . . what? Penniless? What about our old house?" They had not been in this new estate long.

"It was leased. The owners have already let it to new tenants."

"I am not just penniless. I am homeless, too."

Mr. Margate grimaced again. Agatha was starting to wonder if they taught that particular expression as a part of law studies. One could not be certified as a solicitor until one learned the bad news grimace. It needed just a touch of false sympathy to truly qualify.

"What am I to do?" she asked.

"Why, what all impoverished widows do. Seek the kindness of a male relative. Or remarry."

DANBURY HOUSE
THE FRONT HALL
...
TWO DAYS LATER

Mr. Margate was right. Agatha *did* need to seek the help of a male relative. The galling part, though, was that this male relative was her four-year-old son.

"Dominic, please," she said as she waited by the door. "Let Nanny tie your cravat."

"Come, scamp," Nanny said. "It is just a neckerchief."

"More like a hangman's noose!" Dominic howled.

Agatha rolled her eyes. He had no idea.

"Oh ho," Nanny scolded. "Such impertinence."

He grinned at her. It was a smile he never gave to his own parents. Agatha felt a twinge of regret. She would do something about that. She would be a better mother than she had been, but today was not the day for her to tease out his smiles.

"Dominic, stop that at once," she said sternly. "This is an important day, and you must behave."

He looked to Nanny for guidance. She gave him a little nod. "Be a good boy," she said. "Listen to your mother."

Agatha took his hand and led him out to the waiting carriage.

"When are we returning to Nanny?" he asked.

Agatha swallowed. "Dominic," she said, her voice softer than it had been for weeks, "I am sorry you do not know me. I did not know my parents well, either, and I know it must be very frightening to leave Nanny like this. But I am your mother, and your father is gone to the angels, and now you are the man of the family."

He looked at her with solemn four-year-old eyes. "The man of the family."

God help them.

Agatha soldiered on. "Your family needs you to do your duty."

"All right, then." He thought about that for a moment, then brightened. "We are going to meet a princess?"

"We are."

"A real one?"

"Very real."

"Will she be wearing a crown?"

Agatha thought about that. She didn't think she had ever seen Princess Augusta without a tiara. "Probably."

"Will she like me?"

"I do not see how she could not."

Dominic smiled. He peered out the window as they began their journey. It would not take long. The new Danbury House was exceedingly well located, barely a mile away from St. James's Palace.

"Did you know I can count, Mother?" Dominic asked.

Agatha had not known this, but she lied and said, "Of course."

"One. Two. Three."

His little head nodded with each number.

"Four." He paused. "I am four."

"I know."

"The next is five," he said. "That is what I will be soon."

"Perhaps we shall have a party."

"With cake and biscuits?"

"Absolutely with cake and biscuits."

Dominic clapped his hands together and resumed his count. "Six comes next," he said. "Then seven. Eight." He looked back up. "I'll need help after nineteen."

"I can help you," Agatha said.

And thus it was that they found themselves at one hundred and forty-three when they stepped down from the carriage.

She took Dominic's hand. "Just remember to do as I told you."

Agatha handed her calling card to the butler even though he knew very well who she was.

"Is the Princess expecting you?" he asked.

"She is not," Agatha replied. "But she will receive me."

The butler motioned for them to wait on a bench in one of the grand hallways. A few moments later, he returned.

Again, Agatha took her son's hand. It felt small, and yet, he was already older than she was when her fate had been sealed with her betrothal to Herman Danbury.

They followed the butler to Princess Augusta's sitting room. She was in her customary spot on her sofa, her wide skirts taking up almost the entire cushion. As usual, Lord Bute and Earl Harcourt stood behind her, one on each side. Agatha ignored them, instead directing her words directly to the Princess.

"I thought it high time, Your Royal Highness, that you met my son, Lord Danbury."

She gave Dominic's shoulder a little squeeze of encouragement, and he executed a darling bow before saying, "Lovely to meet you, Your Highness."

Princess Augusta smiled, obviously charmed by this display of cuteness. "A pleasure to meet you, Lord—"

Lord Bute let out a violent cough.

Augusta turned away from Agatha and Dominic. "Are you quite all right?" she asked Bute.

"The question of inheritance," he whispered.

Agatha had to pretend not to hear.

"It is far from decided," Earl Harcourt said.

"The concerns involved—"

Agatha wasn't able to get the end of that sentence, but she did hear Earl Harcourt quite clearly when he said to Princess Augusta, "Do you understand the implications?"

Silence.

Princess Augusta turned back to her guests. "Such a handsome boy," she said. "Pray, both of you call on us again soon."

With a flick of her wrist, she bid them gone.

There was nothing more Agatha could say, not right there in front of Bute, Harcourt, and Dominic, so she curtsied and backed out of the room.

"Did I do my duty, Mother?" Dominic asked once they were back in the hall.

He hadn't, but he'd tried. They'd both tried. Agatha knelt before him, taking his little hands in hers. "You showed them who you are."

He looked at her with a solemn expression. "Dominic Danbury. Son of Herman Danbury."

"Yes. You are. And you are Lord Danbury, and you will take your rightful place because you are entitled to it. And because you are *my* son, too. You are the son of Agatha Danbury, born name Soma, royal blood of the Gbo Mende tribe in Sierra Leone. You come from warriors."

"Warriors?" he whispered.

"We win." She squeezed his hands. "Never forget that."

She needed only to remember that herself.

Brimsley

Nearly two months had passed since the King's episode.

Episode.

Brimsley did not know what else to call it, but by God, *episode* seemed far too benign.

He was not sure he could ever forgive Reynolds for keeping a secret of that nature. Yes, he understood Reynolds's need to defend the King, but *surely* the Queen had had a right to know.

Which meant that Brimsley should have been told. He could have supported her. He could have prepared her.

Very well, he could not have prepared her. Nothing could have prepared her for *that*. But he could have tried. He could have done *something* so it wasn't quite so stunningly horrific.

As for the King, he had not been seen at Buckingham House even once since that fateful day. He had departed for Kew and refused to receive visitors.

Not even the Queen.

She wrote him letters. She wrote him so many letters, but she received no response.

Brimsley tried to get answers, but Reynolds told him almost nothing. Just that the King had returned to his scientific pursuits. And that he was receiving treatment for his malady. Brimsley had asked him what sort of treatment (because honestly, what *did* one do for such a thing?), but Reynolds had told him that it was none of his business.

And also to shut up.

Brimsley was not happy with Reynolds these days.

"Are you warm enough, Your Majesty?" he asked. It was mild for January, but still, it was January, and they were standing at the edge of the King's gardens.

"Yes," she replied. "I shall not be outside for long."

Brimsley looked out over the garden patch. It was no longer bursting with life, but several hardy vegetables still grew and bloomed. It was remarkable, really.

"The King is quite talented," he said.

"I beg your pardon?"

"To have cultivated plants that grow through the winter."

"He does like his science."

Brimsley peered down. "What is it? Broccoli? Tiny cabbages? I am sure they are delicious."

"Have them harvested, given to the poor," she said.

"Right away, Your Majesty." He was just deciding who best to contact about this when a footman hurried over.

"Princess Augusta has arrived," the footman said quietly.

Brimsley tried not to audibly groan.

"Has he written?" the Queen asked. There was hope in her voice.

It was the hope that hurt the most.

"I am afraid not, Your Majesty. It is the Dowager Princess."

The Queen made no attempt to hide her displeasure. "What does she want?"

Brimsley looked to the footman.

"She has arrived with Lord Bute," the footman said.

"I am not receiving visitors," Charlotte said, and marched away.

The footman grabbed Brimsley's arm. "There is more," he said urgently. "She has brought the Royal Physician."

The Queen turned around, having obviously overheard the footman. "I absolutely refuse to see the physician."

BUCKINGHAM HOUSE
THE QUEEN'S BEDCHAMBER

Thirty minutes later, the Royal Physician was examining the Queen, who was flat on her back in her bed, skirts up, legs spread. Brimsley was standing at the far wall, scrupulously facing away. Princess Augusta had tried to order him to leave, but the Queen had intervened. She had not said so, but Brimsley rather thought she wanted an ally.

He hoped she saw him as such. It had taken her some time to forgive him for what she had perceived as his disloyalty. He hoped she understood that he had truly not known the extent of the King's illness.

Or really, that he was ill at all.

"You are taking a long time," Princess Augusta said, presumably to the doctor.

"A very long time," Lord Bute added.

"I am precise," the doctor replied.

The Queen let out a sigh. More of a groan, really.

"Your Majesty?" Brimsley called out. He had seen the doctor's devices before she had taken her place on the bed. They had looked like instruments of torture. All shiny metal and weird shapes. Brimsley didn't know a whole lot about the female body (honestly, he'd probably learned as much as the Queen during Lady Danbury's lesson at tea all those months ago), but he did not see how any of these awful contraptions were meant to fit anywhere.

"It is nothing," the Queen replied stoically.

"It is not nothing," the doctor finally said. "She is with child."

Princess Augusta made a sound that approached glee. "It is done, then?"

"Are you certain?" Lord Bute asked.

"There can be no doubt," the doctor stated.

"Doubts are the better part of a woman's insides," Princess Augusta pronounced.

Brimsley winced. What the devil did that mean?

"Are you as sure as you can be?" Princess Augusta continued.

"Oh, quite sure," the doctor said. "In fact, Her Majesty is quite far along. Making magnificent progress."

"Thank God," Lord Bute said. "Can we announce?"

"Not until the quickening," Princess Augusta said with the tone of one plotting a strategic assault. "When will that be?"

"Within a month, I should expect," the doctor said.

The Princess let out another little gleeful chirp.

"Congratulations, Your Highness," Lord Bute said to Princess Augusta. He was beaming.

"I should think congratulations are due as much to you, Lord Bute," she replied.

And what of the Queen? Brimsley wondered. Why was no one congratulating *her*? She was the one growing a baby in her womb. She was the only one in the room who had actually contributed to the making of this royal heir.

Brimsley stole a look at her. He was closer to her head than her feet, so he did not see anything untoward. He caught her eye. She looked to the ceiling, then sighed.

"Is she done yet?" Brimsley inquired. Because honestly, she did not look comfortable.

He was ignored. Princess Augusta moved to Charlotte's head and peered right down at her. "I will have my things moved over to Buckingham House at once."

Brimsley winced. The Queen would not like that.

Augusta patted her on the shoulder. It was probably meant to be maternal, but to Brimsley there was something monstrous about it. Poor Charlotte on the bed with Augusta's face filling her entire vision.

"You carry the crown," Princess Augusta said. "Your safety is most important. I shall not leave you alone for a moment. We shall wait for the future king's arrival together."

"Together," the Queen said weakly.

"Doctor," Princess Augusta said. "That thing is still inside her."

"Oh, right, sorry about that." He pulled something out of the Queen. It looked rather like an iron duck.

Brimsley really wished he had not been watching.

It was not easy being a man who loved men, but by God, it was better than being a woman.

KEW PALACE
THE FRONT PORTICO
...
24 FEBRUARY 1762

"Another one?" Reynolds asked.

"She writes to him at least twice each week," Brimsley said. "You should not be surprised that I am here to deliver another letter."

"We usually meet in the park."

"The Queen has received no replies to the letters I have delivered to you in the park. I thought it prudent to travel to Kew myself."

"Brimsley," Reynolds said on a sigh. He raked his hand through his hair. "Brimsley, please."

"What?"

"Just that—" But Reynolds did not finish his sentence. He never finished any sentences about the King.

"The Queen suffers," Brimsley said. His voice was sharp, sharper than he'd ever used with Reynolds.

Reynolds just shook his head. "You know I cannot. My duty . . ."

"*She suffers*," Brimsley all but snapped.

"I can't . . . I am not able . . ."

"Much as I would love to stand here and help you find your words, I have my own duties to attend to. Deliver the letter to His Majesty."

Brimsley handed him the envelope and started to walk away, but then Reynolds called out his name. "Wait!"

Brimsley turned.

"I want you to know," Reynolds said haltingly, "I deliver them. I deliver them all. Personally."

"And is he reading them?"

Reynolds swallowed uncomfortably. "I do not know. I could not say."

Brimsley very much suspected that meant no. "Perhaps there is something we can do," he said, "to bring them back together. Surely that is what is best."

Reynolds looked dubious, almost pained.

"I have scrubbed the walls clean," Brimsley told him. "There is no more trace of that night. And we can shield the garden. If His Majesty requires time to bathe in the moonlight without his garments, we can build a screen."

"A screen," Reynolds repeated with disbelief. "You think this can be solved with a screen?"

"There is something else," Brimsley said. "Her Majesty—she is in a state I have never seen before. I worry, Reynolds. I fear the Queen teeters on disaster. I wonder if Her Majesty might better see that man again. The King's doctor. For her mind, this time."

"Absolutely not," Reynolds said sharply.

"Reynolds, just listen—"

"*I said no!*" And this time, it was a roar.

Brimsley felt his face grow hot. "You give me nothing," he seethed. "You tell me nothing but lies. I ask for your help, and you refuse to treat me like a partner or equal."

"I cannot help you!" Reynolds thundered.

Or was it a wail?

It was somehow both.

But he clenched the letter from Brimsley in his hand before heading back to the front door.

Brimsley shook his head and headed back to his coach.

"Wait!"

Brimsley turned around.

"Tell her . . . Tell her he misses her," Reynolds said.

"Does he?"

"He does. I am sure of it."

"Has he *said* this?" Brimsley asked.

Reynolds did not answer.

No, then.

Brimsley kept this in mind when he returned to Buckingham House later that day.

"Any word?" the Queen asked him. She was on her way to sit for a portrait and had been dressed in her wedding finery. It was painfully ironic.

"I am afraid not, Your Majesty."

"You are sure he is receiving the letters?"

Brimsley was sure that he was *not* receiving them. Or at the very least, that he was not reading them. But he avoided an outright lie by saying, "I am delivering them, Your Majesty."

The Queen frowned and peered down the hall. "Is *she* still here?" she asked, referring to Princess Augusta. "She has not fallen down a flight of stairs or choked on a cube of meat?"

"I am sorry to report that she remains alive and well, Your Majesty."

The Queen groaned.

"It is time to sit for your portrait, Your Majesty," Brimsley reminded her.

She groaned again, although perhaps not quite as loudly as she had about Princess Augusta. "It is so tedious."

"And yet an indispensable part of royal life, Your Majesty. A Queen must be remembered for the ages."

"It is odd, isn't it? My likeness shall hang on these walls for centuries. And yours shall not."

She did not mean to be unkind. Brimsley knew this. She was simply the Queen. She was different.

"You should also be remembered in some way," the Queen said. "Perhaps we all should."

"That sounds almost revolutionary, Your Majesty."

"It does, doesn't it?" She gave him a humorless smile. "It is probably because I chafe so keenly with the Dowager Princess in residence."

"As do we all," Brimsley murmured.

"You grow bold, Brimsley," the Queen said.

"My apologies."

"None required," the Queen answered, striding into the salon where she'd been sitting for the royal portrait.

"There you are!" Princess Augusta trilled.

"Speak of the devil," Charlotte muttered.

Brimsley tried not to smile.

"Mr. Ramsay has been waiting for you," Princess Augusta said. "Please resume your pose."

"Right this way, Your Majesty," Brimsley said, leading her to her assigned spot. "May I get you anything? Refreshment?"

"She is not drinking a glass of lemonade in the portrait," Princess Augusta said.

"I shall be fine," the Queen told him.

Brimsley moved back to his spot at the edge of the room. This was at least the fourth sitting Queen Charlotte had done. It was excruciatingly dull, but she looked magnificent. Her hair had been dressed like a cloud to support her bridal tiara, just as it had been on the day of her wedding.

How could anyone not love her?

"Are we almost finished?" the Queen asked.

"I am afraid I am not even half done," Mr. Ramsay said.

"Ramsay," said the Queen. "That cannot be true. I am not so large a woman."

"No, Your Majesty, but . . ."

He turned the canvas around. Brimsley stepped forward for a better look. Queen Charlotte was nearly done, and an excellent likeness it was. But beside her . . . nothing but a yawning blank space where the King ought to be.

"We still need the King," Mr. Ramsay said awkwardly.

"He is not yet available," Princess Augusta said.

"Nevertheless," the artist said, "it is a wedding portrait. By His Majesty's request."

"Yes," the Queen said pointedly. "His Majesty requested a wedding portrait."

"His Majesty is quite thoughtful," Princess Augusta said.

Brimsley's eyes flicked from woman to woman. There were entire conversations going on between their spoken words. Diatribes. Wars.

"My skin is too light," the Queen said suddenly. She turned to the artist. "Paint my skin darker. As it actually is."

"Your Majesty," Ramsay said. Brimsley almost felt sorry for him.

"Let me see," Princess Augusta said. She rose from her position on the sofa and inspected the half-finished portrait. "No," she said in that sharp voice of hers. "Paint her skin lighter. Pale. His Majesty wants her to glow."

Queen and Princess stared each other down.

"I shall be painted as I am," Queen Charlotte said.

"You shall be painted as your subjects wish you to be," Princess Augusta said.

"Perhaps we should be done for the day," Brimsley cut in. He scooted between the two women.

"You are tired, are you not?" he said to the Queen.

Her eyes narrowed with rage. "I am——"

"Tired," he cut in before she could say something he would regret.

She wouldn't regret it, of that he was sure. But he would, because he would have to deal with the aftermath.

"You are with child," he said. "You deserve solitude. And restful company." He looked over at Mr. Ramsay with a pointed expression. "And we have lost the light, have we not?"

"Oh," Mr. Ramsay said. "Oh yes. The clouds. They blew in so quickly."

"We are inside," Princess Augusta pointed out.

"Nevertheless," Mr. Ramsay said.

"Another day, perhaps," Brimsley said. He turned to the Queen. "Your Majesty? Perhaps you would like to lie down?"

"Yes," she said.

But there was something about her tone that unnerved him.

"I need to write another letter."

"Another one, Your Majesty?" Brimsley was surprised. She usually waited at least a day.

"I do correspond with people other than my husband," she said, sweeping out of the room.

She did?

"You do?" he asked.

"Stop following me," she said.

"You know I cannot."

"Perhaps I just like to say it."

"Then I shall continue to enjoy hearing it."

She halted in place just long enough to let out a loud, frustrated groan.

Brimsley waited patiently. He was used to this. It was not the first time she had done this.

She marched on to her bedchamber, then stopped at the door. "I assume you will be waiting here until I emerge?"

"Of course, Your Majesty."

"Good. I shall see you when I see you."

She shut the door in his face.

He was used to that, too.

KEW PALACE

THE ENTRY HALL

...

LATER THAT NIGHT

"You are back," Reynolds said.

"I am, and it is not good."

"What do you mean?"

Brimsley tried to ignore the acid burning up his throat. "I have an-other letter."

"Already?"

"It is not for the King."

"Then why have you brought it here?"

"She has written to Duke Adolphus."

Reynolds's surprise showed clearly on his face. "What, the Queen's brother? In Germany? What for?"

"Because she cannot leave England without a country to give her safe haven."

"What?" Reynolds turned away before twisting right back. "No. She would not leave."

"She would. She is miserable, Reynolds. I have tried to tell you."

"And you are sure that she is asking—"

"I am sure." Brimsley was not proud of himself, but he had used ice to freeze the seal so that he could pop it open without breaking it. He'd read the Queen's private correspondence before carefully resealing it.

"Oh," Reynolds said.

"Oh. Oh? That is all you have to say? Reynolds, I have read the private correspondence of the Queen. I am fairly certain that is a hanging offense."

"I shall not tell."

"I *know* that," Brimsley said, frustrated beyond measure. "I tell you merely to demonstrate the lengths to which I am willing to go to protect her. I am worried, Reynolds. I am scared."

Reynolds shook his head, the blank, mindless motion of one who has no answers. "What do you want of me?"

"Help me," Brimsley begged. "Do I post it?"

"You ask me?"

"Yes, I ask you. No one else has the ear of the King. This is . . . She wants to *leave*."

Reynolds looked away, at some far-off nothingness on the horizon.

"I can fail to post it," Brimsley said. "Shall I fail to post it?"

Reynolds swallowed uncomfortably. "That is up to your discretion."

"No. It is our . . . We work together. You can tell His Majesty. He will take action. Come back to her. All will be solved."

Brimsley waited. But still, Reynolds did not answer.

"Shall I fail to post it?" Brimsley asked yet again.

Reynolds closed his eyes. He looked to be in pain. "There is nothing that can be done. Post it."

Brimsley swore. He swore at this untenable situation, and he swore at this man he thought he might love.

"Everything is in danger," he warned. "And you keep secrets."

"They are not my secrets to reveal," Reynolds said.

He walked away.

Brimsley supposed he ought to be used to that, too.

CHARLOTTE

Charlotte was sick of reading. She was sick of needlework, she was sick of directing the servants to prepare baskets for the poor. She was sick of everything. She was bored, and she was lonely, and the only fun she had was trying to devise new ways to avoid Princess Augusta, who she swore must be a witch, because by God, that woman was everywhere.

Unescapablemenaceperson. That was going to be her new word. George had told her it was her right as Queen to make up all the words she wanted.

Overmotherfuss. There was a certain elegance to that one.

Or maybe she ought to go back to the tried and true. *Backpfeifenge-sicht.* A face in need of a fist.

Well. This was the most fun she'd had in weeks.

Brimsley entered the room with a little click of his heels. She thought he might be trying to act a bit more German for her. It was rather sweet.

"Your Majesty," he said, "Duke Adolphus Frederick IV of Mecklenburg-Strelitz has arrived."

Her brother! Charlotte was overcome with a deep sense of relief. Finally, he was here. She could go home.

Adolphus entered the room and made a profoundly formal bow.

Charlotte shot Brimsley a look. "Where is . . . she?" They both knew she was talking about Augusta.

"I believe she is with her modiste."

Charlotte breathed a sigh of relief. "Wait outside, Brimsley."

He didn't look happy about it, but he went.

Adolphus bowed again. "Your Majesty."

She rolled her eyes. "Get up. You look ridiculous."

He smirked. "It is good to see you as well, Sister."

"You could not make it any faster?" she demanded.

"*Mein Gott*, being Queen suits you."

Charlotte pushed herself to her feet—she'd started to become a bit awkward in her own body—and went to his side. She smiled up at his beloved face, and then gave him a hug.

"I would have been here sooner, but it was a hard crossing," Adolphus said. "I still cannot keep food down."

"That we have in common." She stepped back and adjusted her gown, revealing her increasing midsection.

"Your Majesty!" He beamed with delight. "I am to be an uncle. Such happy news."

"Only I am not happy." She clutched his hand in hers. "I want to go home, Adolphus."

"Home? Nonsense. And besides"—he motioned to their luxurious surroundings—"this is your home now."

Spoken with utter pomposity and condescension. God, she hated men sometimes.

"Don't you dare accuse me of nonsense," Charlotte bit off. "You shall take me home. Now. And you cannot refuse me. When we came here, you told me you could not say no to the British Empire, and now I am their Queen."

"You are emotional," Adolphus said.

"Please," she drawled, "say that one more time. I shall have you be-headed."

"Charlotte," he said, in just the most patronizing tone, "inside you ripens the fruit of England. And until that fruit is ripe, your body is but a . . ."

"Do not call me a flower," she warned.

"A tree," he said instead.

Such an improvement.

"You are a tree in the orchard of the Crown. And at such a time as it will bloom—"

"I am a tree," Charlotte said flatly. She was going to kill him.

"I mean to say only that the child inside you is not yours."

"It is my body that is growing it."

"What matter?"

"*What matter?* You grow it, then."

"Your body is not your own," Adolphus said sternly. "To leave the kingdom now would be treason. King-napping. An act of war, perhaps."

"I only want to be home," Charlotte said. She could hear the tears burbling beneath her voice. She'd known she was unhappy, but she had not realized just how desperately so until she'd seen her brother's face. "I want to be at Schloss Mirow. With my own family," she said. She was trying so hard not to cry.

Queens did not cry.

"I am not your family now," Adolphus said. He sounded regretful, but not enough to help her.

"Of course not," she muttered. "I have been bartered like livestock. You *sold* me."

"Charlotte."

"It is true. You sold me, and that means my family is no longer my own."

"King George is your family now," Adolphus said. "Unless—" His face took on an expression of true concern. "Is there something wrong, Charlotte? Something, perhaps, that you could not put into writing?"

"No," she said quickly. Hopefully not too quickly. But she could not reveal George's secret. She was desperately unhappy, but she could never betray him this way. Whatever was happening, it was not his fault.

Adolphus continued to probe. "He is not hurting you, is he?"

"No, of course not. Everything is fine."

She must have convinced him because he said, "That is a relief to hear. It would have been most difficult to take a stand. I would have done so, of course. You are my sister. But still."

She wasn't sure she liked the level of relief in his tone. "What are you saying, Adolphus?"

He noticed a plate of biscuits on a side table and walked over to take one. "I negotiated your engagement brilliantly. I was able to forge an alliance between our province and Great Britain."

"An alliance," Charlotte said. "That is why you married me off to these people?"

"It was good for everyone." He took a bite. "This is delicious."

"Adolphus."

"Sorry." He chewed and swallowed. "But, Charlotte, the lions were at the gate. This alliance, it means Mecklenburg-Strelitz is defended by the might of Great Britain."

"Of course," she said. She already knew all of this. It was simply the first time her brother had said it so explicitly.

"Our fates are tied," Adolphus continued, oblivious to her turmoil. "Which is why it is good you are happy here."

She stared at him.

He smiled cluelessly.

"But what would it matter?" she said with a sigh. "My body is his, is it not? My body belongs to the entire bloody country."

"Charl—"

"We have Tartarian pheasants now," she announced. And she smiled. Her beautiful, empty, queenly smile. "Would you like to see them?"

His entire face lit up. "That would be marvelous. Show me everything. What a life you lead, Sister. Simply glorious."

Glorious, indeed.

BUCKINGHAM HOUSE
THE DINING ROOM
...
LATER THAT EVENING

As usual, Augusta was inescapable. Charlotte had hoped for a relatively informal meal with her brother, but once the Dowager Princess heard that he was in residence, she insisted upon joining them.

"It is so lovely of you to pay your sister a visit," Augusta said. "When I married, I hardly saw my family again. Charlotte, you are fortunate."

Charlotte stared down at her plate. *Sole meunière*. With George gone, they were allowed to eat fish.

"Charlotte?"

"Hmmm?" She broke out of her daze. Her brother was regarding her with concern. So was Augusta. Or whatever it was that passed for concern on her face.

"She's exhausted," Augusta said. "Confinement. I remember it well. Carrying a future king is not easy."

"It could be a girl," Charlotte murmured.

"And of course that would be perfectly acceptable," Augusta said. "I myself had a daughter before my darling George." She turned to Adolphus. "She will likely be married soon. We are in negotiations with the House of Brunswick."

"My felicitations."

Charlotte sighed.

"Where is the current King?" Adolphus asked. "Will His Majesty be joining us?"

"His Majesty has business," Augusta said, dabbing her mouth delicately with her napkin. "Charlotte has been such a support for him."

Charlotte stared at the window. She could go through that window. She'd open it first; she was not that insane. But she could go through it and just walk away.

"*Your Majesty?*" Augusta said pointedly.

Charlotte blinked. "I'm sorry."

"We were talking about what a support you are for His Majesty."

"Oh. Yes, of course." She managed a small smile. "I write him letters."

"Letters?" Adolphus asked.

"He is at Kew," Charlotte replied. She brought a bite of sole to her mouth, then put it down. Too fishy for her pregnant nose. Wasn't that just the most exquisite irony? She finally had fish at the table and couldn't bear to eat it.

"Kew?" Adolphus said.

"It is His Majesty's other London estate," Augusta said quickly. She shot a warning look to Charlotte.

Charlotte closed her eyes. She was tired.

"Is it near to Buckingham House?" Adolphus asked.

"Oh yes," Augusta said. "Very near. It is where he likes to conduct his scientific experiments. He has an observatory."

"Yes," Charlotte said dutifully. "It is a one-of-a-kind magnificent observatory. The only one in England."

"Georgie has quite the brilliant mind," Augusta went on. "Truly, one of the greatest of our generation. He must remain undisturbed while he carries out his work."

Adolphus looked at Charlotte. She nodded and turned back to the window. What would everyone say if she just got up and walked over to it? What would they do?

Would she even be able to get it open? She'd never seen that window open. It might be sticky.

A door would be better. It wouldn't be as dramatic an exit, but there was value in simplicity and ease. Would anyone stop her if she got up and walked out? If she just kept going?

She nudged the uneaten fish off her fork and instead cut a small boiled potato in two. She wasn't really hungry, but she had to eat something, if for no other reason than she'd hear about it later from Augusta.

The King's mother had many opinions on the topic of how best to gestate a future monarch.

So Charlotte ate the potato.

And she didn't crawl out a window or walk through a door, even though she very much wanted to.

Later that night, when they were listening to music in the sitting room, Augusta leaned in and said, for Charlotte's ears alone, "Dearest, the hard part is done. You have done your duty. You have conceived an heir. Now you are free."

Charlotte did not feel free, but what could be the point in saying so?

"As for my son," Augusta went on, "you never even have to see him again, if that is what you want. Well, at least not until we need another heir."

Charlotte gave her a tight, tiny smile. "I'm going to go to bed now," she said.

"Of course," Augusta said. She patted her on the arm. "You are tired. You must have your rest."

But Charlotte was more than tired. It was something different. It was more than a need for sleep. She wanted to lie down, not because she needed rest but because she just couldn't bring herself to keep walking and talking and smiling and doing all the things people expected of her.

She just wanted to lie down.

Close her eyes.

Disappear.

BUCKINGHAM HOUSE

THE GARDENS

...

THREE DAYS LATER

Weather permitting, Charlotte forced herself to go outside for at least an hour each day. The crisp air felt good against her skin. Sometimes the sting of it seemed like the only reminder that she was still alive.

Her brain felt mushy. She was not using her mind, and she was just so tired all the time. Still, some little piece of her backbone forced her to don her cloak and head out into the winter air.

Or maybe it was a little piece of her corset. It was hard to tell the difference these days.

As usual, she found herself wandering near the King's gardens. There was nothing left of note, just some dried-up vines and decaying leaves.

"Shall we replant for next year?" Brimsley asked.

"No," she said. "Let it die."

It was not right to offer hope, even to plants.

"Your Majesty," Brimsley said.

She looked at him. His eyes were filled with concern. And sorrow. She tried to smile. He really did care for her, and she did not thank him for it nearly enough.

"You cannot leave," he said.

"I know that." She shouldn't have written to Adolphus. Deep down she'd known it could go nowhere.

"*England*," he said. He straightened his cravat, tugging on it as if it had suddenly grown a half-inch too tight. "You cannot leave England."

Her eyes held his. Did she understand him correctly? Was he advising her to leave the palace?

"You cannot come with me," she said.

"I must remain by your—"

"No," she said, cutting him off. "You will be blamed if you accompany me. You must stay here."

"But—"

"I will not allow you to take my punishment. You have done—" She swallowed. Brimsley had been her one constant in England, the only person who had always been on her side. "You must remain blameless."

"You know where to go?" he asked. But it was really a statement. They both knew where she would go.

DANBURY HOUSE

THE SITTING ROOM

...

ONE HOUR LATER

"Your Majesty. To what do I owe the pleasure?"

Charlotte crossed the room and sat in the chair Lady Danbury had motioned to. "I am here to offer my official condolences, of course. Sorrows. Prayers."

Agatha was far too polite to point out that it had been several months since her husband had died. Charlotte had been counting on that.

"How very kind," Agatha said. "But Your Majesty should be lying-in. Resting at home. This is a most critical time."

Charlotte's lips began to quiver. No tears. There could not be tears. She was the Queen. She did not cry.

"Your Majesty?" Agatha reached out and took her hand. "Charlotte?"

"Home," Charlotte repeated. "That place is no home. I have left that place and I am never, never going back."

Agatha looked plainly aghast. "But where will Your Majesty go?"

Charlotte let out a loud sniffle. "Why, I have come here."

Agatha blinked. Several times. "Here, Your Majesty?"

"Surely you have an extra room."

"Yes, of course, but—"

"I shall not be a bother."

"It would of course be an honor to host you, but—"

"Thank you," Charlotte said. With great emotion.

Agatha stood. "If you will excuse me for a moment." She hurried to the door. "You will be all right in my absence?"

"Of course," Charlotte said.

"I will send in biscuits."

"That would be lovely."

"Er, tea?"

"Yes, thank you."

Agatha nodded again. She looked a bit frenzied, to be honest. Then she shut the door.

Charlotte sighed and allowed herself to slump into the chair. She was so glad she'd done this. She would be comfortable here.

So much better than Buckingham House.

Agatha

She had to get rid of the Queen.

Now.

Yesterday, if possible.

Agatha very carefully shut the doors behind her. The entrance hall looked somehow both smaller and grander with the assortment of royal guards who had accompanied the Queen. They took up a great deal of space, but their bright red livery was unmistakably regal.

She saw Coral rushing toward her, dozens of questions in her eyes. Putting a finger to her lips, Agatha jerked her head to the side. They needed to speak where they would not be overheard.

"Her Majesty means to stay," Agatha whispered.

"Stay?" Coral gushed. "What an honor."

"No, it is not an honor," Agatha snapped back. "It is terrifying. She is with child. With royal child. She quite literally contains the future of the British Empire in her womb. I cannot be responsible for her."

"But even for an afternoon?"

"She is not talking about an afternoon! She wants to take up residence in one of our guest rooms."

"Ooooh." Coral was entranced.

"Stop. Now." Agatha gave her maid a stern look. Stern and petrified.

Stern and petrified and panicked. "This cannot happen. Do you under-stand me? I would be harboring a . . ."

"Queen?" Coral supplied helpfully.

"She is asking me to commit treason, Coral."

"Oh. My." Coral frowned. "Are you sure?"

"Yes, I'm sure." No, she wasn't sure. But she *was* sure that treason was whatever the Palace decided it was. And keeping the Queen against their wishes would not be looked upon with kindness.

"What would you like me to do?" Coral asked.

"Send a footman to Buckingham House. *Now*."

Coral raced off. Agatha eyed the doors to the drawing room with trep-idation. What should she do? Go back in? Wait outside? She'd told the Queen she'd send tea and biscuits. But she'd already sent Coral away, and she dared not leave this spot to ask the cook to prepare a plate.

She grabbed a chair and shoved it up in front of the drawing room doors. Smiled at the guards. Sat down.

Folded her arms.

She was not moving from this spot.

The fate of a nation depended on it.

Twenty minutes later, Brimsley arrived with a handsome dark-skinned man who was introduced to her as the Queen's brother, Duke Adolphus of Mecklenburg-Strelitz.

"She's in the drawing room," Agatha said, unsure of to which man she should address her comments.

They both charged forward.

She held up a hand. "Perhaps I should announce you. To smooth the way."

She scooted the chair to the side and slipped back into the drawing room, shutting the door behind her.

"Were you going to send tea?" the Queen asked. She was slouched on Agatha's settee, looking exhausted in that way only another woman who had been pregnant could understand.

"My apologies," Agatha told her. "I quite forgot. But I must inform you that your man Brimsley is here."

"So bloody good at his job," the Queen muttered.

"Your brother is here as well."

"I will not see them," the Queen stated.

Agatha cleared her throat, working out how best to proceed. "Your Majesty, I do not pretend to know what problems await you outside. However, I do know that they will not be solved in here."

"They will not be solved anywhere," Charlotte told her.

Agatha let out a shaky sigh. "Would you care to tell me what troubles you?"

"Very much. But I cannot. I cannot tell anyone. All I can say is that I have been lied to and betrayed by everyone in this country but you. You are my only friend."

But she was not. Agatha had not been a friend to Charlotte. She had sold her secrets to Princess Augusta for the price of this house, admission to White's for Lord Danbury, and now possibly for the succession rights for her son.

She had betrayed Charlotte in every way possible.

"Your Majesty," Agatha said, taking a seat across from her, "I am not your friend. But I want to be. However, at this moment, I am purely your subject. And I have been acting as your subject. Not considering your feelings. I have made you into a crown instead of letting you have your humanity. And I am sorry."

She did not know if she would tell Charlotte what she had done. She did not know if anything could be gained by retroactive honesty. But she vowed that she would do better.

"If we are to be friends, we need to start again," Agatha said. "Because I very much need a friend, too."

Charlotte stared at her. For a very long time. And then finally, in a voice that belonged to a girl, not a Queen, she said, "You will be my friend?"

Agatha nodded gratefully. "I will be your friend."

Charlotte took her hand and squeezed it. "This is not the life I wished for."

"I can see that you are most unhappy."

"What would you advise me to do?"

Agatha chose her words carefully. "I cannot advise unless I understand your situation."

Charlotte's mouth trembled. But her eyes were steady when she said, "I will have your discretion?"

"You will," Agatha vowed.

"The King . . . He is . . ."

A hundred things went through Agatha's mind in under a second. None of them was what Charlotte finally said.

"He is . . . ill."

"What?" Agatha gasped. "Is he dying?"

"No," Charlotte assured her. "It is not like that. His illness is . . . in his head."

Agatha's eyes grew wide. She could not even bring herself to reply.

"Not all the time," Charlotte hastily added. "Most of the time—or at least most of the time that I have seen him—he is quite sane. But then . . . once . . ." She caught her lower lip between her teeth. "It was terrifying."

Agatha leaned forward. "I must ask. Did he hurt you?"

"No," Charlotte said, and Agatha thanked the heavens that she did so firmly, and without hesitation.

"No," Charlotte said again. "And I do not think he ever would. But when he was . . . like *that* . . . he did not know me. I do not think he knew himself."

"And no one told you of this before you married him," Agatha surmised.

Charlotte shook her head, and her voice grew brittle. "It was why they chose me." She motioned to her face, to her beautiful brown skin. "They thought I would be so grateful for the position that I would overlook his peculiarities."

"*Peculiarities?*"

Charlotte let out a grim snort. "That is what Princess Augusta likes to call it. It hardly seems sufficient."

"I—I'm not sure—" Agatha had so many questions, but how did one press for details? It was probably treasonous just to inquire.

"I have only seen it happen once," Charlotte said. "I was asleep, and I awoke to him talking nonsense about the stars and the sky and honestly I do not know what else."

Agatha squeezed Charlotte's hand. She had no words; a gesture would have to do.

"He was writing on the walls. And repeating numbers. I think he was trying to make sense of some mathematical equation, and then . . . he . . ." She looked up, her eyes pleading. "You *promise* me. You promise you will say nothing."

"I vow on the lives of my children."

"He ran outside and tore off his clothing."

Agatha gasped. She could not help it.

"He started shouting at the sky. He thought I was Venus."

"Dear God," Agatha whispered. "Who witnessed this?"

"Me. Brimsley, although only part of it. And Reynolds, the King's man. I think he knows more than anyone."

"What did you do?"

Charlotte gave a sad shrug. "We brought him back inside, Reynolds and I. We washed him, put him to bed. He was so tired. He fell asleep instantly. And then the next day . . ."

Agatha leaned forward.

"He was gone."

"Gone?"

Charlotte nodded. "He went to Kew. I have not seen him since."

Agatha tried to absorb all of this. "How long has it been?"

"More than four months."

"What?" Agatha was *not* expecting that.

"He has been at Kew this entire time. I remain at Buckingham House. Alone." Charlotte let out a bitter laugh. "Well, as alone as one can be with a flotilla of staff. *And* Princess Augusta. *Mein Gott*, that woman is everywhere."

Agatha nodded. She had been to the palace. It was clear the Queen had no real privacy. "Is the King receiving treatment?" she asked.

"Yes, there is a doctor. I met him once. I do not like him. I could not tell you why. It was just a sense I had."

"Is he improving?"

Charlotte shrugged helplessly. "I do not know. No one will tell me anything. I write him letters, but I receive no replies. I can only assume he is not getting better. Surely someone would have told me if he were."

Agatha sat back, taking a moment to steady herself. What the Queen had just told her— It had the potential to bring down the monarchy. The government. Their very way of life.

"Who knows about this?" she asked.

"His mother, of course."

Of course, Agatha thought acerbically.

"Lord Bute. Earl Harcourt. But I do not think the three of them are aware of the severity. They did not see him that night."

"Charlotte," Agatha said. "I may call you Charlotte?"

She had called her Charlotte before, but somehow it seemed right to ask this time.

Charlotte nodded.

"What do *you* want?"

Charlotte looked at her blankly. As if it had never occurred to her that her opinions mattered. That she had a voice in the outcome.

"No one has ever asked me that," she said.

"Do you want to leave?" Agatha asked. "Because you can't. Surely you know that. But is that even what you really want?"

"No," Charlotte said. "I'm not even sure why I came here today. It was only that . . ." She shook her head, and it seemed to Agatha that she was only just now truly considering the question.

"There are things you *cannot* do," Agatha advised her. "You cannot leave the country. You cannot divorce the King. But you can, if you want, live apart from him. Not here," she added quickly.

"That is what I have been doing," Charlotte said. "He is at Kew, and I am at Buckingham."

"But is it what you want?"

Agatha had met the King but twice. First at his wedding, when they had exchanged barely a dozen words, and then at the Danbury Ball, when he had changed the world by asking her to dance. It was impossible to judge a man on two meetings, but Agatha felt in her bones that he was a good man, a decent man.

And clearly, a troubled one, too.

"Charlotte," she said, taking both of the younger woman's hands in hers, "what sort of man is the King? Tell me about him. The man he truly is. When he is . . . himself."

Charlotte's lips trembled into a smile. "He is funny. And he is kind.

And he is so very intelligent. I did not expect . . . I know that many think the royals are simply bumbling idiots born into their roles, but he is truly clever. He has a giant telescope. Have you ever seen one of those? No, of course you wouldn't have. He has the only one in Britain."

Agatha watched Charlotte closely. She was like a different person when she talked about her husband. When she talked about him as a man, not as their King.

"He sees me," Charlotte said. "He *sees* me. For me, not just for what I represent or this baby I carry in my body. He asks my opinion. Did you know that before the wedding he said I could leave if I wanted to? There we were, with my brother, and—oh, *Himmel*." She looked toward the door. "Is he still in the hall?"

"He can wait," Agatha said. This was much more important.

"I tried to escape before the wedding," Charlotte said, a look of mischievous glee sparking in her eyes.

"I knew it!"

"What? How?"

"I saw you. Up in the balcony. And everything was running so late. I knew something was amiss." Agatha leaned forward. This had turned into a wonderful woman-to-woman chat, and it was clear they were both desperate for the connection. "Forget about that. Tell me what happened."

"I tried to climb the garden wall."

"You didn't!"

"I did. I mean, I tried. I didn't succeed. And then George came out, and I didn't know who he was, and I asked him to help me go over the wall."

Agatha shrieked with laughter.

"I know!" Charlotte exclaimed.

There was a knock on the door. "Is everything all right in there?" came the German-accented voice of Charlotte's brother.

"Wait one moment," Agatha said. She scurried over to the door and poked her head out. "We need a bit more time."

"We don't have time," Duke Adolphus replied.

Agatha looked at him impassively. "Why not?"

"Because—" He looked at Brimsley, who shrugged. "I suppose we do have time," he said, "as long as she returns to the palace."

"She will," Agatha said. "But right now, she needs a friend." She shut the door on Duke Adolphus's stunned face and returned to Charlotte's side. "What happened next?" she asked eagerly.

"We talked, and he was very charming."

Agatha nodded. "He is very charming. I danced with him, remember?"

"Yes, of course. Anyway, then Adolphus came out, and he was horrified."

Agatha laughed. "I can just imagine."

"And then George said that I was deciding whether or not I wanted to marry him, and Adolphus said something like, 'Of course she's going to marry you,' and then George said, 'No. She's still deciding. It's entirely up to her.'"

Agatha thought that was the most romantic thing she'd ever heard.

"I think I might love him," Charlotte whispered.

"Then you need to fight for him."

Charlotte looked up sharply. "I said that to him once. I asked him to fight for *me*."

"Perhaps he is trying," Agatha said. "In his own way."

Charlotte's eyes took on a sad, pensive look. "I will never understand his way. No one will."

Agatha had no idea what to say to that.

"But I have not even asked about you," Charlotte suddenly said. "I know it has been many months, but you are still mourning a great loss. And the children? Is there anything I can do?"

Agatha's lips parted. Her heart stopped. There was so much Charlotte could do. She could wave her hand, and all of Agatha's troubles would disappear. Dominic would become Lord Danbury in truth, a thousand heads of cattle would be relocated to the Danbury lands, and suddenly there would be income.

And yet . . . Agatha could not ask. Not when she had vowed to be nothing but a friend.

"This," she said firmly. "This is all I need. Spending time with a friend. It helps so much."

"Wonderful," Charlotte said with that unique smile of hers. "Now. I have asked the Royal Physician, and he says getting a baby out of me shall be quick and painless. You have babies. Tell me. Does it hurt?"

"Having children is the worst pain imaginable."

"I knew it." Charlotte's head snapped up. "Wait. Really?"

Agatha saw the queasiness in her eyes and gave a little laugh. "No. It only hurts a little," she lied. "And you will hardly remember it once it is over."

"Oh," Charlotte sighed. "Good."

"You have nothing to worry about," Agatha assured her.

"Except for my brother outside the door and my husband over at Kew doing God knows what with that doctor."

Agatha reached forward and took Charlotte's hands. "We are women," she said. "And the men who hold our fates hardly conceive that we have desires and dreams of our own. If we are ever to live the lives we want, we have to make them conceive it. Our bravery, the force of our will, shall be their proof."

"Yes," Charlotte said. Just that. Just *yes*.

She stood up.

So did Agatha.

"I will never be able to thank you publicly for what you have done for me today," Charlotte said. "For how you have helped me. But please know that in my heart, I will always be grateful."

Humbled, Agatha curtsied. "Your Majesty."

Charlotte bid her to rise. "Right now, to you, just Charlotte."

At that, she walked to the door and opened it. The moment she stepped into the hall, she changed. Her posture, her mien, the very look in her eye.

She was no longer Charlotte.

She was the Queen.

"Brother," she said, "how nice of you to come and fetch me."

The duke's temper was clearly frayed. "Charlotte, you cannot—"

She cut him off with an upraised hand and turned to Agatha. "Please thank your household for their hospitality, Lady Danbury."

"I will, Your Majesty."

As Agatha watched her cross the hall to the front door, Duke Adolphus made his way to her side.

"May I thank you, too, Lady Danbury. For your discretion and grace."

"Anything for Her Majesty," Agatha said.

She meant it.

But then Charlotte stopped. She crossed back to Agatha and took her hand. *Strength*, she seemed to say.

Agatha squeezed back. *Strength*.

"I am ready," Charlotte said.

Agatha followed them to the door—Charlotte, escorted by her brother. Brimsley, five paces behind.

"A Queen's first responsibility is not to her whim, but to her people," Agatha heard Adolphus say.

Poor Charlotte. Lectured at already.

"Queens immemorial have shouldered that burden before you," he continued, "and you shall fare no worse than them. In time you will grow to love your noble responsibilities. It is the natural outgrowth of your noble character."

Charlotte stopped walking.

"Charlotte?" her brother said.

She just stood there. Agatha tried not to gape.

"Brimsley," Charlotte said.

He was at her side in a heartbeat.

She turned back to Adolphus. "You will need to find your own way back to Buckingham House. Perhaps Lady Danbury will lend you her carriage."

"What are you talking about? We have only just retrieved you. Where are you off to now?"

"You sold me off to be the Queen of England." Charlotte stood tall. "I am off to *be* the Queen of England."

On the outside, Lady Agatha Danbury was the epitome of grace and dignity, quietly directing her footman to have a carriage prepared for the German duke.

But on the inside—oh, how she cheered!

CHARLOTTE

Charlotte's feet had barely touched the ground before she was striding away from the carriage. It was time to be Queen.

"Where is the King?" she demanded.

Reynolds came rushing over. She tried to remind herself that he was a good man, that he cared deeply for George's welfare, but just then all she could see was an infuriating obstacle.

He bowed, then said, "I am so sorry, Your Majesty, but the King cannot see you now."

"Nonsense. Take me to him."

"Your Majesty, there is nothing more I would like than—"

"She needs to see him," Brimsley cut in sharply. "It is her right."

Reynolds looked torn. "I wish I could—"

But just then another man came running out, wiping his hands on a rag. It was that doctor. The one she did not like.

"Your Majesty," he said, his voice deep and authoritative. "I am sorry you have bothered yourself to make such a trip. But I am afraid it is impossible for you to see the King."

Charlotte held her ground. "It is perfectly possible. I want to see him. Where is he?"

"No," the doctor said dismissively. "Your Majesty would not want that."

Charlotte had to force herself to maintain her queenly composure. What she really wanted was to go for the man's throat. "Do not tell me what I want, doctor. Now show me to him, or I shall have my men search the entire palace."

The doctor's jaw hardened, and he took a step. It was a small motion, but it was clear that his intention was to block her way.

Charlotte turned to Reynolds. "What is his name?"

"Doctor Monro, Your Majesty."

"Doctor Monro," she said, each syllable cut like a diamond. "*I am your Queen.*"

Still, he did not budge.

And then Reynolds moved between them, turning his back most pointedly on the doctor. "Come with me, Your Majesty. I will lead you to the King."

"No," Doctor Monro protested. "You cannot. My work . . . We are at a most precarious point."

Charlotte ignored him. She and Brimsley followed Reynolds through the palace, past the glorious public rooms, past the comfortable private rooms. Down a long hall they went, finally arriving at a rather unassuming door. Monro followed the entire way, spewing a nonstop torrent of dire warning.

"Someone shut that man up," Charlotte muttered.

"Do not open that door!" Monro raged.

Charlotte shoved it open.

And walked straight into hell.

There were cages on every surface. Some open, some with sad little animals inside. None big enough for a human, thank God, but what were they even doing there?

And blood. There was blood. Not a lot of it, but splatters here and there, along with terrible yellow stains on the floor.

Chairs were overturned, grotesque metal instruments were strewn about. Whips. Chains. And in the center of it all, strapped into a monstrous iron chair, was George.

He moaned incoherently and his head lolled, his hair sticking to his forehead in sweaty clumps. There were bruises on his body, angry red welts. And he was so thin, so desperately, agonizingly thin.

"*Mein Gott*," Charlotte breathed. She could not have imagined. She could never have imagined.

The doctor's assistants did not see her enter, so intent were they on their work. Even though George had been securely tied to the chair, one was still bracing his shoulders as the other pressed a hot poker into his skin.

George screamed in agony.

So did Charlotte.

"Untie him," she said, barely able to choke out the words.

The assistants looked to the doctor for confirmation.

"*Untie the King!*" she roared.

They rushed to undo the knots at his hands. Brimsley and Reynolds worked at the ones at his feet. It seemed to take forever. Charlotte looked around for a knife. Her eyes had just landed on one when Brimsley got the last knot undone, and George was finally freed of his bonds. He burst from the chair and ran to her, sobbing, clinging to her shoulders.

"Everyone out!" Charlotte yelled. "Now!"

Monro and his assistants fled, but Reynolds and Brimsley were hesitant to move.

"Are you sure, Your Majesty?" Brimsley asked. "He is most overwrought. And stronger than you are."

"I am sure."

But even as she said it, George was pushing her against the wall.

"No, yes, Farmer George," he whimpered. He buried his face in the crook of her neck as his mumblings grew incoherent.

Brimsley rushed to her side. "He is too strong. I cannot leave you alone with him."

"It's all right. It's all right." Charlotte craned her neck so she could look over George's shoulder at Brimsley. "He is just trying to get away from that damnable chair. Now go! Please."

He and Reynolds exited the room. Charlotte had every expectation that they would remain five paces away.

"Nobody nobody. I'm nobody but I'll try. I'll try I'll try. I will." His hands gripped her shoulders, and his eyes were frantic. "I'll try. I'll try. Just make it stop. I'll try. I'll do it. I'll do it."

"George, stop," Charlotte pleaded. This was nothing like when he'd run wildly under the stars. This was a man in pain. He was utterly lost, nearly broken.

"No," he pleaded. He shook his head fast. Faster. "No, no. I'll do it, I'll do it. I didn't."

"George," Charlotte said sternly. "Look, George, it is me."

His eyes darted all over her face.

"Venus," she tried. "Venus is here, George."

Still, he did not recognize her. He clung to her, he pleaded with her, but he did not recognize her.

"Oh, damn Venus," she swore. "I am Charlotte. I am Charlotte, and I need you to be George again. I need you to try."

She grabbed his face in her hands, trying to stop the shaking. "You are Just George, and I am Just Charlotte. Come back to me. Please, George. Come back."

He whimpered. Words came whispering from his mouth, but she could not understand them. Desperate, she grabbed one of his hands and placed it on her belly.

"Do you feel that, George? It kicks. It grows. *It is ours.*"

He seemed to grow quieter, and the frantic darting of his eyes began to slow and calm.

"I am Charlotte," she said yet again, "and this is our child, and we need you to be George. Or none of us is anyone."

His fingers curled around hers, and he looked up. "Charlotte," he whispered. "Charlotte."

"Yes," she whispered. She nodded jerkily, and all the tears she swore she could not cry began to roll down her cheeks.

"I am with you," she promised. "I am here, and I will never leave you again."

"I was just trying to be good," he whimpered. "I was just trying to be well."

"And you will be. But not like this."

He nodded, but in his eyes she saw a scared child.

What had they done to him? How could she have allowed it to happen?

"That doctor will never come near you again," she vowed. "I promise you."

"I want to be well." He touched her cheek, almost as if he were re-assuring himself that she was really there. "I want to be well for you."

"You will be," she said, but she had no idea if her words were true. Maybe he would always be ill in this way. She could not see into his mind; she could not reach in and mend whatever it was that caused him to lose himself.

But nothing could be worse than what Doctor Monro had done. Charlotte might not be able to cure George, but she could certainly make him better than he was right now.

"What would you like to eat?" she said, careful to keep her voice soft and gentle. "You are far too thin. Do you want something sweet? Savory?"

"Both?" He gave her a tiny quirk of a smile, and in it she saw a hint of the man she so adored.

"And a bath," she said, trying not to wince at his odor. "We will see to that as well."

"Thank you."

She looked at his face closely. He still looked hollow.

Haunted.

But maybe with the tiniest bit of hope.

She held his hand as she went to the door and opened it. Reynolds and Brimsley were waiting just outside.

"Your Majesties," they both said instantly.

"Reynolds," Charlotte said, "would you please see to the King? He needs a bath and something small to eat while we arrange for a proper meal."

"Anything but gruel," George said to him, and the two shared a look. Charlotte was grateful to witness that moment. It spoke of friendship. It spoke of humanity.

She turned to George. "I will be back with you shortly. First I have some important business to attend to."

She waited while Reynolds led George away, then turned to Brimsley and said, "Come. We must deal with the doctor."

"Gladly, Your Majesty."

They strode back through the palace, unfortunately making one wrong turn before locating Doctor Monro and his assistants in the drive in front of the building. The sun had begun to set, and the air was golden and shimmering with promise.

"You," Charlotte said ominously, pointing at the doctor. "You will leave here and never return."

Doctor Monro came striding over, his posture still that of a man who expected success. "I apologize if Your Majesty—"

"Too close!" Brimsley barked, stepping in front of the Queen.

The doctor took a step back. "We were not expecting you, Your Majesty."

"Clearly," Charlotte said.

"You must understand, that was not the part of our treatment I would have preferred you to see."

"There are *pretty* parts to the treatment?" Charlotte asked. "What would those be? The parts that gave him the welts? The bruises?"

"Your Maj—"

But she was not done. "The part where you *starved* him?" she continued, her voice growing dangerously brittle.

Monro brought his hands together, almost like a priest. "Your Majesty must understand. While my methods are distressing, they are proven. I desire the King's sanity as fervently as Your Majesty does."

"I care not for his sanity," Charlotte retorted. "I care for his happiness. His soul. Let him be mad if mad is what he needs."

"You are wrong," the doctor said.

"Watch yourself," Brimsley warned.

Charlotte jabbed a finger toward the doctor. "You? Are finished."

She turned to the guards, the same men who had accompanied her here. "Remove him from the grounds."

"This is an error!" Doctor Monro yelled. "An error that will destroy him!"

Charlotte whipped around to face him, seething. "Be grateful that I do not order *you* destroyed."

She watched the guards pull him away. She took pleasure in it. And when she could no longer hear him howling his fury, she turned to Brimsley and said, "I will need my things packed. Everything. We are moving to Kew."

KEW PALACE
THE OBSERVATORY
...
AN HOUR LATER

Charlotte had thought she'd find George in his suite of rooms, but she supposed it made sense that he and Reynolds would have gone to the observatory. It was where he was happiest.

He was sitting at a table, freshly bathed and clothed, frantically eating the feast that had been laid out before him. Mutton (of course), warm rolls, his favorite scalloped potatoes. Kew, too, had an orangery, and several oranges had been peeled, their sections fanned out for his enjoyment.

"A warm meal and a bath must be a balm," Charlotte said. "You seem more yourself. You look better."

He stared at her, his fork hovering between his plate and his mouth.

"Do you feel better?" she asked.

Slowly, he set down his fork. "You should not have come."

She swallowed. She should have known this would not be easy. But she kept her smile light and cheerful. "I was most happy to come."

"No." He shook his head. "No. This was a mistake."

"I am so sorry, my love." She started to walk toward him, but his forbidding expression caused her to stop. Still, she said, "I should have come sooner. But do not fear. I shall remain by your side as we—"

"No, Charlotte." He raised his voice. She wasn't sure where he found the energy to do so, but he stood and said clearly, "Listen to my words: You should not have come. I do not want you here."

She didn't believe him. She refused to believe him.

"Go back to Buckingham House," he said. "Please."

She did not speak. He was wrong. She knew it, and she only needed him to understand it, too. Slowly, she walked toward him.

"Do you hear me? I said go back to Buckingham House. That is where you live. That is where you belong." Shaking, he thrust his arm out, pointing to the door. "Go!"

Still, she did not obey.

He rose. Crossed the room to where she was standing. Screamed, "I do not want you. I want never to see you. Leave! *Get out!*"

"No."

His whole body shook. "I order you!"

"No. No, George."

"Charlotte—"

She stood steadfast. "You cannot force me away. I will not go."

"I command it. Go!"

Finally, she roared. "I will stay! *I* command it!"

George was stunned into silence, staring at her as she stalked toward him.

"Please, Charlotte." His voice had gone quieter, and it sounded as if it might crack. "Please go."

She said it again. "No."

"Charlotte, you are not listening."

"I am. I have heard that you wish I had not come, that you want me to go, that you do not want to see me."

"Then listen," he pleaded.

"What I have not heard is that you do not love me."

He went very still.

"I have been suffering and alone and believing I am a failure as a wife and as your Queen because you stay away from me as though I am a disease. And then today it quite suddenly occurred to me that perhaps there is another reason. A better reason. Perhaps you stay away from me because you care for me. Perhaps you stay away because you love me."

She stepped closer. "Do you love me?"

"I'm trying to protect you."

"Do you love me?"

He shook his head. "I cannot . . . we cannot . . . this conversation is not . . ."

She watched him with raised brows.

"I cannot do this," he said.

She would not stand for that. "Do you love me?"

"I never intended to marry," he said, shaking his head. "I never wanted to—"

"Do you love me?"

She was relentless. She had to be.

"Charlotte, please stop." But his face was a picture of heartbreak. Maybe his heart had to be broken so that she could put it back together.

"Is it that you do not believe that I could love you?" she asked. "Because I do. I love you, George. I love you so much that I will do as you wish."

He opened his mouth to speak, but she held up a hand and said, "*If you do not love me.*"

She felt the sudden need to move, to rock the baby growing within her, so she walked the few steps to the window and looked out. "All that you have to say is that you do not love me, and I will go." She turned back around, her eyes meeting his with unflinching clarity. "I will go back to Buckingham House, and we can live our separate lives and I will have this baby alone and make do and fill my days and survive all on my own. I will do that. But first you have to say that you do not love me."

And then: "You have to tell me that I am utterly alone in this world."

His eyes searched hers. There was a heartbreaking tension to his body, as if he were afraid he'd shatter. Or maybe as if he was poised and coiled, preparing for escape. Finally, when the silence stretched taut, he said, "I am a madman. I am a danger."

She shook her head.

"No. Listen. Inside my mind, there are other worlds creeping in. The heavens and the earth collide, and I do not know where I am."

Charlotte asked the only question that mattered. "Do you love me?"

"That does not signify," he said. "You do not wish a life with me for yourself. No one wishes that."

She was so sick of men telling her what she wanted. Especially now, when her very heart was at stake. "George," she implored, "I will stand with you between the heavens and the earth. I will tell you where you are."

"Charlotte, you—"

"Do you love me?" she practically cried.

And there it was. She was begging. She had laid herself bare, given him her pride and her heart and everything she was, and—

"*I love you.*" The words sounded as if they'd been ripped from his soul. He'd been holding this back, denying his own heart. She could see it in his eyes as they filled with tears.

"George," she whispered.

"No, let me finish. From the moment I saw you trying to go over the wall, I have loved you desperately. I cannot breathe when you are not near. I love you, Charlotte." He took her face in his hands. "My heart calls your name."

His kiss was one of love, and hunger, and desperation. He kissed her as if he could not get close enough, as if he could never get close enough.

As if he would never let her go.

"I wanted to tell you," he said. "I wanted you to know, but this madness has been my secret my entire life, this darkness is my burden. You bring the light."

"George." She looked up at him, at his beloved face, those dark brows, and the full lower lip he liked to bite when he was amused. She knew him, she realized. She knew the man he was inside, and if sometimes that man was submerged under tortured waters, she could help him rise to the surface. She would not leave his side.

"It is you and me," she vowed. "We can do this. Together."

BRIMSLEY

Brimsley decided he rather liked living at Kew.

It was much more casual than Buckingham House, to whatever extent a royal residence could be called casual. He and Reynolds were treated like the most senior of servants, despite there being a butler and house-keeper. But most of all, Kew was delightful because the King and Queen were delightful—and delighted with each other.

The first few days were difficult, though. It took time for the King to recover from his ordeal. Brimsley would never profess to know much about medicine, but he did not understand how anyone might think that torturing the King would help set his mind at ease.

He was also beginning to realize the strain that Reynolds had been under, caring for the King while keeping all of this a secret. That first night, when the Queen had so magnificently dispatched Doctor Monro, Brimsley had tried to offer his assistance, but Reynolds was so used to bearing his burden alone, he found it difficult to accept help.

Once the furor had died down, and the King and Queen had retired for the night, Brimsley and Reynolds had gone for a walk and found themselves in the stables. It was raining lightly, and so they'd gone in-side to keep dry. It didn't smell as bad as Brimsley had feared; clearly the stable hands were excellent at whatever it was they had to do to keep the place fresh.

The two men found a place to sit, leaning against a bale of hay. Reynolds sighed. Brimsley did not think he had ever seen him so tired.

"Have I ever told you how I came by this job?" Reynolds said.

Brimsley tipped his head, letting the side of his forehead kiss against Reynolds's shoulder. "I imagine you were marked from a young age for your unmatched unction and superciliousness."

Reynolds gave him a little smirk, but there was a hint of good nature to it. "The King and I grew up together. I was His Majesty's playmate. We fished and climbed trees and were boys together."

Brimsley nodded. Reynolds had mentioned this. Not often; he tended to be circumspect about his background.

"I'm still not sure why the Palace allowed it," Reynolds continued. "They were monstrously strict about who got to spend time with the princes and princesses. I suppose it was because my mother was a trusted maid and my father a palace goldsmith. And I was the right age. Our birthdays are just two months apart."

"Who is the elder?" Brimsley asked.

"Me." Reynolds gave him one of those smiles he loved so much. "Of course."

"Of course."

"There was no one else for him unless some foreign dignitary or prince came to visit, but those were always awkward affairs. Two little boys dressed in their ridiculous finest and ordered to be friends."

"That does not sound as if it would go well."

"No," Reynolds mused, "it never did. Half the time they didn't even speak the same language. So it was just me. Me and George. I still called him George then."

"You don't now?"

Reynolds gave him a look. "You know I don't. And I certainly never did when anyone else was around when we were children."

Brimsley chuckled. "No, I can imagine that would not have gone over well."

"Of course I knew my station, but I liked Georgie. I liked him even when adults pushed me aside in their haste to bow and scrape to him." Reynolds looked up and grinned. It was a sentimental sort of smile, with the barest hint of something sad.

"He was affable," he continued. "And full of good humor. He put on no airs. I was perhaps the first to recognize his . . . peculiarities. But I liked him no less. I was the closest thing he had to a friend, so I kept his secret. I sang distracting songs when he lost control of his thoughts. Held his arms down when they trembled."

He looked at Brimsley more directly. "I hid him from his monstrous grandfather."

"That was good of you," Brimsley said quietly. He had heard about George II. He had not been a kind man.

Reynolds nodded slowly, the kind one did not when one is agreeing, but when one is remembering. "When it came time to follow my father into the Goldsmith's Guild, I asked to stay with George instead. It would not be as lucrative, but I made the choice gladly. Because he needed me. And because—"

He swallowed.

"Because he knew my secrets, too. My own . . . peculiarity. And he did not care. He kept my secret as I kept his. As I had to. Even from you."

"I'm sorry I was so angry with you," Brimsley said.

"I would have been the same way," Reynolds admitted.

"It was just . . . the Queen . . ."

"I understand."

"It is my sworn duty to protect her."

Reynolds gave him a little smile. "It is my sworn duty to protect the King."

"What odd lives we lead," Brimsley mused. "When do we get to protect ourselves? Or each other?"

Reynolds kissed him on the cheek. "Hopefully every day. But we never come first."

Brimsley faked a dramatic sigh. "I suppose if I have to come second, it might as well be to the King."

Reynolds chuckled, but he grew serious soon after. "His secret is no longer just ours. I could not keep it. I tried. But first there was his mother, and then Bute and Harcourt. Every damn chambermaid around here whispers of him now. Then that doctor." Reynolds grabbed Brimsley's hand. Tightly. "You understand now why I begged you to keep him away from the Queen."

"Yes," Brimsley said quickly. "I cannot even imagine. It makes me sick even to think of it."

"His Majesty has suffered so much. I could not begin to describe it."

"The little I saw . . ." Brimsley said.

"I tried to intervene," Reynolds said. "I could have tried harder, I suppose."

Brimsley could take it no more. He could not bear the pain in Reynolds's eyes. He just wanted to make it go away, even if only for a moment. Reaching up, he took his face in his hands and kissed him.

Tenderly.

With love.

With a promise he did not know if he could keep.

KEW PALACE
THE QUEEN'S SITTING ROOM
...
1 JUNE 1762

The Queen was doing embroidery, which Brimsley always found odd. He'd never thought she had the temperament for such a repetitive pastime, but she seemed to like it, and he liked that she liked it, especially since she had told him he could sit in a chair by the door rather than stand at attention the entire time.

But then the King came bounding in, which meant that Brimsley most certainly had to rise to his feet. Reynolds arrived five paces behind and stood next to him.

"I am off to work in the fields," the King said, and indeed he was dressed for farm work, with none of his usual finery. "We are cycling millet." He leaned down and gave the Queen a kiss on the top of her head. "Would you like to join me?"

"Never," she said with a chuckle. "I shall stay here and grow our little King."

He kissed his fingers, then touched her belly, and made off to leave.

"George!" the Queen suddenly called. "I almost forgot. You received a letter. Where is it?"

"Right here," Brimsley said, stepping forward. He retrieved it from a side table and handed it to the King. "It is from Princess Augusta."

"My mother is writing to me?" The King rolled his eyes and tossed the unopened letter into the fireplace. Brimsley didn't know whether he was horrified or delighted.

But the King's happiness was certainly infectious. He strode back to the Queen and kissed her again. "You are beautiful!" he proclaimed. "My wife is beautiful!"

And then off he went.

Brimsley blinked. It was as if a whirling ball of sunshine had just rolled through the room. It had been some weeks since the Queen had rescued him from that horrendous doctor, but still, the difference was nothing short of miraculous.

He turned to share a smile with Reynolds, who had not yet left to follow the King, but Reynolds was regarding the Queen with a contemplative expression.

"Did you want to say something, Reynolds?" she asked.

"No, Your Majesty."

Brimsley watched the exchange with interest. Reynolds *clearly* wanted to say something.

The Queen looked up again from her embroidery to find Reynolds's eyes still on her. "Speak," she said.

He cleared his throat. "His Majesty has good days. And down days."

"He did," the Queen replied. "But now that I am here, his days are good. He is better. Is he not?"

"He is better now," Reynolds agreed. But his face told a different story. Brimsley knew him well enough to see the worry in his eyes.

"But?" the Queen prodded.

"Perhaps caution would be—"

"Reynolds," she cut in, "let him be. All he needed was his wife and a routine and to get rid of that dreadful doctor. He is well."

Reynolds did not look convinced, but he bowed and said, "Of course, Your Majesty."

"Will you accompany him to the fields?" she asked.

"Yes, Your Majesty, I enjoy cycling millet above all things."

Brimsley choked on a laugh.

The Queen gave Reynolds a sly look. "You are a good man, Reynolds."

"Thank you, Your Majesty."

"Enjoy your millet."

"Yes, Reynolds," Brimsley said, "enjoy your millet."

Reynolds gave him such a scowl on the way out that even the Queen laughed.

Brimsley sat back down in his chair by the door and smiled. This was how life ought to be.

KEW PALACE
REYNOLDS'S QUARTERS
...
LATER THAT NIGHT

It was late, and the King and Queen had both retired, which meant that Brimsley and Reynolds were, theoretically, off duty.

As Reynolds had a full-sized tub, that was where they had chosen to spend the evening.

It was a perfect end to a lovely day.

"Do you think it will last?" Brimsley asked.

"What do you mean?"

"The King. Will he stay as he is?"

"One can hope," Reynolds said cryptically. He started lathering Brimsley's back. It was heavenly.

"Reynolds?"

"Hmm?"

"If it lasts, they would have one another. They would be together. Have a true marriage. Grow old as one."

Reynolds poured water on Brimsley's back, rinsing off the suds.

"We would serve them together," Brimsley said quietly.

"A lifetime," Reynolds murmured.

It was the sort of thing men like them never dared to dream of. Like the King and Queen, they too would be together. Have a true partnership. Grow old as one.

Brimsley turned so that he could see Reynolds's face. He was so handsome, so noble. The other servants liked to joke that he had the mien of a duke, and they weren't far off. Sometimes Brimsley couldn't believe that a man like Reynolds had chosen to be with him.

And then he reminded himself that Reynolds was lucky, too. Brimsley might not have the face of an Adonis, but he was no troll. And more important, he was clever, and he was steadfast. He was a good man, and he knew his worth.

"Do you think it's possible?" Brimsley asked.

Reynolds nodded. "I do not know. Perhaps. Great love can make miracles."

"It can."

And maybe, God willing, it would.

AGATHA

Agatha sat at her vanity while Coral prepared her hair for bed. It could be a complicated procedure, depending on how formally she planned to dress her hair the following day.

This evening's preparations were complicated indeed. Agatha had received a summons from Princess Augusta. Another one of their afternoon teas. She knew what the Dowager Princess wanted: inside information on the Queen's recent move to Kew.

Rumors had begun to circulate about the royal couple. Nothing about the King's mental faculties; that, at least, had not spread outside the palace walls. But the *ton* wanted to know why the King and Queen had become recluses, why they never left Kew. Parliament was growing restless; just yesterday, Agatha had heard a man in a shop say that if the King did not address the body soon, he ran the risk of losing their confidence.

Princess Augusta would be growing nervous. Very nervous. Hence the invitation.

"What will you say to the Princess?" Coral said.

"Nothing. What can I say?"

"I am sure you could give Princess Augusta the smallest of details. Pears. Her Majesty asked for pears while she was here."

Agatha did not recall anything about pears, but that mattered little.

Augusta was not going to be satisfied with stories about fruit. "I will not engage with the Princess," Agatha told Coral. "I have promised the Queen my friendship."

"If you are friends, perhaps you could ask Her Majesty to intervene," Coral said. "She seemed so kind. I am sure she would make little Dominic Lord Danbury if you asked."

"Her Majesty has gone to Kew," Agatha said firmly. "I cannot simply turn up there and beg a favor. And she is with child. She is in a state. I cannot do anything that might cause her upset or worry."

"She has enough of that as it is," Coral said with a dramatic sigh.

Agatha turned around sharply. "What do you mean?"

Coral tied one of the rag curls and picked up another strip of cloth. "Well, there are the rumors to consider."

"Rumors?" This made Agatha nervous. Servants always heard different rumors than the *ton*. And theirs were likely more accurate.

Coral gave up the pretense of doing Agatha's hair and took a seat in front of her. "I am hearing that the Palace stands not on firm ground. That the King is ill or injured or . . . well, something is not right."

"Coral, that is *gossip*."

"No. I am not a person for gossip. If I were," Coral said pointedly, "I would say that I heard from several kitchen maids that the members of the House of Lords were concerned for the King's welfare. There is talk that the Palace is in jeopardy."

"But you are not one to gossip."

"Never."

Agatha let out a weary sigh. This only confirmed what she had overheard in the shop. "I certainly cannot ask Her Majesty for help if that is true."

"No," Coral said, "but again, if I did gossip—which of course I do not—I would say that I have heard that all the power lies with Princess Augusta and Lord Bute now."

Agatha stared at her reflection as Coral went back to setting her hair. What was she to do? She could not betray the Queen. She *would* not. But the only way to secure the future of the Great Experiment was through Princess Augusta.

And she demanded secrets.

ST. JAMES'S PALACE
PRINCESS AUGUSTA'S SITTING ROOM
...
THE NEXT DAY

She was back.

Back in Lady Augusta's oh-so-formal sitting room, where everything was edged in gilt and even the ceiling was a picture of elegance: an oval dome with a painting that Agatha thought must rival the Sistine Chapel.

"Thank you for seeing me, Your Highness," Agatha said.

"Thank *you* for paying me a visit, Lady Danbury."

"I am so glad that you met Lord Danbury." Agatha took an intentional pause. "The new Lord Danbury."

"Did I?" Princess Augusta waited while one of her ladies prepared a cup of tea. She motioned for her to give it to Agatha. "I know I met your son. He is very handsome. Such a sweet boy."

Agatha waited until Princess Augusta had sipped her own tea before she did the same.

"I have been told," Princess Augusta said, "that you had the honor of a visit by Her Majesty."

"It was two months ago," Agatha said. She wanted to make it clear that she had not seen the Queen since her departure for Kew.

"Yes," Princess Augusta said. "I'm aware."

Of course she was.

"It is not common for the Queen to visit her ladies-in-waiting in their homes," Princess Augusta continued.

"The Queen was kind enough to offer her sympathies upon the loss of my dear husband. The late Lord Danbury."

"Yes. My condolences. Losing a husband is . . . inconvenient." Princess Augusta smiled, but her lips barely managed a curve. "The Queen must be very fond of you. To come out during her confinement."

"Yes," Agatha said. She knew what game Augusta was playing, and she refused to take part. Not this time. She had made a vow to be a true friend to Charlotte.

"Yes," Princess Augusta repeated.

Agatha regarded her over the rim of her teacup.

Princess Augusta did the same.

Agatha took a breath. It was now or never. "As it is a fact," she said, "that my son will inherit his father's title—"

"Is it?" Princess Augusta interrupted. "A fact?"

"Is it not?"

"Whether or not the Great Experiment will go on past this generation is something only His Majesty can determine." Princess Augusta set down her cup and made some sort of meaningless gesture with her hands. "Such a complicated debate," she said with a sigh.

"I see."

"Of course," the Princess continued, "I am sure I could expediate your answer. If you have information that may be useful."

"I am not sure what information I could possibly possess that one as brilliant as Your Highness could not obtain yourself."

And honestly, this was true. What did Agatha know? That the King was ill? Princess Augusta already knew that. But she might not know the extent of it. What Charlotte had shared was damning indeed.

Still, she would not speak of it. To anyone. She had sworn her fidelity to Charlotte, and she would not break this promise.

Women had so little power. They needed to stick together. Even, as in this case, when they were pitted against another woman.

"Well," Princess Augusta said. "I believe the matter of title inheritance shall be difficult to settle. More tea?"

"No," Agatha said. "Thank you. I believe it is best if I went on my way."

"You have much to think on," Princess Augusta said.

"I always have much to think on."

The Princess actually laughed at that. And not unkindly. "You are a very intelligent woman, Lady Danbury."

"I take that as the highest of compliments," Agatha said, "given that you are one as well."

Princess Augusta nodded regally. "Women must navigate this world differently than men. I believe you understand that."

"I do, Your Highness." And it was the reason her heart felt like a rock every night when she tried to sleep.

"I hope we shall meet again soon," Princess Augusta said.

Agatha nodded, curtsied, and let herself out. It was all she could do not to collapse against the wall and heave a giant breath.

"Lady Danbury!"

She looked up. It was the Queen's brother, Duke Adolphus. He was striding toward her with some purpose. He was a handsome man. Not surprising, given that his sister the Queen was quite beautiful.

"Oh, good afternoon," she said with a curtsy. "I was having tea with Princess Augusta."

"How nice. Are you friends?"

"Of a sort," Agatha hedged.

"It is lovely to see you," he said. He spoke English perfectly, and his accent was charming.

"And you," Agatha said.

"May I walk with you?" he inquired.

"Of course."

He smiled genially. "With the impending new arrival, it seems I may be in England longer than expected."

"How lovely for you. I mean, I assume it's lovely. Perhaps you have duties you must return to."

"I do, of course, but nothing that cannot wait. It is not every day a man gets to witness the birth of his nephew." He leaned in with a bit of a grin. "Who happens to be a future king."

"It might be a girl," Agatha reminded him.

"True. And if that is the case, I wish King George the very best of luck. My own father passed when Charlotte was but eight. I had quite a hand in raising her."

"Why do I get the impression you are trying to tell me she was a handful?"

"Far more than a handful," he said with a laugh. "But her spirit does her credit. I believe she will be a great Queen."

"I believe you are right."

He smiled at her again. Agatha felt a little flip in her stomach. When had such a handsome man ever flirted with her before? She'd been promised to Herman when she was three, and her parents had kept her out of society until her wedding. There was no point in bringing her out if a match had already been secured.

"Do you think the Queen misses her home in Mecklenburg-Strelitz?" Agatha asked.

"I think she misses some of it," Adolphus answered. "I hope she misses me."

Agatha laughed.

"I would imagine she misses some of the freedom," he added. "But with the loss of freedom comes great power. If I know my sister, I know she likes that power."

Agatha laughed again. What fun this was. What a pleasant surprise after such a fraught afternoon with Princess Augusta.

"But she does feel alone at times," Adolphus said. "I am glad she has you."

"I am honored to be her friend."

"It can be difficult for those in power to find true friendship," he said. "I am sure she will find others in due time. But for now, she has you, and that is a good thing."

"Thank you," Agatha said. "Or should I say *danke*."

He let out a delighted laugh. "*Danke schön*," he said, "if you want to be truly grateful." He leaned in with a twinkle in his eye. "It means 'thank you very much.' I should not want to advise you to say something without giving you the proper meaning."

"Well, now I *am* truly grateful."

He smiled.

She smiled.

They reached the front door to the palace, and he walked her to her waiting carriage. "Lady Danbury," he said, "since I *am* to be in England a bit longer, I wonder if I might call upon you."

Agatha nearly tripped over her own feet. "On me?"

"Yes. You are out of mourning? Or am I mistaken . . . ?"

"I am out of mourning," she said. "Or nearly so. Half-mourning," she explained, indicating her lavender dress.

"Ah. Then I hope you will not think me too bold."

"No," she said.

"Then I may call?"

"I would like that very much."

He took her hand to help her up into the carriage. She faced front, as was her custom, but when they were a half-minute or so into their journey, she turned around.

Duke Adolphus was still watching her.

DANBURY HOUSE
LADY DANBURY'S BEDCHAMBER

...

LATER THAT NIGHT

Agatha sat at her vanity while Coral prepared her hair for bed. It was a much simpler task than the night before. She had no plans to go anywhere beyond her own sitting room the next day.

"Coral," she said, "I believe I have solved my problem."

Coral scooted around front so she could face her. "You asked Princess Augusta? She will secure the title?"

"No. She was intransigent as always."

"Then . . . ?"

"I spoke to the Queen's brother."

"Prince Adolphus? What can he do?"

"He says he would like to court me. I said yes."

"A prince!" Coral said.

"Technically, I think he might be a duke."

"Either way!" Coral exclaimed.

Agatha chewed on her lower lip in thought. "I believe I shall marry him."

"He is German," Coral pointed out.

"He is a nice man. Certainly nicer than Lord Danbury ever was. He made me laugh. Several times."

"Well, that is certainly something Lord Danbury never did."

Agatha nodded. "He rules his own land, and not because of an experiment. His title is his own."

Coral blinked rapidly, trying to take this all in. "You shall have to learn German."

"I shall." She grinned and patted Coral on the arm. "You shall learn it, too."

"Me?" Coral said with some surprise.

"I could not survive without you. Surely you know that."

"Do you think I'm clever enough to learn German?"

"Of course you are. I already learned a bit this afternoon. *Danke schön.*"

"What does that mean?"

"'Thank you very much.'"

"I suppose that's useful."

"Almost as useful as 'Where is the chamber pot?'"

They both had a laugh at that.

"Are they nice in Germany?" Coral asked.

"The Queen is nice. Her brother is very nice."

"Germany," Coral said. "Imagine that."

Agatha nodded. "Imagine that."

CHARLOTTE

Several months had passed since Charlotte had come to Kew. George regained weight, and his bruises and welts healed until they were no longer visible. Charlotte decided that this was their true honeymoon. They were relatively alone, able to enjoy each other's company.

Able to become friends as well as lovers.

He did not have another episode, but she learned how to notice the signs that indicated he was struggling. His hands might shake. He would close his eyes in an odd, tremulous manner, almost as if he were fighting against his own thoughts. Sometimes he would repeat a few words, usually about Venus, or the Transit of Venus, or the date 1769, which she now knew was when the Transit of Venus was next expected to occur.

"I had assumed it would be sooner," she said to him one day in the observatory. "From the way you talked about it."

He looked up with a smile. He seemed to enjoy when she interrupted his work. "Actually, it happened in June of last year."

"What? And you didn't tell me?"

"You weren't here."

"Yes, but it's obviously very important to you. I would have thought you'd have told me about it."

He gave her a dry smile. "For much of the time, I was otherwise engaged."

"I don't know how you can joke about that monster," Charlotte said. She wanted to have Doctor Monro arrested for his treatment of George, but he convinced her that it would only create more problems.

He shrugged. "Sometimes humor is the only way to cope."

"If you say so." She walked over to the telescope, idly trailing her fingers along the long tube. She was careful not to touch any of the knobs or buttons or anything that could be knocked out of place. George tended to have everything set very precisely.

"How was the Transit?" she asked. "Was it glorious?"

"Unfortunately, we were not able see it in its entirety from here. It's a shame. I wouldn't have had to travel far. Just up to Norway."

"Why didn't you go?"

He gave her an indulgent look. "I am King. I cannot just traipse up to Norway to view the stars."

"I would think that is exactly what a King could do. Are you allowed none of life's pleasures?"

He smiled wickedly. "I have you."

She waddled over to his side. "That you do. More of me, every day."

George touched her belly. "When will he come? Our little King."

"Soon, I fear. Very soon."

He leaned down and spoke right up to her belly. "Hello, Little King. Hello."

Charlotte laughed when she felt a kick. "I believe he just returned your greeting." She took his hand and laid it upon her. "Just wait a moment. He'll do it again."

"Are you sure?"

"He never stops."

George smiled. "A good, healthy lad."

Charlotte walked back over to the telescope. "May I look?"

He followed her. "Of course, although I'm not sure what there is to see right now. Middle of the day, and all that."

"Clouds, perhaps. I like clouds."

"I like that you like clouds."

She rolled her eyes. He was incorrigible. And she loved him.

She peered up through the telescope, which, as he had warned, did not reveal anything terribly exciting. "Will you be able to see the next Transit of Venus?" she asked.

"If our calculations are correct, we will again have a partial viewing."

She pulled her face away from the eyepiece to look at him. "Can you travel to a better location? I think you should."

"Alas, we are even less well-suited than last time. I would need to head to the Americas. Or the South Seas."

"Goodness. You should have gone to Norway."

"Perhaps. But we are lucky that we shall have partial viewings for both transits. Not many geographical areas are so fortunate."

"What will happen for the next one. In . . ." Charlotte did some mental calculations. "1787, correct?"

"Incorrect, I'm sorry to say."

"It's not every eight years?"

"I'm afraid not. It's actually a two-hundred-forty-three-year-long cycle."

Charlotte stared at him, certain she must have heard incorrectly. "And yet we went eight years this time?"

"Yes, it makes perfect sense, actually. It goes a hundred and five years, then eight years, then a hundred and twenty-two years, then eight years again."

"Perfect sense," she echoed.

"Well, it's actually one hundred and five and a half years."

"Of course."

"Right," he said, completely missing her sarcasm. "And one hundred twenty-one and a half years, too."

She could not help but smile. She loved seeing him so passionate, even if it was regarding a subject about which she understood little.

"What does it look like?" she asked.

"The Transit?"

"Yes. You say that it can be observed. What does it look like?"

"A black dot, traveling across the sun. Here." He moved to his piles of charts and began shuffling through them. "I've got a diagram somewhere. Just give me a moment . . . Here we are!" He pulled out a large sheet of parchment and spread it flat on a table.

Charlotte looked down. It was exactly as he said. A small black dot traveling across a large orb.

"It's more impressive in real life," George said.

"I imagine so." She sat down, suddenly weary on her feet. "I should like to learn more about astronomy."

"Yes, you'd mentioned."

"But I think I'd rather learn more about different sorts of sciences. Things that aren't quite so far away."

"Like what?"

She thought about that. "Medicine, perhaps. No," she decided, "locomotion."

"Locomotion?" He looked surprised. In a delighted sort of way. "What do you mean?"

"Think about how long it takes to travel from one location to another. I would like to visit my home again someday. I have very fond memories of Schloss Mirow, and I would love to show it to you. But it is most impractical. You are King. If you do not have time to visit Norway to view the Transit of Venus, you do not have time to travel to Mecklenburg-Strelitz to see my childhood home."

"Perhaps your childhood home is more meaningful to me than the Transit of Venus."

"Now I know you're simply trying to be a romantic poet," she scolded. "But think about it . . . What if there were a way to move faster than we already do?"

"Better roads," he suggested. "They make a great difference. Expensive, though."

"I suppose. I don't know that I have any answers. In fact, I'm quite certain that I do not. But I think it would be an interesting topic to read about and study."

"Then we shall find you books. I have a man who does that for me all the time."

"How convenient it is to be King."

He gave her a look. "Most of the time."

It wasn't exactly the opening she was looking for, but she decided to take it, anyway. "How are you feeling lately, my love?"

He motioned to his head, his finger pointing rather like a gun. "You mean this?"

"I might have used a different motion to indicate," she said.

"Better." Then he seemed to change his mind and instead said, "Improved." He went to his desk and shuffled some papers. "I don't want to talk about it."

"I wish you felt that you could."

He sighed. "It is too difficult to explain."

"You could try."

"Not when I am feeling so well. Why would I want to remind myself?" He held out his arms, motioning to the glorious round room of his observatory. "I have all this. I have you. My mind is behaving. *Why* would I want to think about the unpleasantness of when it is not?"

"To learn how to avoid it?"

"It is unknowable," he said with harsh finality. "Trust me. I have tried. I can create a peaceful world, and that does help a bit, but it is not infallible. There is no knowing, and there is no stopping. And that is why I am so dangerous."

"George." She reached out for his hand, but he did not let her take it. "You are not dangerous. You are sweet. And you are kind. You are a wonderful King, and you will be a wonderful father. We will just keep ourselves in this lovely cocoon. You, and me, and soon the baby. We shall be happy."

"I have never been so happy as I am right now," he told her.

She reached out her hand again, and this time he took it.

"Just us three," she said.

"Just us three."

And for a little while, it was true.

KEW PALACE

THE SITTING ROOM

...

8 JULY 1762

"Princess Augusta has arrived, Your Majesty."

Charlotte looked up at Brimsley, not bothering to hide her displeasure. "Is there any chance we can convince her that we are not here?"

"None," he confirmed. "She has already proved most intractable."

"Well, show her in," Charlotte said with a sigh. "But only to the sitting room. Under no circumstances is she allowed to see the King."

The King's mother was not a restful presence, and Charlotte was determined to keep George's life as free of stress and strife as possible.

"Your Majesty," Augusta said when she was shown in. "You are looking well."

Charlotte stood to greet her, even though, strictly speaking, she did not have to. She did outrank Augusta, after all. Still, it seemed a polite gesture for one's mother-in-law, especially one's mother-in-law whom one was about to disappoint.

"Thank you," she said, coming forward to kiss Augusta on both cheeks. "Larger by the day, I'm afraid."

"That is wonderful news. Uncomfortable for you, but wonderful for the nation."

Charlotte patted her midsection. "We do what we must."

"I did what I must nine times," Augusta said with remarkable serenity. "Perhaps you shall even outdo me."

As Charlotte could not begin to count the number of times she had thrown up at the outset of her pregnancy, she did not want to contemplate reaching the double digits of childbearing. "That is a race I may well be happy to let you win," she said with a laugh.

"As long as you produce at least one healthy boy," Augusta said. "For now. You'll want an extra just in case." She must have seen the look of shock on Charlotte's face, because she added, "Do not think me so cutthroat when it comes to my children. I love them all. Dearly. But we cannot lose sight of the fact that we are royal, and we have different duties and responsibilities than the rest of the world. Just look at George."

"What do you mean?" Charlotte asked carefully. She sat back down, indicating that Augusta should join her.

"Why, we were certain he was going to die shortly after his birth. He was quite premature."

"Yes, he's mentioned."

"Even the first few years, it was always a worry. It is always a worry even if a child is born fat and healthy. George's father and I rested much easier when Prince Edward arrived. Just nine and a half months later," she added with pride.

"Nine and a half months?" Charlotte asked queasily.

"I take my responsibilities seriously."

"You are most admirable," Charlotte said.

"Now then," Augusta said, getting down to business. "The reason for my call. I need to speak with the King."

"Ah," Charlotte said, clasping her hands in front of her like a serene little doll. "I'm afraid that is not possible."

Augusta's mouth pinched. "I do not understand."

"The King is not receiving visitors at this time."

"I am not a visitor. I am his mother."

"You are most welcome to return some other time in the future."

"I am here now."

Charlotte schooled her features into an expression of regret. "George is not available now."

"Does he even know I am here?" Augusta demanded.

Charlotte shrugged. "He is occupied."

"I may be forced to worry that you are holding the King against his will," Augusta warned. "Which would be—"

"Treason," Charlotte supplied, almost cheerfully.

"Yes. It could be considered treason if you do not allow me to see him."

"I am sorry, but the King does not wish to receive at this time."

"You dare to speak for him?" Augusta seethed. "You are not the King."

"No," Charlotte answered, deciding that it was time to play dirty, "but I am *your* Queen."

Augusta gasped. "Well. You certainly have become comfortable."

Charlotte took a sip of her tea. "You chose me well."

"You carry just one king in your womb," Augusta said with sharp precision. "The other king? George? I carried that king. And while your little king can hide out, cozy and warm in the embrace of your belly, *my* king cannot."

She stood, pacing across the room before turning back with a blazing expression. "How do you not know what I have always understood? From the moment a king is born, there is no hiding for him. There is no room for illness or weakness. There is only power. I have done all I can to ensure his power. And you are undoing it."

"That is not—"

"He is not even trying," Augusta bit off. "And you are allowing it. You cannot allow him to hide. His crown will not survive. He has a country. He has people. He must *rule*. Lord Bute is waiting. The government is growing restless. And suspicious. George must face Parliament."

"Your Highness . . ." Charlotte began, but truthfully, she did not know what she could say. Augusta was right.

"This is on you now," Augusta said as she strode to the door. "He is yours."

Charlotte knew that Augusta did not really mean this. She could no sooner stop meddling than she could stop breathing.

But this time Augusta was not wrong. George was King. And he could not hide away forever, no matter how desperately Charlotte wanted to protect and comfort him.

With a weary sigh, she stood up and headed to the one place she knew she'd find him.

KEW PALACE
THE OBSERVATORY
...
TEN MINUTES LATER

"Charlotte!" George called cheerfully when he saw her walk in. "How goes the day?"

"Your mother was here."

George's fingers, which had been fiddling with one of his scientific instruments, went still. "I do not want to see her."

"I know. I sent her away."

He smiled. It was a smile of love and thankfulness. She understood him. She protected him. She gave him what he needed. She knew how grateful he was for that.

Just as she knew she had to finally draw a line between what he needed and what he wanted.

"However," she said, "we must away as well. Back to Buckingham House."

"No," he said. "Charlotte, no."

"You have to address Parliament. The people need their King."

"I'm not ready."

"You can be. You will be."

"No." He shook his head. "I'll have to make a speech. I'll have to write a speech."

"And it will be brilliant. I will support you in every way. Besides, your garden at Buckingham House has been terribly neglected. I'm sure it's overgrown with weeds by now."

"You know the gardeners would never allow that," he said.

"Fine," she conceded, "but it won't be the way *you* would have it done."

He smiled a little. Caught his lip between his teeth.

"It will be different this time," she told him. "This time we are together. We are one."

He touched her belly. "We are three."

"We are three," she agreed. "And one." She lifted up to her tiptoes to kiss him. "You are a great king, George. And an even greater man. You can do this."

He nodded, but it was a little shaky. "I can do this."

Charlotte managed to get out of the room and all the way down the hall before she sagged with relief. Dear God, she hoped he could do this.

BUCKINGHAM HOUSE
THE KING'S OFFICE
...
11 AUGUST 1762

"I can feel you watching me."

Charlotte moved sheepishly from her spot in the doorway. She'd been spying on George for several minutes. "I like watching you."

He looked up and raked his hands through his hair. His fingers were stained with ink. "You make it more difficult for me to write."

"You are doing a fine job, of that I am sure."

"This is a speech to Parliament. I cannot do a fine job. I must be brilliant."

Charlotte wandered over to his desk, which was littered with discarded drafts. She picked up the one on top and skimmed it. "These are certainly the words of a brilliant man," she told him. She motioned to the rest. "And so are these."

"You haven't even read those."

"I don't need to. You are brilliant, George. Ergo, so will your words be. I have faith in you."

But he did not look as if he had faith in himself.

She walked back to him and placed her hands on his shoulders, massaging his muscles. "Perhaps you need a bit of a distraction," she said, a trifle cheekily.

"Distraction?"

"Yes. I believe I have just the distraction to help." She leaned down and kissed him on that tender spot behind his ear.

But he could not be deterred from his task. Or his anxiety. "I do not need distraction. What I need is to deliver a perfect speech before all Parliament. Or do you wish me to no longer be King?"

"George, no . . ."

"Perhaps I should simply surrender and offer them my head. Put an end to the monarchy. Let them call me Mad King George and laugh. Is that what you wish?"

"Stop." She could not bear to hear him talk this way.

"I'm sorry," he said immediately. "I need this to be . . ." He squeezed his eyes shut and moved one of his hands near his face, almost as if he were making little chops in the air. "This is important. It might be best if we left the distractions for another time."

He was right, she supposed. The speech *was* important. Critically so. And no matter how she tried, she would never truly be able to understand the pressure he was under to get it right. But—

She winced.

Grabbed her belly.

"George?"

"Not right now, Charlotte. I must get back to work."

Another squeeze. Harder, this time.

"The baby . . ." she said, as calmly as she was able. "It is coming."

He flew out of his chair. "Now?"

"I believe so." She looked up at him with a shaky smile. "I've never done this before."

George ran to the door, utter panic seizing his face. "You're sure?"

"As sure as I can be."

He wrenched open the door and bellowed, "*REYNOLDS!*"

Charlotte almost had to laugh. Because who else would he call for when his wife went into labor?

George

It was time. The baby was coming, and as God was his witness, it was going to be the easiest birth in the history of man.

He was King. That had to count for something.

Charlotte had been taken to her bedchamber, which had been meticulously transformed into a birthing room. George had seen it only briefly; he'd been quickly shooed out by, well, everyone.

He'd kept an ear to the door, though, and every now and then a maid would pop out to get towels or tea or some such, and the poor girl would then get grilled by the King.

One or two had fled in tears.

But at least he was getting regular updates.

Charlotte was doing well.

But she was in pain.

But that was normal.

But she was in pain.

But again, Your Majesty, that is normal. And she is bearing it like a Queen.

"What the hell does that mean?" he'd demanded of the maid.

She'd burst into tears. That made three.

It was at that point he'd decided it was well past time that the physician should have arrived to attend to her. She was the Queen of Great

Britain and Ireland, for the love of God. Every medical mind in the nation ought to be by her side.

Except for Doctor Monro. That went without saying.

He took off down the hall, searching for Reynolds. At this point, he was the only person George trusted, except possibly Brimsley, but for some reason Brimsley had been allowed in the birthing room. He'd spent the last four hours facing the window, George was told.

"Reynolds!" George bellowed.

Two footmen came rushing toward him.

"Get out of my path!" George roared.

The footmen fled.

George skidded around a corner, stopping just before he crashed into Reynolds.

"Where is the doctor?" George demanded. "Why has he not arrived? She cannot do this without a doctor. Opium! She needs opium!"

"I was searching for you to tell you that the Royal Physician has arrived. Just moments ago. I believe he is now with Her Majesty."

It took George about a half-second to take that in, then he turned on his heel and ran back the way he had come. Only now, when he reached Charlotte's bedchamber, there were six men gathered by the door. Good Lord. Was there to be no privacy?

"Your Majesty!" the men chorused.

George tried to greet them all. "Archbishop. Prime Minister. Lord Bute. Hello. Thank you for coming. If you'll excuse me." He brushed past them to head into the room so he could confer with the physician, but the archbishop grabbed his wrist.

"Your Majesty," Lord Bute said, "surely you are not entering the birthing room. There is womanly work afoot."

"We will wait out here," the archbishop said serenely.

"Right," George said, tapping his hands nervously against the sides of his thighs. "Yes."

He paced. Looked to Reynolds for support. Paced some more. Flinched when the air was rent with a scream.

"Charlotte," he whispered, lurching forward.

This time it was Reynolds who put a hand on his arm. "This is normal," he said in his deep, soothing voice.

"You know this . . . how?"

"Er, I've heard things."

"You've heard things," George repeated crossly.

"I have sisters. They both have children."

"Were you present for the births?" George wasn't sure why he was being such an ass to Reynolds. Probably he just needed to be an ass to someone, and he couldn't very well do it to the archbishop.

"I was not," Reynolds said in that ever-calm manner of his. "But they are both prodigious storytellers, and I was informed of every last detail."

Another scream, although perhaps not as piercing as the last.

"This cannot be normal," George said.

Reynolds opened his mouth to speak, but just then the door opened, and Lady Danbury poked her head out.

George regarded her with some surprise. When had she arrived?

"Your Majesty," she said. "She is asking for you."

"He cannot be in there," the archbishop interjected.

Lady Danbury looked at George with a firm, direct gaze. "Your Majesty."

George turned to the archbishop. "Do you like being Archbishop of Canterbury? Would you like to remain Archbishop of Canterbury?"

The archbishop's chin drew back into his neck. "Your Majesty—"

George put his face right up next to his. "Do you believe you can remain archbishop by defying the Head of the Church of England? MOVE!"

The archbishop's mouth slid into an upside-down arc that would not have looked out of place on a turtle. With a little mumble of assent, he stepped out of George's way.

"This way, Your Majesty," Lady Danbury said, leading him to Charlotte's side.

"My darling," he said, taking her hand. "I am here now."

She managed the wobbliest of smiles. "I don't want to do this."

"Too late, I'm afraid." He gave her a smile of his own, trying to offer strength through good cheer. "But I am with you. I would take the pain if I could."

"Perhaps a new science experiment," Charlotte said.

"I shall get on it right away," George tried to joke, and they both had a little laugh, which was enough to hold them over until Charlotte was overcome by another contraction.

"Aaaaaaaahhhh!" she moaned.

"Is there nothing that can be done for her pain?" George demanded.

"I have already given her laudanum," the doctor said. "But I dare not give more. The dosing must be precise."

George turned to Lady Danbury. "Something she could bite on. Would that help? You have done this, have you not?"

"Four times, Your Majesty," Lady Danbury confirmed.

"And? What are your thoughts?"

Lady Danbury shot a look at the doctor, then said to George, "She is losing blood."

"Is that normal?"

"Yes," Lady Danbury said hesitantly, "but this seems like a lot."

"Doctor!" George barked. "What is happening? Why is there so much blood?"

"A woman must lose blood during the birth," the doctor said condescendingly. "It is part of the lining of the—"

"I *know* anatomy," George snapped. "I want to know why she is losing *so much*."

The doctor moved back between Charlotte's legs. He pressed on her belly, and then reached up inside her. George winced; every one of the doctor's motions caused Charlotte to whimper with pain.

"The baby is breeched," the doctor finally said. "We must await the natural evolution."

"How long?" George demanded.

The doctor shrugged. "There is no way of knowing. It is different with every patient."

George looked at Lady Danbury. She shook her head.

"This is all very natural," the doctor said. "All normal."

"Doctor," George said, "were we to leave all decisions to nature—"

Charlotte cried out yet again. George rushed back to her side, dabbing at her neck and brow with a cool cloth.

"Charlotte, no," he tried to tease. "This will not do. You shall wake the neighbors."

"Of which we have so many," she muttered.

"That's my girl," he said, squeezing her hand. That she could joke at such a time . . . She was magnificent. He'd known that from the first moment he'd seen her. But right now, she needed his help.

He turned back to the doctor. "I had a horse, my favorite as a boy. He was breeched in his mare. The stable hands, they . . . I've seen it too with sheep, with calves . . . There are ways to aid in this situation. To turn the baby? Are there not?"

The doctor was visibly horrified. "There are methods, yes. However, with a royal patient—"

"Prepare them!" George ordered. "Now!"

"Your Majesty, she is not a horse. Or a sheep."

"We are all animals, doctor, and it is clear to me that this baby must come out. If we can do it with a calf or lamb, surely we can do it with a tiny human."

"How may I help?" Lady Danbury asked.

"The two of us will need to hold her while the doctor works," George said.

She nodded and moved quickly to his side.

"I believe we need you moved," George said to Charlotte. "Just there to the edge. Put your arms around my neck." To Lady Danbury, he said, "Hold her steady around her shoulders."

"I am ready," the doctor said.

"I'm not," Charlotte cried.

"You are, my love," George said. "Remember? Together. We can do anything together."

"You are the strongest woman I know," Lady Danbury said.

"And you could have made it over the wall if you hadn't been wearing all those skirts," George said. "Although I'm very glad you didn't."

"I need you to teach me to swear in German," Lady Danbury said.

"What?" Charlotte asked.

Lady Danbury looked at George and shrugged. Together they were doing a fine job of distracting Charlotte while the doctor moved the baby.

"She likes to make up words," George said to Lady Danbury. "Did you know that?"

"I did, actually. It's a German thing."

"It's a German thing," Charlotte managed to say.

"Yet another thing you can teach me," Lady Danbury said.

"Why do you want to know—OW!—German?" Charlotte asked, panting through the pain.

"Oh, expanding my mind. Plus, we are friends. Would it not be fun to have a secret language?"

"Not so secret," George said. "Half the palace speaks it."

"Almost done," the doctor said.

Thank God, George thought.

"Did you hear that?" Lady Danbury said. "He's almost done, Your Majesty. Soon you will—"

"There," the doctor announced. "The baby has been turned."

Everyone sagged with relief.

"What now?" George asked.

"We wait for it to come like any other baby."

"Are you serious?" George nearly yelled.

"I have every faith that it will not be long now," the doctor said.

And indeed, it was not. Thirty minutes later, George held his newborn son in his arms. "He is perfect, Charlotte. Would you like to hold him?"

She nodded.

Carefully, George placed the babe in her arms. Once they were settled, he turned to Lady Danbury, who he frankly had more confidence in than the doctor. "Does all look well to you now?"

"Yes," she said. "The afterbirth has been delivered, and the bleeding has stopped." She glanced over at the doctor and then back at George. "If I might speak freely, Your Majesty."

"Of course."

She spoke quietly. "I believe Her Majesty—and his little Highness— might owe their lives to you. I am no expert on childbirth—"

"Other than having done it four times," George interjected.

"Other than having done it four times," she repeated with a smile, "but women talk. I hear stories. A woman cannot labor indefinitely with a breeched baby. It was time to take action."

George swallowed. He was not sure if her words buoyed his confidence or filled him with terror. It could all have so easily gone wrong. "Thank you," he finally said. "For being here. You were a tremendous support to the Queen. And to me."

Her eyes widened at the compliment, which she accepted with a gracious nod. Then she motioned to the door. "I think there are a few people who would like to meet the new prince."

George raised his brows.

"Your mother," Lady Danbury clarified, "and Her Majesty's brother."

"Ah. I suppose I had better not keep them waiting."

"No," Lady Danbury said with a knowing little chuckle.

"That's right," George said. "You've grown acquainted with my mother."

"She has invited me to tea on several occasions," Lady Danbury confirmed.

"We won't be rid of her until she sees the baby," George said, "and I do not wish to invite her in. Charlotte needs to rest. Will you stay with her while I take the prince?"

"Of course," Lady Danbury said.

George went back to Charlotte and kissed her on the brow. "May I borrow him for a moment?"

"Yes," Charlotte said. "I'm very tired, actually."

"Rest," George told her. "Lady Danbury is going to stay with you while I present our son to my mother and your brother."

Charlotte nodded sleepily and closed her eyes. George carefully cradled the swaddled babe in his arms and took him out to the hall, where Augusta and Adolphus were waiting.

"My grandson!" Augusta exclaimed.

"He is magnificent," Adolphus said. "How is Her Majesty?"

"Taking a well-deserved rest," George said.

Augusta moved closer. "Is he healthy? Oh, I wish I could count his fingers and toes."

"I can assure you there are ten of each," George said. "And I have been warned by the nurse that under no circumstances am I allowed to release him from the swaddling."

"It appears to be a highly engineered set of folds," Adolphus joked.

Augusta peered down at the little prince's face. "So beautiful," she said softly. And then, after casting a furtive glance at Adolphus, she quietly asked George, "Are there any signs of . . . ?"

"Of what, Mother?" George said, almost daring her to say it.

But Augusta was all too aware of Adolphus's presence, so all she said was, "I am only asking . . ."

"He is our next King," George said. He looked his mother straight in the eye. "Could he be anything but perfection?"

CHARLOTTE

"Your Majesty," Brimsley said. "He needs you."

Charlotte nodded and hurried out of the nursery. She should have been with George already, but little George had been fussy and had required more of her time than usual.

Today was the day. George's speech to Parliament. He had been working so hard. Draft after draft of his speech. Charlotte had read them all and offered her thoughts and opinions, but she was still new to this country. There were cultural subtleties that she didn't fully understand.

"How is he?" she asked Brimsley.

"Nervous. Reynolds looks concerned."

Charlotte bit her lip. Reynolds was such a stoic. If he looked concerned, then George was definitely in need of help.

"Walk with me," she said to Brimsley.

"I always walk with you."

That elicited a little smile. "So you do."

"If I may speak freely, Your Majesty . . ."

"You often do that as well."

He acknowledged this with a nod, then said, "I think perhaps he simply needs some good cheer."

"Encouragement, you mean?"

"Yes, Your Majesty. He has been very well lately. Would you not agree? This is probably just nerves. Anyone would be nervous in such a situation."

"This is true," Charlotte said. "Even I."

Brimsley bit back a smile.

"You are not so stoic as Reynolds, are you?" she murmured.

"I beg your pardon?"

She waved this away. They had arrived in the formal sitting room. George was pacing near the window, mouthing words and making hand gestures. Reynolds was watching him with a worried expression.

"Here I am!" she announced, her voice cheerful and bright.

"I have been waiting," George said. He looked magnificent in his formal military uniform, but his hands were shaking.

"I was with the baby," Charlotte said. "I am not late. There is plenty of time."

George nodded, but it was a shaky, jerky motion.

"You look very handsome," Charlotte said, brushing an imaginary piece of lint from his coat. "Do you have your speech?"

"In hand," he confirmed. "Though I am rethinking the middle section on the Colonies . . ."

"Parliament will appreciate all of your thoughts," she assured him. "You have worked so hard. You are ready."

She reached up to kiss him. He rested his forehead against hers, and the connection seemed to help him settle. She took an extra moment to take his hands in hers. She held them long enough for the shaking to subside.

He let out a long breath. "Thank you."

"Off you go," Charlotte said. It was now or never. And they both knew that never wasn't an option.

George departed, Reynolds right behind him. Charlotte counted to ten, then turned to Brimsley. "He is going to be brilliant," she said.

"Of course, Your Majesty. He is the King."

BUCKINGHAM HOUSE
THE QUEEN'S SITTING ROOM
...
ONE HOUR LATER

"Your Majesty."

Charlotte looked up to see Reynolds standing in the doorway. This was a surprise. She would not have thought he'd be back so soon.

And the look on his face . . . it was not good.

Dread began to pool in her stomach. "What was it? Did his speech not go well?"

Reynolds glanced at Brimsley, then looked at her with a pained expression. "His Majesty did not deliver a speech. He never got out of the carriage."

Charlotte stood. "What do you mean, he never got out?"

"His Majesty *could not* get out of the carriage."

"Well, what happened?" Charlotte demanded. "What did you do? He was quite fine when he left here."

"He was not fine!" Reynolds exploded.

Charlotte froze, and beside her Brimsley audibly gasped at Reynolds's outburst.

"Your Majesty," Reynolds said. "Forgive me. Please. It is only . . . He was not fine. He was not. That was merely . . . hope."

"Hope," Charlotte repeated.

Reynolds nodded. His eyes were sad, and so very tired. "I have tried to say . . ." he began.

"I know," Charlotte said. It was just that she had not wanted to know. But now she had no choice. "What happened?" she asked Reynolds. "Tell me everything."

"It started well," Reynolds said. "I rode on the footboard so I could see through the back window. He was studying his speech. Practicing, mouthing the words. But as we grew closer . . ."

Charlotte took a shaky breath.

"His hands started to tremble."

Charlotte's heart sank. She knew what this meant.

"And he started to . . ." Reynolds looked up at her with the most tortured expression. "I don't know how to describe it, Your Majesty, except that he began to shrink."

"To shrink?" Brimsley asked, when it became apparent that Charlotte could not.

"It was as if he were closing in on himself." Reynolds demonstrated, his shoulders hunching, his belly going concave. "And then before I knew it, he was on the floor."

Charlotte's hand flew to her mouth. "The floor? Of the carriage?"

Reynolds nodded. "He was on the floor, but no one knew but me. I was the only one riding on the footboard. I didn't know what to do when we stopped in front of Parliament. I got down as fast as I could. I wouldn't let anyone else near the door."

"Thank you," Charlotte whispered.

"I tried to open it, but he'd locked it from the inside."

Charlotte closed her eyes. "Oh no."

"Were there many people there?" Brimsley asked.

"Yes," Reynolds said, with just the barest tinge of what could only be termed hysteria. "Yes, there were many people there. All of Parliament was waiting for him. I did the only thing I could think to do. I climbed up and looked in the carriage."

Charlotte and Brimsley both looked at him, as if to say, *And?*

"He was still on the floor, but it was worse than before. He'd curled into a tight little ball, as if he were trying to make himself as small as possible. As if he were trying to disappear."

Charlotte choked back a sob.

"I told everyone the door was jammed," Reynolds said. He looked at Charlotte with regret. "I don't think anyone believed me."

"There was nothing else you could have done," Brimsley said. He started to reach out a hand, as if to console, but he pulled it back.

Reynolds swallowed spasmodically. For a moment, Charlotte thought he might cry.

"I will go see him," she said.

"Your Majesty," Reynolds said. "I don't know . . ."

"I am his wife. I will go see him."

Before she reached the door, Brimsley was there, holding out a small cordial glass. "Apple schnapps," he said.

She took a sip. Then another. It tasted like home. No, it tasted like Mecklenburg-Strelitz. London was her home now.

"I am ready," she said.

Brimsley took the glass back and nodded. "I will take you there."

BUCKINGHAM HOUSE
THE KING'S BEDCHAMBER
...
A FEW MINUTES LATER

The room was dark when Charlotte entered, the curtains drawn tightly against the late afternoon sun.

"George?" she called out. "George? It is me."

"Charlotte?" His voice was muffled. She looked around. She did not see him.

"Yes, darling. It is me. Reynolds told me what happened. I am here, George." She walked to the windows and pulled back the curtains. Light flooded in, but still, she did not see him.

Behind his dressing screen? No. At his desk? Under his desk? No.

"George? George, where are you?"

And then, in the tiniest, saddest voice, "I am sorry."

It took her a moment. She lowered herself to the floor and looked under the bed. George was there, flat on his back, still in his splendid uniform.

Her heart breaking, she said, "George, dearest. Can you come out for me?"

"I want to," he said. "But I cannot. It is the heavens. They cannot find me under here. I am hiding."

"You are hiding," she repeated patiently. "From the heavens."

"They are thwarted under here."

"George, all is well."

"No," he told her. "All is very, very wrong."

She did not know how to lie to him any longer. He was correct. All *was* very wrong. She took a deep breath, lay on her back, and scooted herself under the bed until she was lying right beside him. Staring up at the underside of the bed.

"Tell me," she said.

"I could not get out of the carriage. I could not even read the words on the page. I am not a king. I am no one's king."

"You will do better next time," she said reassuringly.

"No. There is no better. There is no cure. This is who I am."

"I love who you are," she said.

He shook his head. "You don't understand. I will be here sometimes and sometimes I will be . . ." He looked at her, his eyes tortured. "You can leave me. I would understand, and I would let you go."

"George," she said, "I will not leave you."

"You should."

"I will not."

"You have half a husband, Charlotte. Half a life. I cannot give you the future you deserve. Not a full me. Not a full marriage. Only half. Half a man. Half a King. Half a life."

"If what we have is half, then we shall make it the very best half. I love you. It is enough."

She reached out and took his hand, laced their fingers together.

"I am your Queen," she said. "And as long as I am so, I will never leave your side. You are King. You will be King. Your children will rule." She gave his hand an extra squeeze. "Together, we are whole."

They lay there, staring up.

"It is quite dust filled under here," George finally remarked.

Charlotte stifled a tiny laugh. "It really is."

He motioned with his free hand. "That one looks like a cumulus cloud."

She motioned with her free hand. "That one looks like a deformed bunny."

"You mean a Pomeranian?"

"No, I mean a deformed bunny. Pomeranians are regal and dignified."

He smiled. She did not see it, because she was not looking at his face, but she could hear it in the tenor of his breath.

But then his voice grew serious. Rueful. "I am so sorry that I did not give you a choice. That I did not tell you the truth of who I was before we wed."

"You did tell me the truth. You said you were Just George. And that is who you are. Half King. Half Farmer. But always Just George. That is all you need to be."

They lay in silence for several moments, the only sound the air from their lips, slowly evening out until they breathed in unison.

"I do not know how to repair what happened at Parliament," George said. "I fear it will overtake my Crown."

"If the Crown cannot go to Parliament, we shall bring Parliament to the Crown. Perhaps it is time we opened the doors to Buckingham House."

"What do you mean?"

"A ball."

"Here?"

"Why not?"

"It will be very crowded."

"It was crowded at the Danbury Ball," Charlotte reminded him, "and you performed beautifully."

He turned to face her. "That was because you were with me."

She turned to face him and smiled. "Exactly."

Agatha

"It is a surprise to see you again so soon," the Princess said to Agatha. "You have news?"

"News?"

"Of Buckingham House."

"No," Agatha said. "I do not have news."

Augusta raised her brows as if to say—*Then why are you here?*

Agatha took a deep breath. "I need to know, Your Royal Highness. Has there been a decision?"

But Augusta had clearly decided to feign ignorance. "A decision about what?"

"About the title. Is my son to be Lord Danbury?"

That was the question—along with so much that was left unsaid. Would Lord and Lady Smythe-Smith get to pass their titles to their children? Would there ever be a second Duke of Hastings? The fate of many rested on this one decision.

"As I told you before," Princess Augusta said, "that is a decision only His Majesty can make. I would think you would have news on the issue yourself. You are close to the royal couple. You were there at the birth. The birth of my grandchild."

"I cannot . . ." Agatha swallowed, trying to hold herself together. "I could not speak to the King or Queen on such matters."

"Such a shame. I could be so helpful." There was a moment of silence, and then the Princess leaned forward, her eyes sharp. "Her Majesty is attempting to run the Crown. I am sure of it. What do you know?"

Agatha held her tongue. She would not betray Charlotte again. No matter how high the stakes.

"The ball, then," Princess Augusta said. "I have been informed that they intend to host a ball at Buckingham House. What know you of that?"

"I know nothing," Agatha said quite honestly. "I have not received an invitation."

"They have not yet gone out," Princess Augusta said. "I am sure you are on the guest list. As is the rest of the *ton* . . . both sides, I think?"

Agatha just shook her head. "I do not know, Your Highness. I have not seen Her Majesty in several weeks."

Princess Augusta's mouth clamped into a straight, irritated line. "I suppose you heard what happened at Parliament."

"Only that His Majesty was not feeling well," Agatha said carefully. "A throat ailment, I heard."

She had heard nothing of the sort, but she had a feeling it was what the Princess would most want to hear. Agatha's knowledge of the King's condition had led her to all sorts of terrible speculation as to what had *actually* happened. But she would never ask the Queen. It was not her business. And it was certainly not her place to discuss it with the King's mother.

"What do they hope to achieve with this ball, I wonder," Princess Augusta said.

"Again, Your Highness, I could not begin to speculate. Until this afternoon, I did not even know a ball was being planned."

The Princess eyed her suspiciously. It was clear that she was not sure if she believed her. "Well," she said, "how unfortunate that you will not speak freely to me. We had a very fine arrangement, did we not? Were not all your needs met? Would it not be a shame for you to lose the very fine estate in which you now reside?"

Agatha's breath caught. She had not thought she might lose her home. Granted, she had no money, and there was every possibility that Dominic would not inherit the Danbury title, but it had never occurred to her that the Crown might swoop in and repossess Danbury House.

And then . . .

Oh no . . .

Please God, no . . .

She burst into tears.

Ugly, loud tears.

Augusta stared at her in patent horror. "Hush," she said awkwardly. "Stop that. Do not do that. No. No."

But Agatha couldn't stop. All the stresses of the past year. All the stresses of her *entire life* . . . They had somehow coalesced into this single, mortifying moment, and she could no more stop the tears than she could stop her very breath.

She cried for her years with Herman, who never once saw her as an actual person.

She cried for all the work she'd done to support the Great Experiment, for which she'd never get an ounce of credit.

She cried for the fact that all that work would be for naught, because Princess Augusta and Lord Bute and the rest of them were too damned selfish to open their hearts and minds to people who did not look as they did.

She cried for her son, and she cried for herself, and she cried because she just damned well needed to cry.

"Go, go," Augusta was saying, waving the servants out of the room. And then back to Agatha, "You must stop this."

Agatha couldn't. She had years of tears inside her. Decades.

Augusta pulled a flask out from under a seat cushion and poured some liquid into Agatha's tea.

"Pear brandy," she said. "I have it shipped in from Germany. Now drink. And cease crying this instant. Please."

Agatha drank. "I am sorry," she managed to get out. "I—"

"No," Augusta said firmly. "I do not want to know your burdens or hear what problems plague your life. Nor do I care."

Agatha stared at her with watery eyes. The Princess was the strangest creature. Acting maternal and then speaking with harsh finality.

Agatha drank more of the brandy. It was good. And it actually helped. Augusta refilled her cup.

"I want you to listen to me," Augusta said. "When my dear husband died, I had to throw myself on the mercy of his father, the King. George II. I expect you did not know him. He was a cruel, evil man. My husband loathed him. I loathed him. He was vicious with Georgie. The bruises. I had bruises as well. But there were no other options."

Agatha had never thought she'd feel a kinship with this woman, but just then, just a little bit, she did.

"I endured," Augusta said. "And over the years I learned I need not be content to surrender to the uselessness of female pursuits. Instead, I secured my son as King. I found a way to control my own fate."

She held out the brandy again. Agatha nodded and accepted another splash.

"I do not like you," Augusta said starkly. "However, you have been an admirable adversary thus far. Our battles bring me satisfaction. So this?" She waved her hand in the air, motioning toward Agatha's tearstained face. "Will not do. You are not allowed to come here and sob. You may not quit. You are a woman. Cover your bruises and endure. Do not lose control of your fate, Agatha."

Agatha nodded, taking a few breaths to compose herself. Maybe there was a way. Maybe she didn't have to betray Charlotte. Maybe she could keep Augusta happy with tiny bits of nonsense. Or at the very least, maybe she could buy herself a little time.

"Now tell me," Augusta said, "how goes life at Buckingham House?"

Agatha lifted her chin. She could figure out something to say that would not compromise her devotion to the Queen. "I believe that news depends on what is to become of my son's title, Your Highness."

Augusta smiled. Her adversary was back.

DANBURY HOUSE

THE SITTING ROOM

···

23 SEPTEMBER 1762

"You are quiet today," Adolphus said.

Agatha smiled up at him. The Queen's brother had called upon her quite frequently since the birth of the little prince. They had formed a friendship.

"I do not mean to be," she said. In truth, she was still thinking about her conversation with Princess Augusta. She had spun a tale about having heard gossip that the King had laryngitis, but she did not think it was enough to persuade the Princess to act on her—and Dominic's—behalf. After all, Agatha had not provided any *real* intelligence about the King and Queen. It had been nothing but gossip, and false gossip at that.

"Come," she said to Adolphus. "Tell me of your week's adventures."

"I made some headway with trade agreements," he said with some pride. "The British are an obstinate lot." He tipped his head flirtatiously. "I do not speak of the ladies, of course."

She nodded graciously. "Of course.

He smiled, but her mind was still on Princess Augusta. She did not like that woman. She likely never would. But she respected her. How long ago had Prince Frederick died? It had been more than ten years. During that time, Augusta had fought for her family, and for herself. She was surrounded by men who were constantly telling her what to think and what to do, and through it all, she had remained fundamentally independent.

Agatha didn't necessarily agree with Augusta's methods or opinions, but she could not help but admire the way she had carved out a place in this world that was ruled by men.

"Agatha," Adolphus said, "my business is complete. My nephew is born. I am to return home soon."

"I did not think you would stay," Agatha said. "But I do hope we shall see one another again on your next visit."

"No," he said. "That is to say . . . I was hoping . . ."

She watched him curiously. He normally carried himself with such style and confidence. His stammering was highly out of character.

"Agatha," he said again, "would you consider returning home with me? As my wife?"

"I—I—" She shouldn't have been surprised. He had quite clearly stated his desire to court her, and she herself had told Coral that she

saw him—and his inevitable proposal—as a solution to her problems.

But now that it was happening, she didn't know what to do.

"I know," Adolphus said. "It is quite soon. You are just barely out of
mourning, and we have only just begun to court. But I believe we could
be happy together."

"I'm not sure what to say," she murmured.

"You do not need to say anything just yet," he told her. "I will not say
words with hearts and flowers because I know you are not a hearts and
flowers woman, but I believe there is something here."

He sat next to her. Touched her chin. "There is something between
us," he said. He kissed her, gently at first, but then with a growing spark
of passion.

"Do not answer me now," he said. "Think on it. I shall await your
response."

He stood, his posture perfect, and gave her a smart bow before de-
parting. Agatha sat in stunned silence for about a minute before Coral
came running in.

"Are you going to say yes?" Coral demanded.

"Were you listening at the door?"

"Would you believe me if I said no?"

Agatha rolled her eyes.

"He is quite a handsome man," Coral said.

"Yes."

"And you would not have to worry about your future."

"Yes."

"Or the title issue."

"Yes."

"And it does signify that his sister is Queen Charlotte. Imagine, stay-
ing at the palace when we come back to visit."

"Yes," Agatha said, yet again.

Coral plopped down next to her on the sofa, not something she ordinarily did. "I have been practicing my German. *Ich diene der Königin.* That
means 'I serve the queen.' That's you. You would be a queen. Never have
another moment's worry when you are royalty—"

"Stop talking, Coral," Agatha begged. She needed to *think*.

Coral pulled a bit of a face, stood up, and headed for the door. At the last moment, she turned back around. "You *are* going to say yes to his proposal?"

"*Go*, Coral," Agatha said.

Because she had no idea what she was going to do.

George

"It's a fine likeness, don't you think?"

George held his wife's hand as he stared at his wedding portrait. "A portrait for which I did not even sit. I am an insertion."

"It is still us," Charlotte said. "You and me."

"Yes. But not real." And that was what worried him. There was so much in his life that was not real. Charlotte didn't know the extent of it; he had become adept at hiding all but the worst of his mental jumbles. But the heavens never stopped. Even when he was able to talk and act normally, he felt them encroaching.

Even now. Even with his beloved by his side, in this palace he called home, a little piece of his mind was marching off in its own direction.

Venus, it called. *Venus*.

"George," Charlotte said.

He forced himself back to the moment and looked at her again. She was magnificent, every inch a queen. She was wearing a wig—the first time he had seen her do so—but it was colored to look like her natural hair. It added nearly a foot to her height, made her taller than he was, even.

"Look at you," he said. "You are a rare jewel."

He reached out to touch her face, but his hand was trembling. Uncontrollably. He could not remember the last time he had seen it shake so.

His gaze moved from her face to his hand. He could not take his eyes off his fingers. They shook and shook, and yet somehow it was Charlotte's face that looked blurry behind them.

He did not touch her. He dared not. Not with that hand.

But Charlotte dared. She always dared. She took his hand in hers and held it steady. "You and me," she said.

He managed the tiniest of nods. "You and me."

"You ready?" she asked.

"Yes," he said. He prayed it was true.

They walked to the ballroom, already filled with guests. Reynolds and Brimsley trailed behind them, just in case.

Just in case.

George hated that. Charlotte shouldn't have to spend her life with someone who always needed a *just in case*.

"Your Majesty?" Reynolds asked when they reached the door.

George gave him a nod.

Reynolds stepped forward and announced, "His Majesty King George III and Queen Charlotte!"

Venus. Transit of Venus.

George grabbed Charlotte's hand. Hard.

"I am here," she whispered. "I am Charlotte."

He nodded jerkily, but his feet wouldn't move.

The crowd had gone quiet at Reynolds's announcement, but when the royal couple did not immediately appear, a low rumble began to hum through the air.

So many voices.

So many people.

Venus. Venus.

And then, somehow, Lord Bute's voice. "If he cannot even face his people, he is finished."

"I cannot," George said to Charlotte.

"You can. You and me," she reminded him. "Together. We are one."

He nodded again, and somehow—he would never know how—his feet began to move. He entered the ballroom, Charlotte at his side.

So much noise.

So many faces.

"George," came Charlotte's voice. "George?"

He focused on her face. Her smile.

"Do not feel nerves," she said.

"I am fine," he said. "Do I not seem fine?"

"You are hurting my hand."

He looked down. Dear God, he was clutching her fingers with a death grip. Instantly, he released her. "Charlotte," he said. "I did not mean to— This was a mistake."

He had to go. He started to turn.

But she took his hand again. Gently.

"George, look at me," she said. "Only at me. Squeeze my hand if you must. It is all right. Softer. There. Now. Let us smile and wave. Ready?"

He smiled. It was forced, but it was good enough.

"Now we wave," she said.

And they did. They smiled, and they waved, and the crowd cheered.

"You are Just George," Charlotte said. "*My* George. Let us dance."

Together they walked to the center of the dance floor. "Keep your eyes on me," Charlotte said. "Do not look at anyone else. There is no one here but us."

"You and me," George said as the music began.

"You and me."

The first few notes floated through the ballroom, and the music swelled. George never took his eyes off Charlotte's face. He didn't need to. The steps of the dance were as ingrained in his muscles as walking or riding a horse. His body knew what to do. And his mind . . . all it needed was to focus on Charlotte.

Just Charlotte.

Their hands touched, then separated. They came together, stepped apart. They circled. They nodded. And as the music moved through him, something miraculous happened. That little piece of his brain, the part that was owned by the heavens . . .

It went silent.

It would not be forever; he knew that. But for this moment, in this room, with this music and most importantly, this woman . . .

He was here.

All of him.

When the music ended, he took his Queen's hand and kissed her fingers. And then he thought—

That is not enough. That will never be enough.

Right there, in front of all the *ton*, in front of his mother and Lord Bute and all the rest, he kissed her. He kissed his wife, his Queen.

His Charlotte.

Maybe he was mad, and maybe he was growing worse. But he would not let this moment slip away. Everyone would know that he loved her, that she was the Queen, that if anything happened to him, it was *she* they should turn to.

"George?" she whispered, breathless at the end of the kiss.

"I will be all right," he assured her. "I *am* all right."

Her smile grew wide. "Just George."

"*Your* George. But if you'll excuse me, I have some kingly responsibilities to take care of."

"By all means, Your Majesty."

Off he went. He had nobles to charm, members of Parliament to reassure. There was much to do, and he knew he must take advantage of this moment, when he felt so well.

He spent an hour or so playing his part. He danced with several ladies—his mother, of course, and Lady Danbury, to whom he would always show favor. He chatted with Lord Bute, and he joked with Charlotte's brother, and all in all, he acted exactly as a king ought.

He was proud of himself.

But he wanted Charlotte again. He'd done his duty; now it was time to dance again with his wife.

He heard her before he saw her. He was just about to round a corner when he overheard her speaking with his mother. He stopped, shamelessly eavesdropping.

"It is a lovely ball," his mother said.

"It is," Charlotte replied. "We enjoy hosting."

George almost laughed. It was an outright lie. He hated hosting. But he would do it. If it meant more moments like these, he would do it.

"We shall do it more often," Charlotte said.

"Good," his mother replied.

"Yes."

It was growing awkward. Perhaps he should intervene.

But then his mother said, "I have only ever wanted him to be happy."

"He *is* happy," Charlotte said.

"You make him happy."

George bit back a smile. His mother was not an easy woman, and she had an overabundance of pride. She had devoted her life to his kingship. And now she was ceding her place to Charlotte.

He peeked around the corner.

"Thank you," his mother said to Charlotte. She swept into a curtsy, the deepest he had ever seen her perform. She looked up at Charlotte and said, "Your Majesty."

Then she stood, straightened into her usual stiff posture, and the moment was gone. "I must see to Lord Bute," she said, and she walked away, leaving Charlotte vaguely stunned.

George stepped forward and wrapped his arms around her.

"Did you see that?" Charlotte asked.

"I did."

"I am not sure—"

"Don't question it." He smiled. "Shall we dance?"

"Yes, but . . ." She glanced about.

"What is it, my love?"

"Let us have one dance just for us. Where no one can see."

"Does this mean I will be able to kiss you?"

"You mustn't disturb my hair," she warned him.

"I would not dare."

"To the gardens?"

He nodded, grabbed her hand, and took off, the pair of them giggling like truant schoolchildren.

"Shhh . . ." Charlotte admonished. "Someone will hear."

"Who will hear?" he whispered.

"I don't know. But we should still be—"

She stopped short.

"Wha—"

She elbowed him, then jerked her head toward something ahead of them.

George followed her line of sight. It was another couple, dancing.

Reynolds and Brimsley.

George put his finger to his lips and pulled Charlotte behind a hedge.

"Did you know?" she whispered.

"I knew that Reynolds preferred men, but I didn't know about Brimsley."

Charlotte peeked out. "They look so happy."

George yanked her back so he could see. They were dancing like a couple in love. Reynolds was leading, probably because he was taller. They were laughing and whispering, and it occurred to George that they looked rather like Charlotte and him.

In love.

Happy.

"Let us go," he whispered to Charlotte. "They need this moment more than we do."

She nodded, and they tiptoed back to the palace. King and Queen, tiptoeing like thieves.

"Well," Charlotte said, once they were out of earshot.

"Well."

"That was . . . surprising."

"But nice."

She nodded slowly. "It was. It is."

George cleared his throat and glanced toward the ballroom. "It is probably time I make a toast."

"Wait," she said. "I have something to tell you."

He gazed upon her with indulgence. She looked suddenly shy, and this was not an emotion he normally associated with her.

"You and I, George," she said, "we have changed the world with our love. But the Crown can be fragile, and the fates of many rest on us securing our line."

While he was digesting that comment, she took his hand and placed it on the pale green silk covering her belly.

"Our line," he murmured, regarding her with something approaching wonder. "You and me."

"And them," she said. "Little Georgie and whoever this might turn out to be."

He kissed her, and then he kissed his fingers and touched them to her belly. "This is just our news for now, though, yes?"

"Oh, most definitely."

"I would very much like to retire for the evening," he said with regret, "but I'm afraid we must go be King and Queen again."

Off they went, back to the ballroom. Wine was poured, and George stood in the center of the crowd. Charlotte's pregnancy would be a secret for several more months, but they did have their young son to celebrate.

George raised his glass, waited for the noise of the crowd to subside, then said, "We thank you all for joining us to celebrate the arrival of our new prince."

Everyone cheered. A baby was always a magical thing. A royal baby, even more so.

"Unsurprisingly, given that I am the third, we have chosen to name him George IV!" He raised his glass again. "To your future King!"

The crowd joined in. "To our future King!"

To the future.

Whatever it might hold.

AGATHA

BUCKINGHAM HOUSE
THE GARDENS
...
SHORTLY AFTER THE TOAST

Agatha did love a good party, much more so now that Herman was gone, and she did not have to monitor his behavior. Or her own, with which he had always managed to find some fault or infraction.

But this party was wearying. It was full of secrets, and of hidden struggles. She had seen the look of terror in the King's eyes when he and the Queen first stepped into the ballroom. She had seen how Charlotte had held his hand and whispered words that no one else would ever hear.

But Agatha had been granted unfathomable access into their secrets, and she had a good idea of what those words might be.

She felt for her friend.

She could not know what the future might hold—none of them could—but she suspected that Charlotte had many years ahead of her of holding the King, keeping him safe and well. Protecting him from gossip and intrigue.

At some point he would falter, and she would *be* the Crown. It was a heavy burden.

The party was still very much in full swing, but Agatha decided she needed a break, so she'd wandered out into the gardens. Not too far—a lady had her reputation to think of, even respectable widows like her—but the air was fragrant and cool, and it brought a welcome sense of peace.

After a few minutes, however, she discovered she had company. Adolphus. She had a feeling he'd been looking for her.

"You dislike crowds as much as I do," he said once he reached her side. "Another way we are a match."

"True. I needed a moment to breathe. It is such a crush in there."

"My sister is a shining success," Adolphus said. "I am happy for her."

Agatha gave him a small smile. Charlotte had shared none of her problems with him; of that, Agatha was certain. Adolphus knew nothing of George's illness, of the strength and steel Charlotte would need to draw upon to navigate the years ahead.

He saw a glittering queen.

And she *was* a glittering queen. But she was so much more.

Adolphus stepped closer. "It would be nice to be happy for myself as well."

Agatha did not pretend that she did not understand. "What would our life be like?" she asked. "If we married and I went back home with you?"

He smiled broadly, his chest puffing with pride. "It is probably treason to say this here, but my province is the greatest place in the world. It is exquisitely beautiful, with green fields and glittering lakes. The best people, the best food . . ."

"That sounds nice."

"It is. I rule, of course, but as my consort you would have certain duties as well. We are more egalitarian there."

Egalitarian sounded good.

"Most of the wives at court are older than you, but you will like them," Adolphus continued. "Once you learn the language."

"Of course," she murmured. She'd known that would be a requirement.

"And it is good that you are young. It means you can have more children."

"More children," she echoed. Dear God. She already had four. She did not want more. She had not enjoyed being pregnant, and she *really* had not enjoyed giving birth.

Not that anyone did, but she was well aware what a perilous endeavor it was. Charlotte had nearly died giving birth to the new Prince of Wales. It had been terrifying.

And all too common.

"Agatha," he said, "I will raise the Danbury children as my own. I will care for them as I do you. But you know that I must have an heir of my own. Perhaps two or three."

"Two or three." She swallowed. Two or three more children. She did not want two or three more children.

"You can travel with me," he said happily. "We can even come back here to England every few years if you are worried about missing home. But you will not miss home for long. There will be festivals and balls and charities and—"

"No," she blurted out. She'd had no idea she was going to say it. It just came from her. Unbidden, but no less true.

"Agatha," he said, clearly surprised.

"I cannot marry you." She was realizing the truth of this as she said it. "I am sorry."

His face betrayed his confusion. "I have made you nervous with so much talk of change."

"No. I cannot marry you. But only because . . ." And that was when she understood. "I cannot marry anyone."

He took a step back, an uncomprehending look on his face.

"You are a wonderful man," she told him. "And when you courted me, something in me was awakened so I felt hopeful. You would have saved me from a thousand different problems. You would have rescued me. You would have listened to me and cared for me."

"Then let me," he implored.

She shook her head. "It does not change what I know to be true. I cannot marry you. I cannot marry anyone. I never want to be married again. Adolphus, I have spent my life breathing someone else's air. I did not know any other way. It is time I learn to breathe all on my own."

"Agatha," he said. "Do not do this. You are . . . this is a terrible mistake you are making."

"Perhaps I am making a terrible mistake. But it is mine to make. I do hope you will forgive me." She smiled gently and gave him a kiss on the cheek. "Goodbye, Adolphus."

She took a step. And then another. Walking by herself. On her own. She was her own person.

Finally.

BUCKINGHAM HOUSE
THE BACK ENTRANCE
...
AN HOUR LATER

It was time to go. It had been a wonderful night, but a momentous one, and Agatha was exhausted. She made her way to her carriage, but before she could step up, she heard the unmistakable voice of the Queen.

"Lady. Danbury."

Agatha had never heard her use that tone before. Not on her. Not on anyone. She was marching toward her with a purpose and stride that was frankly unsettling.

"Your Majesty," she said quickly, dropping into a curtsy. "Thank you so much for—"

"You refuse my brother?" Charlotte demanded. "Offer him hope of a union, of happiness, then break his heart? At my ball? *In my home?*"

Of course Charlotte had been aware that Adolphus had been court-ing her. Agatha did not recall speaking with her about it specifically, but Adolphus must have done so. And now he must have told her that Agatha had said no.

Agatha's heart dropped to her knees. Which very nearly buckled. "Your Majesty, I . . ."

"His humor may lack wit," Charlotte went on. "And yes, his conde-scension knows no bounds. He is, however, a person of fine character and pure heart and someone in your position could find much worse options, *could they not?*"

"They could indeed," Agatha said hastily. "Your Majesty. Please, I beg of you to accept my apology. Tell me . . . what might I do in order to—"

"Adolphus will survive," Charlotte said curtly. "What concerns me is what I am to do with *you.*"

"Me?"

"The fact that you did not bring your concerns to me. Your fears regarding your inheritance. Your title. The fate of your family. Of all the families recently titled."

"How did you know?" Agatha very nearly whispered.

Charlotte raised her brows. "Does it matter?"

"No, of course not."

"I am Queen. It is my job to know these things. My duty. And I must be able to rely upon my most trusted friends to come to me with honesty and openness."

Agatha bowed her head. "I apologize, Your Majesty. I only did not wish to place my burden on top of your own. Yours, which seems so . . ."

She did not finish the sentence, so Charlotte prompted her. "So . . . ?"

"One crown is heavy enough," Agatha said quietly. "But to carry two . . ."

Charlotte did not speak right away. She stared at Agatha with an intensity that made her wonder if she'd made a mistake. She should not have alluded to the King's troubles, to Charlotte's impossible responsibilities. She should have been more circumspect.

But then, finally, Charlotte spoke. And when she did, it was with the authority of one who had been born for this very moment.

"We are one crown," she said. "His weight is mine, and mine is his. One. Crown. We rule for the welfare of our subjects. New and old. Rival and foe. Titled or not. You tell me my palace walls are too high? I tell you they must be. High as the sky if necessary. To protect you, to protect all our worthy subjects."

Agatha could only stare, feeling that she was somehow witnessing the birth of something great. Something miraculous.

"I suggest you shift your fear to faith. Come to *us* with your concerns," Charlotte said, her expression softening slightly. "Directly. To do otherwise would suggest that we are incapable of addressing them. Unless that is what you believe, Lady Danbury?"

Agatha could not speak. This girl—*this woman*—she was a wonder. She was going to change history. She already had.

"You may go," Charlotte said. "I shall send for you soon."

"Your Majesty," Agatha somehow managed to say. She curtsied. Deeply.

Charlotte turned to go, but after only a few steps, she turned and said, "Do give my regards to young Lord Danbury. Dominic, his name is, yes?"

Hope and, yes, joy, bloomed in Agatha's chest. "Yes, Your Majesty. Dominic."

"He is a handsome little one. Not as handsome as my Georgie will surely be, of course."

Agatha bit back a smile. "Of course."

She waited until the Queen had departed, then took a footman's hand to help her up into her carriage. As she rode home, to her marvelous mansion that *she* had secured for her family, she settled back against the cushions with a sigh and smile.

The Great Experiment?

Was no longer an experiment.

It was a fact.

And it was very, very great.

Fifty-Six Years Later . . .

CHARLOTTE

It was not a long distance from Buckingham House to Kew, but to Charlotte, Queen of the United Kingdom of Great Britain and Ireland, it felt as if she were traveling to an entirely different planet.

She did not make this journey as often as she ought. It *hurt* to see George. It hurt her heart. It hurt her bones. It hurt her soul. She had spent so many years watching him slowly whisper away, and now . . .

He did not recognize her. Perhaps once in the past year she had been able to reach him. Twice in the year before that. It was heartbreaking. To have that fleeting connection, that brief moment when she could remember Just George and *be* Just Charlotte.

The joy of it wasn't worth the pain that inevitably followed, when he returned to his madness, with his heavens and stars and equations. And more lately, his absolute nonsense. She'd used to be able to understand what he said, even if it made little sense. But now it was usually just gibberish.

Her George was a ghost, just waiting to die.

But today she had important news. And she would tell it to him, whether he heard her or not. He was her love, and he would always be her love. She owed him this.

Charlotte entered his room to find him writing on the walls, as he often did. An attendant sat in the corner. He'd been instructed to let George draw whatever he wanted, wherever he wanted.

It made him happy. And that was what Charlotte wanted most. For him to be happy.

"You may go," she said to the attendant.

He gave her a look that said, *Are you certain?* George did sometimes have difficult outbursts.

She gave him a look that said, *I am your Queen. Get out.*

He got out.

"George," Charlotte said once the attendant had shut the door behind him.

George didn't turn around, but he did wave his hand as if shooing her away. "Do not bother me in the sky."

"George, it is me. It is your Charlotte."

Still, he ignored her, mumbling words she could not make out.

"I have some news, George. Wonderful news." She stepped toward him. "George? George?"

It was as if she weren't there. He kept mumbling and writing on the wall, and Charlotte wondered if *she* was the ghost, just waiting to die.

She looked at his bed. It was not the same one from his room in Buckingham House, but it was still a bed. And she thought— *Maybe, just maybe . . .*

She got down on her knees, clearing her throat loudly as she did so.

He looked over and frowned.

She lay on her back and scooted under, not an easy feat in her gown. "Just George?" she called out. "Farmer George?"

She waited, holding her breath. And then there he was, peering under the bed at her.

"Come," she said with a smile. "Hide from the heavens with me."

He pondered her request for a brief moment, gave a little nod, and joined her. "Charlotte!" he said, with the greatest delight. "Why, hello."

"Hello, George." She didn't cry, because she *did not cry*. But her eyes felt rather odd.

"It is quiet here," he said.

"George," she said, "we have succeeded. Our son Edward has married, and his wife is with child."

"Edward is going to be a father?"

"Yes. Your line will live on."

"Our line," he reminded her.

"Our line," she repeated.

And then, very sweetly, he kissed her. It tasted like the past. It tasted like her very heart.

"Fancy meeting you here," he said.

She burst out laughing. But then he looked at her with an expression she rarely saw on his face anymore. Sober, serious, but still full of love.

"You did not go over the wall," he said.

She smiled. "No, George. I did not go over the wall."

ABOUT THE AUTHORS

#1 *New York Times* bestselling author JULIA QUINN began writing one month after graduating from college and aside from a brief stint in medical school, she has been tapping away at her keyboard ever since. Her novels have been translated into forty-three languages and are beloved the world over. A graduate of Harvard and Radcliffe colleges, she lives with her family in the Pacific Northwest.

SHONDA RHIMES is an award-winning television creator, producer, and author, as well as the CEO of the global media company Shondaland. In her career, Rhimes's work has been celebrated with numerous awards including induction into the Television Academy Hall of Fame. She has shifted the entertainment industry's business model and changed the face of television.